Shivering uncontrollably, Tara heaved herself into a sitting position. Freezing chills raced over her skin as she glanced around the familiar slime-walled hallway of the nightmare dungeon. She looked toward the closed iron door that sealed her off from the corridors beyond. Her heart sank to the floor. No red griffin lay embedded in its smooth surface.

A soft scraping sound floated through the air, drawing closer. The reek of rotting flesh filled the hallway. Tara staggered to her feet, her gut twisting in panic. She backed away from the churning darkness at the other end of the hall. Malevolence radiated from the depthless black, hatred mixed with anticipation. The creature had been waiting for her.

Also by Lori L. MacLaughlin:

LADY, THY NAME IS TROUBLE

Trouble, BY ANY OTHER NAME

Lori L. MacLaughlin

Book and Sword Publishing

Lori L. MacLaughlin/Book and Sword Publishing, LLC
Milton, Vermont, USA
www.bookandswordpublishing.com

Publisher's Note: This is a work of fiction. Names, characters, places, and incidents are a product of the author's imagination. Locales and public names are sometimes used for atmospheric purposes. Any resemblance to actual people, living or dead, or to businesses, companies, events, institutions, or locales is completely coincidental.

Cover Design: Lori L. MacLaughlin and Forward Authority Design
Cover Art: © iStock/fotofrankyat; iStock/Alexander Podshivalov; iStock/Mikesilent; iStock/Olga Brovina; iStock/CURAphotography; iStock/coloroftime; iStock/Ricardo Reitmeyer; iStock/Tom Tietz
Book Layout © 2014 BookDesignTemplates.com
Maps: © 2015-2016 Lori L. MacLaughlin

Trouble By Any Other Name/ Lori L. MacLaughlin. -- 1st ed.
ISBN 978-1-942015-02-4

Library of Congress Control Number: 2016906083

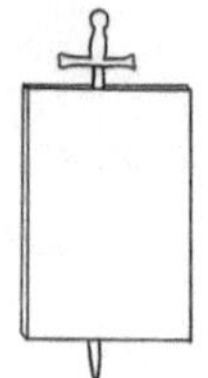

Book and Sword Publishing

ACKNOWLEDGEMENTS

In 2014, I released my first book, *Lady, Thy Name Is Trouble*, and accomplished my dream of being a published author. This wonderful dream-come-true continues with the release of my second book: *Trouble By Any Other Name*.

I am so grateful to everyone who helped me bring this book to life. Heartfelt thanks go out to my writing group, the ELFS: Kari Jo Spear and Jody Wood; to freelance editor Meg Brazill; to editor and wordsmith extraordinaire Sue Archer; to designer Carrie Butler of Forward Authority Design for taking my vision for the cover and making it beautiful; to the always inspirational League of Vermont Writers; and most of all to my amazing family and friends for their support and encouragement. I can never say thank you enough.

For My Family

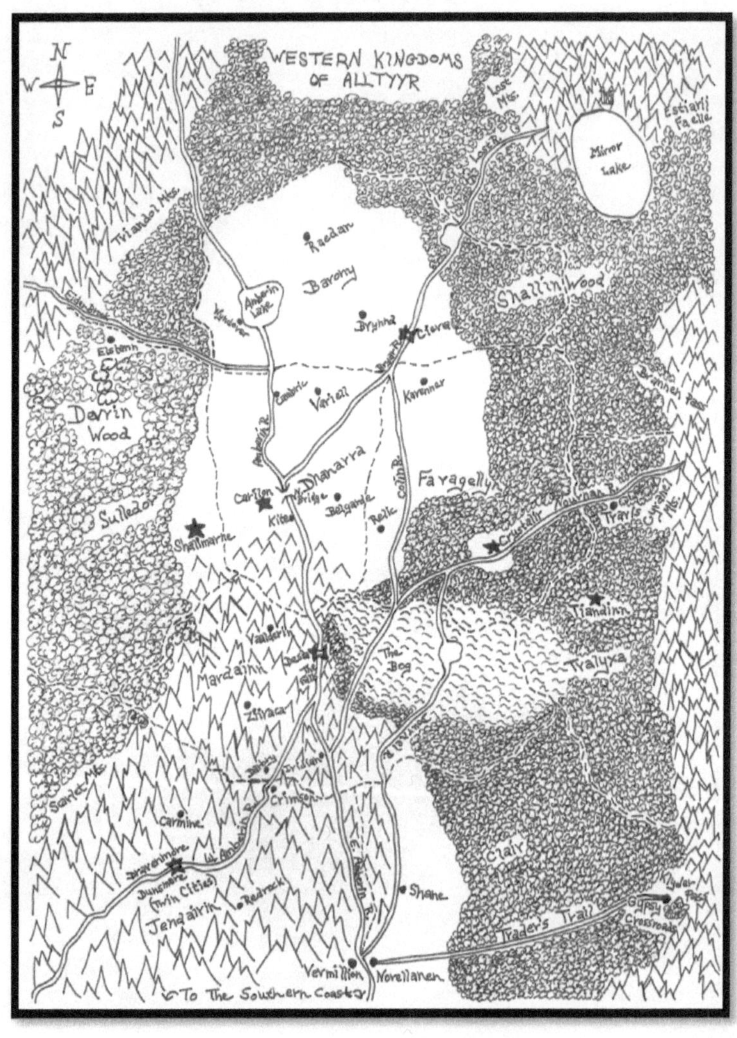

WESTERN KINGDOMS OF ALLTYYR
N W E S
Triandol Mts.
Raedan Barony
Amberin Lake
Yeneldor
Elsbinn
Devrin Wood
Sulledor
Embrli
Varieli
Bryhha
Lost Mts.
Mirror Lake
Estiarii Faelle
Shallin Wood
Lieva
Karennar
Ambrenin R.
Dhanarra
Carilon
Kites
Bridge
Belgande
Reik
Shellmarne
Favagelly
Coltan Rd.
Cuirelir
Travis
Cuirani Mts.
Tlandinn
Trallyxa
Vanderi
Mardainin
Zilvara
The Bog
Yanin R.
Eridune
Crimsen
Sande Mts.
Carmine
Mt. Ambrose
Bravenmore
Juncimore
(Twin Cities)
Jendairin
Redreck
Clair
Shane
Cedar Forest
Gipsy Crossroads
Trader's Trail
Vermillion
Novellanen
To The Southern Coast

N
Alltyyr
Eastern Frontier
To the Western Kingdoms
Barren Mts.
To the Northlands
Black Mts.
Valley of Kamar
Lake
Cyranel Mts.
Brannen Pass
Floresta
Dhavalwood
Roane Valley
Ravnauli
Annor
Ravnauli's Keep
Falton
Wood
Aragriffs
Gypsy Crossroads
Kinder Pass
Aldontis
Rinpool
Jhaurrian Swamp
Alltairryn
Rhylaena
Teherlis
Mandir
Tairrn
Loneir R.
Orroon
Bran
Wood
Saedinn
Eldranat
Isalte
Silvadel R.
Aalinyr
Bran Wood
Janneere
Inigaerra
Kievunn
To the Southern Coast
Aerintel

Trouble,

BY ANY
OTHER
NAME

CHAPTER 1

Tara Triannon hurried down the hallway, glancing behind her every few steps to make sure no one was following. Torchlight glimmered off the white stone walls, driving back the night's shadows. She heard the scuff of boots and distant voices. She ducked around a corner, her left hand flying to her sword. Chiding herself, she let go of the hilt. Castle Carilon, the capital of Dhanarra, was safe now. General Caldren and his Sulledorn army had been defeated and the castle retaken. There were no enemies left to fight within its walls.

The voices and footsteps faded, and Tara continued on down the corridor to an arched wooden door emblazoned with the coat of arms of the Royal House of Dhanarra: a leaping white stag on a field of dark green. She eased open the door to the royal suite and peered inside, her nose wrinkling at the reek of disinfectant. The room was dark. Where was her sister? She'd said to meet her here at midnight. Candles glowed in the chamber beyond like spots of foggy moonlight. Tara stepped inside, closing the door behind her with a faint click.

"Tara, is that you?" came the soft whisper of her sister's voice from the other room. Laraina Triannon approached from the far chamber, sword in hand, her pale blue dress swishing around her legs as she walked. She'd tied her long red curls back with a leather thong.

Tara blinked at the odd image. She still wasn't used to seeing her sister in royal attire. "Yes, it's me."

"In here." Laraina gestured for Tara to follow.

Laraina led the way into the far chamber, stopping beside the large four-poster bed where Prince Kaden of Dhanarra lay tangled in satiny, dark green sheets. Flushed with fever, his brown hair sweat-plastered to the pillow, the tall prince moaned and twitched in his sleep. Tara frowned, surprised by his condition. She had known he was sick, but not that it was this bad.

Ten days ago, the medics had operated on his shoulder to try and repair the damage done by the burning Mardainn arrow that had lodged there, a wound suffered during the recent battle with the Sulledorn-Mardainn army. The operation had been unsuccessful. Despite their best efforts, the wound had become infected. *At this rate*, Tara thought, *the kingdom of Dhanarra will soon be losing their prince.* She wouldn't have cared, except that her sister was in love with him. They were to be married in two weeks.

Laraina sat on the edge of the bed. "I sent Kaden's guards on an errand and said I would watch him until they got back." She touched Kaden's hand. The prince moaned again and tossed restlessly. "His skin is so hot. He hasn't been conscious enough to take any water or food for two days now, and he's getting worse. I don't know what to do."

Tara raked her hand through her long silver-blonde hair. "Why didn't you tell me he was… like this?" She couldn't quite bring herself to say *dying* to her sister.

"I didn't want you to feel like you had to heal him." Laraina turned toward her. The plea in her eyes tore at Tara's heart. "I know what will happen if you do, and I can't ask that of you." Laraina looked down at her love. "But I don't want him to die." A sob escaped her, and she bent her head.

"Raina..." Tara put her hand on her sister's shoulder. "What could be worse than watching you suffer and knowing I could have eased your pain and didn't? How could I live with that?"

Laraina looked up. "You'll do it?"

Their eyes held for a long moment, then Tara nodded. She took Laraina's hand and pulled her sister up beside her. "Go. Keep watch."

Laraina hugged her hard. "I'm sorry."

"Go." Tara gently pushed Laraina toward the door. "I'll tell you when I'm done."

Laraina hurried away.

Tara turned back to the prince. A fleeting thought crossed her mind. If Kaden died, Laraina might stay with her instead of settling down, and they could go back to their adventurous ways. She immediately dismissed the idea, angry with herself for even thinking it. Laraina no longer wanted to be a soldier of fortune. Regardless of whether Kaden lived or died, Tara was on her own.

She drew her dagger and ran her thumb along the blade, testing its sharpness, feeling the bite of its well-honed edge. Tendrils of fear curled around her spine, sending cold shivers over her skin. The nightmare would come. She could feel the evil presence that haunted her dreams, hovering just outside her consciousness, waiting for the chance to claw its way back into her mind. She only hoped she could handle it without Jovan's help. He'd warned her against using her healing power again. With any luck, he wouldn't find out her intention.

Prince Kaden moaned softly. Tara looked down at him, then at the door through which Laraina had exited. What choice did she have? Balling her hand into a fist, she squelched her emotions. She had no time to waste. She took a deep breath and knelt beside the prince.

*****

Jovan Trevillion jogged down the sloping passageway that led to the white stone stables of Castle Carilon. He wanted to catch the courier from Relic, the Faragellyn border town to the east, before the man left for home. He had heard the courier's report detailing the reconstruction of Relic in the aftermath of the battle with Sulledor, but he still had one question he needed answered. He reached the stables and looked about. The smells of horse and hay and leather clung in the damp air. At the far end of the stable, a man in a dark gray uniform was leading his mount toward the open door that led outward into the night.

"Corporal Gendron," Jovan called.

The man in gray stopped. "Sir?" His horse snorted and nipped at him playfully.

"I'm sorry to delay you." Jovan came up beside him. "I had one more question."

"Yes?"

"In your cleanup efforts, did anyone find the body of Captain Natiere?"

"The Butcher? No. We've been looking as you requested, but no one matching his description has been found, alive or dead."

Jovan scowled. "How can a dead body just disappear?"

"I don't know, sir." The corporal's horse snorted again and pawed the dirt floor.

"Did your men search outside the city?"

"Yes. We found lots of tracks, but nothing more."

"What kind of tracks?"

"Wolf tracks. A small pack had been wreaking havoc with the livestock. We hunted for them, but couldn't find them. About three weeks ago, the attacks stopped. We haven't seen any new tracks since then."

Jovan's eyes narrowed. "Sounds like they've moved on." *To where?* he thought silently.

"We alerted the fortress at Belgarde, in case they went west. They may be headed your way."

"We'll watch for them." Jovan stepped back. "Thank you for the information. Have a safe ride back."

The corporal nodded. He led his horse out the door, mounted, and galloped away into the night.

A groom closed and locked the stable door. Jovan strode back through the stable and on up the sloping passageway into the castle, cursing to himself. Natiere had to be dead. Tara had defeated him in a grueling duel. Jovan had seen Tara drive her sword into the Butcher's chest, had seen him fall. And yet, corpses didn't just melt into the dust.

A square of moonlight painted the floor, streaming through a small window cut into the passage wall. Jovan stopped and looked out, separated from the night by a thick pane of wired glass that distorted his view of the white stone city below. *Where are you?* he thought. Captain Natiere, as General Caldren's executioner, had relentlessly pursued Tara, Laraina, Prince Kaden, his cousin Aurelia, and Jovan through the kingdoms of Dhanarra, Mardainn, and Faragellyn, finally confronting them in the epic battle in the Faragellyn city of Relic. Natiere had formed some sort of mental link with Tara, similar to the link Jovan shared with her, and Jovan had the distinct impression Natiere wanted more. *If you come after her again, I will kill you,* Jovan swore silently. He pounded the stone sill with his fist. *How can I protect her against both the creature in her dream and the Butcher?*

You must find a way. The ancient voice, cold and implacable as a mountain, resonated in his mind. *She must survive. She is the last of her kind.*

What kind? Jovan shot back.

Her kind, the voice intoned. *The time is near. If she fails, the evil will escape, and all will be lost.*

Tell me what she has to do, and I will tell her.

No. She must discover for herself who she is and what she must do.

Why?

It is the way.

Jovan's jaw clenched. *How can I help her if I don't know —*

You will know what you need to know when you need to know it.

So you keep telling me. What do I do in the meantime?

Stay with her. Keep her safe.

Jovan stifled a grim laugh. *Trying to keep Tara Triannon out of trouble is like trying to keep the wind from blowing. It's impossible. At least let me tell her —*

No. You can tell her nothing. It is the only way to hold the balance.

Jovan dipped his head and exhaled loudly. *I don't see —*

If you cannot fulfill the task entrusted to you, we will find another protector.

Jovan's head shot up. *No.* A niggling of unease crept into the back of his mind, a stirring in the connection between Tara's mind and his. He felt a brief surge of power, then the link closed abruptly. *Tara, what are you doing?* He bolted down the corridor.

*****

Tara pulled back the blankets to uncover the prince's bandaged shoulder. She sliced through the wrappings with her dagger, exposing the festering wound. Then she cut a gash across the palm of her left hand and placed her bleeding hand over the wound. Power flowed through her, warm and strong, filling her being. She closed her mind, trying not to broadcast what she was doing. Focusing her thoughts, she sent her power coursing into Kaden. Pain split her shoulder as if she were the one who had been hit by the arrow. She sucked in a breath, gritting her teeth. The spasm passed, and her power sang through Kaden's body, healing flesh and bone, rooting out the infection that threatened his life.

When his blood was clean and his shoulder nearly healed, she reined in her power and began to ease it back into herself. Icy jabs of warning froze her in mid-thought. Something was wrong. Panic crawled into her throat, and she couldn't breathe. Forcing herself to calm down, she closed her eyes and searched the stream of power, pulling it slowly back, her mind probing for whatever had set off her danger sense. She gasped as her mind touched blackness. The evil presence, the creature of her nightmares, had dug its claws into the power stream and was riding it back into her.

"No!" she cried, her hands flying to her head. She flung up a mental wall and thrust outward again and again, pummeling the creature until it let go and sank with a shriek back into its dungeon prison. The power snapped back into her, knocking her backward. She lay on the floor, panting. Her head spun like a maelstrom. Another presence touched her mind, cool and inquisitive, unfamiliar. She recoiled violently. Her mental wall rammed against it, and the touch vanished.

"Tara!" Jovan Trevillion's voice rang out as the door banged open.

Tara heard running footsteps. Then Jovan and Laraina appeared beside her. She sensed more than saw them, their blurred faces whirling around her in dizzy circles.

Jovan scooped her into his lap and cupped her face with his hand. "Tara," he said urgently.

"I'm fine," she whispered. "Just dizzy." She closed her eyes, waiting for the swirling of the silver and blue color of her eyes — one of the side effects of using her healing power — to stop, so she could see clearly again.

Jovan cradled her against his chest, holding her close. She could feel his heart pounding. She sensed fear, relief, and apprehension. "I told you not to do it," he murmured against her hair. "Why won't you listen to me?"

"It's my fault," Laraina said.

"No, it's not." Tara sat up with an effort.

Jovan glared at Laraina. "I can't believe you asked her to do it."

"I-I'm sorry," Laraina stammered. "I —"

"Leave her out of this," Tara said, hearing the tears in her sister's voice. "It was my choice."

Prince Kaden stirred, muttering in his sleep. Laraina hurried to his side.

Tara squinted and tried to focus. "You'll have to rebandage his shoulder. I don't think it's completely healed."

Jovan caught Tara's left hand in his and ran his thumb over her palm. The gash had healed without a scar.

Laraina turned. "It looks good, and his fever is gone." She hesitated, her eyes flicking to Jovan and back. "Thank you, sister. I don't know what I would have done if…"

"I know. You're welcome."

"Will you be all right?"

Tara nodded.

"I'll stay here until Kaden's guards return," Laraina said. "It should only be a few more minutes."

Jovan rose and helped Tara to her feet. She swayed. "I need some air."

He lifted her in his arms and carried her out the door and down the hall. She opened her mouth to protest, then changed her mind and settled against him, enjoying the feel of his arms around her. She'd fought her attraction to him for a long time, before finally giving in to her passion after their fight with Captain Natiere.

Jovan set her down beside the nearest window and threw open the casement. Cool, moist air in the wake of a summer rain swept in, teasing back her hair and flickering the torch fires. She breathed deeply, washing the smell of disinfectant out of her lungs. Her lightheadedness receded, and her vision cleared.

Jovan leaned back against the wall beside her and stared straight ahead, his arms folded across his chest.

She shot him a glance, her gaze lingering for a moment on his tousled black hair, the beginnings of a dark beard along his jaw, his broad shoulders... Feeling the heat rise within her, she looked back out the window and let the fresh air fan her warm cheeks. "Jovan, I'm sorry. I didn't purposely ignore your warning, I just... for La-raina's sake, I couldn't let him die."

"I know," Jovan said without looking at her. "What happened?"

"Everything was fine until the end. As I was drawing the power back in, I felt the presence. I fought it the way you told me, and it let go." She shivered at the memory, still close to the surface.

"The presence has never been able to reach you this far away while you were awake."

"It's getting stronger, feeding off my power somehow. And there's something else."

"What?"

"When the presence let go of the power, it shot back into me, hard. I was stunned for a minute, and then I felt another presence, something different, touch my mind."

Jovan's head snapped around. "What was it like?"

"I don't know. It startled me so badly that I shoved it out of my mind before I really knew what it was."

"Was it familiar in any way?"

"Familiar? Like what?"

"Like, for example, Natiere?"

Tara caught the moment's hesitation in Jovan's voice before he said the Butcher's name. "No, it wasn't like him at all." She tried to read Jovan's eyes, but the expressionless mask he so often wore had come down. "It couldn't have been him anyway," she said slowly. "He's dead. Isn't he?"

"Yes. I only used him as a point of comparison."

You're hiding things again, she thought, anger flaring. She could always tell when he was holding back. She looked away and gripped the windowsill, letting the cold of the stone seep into her and calm her flash of temper. She had said she would trust him. She would not go back on her word. "Any ideas who it might be?"

"No. What did it feel like?"

Tara searched for words to describe the touch she'd felt. "Cool and curious, like someone who was used to mental links and had stumbled into the connection by accident."

Jovan stared at the floor in silence, lost in thought. She sensed that this time he had told the truth. He really didn't know anything about the new presence. She felt the turmoil within him and wished for the thousandth time he could share what he knew.

"What are you going to do now?" he asked.

Tara straightened and took another deep breath of the damp night air. "I'm going to bed. Whether I sleep now or ten hours from now, the dream will come. I can't stop it, so I might as well get it over with." She swung the casement shut and latched it, then started up the hall.

"He'd better appreciate your sacrifice," Jovan said as he fell in beside her.

"Who, Kaden? He probably won't. He has as much use for me as I have for him."

"He is a good man. He proved himself in Relic."

"That doesn't mean I have to like him."

They made their way through the empty halls to Tara's room in the east tower. She reached for the door handle, then stopped and turned. "You will stay? In case..."

"Need you ask?" he said softly.

She smiled, her pulse quickening at the intensity in his dark eyes. She took his hand and led him into the firelit room, closing and locking the door behind them. "I didn't want to take anything for granted."

His arms closed around her, and he kissed her fiercely. "Never doubt me," he whispered. Then he kissed her again, a deep, sensual kiss that ignited every nerve in her body. She kissed him back, her hands sliding up under his shirt, wanting to feel the warmth of his skin against hers. Their clothes came off in a flurry, and they tumbled onto the bed, passion taking them.

Sometime later, Tara stirred. She moved to the edge of the bed and reached for the clothing they had dropped. She found Jovan's shirt and her leggings. Sleepily, she pulled them on. Jovan rose, crossed to the hearth, and added more wood to the fire. He picked up his trousers and dug something out of the pocket, then climbed back into bed. Tara lay on her side. Jovan curled his body around her, his chest tight against her back, his arms drawing her close. She put her hand over his and felt a hardness around his finger. He had put on the ring — the gold ring with the red jewel shaped like a griffin, the insignia of the High Kings — that she had brought back from the dungeon of the evil presence. In her last dream, Jovan had used the ring to transform himself into a griffin to fight the presence in its creature form and rescue her from the dungeon. She shivered and hoped he wouldn't have to repeat the effort.

Jovan's arms tightened around her. "Open your mind, Love. Let me in now. We will fight it together."

She eased her mind open until she felt his touch, strong like a rock that could shelter her from any gale. She strengthened the connection, letting her essence meld with his. Floating on a euphoric cloud, she drifted into sleep.

CHAPTER 2

A persistent numbing chill woke Tara from deep slumber. Her head ached, and her throat felt dry and tight. Needles of ice jabbed down her spine, prodding her into alertness. Opening her eyes a fraction, she scanned as much of her surroundings as she could without moving her head. The scene was hauntingly familiar.

She lay on her side in a long hallway hewn out of solid rock. Yellowish ooze coated the walls. Cobwebs dripped from the low ceiling. Four widely spaced torches, ensconced along the walls, burned steadily. Wisps of smoke rose above the flames, blackening the spiders' lace.

Sweeping back her tangled hair, Tara lurched to her feet. Cold fear flooded her mind. Balling her fists, she fought the panic that wobbled her legs and squeezed the breath from her lungs. *Stay calm,* she told herself vehemently. She wished she had her sword or even her dagger, but whether she wore them or not when she went to sleep, her weapons never came through into the dungeon.

Pressing her fists against her throbbing temples, she looked down the hallway. Just beyond the last torch, blackness filled the corridor, thick and palpable as a tar pit. She had the feeling that if she were to stick her hand into it, her hand would come out soot-black and withered. Somewhere in that blackness lurked the creature.

She looked back toward the other end of the hall. A massive iron door blocked the passageway, closing her off from the rest of the dungeon. She stared at the blank door. The last time she'd been here, the figure of a griffin, blood-red like the jewel in Jovan's ring, had been embedded in the door. Somehow, with the ring, Jovan had entered her dream, shape-shifted into a griffin's half-eagle, half-lion form, and pulled her out when the creature attacked. She knew he had put on the ring this time, too. Where was the griffin? Why wasn't he here?

Working through the pounding in her head, she probed the mental connection they had formed before going to sleep and found it still open. She could feel Jovan's mind linked to hers, but there was something different, a subtle barrier between them. It made no sense. He'd said they would fight the creature together. Why would he suddenly shut her out?

Jovan? she called tentatively, wary of opening her mind any further. He didn't answer.

An odd scraping noise drifted out of the blackness. Something dragged itself toward her. Biting cold shivered over her body as if she'd stepped into an icy cascade. The stink of carrion fouled the air. Her left hand flew to her side, though she knew her sword wasn't there. Cursing under her breath, she dashed to the iron door and yanked it open. Another familiar sight met her eyes. A long, gloomy corridor stretched out before her, branching into countless passageways, each lined with identical iron doors. She slipped into the corridor and closed the door behind her.

A harsh scraping sound grated across the stillness on the other side of the door. Tara jerked away. Panic seized her. She bolted down the corridor and darted into one of the side passages. The creature slammed the door open and shambled after her, its murderous thoughts digging into her mind. With a mental shove, she thrust the creature out. The creature's furious shriek ratcheted through her head. Clapping her hands over her ears, she kept running. A single thought drove her — escape.

She wasn't sure how far she'd run when reason finally began to reassert itself. Gasping for breath, she stumbled to a halt at a four-way intersection. The ghostly corridors around her were silent, empty. Only the sound of her ragged breathing broke the eerie stillness. Shivering, she sank to a crouch. She was completely disoriented. Putting her back toward the wall, she closed her eyes.

Calm down! she rebuked herself. *You're not going to get anywhere this way.* She sucked in the chill, damp air and let it out slowly; her lungs burned as if she had breathed in the torch flames. She focused on the pain until she could suppress the hysteria that threatened to overwhelm her. There had to be a way out. She just needed to find it.

Slowly, she rose to her feet. Rubbing her arms to warm herself, she studied the blank faces of the closed iron doors that lined the passageways. Should she try to open one? In previous dreams, they had all been locked... all except one. The one door she'd been able to open had led to a yawning pit of blackness — a limitless void that had nearly swallowed her alive. She shuddered at the memory.

Taking a firm grip on her resolve, she stepped up to one of the doors, undid the latch, and pushed. To her surprise, it opened. Hot, humid air poured out into the corridor as the door swung inward on silent hinges, revealing a small, bare room wreathed in shadows. Reddish slime dripped from the walls like gore from an open wound. On the floor in the center of the room was a single burning candle — a stub of crimson tallow, rising from a shallow bowl of red clay. The bowl was half-filled with a dark red substance that looked like congealed blood. Beside the candle lay a shriveled body.

Tara stared, her gut twisting into knots at the bleeding walls, the shrunken corpse. The corpse lay on its side facing away from her. A tattered gray robe that looked strangely familiar covered its thin form. A smooth, oval stone, black as a moonless night, hung from a silver chain draped over the back of the corpse's neck.

Tara ignored the warning chills that jangled her frayed nerves and stepped into the room. The candle flame guttered and nearly went out. Tara froze. She watched, holding her breath as the tiny flame sputtered, then grew steady once more. Heart hammering, she approached the withered body. The stifling heat grew more intense the farther she went into the room. She reached the corpse — a woman, she saw — and knelt beside it. Blood clotted the strands of silver hair that spilled over the dead woman's face. With shaking hands Tara eased the corpse onto its back. The battered skull lolled to one side. Two silver-blue eyes stared sightlessly back at her from a face distorted by terror and pain.

Gagging, Tara stumbled to her feet and backed into something solid. A screeching hiss echoed in her ears as the stench of rotting flesh filled her nostrils. Vise-like arms closed around her. She screamed and fought wildly.

Tara, stop! a voice commanded. It blazed into her mind, cutting through the hysteria to reach what was left of her sanity.

She froze again, ice cold. Her eyes flew open. She was sitting in a large canopied bed in a cool, dark chamber. Jovan gripped her arms.

"Tara?" he said hoarsely.

Tara whipped around, searching the darkened room, not quite believing she was out of the dungeon. She had thought... the dead woman...

"Tara!" Jovan pulled her back to face him.

She stared at him blankly for a moment, then blinked and shook her head, trying to banish the image. "Jovan?"

Jovan eased his grip. He released her with one hand and brushed back her sweat-dampened hair. "I'm here, Love."

"Did you see? The woman..." Tara began to shiver so hard she could barely get out the words. "She... she looked like..." She couldn't finish the thought.

Jovan crushed her close. "It wasn't you." He held her tightly, warming her with his own body heat. His voice dropped to a whisper. "It wasn't you."

Surprised at the depth of his reaction, Tara eased back until she could see his face. His expression mirrored the turmoil she sensed in him.

"Love, I'm sorry. I should have been there sooner," he said.

She took a deep breath and let it out slowly, her limbs still trembling. "What happened? The connection was there. I felt you in my mind, but I couldn't reach you. It was like there was some kind of barrier between us."

"I don't know what happened. I could see everything that you saw, but I couldn't get through." He drew her close again. "I thought I was going to lose you."

Tara rested her head on his chest. She, too, had thought herself lost. She closed her eyes and let his hands, stroking her back and hair, work the tension out of her body. Slowly, she began to relax. "The woman — who was she? Do you know?"

"No, I don't." Jovan slipped the shirt off over her head and helped her slide out of her leggings. Then he gathered her into his arms. She pressed against him, opening her mind to his again, melding body and soul. His lips brushed across her hair, slipped to her forehead, her eyes. Every move was slow and gentle, the reaffirmation of life in the wake of the brutal death in her dream. She raised her lips to his, and he kissed her with an aching tenderness that left her dizzy. She closed her eyes and let herself go, her body responding to his, her mind filled with surging emotions until there wasn't room for anything else. Everything — the terror, the revulsion — was swept away in a sweet rush of passion.

*****

Jovan Trevillion snapped awake, feeling like he was being watched. Raising his head, one hand sliding to the knife under his pillow, he glanced about the dimly lit room. Nothing moved. Feeble embers hissed behind the grate, spitting weakly onto the hearth. Jovan waited a few minutes, watching, listening, but everything was still. Knife in hand, he sat up slowly. Tara stirred beside him, but didn't wake. He relaxed a bit, knowing her danger sense would have awakened her if there had been any real peril. Stashing the knife back under his pillow, he tucked a blanket over Tara's shoulders, then slipped out of bed and pulled on his trousers.

He stepped to the fireplace and added more wood, building the fire back up to a roaring blaze. Heat and light spread outward into the room, banishing the cool dark of the early morning hour. He looked around again, puzzled. He could see no intruders, yet he still felt like someone was watching him, noting his every move. Carefully, he searched the room, looking for peepholes or some other outlet. He found nothing.

Moving to the window, he stood to the side where he couldn't be seen and looked out into the darkness. From this vantage point in the east tower he could see a limited stretch of the city of Carilon. The white stone buildings extended eastward for a short distance, then dwindled into darkened fields and meadows. The main body of the city lay to the west. Lighted street lamps chased back some of the gloom, but they could not dispel the blackness of the moonless night.

Jovan studied the silent city below. The streets were empty. No one stirred; not even a dog barked. Frowning, he turned away from the window, his eyes sweeping the room once more. The uneasiness that prickled the back of his neck abruptly vanished. He was no longer under scrutiny. He glanced at Tara, but she was still asleep. His eyes narrowed. *Someone was watching us.*

Yes, the ancient voice whispered. *A wizard. Be wary of him.*

A wizard? Jovan scowled. Just what he needed — another player in this impossible game. *Who?*

Validar Melodian.

Melodian, Jovan repeated. The name was familiar, but he couldn't remember why. *Who is he? Why was he watching?*

You will know in time.

Jovan gritted his teeth. *That doesn't help me now.*

Time illumines all things.

Was he the one who interfered in the dream and kept me from entering?

No, but it was he who touched her mind earlier.

It was you, then, wasn't it? You created the barrier that locked me out of her dream.

It was necessary. She needed to see —

Jovan's anger boiled over. *I almost lost her!*

The resonant voice remained impassive. *She lives.*

Don't do it again. Do you hear me? He glanced around at the ceiling, wishing he could see the Being that plagued him. *I will take her far from here, and you can fight your own battle.*

Fool! The voice cut through his mind like an icy blast. *We gave your life back to you. We can take it away.*

He winced, then straightened, his fury tightly reined. *You will find I do not respond well to threats. If you want our help, stay out of our mental connection.*

You will do your part, or you will be replaced, the Being intoned, then faded from his mind like a ghost moving through a wall.

Jovan stood for a moment, considering his options. He couldn't really take Tara away. There was no place he could go where the Being wouldn't find him. He'd tried ignoring the voice in the past, and it had nearly driven him mad. And he couldn't send her off on her own, away from him. The creature in her dream would eventually devour her. No. If he wanted to free Tara from the nightmare, he would have to continue playing whatever hand was dealt to him. The Being knew everything about the dream dungeon, the creature, and Tara's magical abilities. Somehow, he had to find a way to pry out that information. The creature must be destroyed.

His eyes focused on Tara. He hated not being able to share what he knew. Secrets bred mistrust. She had said she would trust him, but for how long? She was not a trusting person by nature. Her past had jaded her, made her suspicious of everyone. Very few people got closer than the length of her sword.

He crossed to the bed, undressed, and climbed back in. Tara turned toward him in her sleep as if sensing his presence. He slipped his arms around her, and she settled against him. It had taken him a long time to win her trust. He wasn't about to lose it. He rested his chin on her head, his thoughts chasing each other through his mind. The Being, the creature, the Butcher, and now a wizard to contend with. How much worse could it get?

*****

Laraina sat on the edge of Prince Kaden's bed, her skirts tucked around her, her sword belt on the floor by her feet. The guards had returned to their post outside the hall door a few minutes after Tara and Jovan had left. Laraina watched the rise and fall of Kaden's chest, half of her thanking the gods that Tara had agreed to heal him, the other half worrying about her sister's nightmare. At least

Jovan was with her. He seemed to be able to get her out of whatever dungeon it was she fell into.

Laraina rubbed her eyes, wishing she could understand what was happening to her sister. The revelation in the Bog of Tara's healing power had shocked her, but this murderous creature attacking Tara through her dreams... Laraina didn't know what to think or what to do about it. She had never before encountered an enemy she couldn't fight with a sword. What if her sister slipped into the dream and never woke?

A wave of guilt rocked her, leaving her cold and hollow. Tara had said she couldn't live with herself if she caused Laraina anguish by not healing Kaden. Laraina looked down at the sleeping prince, her hand sliding over his chest. She loved him so much. But could *she* live with herself if Tara died as a result? She looked away, staring blindly into the candlelit dark. She wasn't even sure how Kaden would react to being healed. She had the uneasy feeling he wouldn't be happy about it. He wanted no contact with her sister and had gone out of his way to avoid her. Laraina hadn't been able to figure out why. But there had been no other way to save his life.

He stirred under her touch, moving restlessly. She turned back to him, her other hand brushing his face. He opened his eyes. "Raina," he croaked, reaching a weak hand upward.

She caught his hand and held it against her cheek. "Shhhh. Rest."

"Water," he whispered.

She rose and poured a cupful from the pitcher on the bedside stand. Carefully, she held the cup to his lips.

He drained it, then lay back. "Thank you." He glanced around the chamber, then looked down at his shoulder. A puzzled expression crossed his face. "I feel... different somehow."

Apprehension prickled Laraina's spine. She had to tell him, but suddenly she didn't want to.

Kaden moved his shoulder, gingerly twisting his arm in a circle. Relief and bright hope lit his face. "The surgeons were successful?"

Laraina hesitated. "Not exactly."

"What do you mean?"

"The surgeons couldn't repair the damage. The wound became infected. Blood poisoning set in. Your fever was so high they had to bathe you with ice." Laraina swallowed hard. "You were dying."

Anger flared in Kaden's eyes. "She didn't..."

Laraina glared back. "She did. At my request. And you would be dead now if she hadn't."

Kaden's hand curled into a fist, and he looked away, cursing.

"Why does it matter that she healed you?" Laraina demanded.

"Because my blood is now tainted." He glanced around as if to make certain no one could hear him.

Laraina's eyes narrowed. "Her *taint* is mine, too."

"It's not the same thing."

Laraina crossed her arms in front of her chest. "Why isn't it?"

Kaden ran his hand through his hair. "Because she has the true magic of the Ancients. It's in her blood, innate. I don't know how. You don't have that."

"Aurelia's magic never bothered you," Laraina said hotly.

"Aurelia's magic is not the same as your sister's. Aurelia uses incantations to focus the elemental energies, as she calls them, to cast simple spells. It's book magic, not very powerful — taught to her by a mage, who is skilled, yes, but whose magic is also from books. It's not true magic — the kind of inborn power like the Ancient ones of lore. People feared the Ancients and the wizards and witches of old who rose to great power by feeding off the Ancients' knowledge. The mages of this era are simple spellcasters, so the people don't fear them as much. They are accepted, at least, in the more learned cities."

He took a deep breath and said slowly, as if choosing his words with more care, "Your sister is different. If my people... our people... found out about her healing power, they would shun her."

"Even though that same power could save their lives?" Laraina threw her hands up in exasperation. "By all the gods, she has already saved them. If not for her, Dhanarra would still be under Sulledorn rule."

"It doesn't matter. People still remember the Cataclysm and the Wizards' War, and the death and devastation they caused."

"That war was over two hundred years ago, and the Cataclysm longer ago than that," Laraina snapped.

"It doesn't matter," Kaden repeated. "No one remembers the details — those have been forgotten or exaggerated — but all remember the fear. Fear of the Ancients, of wizards and witches with the power to control and destroy. That fear has passed down through the generations, deep-rooted and unrelenting. And there has been no reason for people to think otherwise. The Ancients have all disappeared, their realms hidden from us, if they even exist at all. There are no wizards or witches in the kingdoms of the West, and the few who still walk the Eastern Frontier are said to be crazed hermits, permanently damaged by the war. They certainly have done no good works to ingratiate themselves back into our world."

"The world would not have them if they did," Laraina muttered. She remembered Wyndover, the village where she and Tara had grown up, remembered how the people had shunned Tara then, because of the silver in her hair and eyes. Every day Laraina had lived in fear that Tara would mistakenly do something to anger the intolerant villagers. They had threatened to stone her sister more than once. She shook her head. "But I still don't see why her healing you is so bad."

Kaden sat up, only slightly wobbly. "Raina, you have to understand. Your sister has what the people would call 'witch blood.'" He held up his hands to stem the argument Laraina had been about to make. "Please let me finish. I know you have some of her blood in you because she healed you, but it hasn't changed you outwardly, and it hasn't given you any magical powers. It hasn't changed me, either, except for healing my shoulder. But our children, Raina — with witch blood in both of us, we could produce a witch child. Don't you see how damaging that would be?"

Laraina folded her arms again. "To whom?"

"To us, of course. If we had a witch child, all of Dhanarra would consider us cursed. We would be forced to give up the throne and be sent into exile."

"So this is why you didn't want Tara to heal you? Because of your throne?"

"The kingship of Dhanarra has been in my family since before the Wizards' War," Kaden said vehemently. "My ancestors were great kings, proud warriors. I have a duty to them and to the people of Dhanarra, and I will not sully the line with a witch child."

Laraina rose, shaking with rage. "If not for that 'witch blood' you so abhor, you would be dead and your line of 'great kings' would have died with you." She retrieved her sword. "Since your ancestors are so much more important to you than I am, I suggest you wed someone else." She turned her back and strode from the room.

*****

Tara woke to the sound of sparrows chirping noisily outside her window. She came to awareness slowly, her mind still hazy with the mingled remembrances of love and the dream. She felt Jovan beside her, his arms around her. When she finally opened her eyes, she found him watching her, a mixture of deep love and concern in his dark eyes.

She smiled. "Good morning."

He smiled back, and she caught a glimmer of relief in his expression. He brushed a stray silver lock from her cheek, his fingertips caressing her face. "How do you feel?"

"Fine, now."

He drew her closer. She twined her arms around his neck, and their lips met in a lingering kiss.

After a while, they broke apart and lay back against the pillows, watching the golden glow of the rising sun pour through the window.

Outside, the white stone city of Carilon was awakening. The bustle of activity could already be heard. Preparations for the grand wedding and coronation of Kaden and Laraina were nearly complete. Every day, more dignitaries from the surrounding allied kingdoms arrived to join in the festivities. Apparently, no one had told the people how seriously ill Kaden had been.

Jovan swung himself out of bed and stepped into his trousers. The fire had died down again, but the room was still pleasantly warm. Bright sunlight spilled across the thickly carpeted floor, illuminating the myriad particles of dust that floated and swirled throughout the small chamber, stirred by imperceptible air currents.

Tara sat up and watched him from the bed as he strode to the window and threw it wide. Warm, fresh air burst into the chamber, filling it with the fragrances of midsummer — floral perfume from the nearby gardens, the tang of horses and livestock in the stable, exotic aromas from the markets, and mown hay from the fields beyond the city. The vibrant hum of daily life rose from the streets below and drifted into the room.

Jovan turned from the window. He came back slowly and sat down on the bed. "Tara... your dream..." He stopped, scowled, then his expression hardened. "Something interfered with our connection and prevented me from entering your dream until it was almost too late. I can't explain it, and I can't guarantee it won't happen again." He looked away.

Tara felt the anger radiating from him and swallowed her questions. She moved over beside him. "It's enough that you were there when you were."

"No, it's not enough!" He closed his eyes and, leaning forward with his elbows on his knees, rested his head on his fingertips, his face hidden. "I'm sorry. I didn't mean to snap at you."

"I know." Tara slipped her arms around him. Their eyes met and held. Tara searched the brown depths, but she could not see through to the soul within. She sat back, trying to hide her disappointment.

Jovan swore and rose abruptly. He took a few steps, then turned around. "I want you to promise me you'll do no more healing until we solve this... puzzle."

Tara shook her head. "I can't promise that. If I were to get hurt somehow, my body would heal itself, whether I wanted it to or not." She rubbed her temples. "I just wish I knew where to start."

"You should tell Laraina your dreams are getting worse."

"And ruin her wedding by having her worry over me? No."

"Love, she needs to know, in case..." He hesitated, came back and sat on the bed again. "In case I can't get you out the next time. We don't know how bad the dream will get. If something should happen to you..." His voice had grown rough. He cleared his throat and stared hard at the floor. "She'll never forgive you, or me, if we don't tell her."

Tara was silent. The undercurrent of anxiety in Jovan's voice told her he was far more worried than he was letting on. "All right," she said reluctantly. "I'll talk to her."

"Good." He rose, picked up his shirt, and finished dressing. "Why don't you go find her now, before she gets busy with the wedding arrangements? I'll wait for you in the breakfast chamber." He bent his head and, lifting her chin with his fingers, kissed her lips with a hard pressure. Then he turned and left the room.

Tara pounded the pillows. What was happening to her? She was losing control and the realization of it both frightened and infuriated her. Never had she felt so helpless, so frustrated. Someone, or something, was playing games with her mind, and she wasn't able to stop it. Yet. *But I will*, she thought fiercely. *As soon as the wedding is over, I will find out who's responsible. And when I do... watch out.*

She slipped from the bed and pulled on her clothes. A temple bell outside rang, startling her as it marked the hour. Annoyed at her nervousness, she splashed cold water on her face from the bedside basin and combed out her hair with her fingers. Icy prickles crept down the back of her neck, and she had the sudden feeling she was being watched. She whirled, eyes searching the room. She saw nothing out of place. The chamber was empty, save for her.

After a few moments, the chill faded, then disappeared altogether. Glancing around uneasily, she stomped into her boots and reached for her sword belt that leaned against the head of the bed near her pillow. She picked it up, looked down at the leather-wrapped scabbard, and hesitated. Laraina had asked her not to wear it around the castle, as she and Kaden were trying to promote peace. For the security of the visiting royalty and nobles, they had asked that all weapons be put aside, except for those of the castle guard. Against her better judgment, Tara set the sword belt down and quit the room.

CHAPTER 3

As Tara descended the long curving staircase that led to the main body of the castle, the first thing she noticed was the noise. The steady hum of voices that first reached her ears about halfway down grew to a dull roar by the time she reached the landing that opened onto one of the upper levels of the castle.

She emerged from the tower and leaped to one side as a servant carrying an urn filled with orange-red dragonfire lilies hurried by. Harried servants dashed up and down the halls and in and out of empty chambers, cleaning and decorating furiously to make room for the overflow of guests and their entourages. Lackeys in green and white livery followed after, barking orders. More servants, perched on ladders, were stringing up garlands laced with brightly colored ribbons, while still others polished the heraldic swords and shields and suits of armor that lined the corridors.

Wishing she could be somewhere else, Tara flagged down one of the lackeys and inquired as to her sister's whereabouts. "The kitch-en" was the hurried reply.

Tara slipped through the crowded halls and down three flights of stairs to the kitchen. The clatter and clang of pots and pans, the roar of cooking fires, and the murmur of voices assailed her as she stepped inside. White columns of steam rose from numerous bubbling cauldrons, obscuring the high ceiling. Savory aromas spiced the humid air. Her shirt sticking to her back from the stifling heat, Tara wended past tables and countertops laden with countless varieties of fruits, vegetables, breads, and meats. The cooks and scullery maids shrank away from her and kept their eyes downcast, studiously avoiding her gaze. Tara ignored them, refusing to let it bother her. Laraina's voice, sharp and angry, rose above the noise. Tara hurried forward, wondering what had put her sister in such a foul mood.

Laraina strode out of the steam clouds and snapped at one of the cooks. When she saw Tara, a strange expression slid across her face. Tara halted.

"We need to talk," they said simultaneously.

"What's wrong?" they asked, as one again. Tara felt a sudden apprehension chill her.

"Come with me." Laraina led the way out of the humid kitchen and into the corridor beyond.

"Where are we going?" Tara asked.

"The gardens — where we can talk without being overheard."

"Is that possible, with all the visiting —"

"I know a place," Laraina said.

A few minutes later, they descended the short flight of steps into the luxuriant gardens. The pathways were paved with slabs of white stone; velvety green moss grew between the cracks. Laraina chose a path that led to the rear of the vast expanse of greenery, winding through flower beds bursting with fragrant blossoms and dotted with splashing fountains and white stone statues of deities and forest animals. After making certain they were alone, they sat on a bench in a sunny arbor, a high hedge shielding them from view.

"You go first," Tara said, keeping her voice low.

Laraina drew in a breath, then let it out quickly. "I had a fight with Kaden. The wedding is off. I haven't told anyone yet, and it doesn't look like he has, either."

"What?" Tara demanded. "After what I went through to heal him, and the dream?" She shook her head. "No. Either you marry him, or I'll kill him."

"We fought about you."

Tara stared at her sister. "Granted, he and I don't like each other, but that's no reason to fight."

"He said some things about you..." Laraina looked away, then looked back again. "About your having witch blood and how your powers are different than the book magic of Aurelia, and how the people would fear and shun you if they knew."

Tara's eyes narrowed. "What does this have to do with you?"

"He said that since your blood was now in both of us, there was a chance we might have a... a witch child — which would be fine with me," she said hurriedly, "but Kaden..."

Tara watched her impassively, her mind devoid of emotion. All of the walls she had built to shut out the hurt of constant rejection while growing up in Wyndover, the walls that had been slowly coming down, now snapped back into place. She was in her childhood world again, surrounded by people, yet alone.

Laraina shoved her hair away from her face. "Anyway, that's not what's important right now. What's important is you. What he said made me think... made me remember something that happened — something I've done my best to forget." She glanced around, checking for unwanted listeners.

Tara opened her mind, her senses probing the greenery around them. "There's no one near."

Laraina hesitated, then faced her sister squarely. "There is something about our family that you need to know."

"Like what?" Tara asked, tension threading through her like a string tightening into a knot.

Laraina took another deep breath. "We're not full-blooded sisters. We're only half-sisters."

Tara was silent, stunned.

"Your mother was a recluse. She lived alone in a small cottage on the outskirts of town, down near the lake. No one knew where she came from. One day she was just... there. She made medicines from an herb garden. She could cure any malady. The townspeople were suspicious of her because of her strange ways, but her potions always worked, so they left her alone."

"You don't need to go into detail," Tara cut in bitterly. "I am quite familiar with the suspicions and prejudices of the people of Wyndover."

"Yes, I know, and I'm sorry." Laraina squeezed her sister's arm gently. "She was treated much like you were. They thought she was a witch." Laraina paused. "I was five years old when she and our father met. Not long after, she became pregnant." Laraina hesitated, wiping tears from the corners of her eyes. "I don't blame Father really. She was young and beautiful in an unusual sort of way, and Mother was sickly and bedridden a great deal."

"What was her name, and what did she look like?" Tara asked, still feeling numb inside.

"Her name was Tamara, and she looked just like you. I only saw her a few times, but she had the same build, the same features, the same hair... the same eyes..."

"What happened to her?"

"She died the night you were born."

"You mean she died in childbirth?"

"No." Laraina swiped tears from her eyes again. "She... they stoned her."

"What?" Tara cried.

Laraina nodded. She started to speak, then choked on her words as tears poured down her face.

Tara's anger turned to bewilderment, then concern.

"Raina, what's wrong?" she asked urgently.

"I'm sorry. It was my fault." Laraina buried her face in her hands.

Confused, Tara embraced her sister, comforting her silently.

"It was my fault," Laraina repeated between sobs.

"What was?" Tara asked gently.

"What happened that night."

"What did happen?" Tara was surprised at how calm her voice sounded. Her insides churned like a storm-enraged sea.

Laraina took a shuddering breath. "Mother died the night you were born. Father was at the cottage with Tamara, helping with the childbirth because no one else would." Laraina began to sob once more. "I was so furious with my father for not being there to save my mother that I told the Elders the witch had cast a spell over him to keep him with her... and that she had cursed my mother because she wanted to take her place."

"Oh, no," Tara whispered.

Laraina nodded, her tears flowing unchecked. "They stoned her and burned the cottage that same night."

"Why wasn't I killed as well?" asked Tara, her voice hard.

Laraina brushed the back of her hand across her eyes to try to stem the tears. "Father refused to give you up. He couldn't stop them from taking Tamara, but he wasn't about to let them take you. He said they would have to kill him first. They relented. They didn't blame him for anything because he supposedly had been bewitched, and even they couldn't bring themselves to murder an infant, so you were spared. You became a part of our family.

"I hated you at first. I blamed you for Mother's death. But then Father explained things, said everything was his fault, not yours. He swore Tamara was not a witch and that the townspeople would pay for the shedding of innocent blood.

"I was horrified. I couldn't bring myself to tell Father that I was the one who had condemned her. So I tried to make up for what I had done in the best way I knew how. I became your mother. Since I was responsible for her loss, I felt that it was my duty to take her place."

"But you were only six years old."

"Yes, but guilt is a heavy burden. It makes one grow up very quickly."

"You were not to blame," Tara said roughly. "The townspeople — gods, how I hate them — the townspeople would have come to the same conclusion regardless of what you said. In their minds, she'd been condemned long ago."

Laraina wiped her eyes. "I... I suppose you're right."

"I *am* right. But why, by all the gods, didn't you tell me this before?"

"I couldn't. Father made me promise —"

"What right did he have —"

"Please," Laraina begged, "let me finish."

Their eyes locked, and Tara felt her resentment cool somewhat under her sister's pleading gaze. She tore her eyes away and stared blindly out across the gardens. "Go on."

Laraina rummaged in her belt pouch. "Four years later, the black fever hit. It wiped out most of the town. All of the Elders and everyone else involved in Tamara's murder died."

"I'm surprised they didn't blame me for it," Tara muttered.

"They couldn't because you were sick, too. So was I. But we recovered. So many others didn't, including Father."

Laraina pulled a small object bound in leather out of her pouch. Slowly, she unwrapped it. "Just before Father died, he gave me this. He said that Tamara had given it to him on the night you were born and asked him to keep it for you until you were older. He said she acted like she knew she was going to die." Laraina paused reflectively. "You are like her in that way — the way you always seem to know things you couldn't possibly have any way of knowing. I always thought it was strange, but I never made the connection." She shook her head. "Father said that when the time was right, I was to give it to you. I asked him when that would be, and he said I would know." Laraina looked down at the object in her hand. "I think — no, I am certain — that time is now."

She held out her hand. A small black key encrusted with smooth, smoke-gray jewels lay on her palm.

Something stirred in the back of Tara's mind. The key looked familiar. Why? She picked up the key and turned it over in her fingers. It was much heavier than she'd expected. The smooth gray crystals shimmered and winked at her. She frowned. A trick of the light, that was all.

"I don't know what it opens," Laraina said, "but there's only one logical place to start looking."

"Wyndover? No! Never!"

"Now, don't get angry at me," Laraina protested. "I was only making a suggestion."

Tara capped the well of fury that had erupted. "I'm sorry, but you know how I feel about that place."

"Yes, I know."

Tara looked down at the key. Touching it evoked strange sensations inside her, similar to what she felt when she used her healing power. Half of her wanted to cling to it — the feel of the smooth stones was somehow soothing — while the other half wanted to fling it as far away as possible. "I swore I would never go back."

"You also swore off men, after Myles, as I recall," Laraina reminded her gently, "and that didn't stop you from falling in love with Jovan."

Tara smiled faintly. "You've got me there, sister." Jovan's image rose unbidden in her mind, and she grew warm inside, as she always did when she thought of him. No, she was not sorry she had allowed him into her heart. This, however, was an entirely different matter. "You think I should go."

Laraina hesitated. "I know how much it would hurt you, but... yes."

Tara looked up, and their eyes met once more. Laraina's expression was deeply troubled.

Tara looked back at the key. Something tugged at her from some deep well in her mind — voices, images long buried, hovering just beyond her consciousness. She couldn't quite bring them to the surface. "I... will consider it."

Laraina took a deep breath and let it out slowly. "Now what were you going to tell me?"

Tara pulled her mind away from the key. "My nightmares have been getting worse. Jovan had trouble getting me out of this last one."

"After healing Kaden?"

Tara nodded. "And I can't seem to get out of them myself. I don't know why."

Laraina squeezed her sister's arm again. "I'm sorry. In what way are they worse?"

Still turning the key over in her hand, Tara described her last dream. The horror on Laraina's face mirrored her own feelings.

"Jovan said the dead woman in the dream wasn't me, but the similarities..."

Laraina shook her head in bewilderment. "What could it possibly mean?"

"That's what I have to find out," Tara answered grimly.

"There must be someone who would know."

"Who?"

"Perhaps someone who has studied magic — not book magic, but real magic — the powers of the Ancients, like a wizard or a —" Laraina stopped abruptly, and Tara knew she'd been about to say "witch."

Tara clamped her emotions down. "I didn't think there were any left."

"Most died in the Wizards' War. The few that survived were banished, but the stories say that wizards still live across the Cyran-el Mountains in the Eastern Frontier. I don't remember all their names, but there was the Gypsy Wolfgren and Melodian, for a start. We used to hear about them sometimes at that old inn at the Gypsy Crossroads."

Tara frowned. "I always thought those stories were just tall tales." She shook her head. "I don't think seeking out more magic is a good idea. The power I have is causing me enough trouble. If anyone found out about it I'd be stoned to death... like my mother," she whispered, half to herself.

"Well, you have to do something." Laraina rose. "Those nightmares..."

"I know." Tara slipped the key into an inner pocket of her tunic and stood. "What about you and Kaden?"

Laraina's eyes slid away from hers. "I don't know. I haven't seen him since we fought."

"You should talk to him. Settle things one way or the other."

"All right. Let me know what you decide to do about... what I told you." Laraina gave Tara a quick hug, then hurried off through the garden, back toward the castle.

CHAPTER 4

Tara walked slowly back up the garden path, her mind still reeling from her sister's stunning disclosure. She was glad Laraina had left her alone. She needed time to collect her scattered wits.

The warm breeze ruffled her hair, and she brushed it back out of her face, thinking as she did so of another woman who, according to Laraina, had been her mirror image. If only she could have known her mother. She had so many questions. What had she been like? A healer, Laraina had said, tolerated by the townspeople only because of her great skill. A rose in a field of nettles. Tara steeled herself against the stinging in her eyes and sudden tightness in her throat. Laraina had looked out for her as best she could. But to have had a mother who would have loved and wanted her...

Anger burned as Tara contemplated what she had lost, what had been taken from her. She pictured the small town of Wyndover with its rutted wagon track for a main street. The tiny cottage near the lake — charred corner posts overgrown with thorn trees were all that had remained the last time she'd seen it; what must have been the herb garden had been little more than a patch of weeds. She hadn't known the significance of the place then, had never explored it. Now that she knew about it... She clenched her fist. No. She did *not* want to see it.

Loneliness welled up, and Tara's eyes brimmed with tears again. She refused to let them fall. It had been nine years since she and Laraina had left Wyndover. She'd been sixteen at the time, and she'd sworn she would never go back.

She could still see with vivid clarity the grim faces of the townspeople eyeing her with suspicion, disapproval, hatred. She'd been shunned by everyone except Laraina and the one childless couple who had grudgingly taken them in after their father died. How she'd hated them all, still did. It was like a poison deep in her soul, a festering stab wound that had never healed. She'd never forgiven them for their cruelty, and now she despised them even more.

Tara left the gardens and reentered the castle, pausing for a moment to let her eyes adjust to the shadowed interior. The castle was crawling with people. It was nearly midmorning, and the visiting lords and ladies were up and about, wandering through the festooned hallways, exclaiming over the decorations. Tara ducked into a side passage and took the long way around to the small breakfast chamber where Jovan had said he would wait for her.

She slowed her pace as she neared the breakfast room, her mind wrestling over how much she was going to tell him. She knew that if he heard the whole story he would agree with Laraina — that she should go back to Wyndover — but she recoiled from that idea the way she had recoiled from the gruesome corpse in her dream. The first sixteen years of her life had been worse than slow torture. The last thing she wanted to do was live them over again. Yet that was what would happen if she went back. The hateful memories she'd locked away would burst forth to torment her. *I don't know which would be worse,* she thought with a grimace, *the memories or the nightmares.*

Then the irony of her thoughts struck her, and she halted. How many times had she been frustrated with Jovan for not telling all he knew, and now here she was, plotting to keep secrets from him.

A hand closed over her shoulder with a grip like ice. A searing chill raked her flesh. She wrenched away and whirled, her left hand flying to where her sword normally hung.

A man stood before her in ill-fitting livery. He was pale and wasted, his face gaunt under long, unkempt blond hair.

"What do you want?" Tara asked warily. Her shoulder tingled where the man had grasped it, and she wished she'd trusted her instincts and worn her sword.

The liveried man didn't move. "I have a message for you from Jovan Trevillion. He asks that you meet him in the stable."

"The stable? Why?"

"He did not say."

Tara frowned. The man looked like a drug-ridden derelict. His unblinking stare was giving her the shivers. She could feel the hairs on the back of her neck standing on end. If this was one of the regular lackeys, then she was a four-eyed nanny goat.

"Who are you? And how did you get in here?" she asked sharply.

"I am Skuldrist. Come." He reached out a bony hand toward her.

Tara backed up a few steps. "I prefer to go alone, thank you." She dashed to the breakfast chamber.

Two noblemen and their ladies, late risers, were just sitting down to eat. A quick glance told her Jovan wasn't there. She looked back down the long corridor. The hall was empty.

"That's impossible," she muttered. She jogged the length of the corridor. Only two rooms opened off from it besides the breakfast chamber. Both were empty. She walked back to the spot where she'd encountered the gaunt lackey and stood for a moment, perplexed. Where could he have gone? There hadn't been time for him to get to the end of the corridor, and she would have heard him running if he'd tried to escape that way. Had she imagined the whole thing? No, her shoulder still tingled. She rubbed it as she set off for the stables. Why would Jovan have gone there? Maybe he ran into Laraina, and she told him… no, she wouldn't do that. There had to be some other reason. Perhaps another courier had arrived.

She slowed at the stable entrance and scanned the interior. There was no one in sight. *That's strange,* she thought. Where were the grooms? She stepped forward into the building. The dirt floor had been recently swept clean. Well-oiled bridles, harnesses, and other gear covered the walls, hanging from iron pegs that had been driven into the stone. Tara crossed over to the box stalls to check on the horses. The first two animals munched on fresh bundles of hay. The other horses stamped and snorted impatiently, whickering at Tara as she drew near. A mound of the sweet-smelling hay stood close by. A pitchfork stuck out from the center of it as if someone had been interrupted in his chore.

A low moan rose from behind a nearby pile of grain sacks. Tara started forward, then an icy chill shocked her. Something grabbed her from behind. An arm closed around her throat. A cold tingling shot through her, numbing her senses. She grasped the arm, shifted her weight, and threw her assailant over her shoulder, slamming him to the ground. More hands clutched at her. She dropped to a crouch and leaped toward the haystack. Rolling to her feet at the base of the mound, she yanked out the pitchfork and jammed the handle into her attacker's throat. He choked and fell, clutching his crushed windpipe. Tara jumped over him and, reversing the pitchfork, buried it tine-first in the next one's belly. His mouth gaped in a silent scream. Tara levered her foot against his chest and shoved him away. He crashed against one of the box stalls and slid slowly to the ground. The horses reared and whinnied, frightened by the ruckus and the smell of blood.

Pitchfork in hand, Tara faced her remaining assailants. She was surprised to find they were weaponless. There were three left, including the man she'd thrown over her shoulder. He was just now getting to his feet. Waves of coldness rolled over her. It was Skuldrist, the ghastly lackey she'd met in the hall on her way to the breakfast room.

Skuldrist rose jerkily, his uniform askew, his long hair tangled and dirty. "You are to come with us."

"Where?" Tara asked guardedly.

"To the Master."

"Who is your Master?"

Skuldrist's gaunt face remained expressionless. "The one who commands us."

"That tells me a lot," Tara muttered in disgust. She edged back toward the castle entrance.

Skuldrist cut off her escape. "You will come with us."

"Why?" Tara brandished her pitchfork to keep him at bay.

"The Master commands it." Skuldrist advanced toward her.

Tara backed away, further into the stable. The other two moved to surround her. They appeared to be robust, unlike their gaunt leader. Tara watched them carefully and maneuvered to keep them in front of her. Their blank faces and vacant eyes chilled her.

"Tara!" Jovan's voice cut through the still air, coming from the direction of the castle.

"In here!" Tara waved the pitchfork menacingly as her attackers closed in.

Pounding footsteps reverberated through the connecting passageway, and Jovan burst into the stable, followed by six of the castle guards.

Tara's assailants abruptly straightened up, shimmered, and vanished.

Tara blinked in astonishment.

Jovan raced to her side. "What happened? Are you all right?"

"I'm fine. Did you see them?"

"See who?"

"The men."

"What men?"

"The men who attacked me," Tara cried in exasperation.

"I didn't see anyone." Jovan glanced at the guards. They all shrugged and shook their heads.

"How could you not see them? You must have practically tripped over one of the dead ones on your way over here." Tara pushed past them and strode to the spot by the haystack where the man with the crushed windpipe had fallen. He wasn't there. "This is impossible."

"Tara —" Jovan said.

"I didn't imagine it. See this?" She held up the pitchfork, displaying its bloody tines. "And that?" She pointed to the bright red stain dripping down the side of the box stall. "Five men attacked me."

"I believe you." Jovan gently took the pitchfork from her hands. "I never said that I didn't."

Tara breathed deeply and closed her eyes for a moment, calming herself. "I'm sorry. The men who attacked me... they just vanished. One minute they were here in front of me, and the next, they weren't. If I hadn't seen it happen, I would doubt my own sanity."

"I don't doubt you." Jovan examined the pitchfork. "Why did you come to the stable?"

"I was told to meet you here by a ghoulish-looking man dressed as a lackey. I met him in the hall near the breakfast room. He was one of the men who attacked me just now. Where were you? Why weren't you in the breakfast room?"

Jovan handed the bloody pitchfork to one of the guardsmen. "A page gave me a message, supposedly from you, that said I should meet you in your room. When I got there, the room was empty. Then I sensed you were in trouble and knew you were here."

A low groan emanated from behind the grain sacks.

They rushed toward the sound. Half buried under a pile of loose hay lay one of the grooms. Tara and Jovan uncovered him and eased him into a sitting position. His face was white, his skin ice cold. Jovan snatched up a horse blanket and wrapped it around him, then motioned to the guards. "Take him to the infirmary. Alert the rest of the guard that there are intruders in the castle and inform Prince Kaden." He gestured toward the bloodied box stall. "And get someone down here to clean that up."

Tara caught Jovan by the hand and hurried back through the connecting passage into the castle. "I need to talk to you, but first I want my sword."

Jovan followed as Tara pushed through the crowded hallways to the east tower. They ascended the spiraling staircase, leaving behind the noise and chaos of the wedding preparations.

Flinging open the door to her room, Tara ran inside. She caught up her sword belt and buckled it around her waist. "Now I feel better."

Running footsteps pounded up the stairs and onto the landing outside the door. Tara whirled, sword in hand.

Laraina burst into the room. "I just heard the craziest story —" She stopped short, eyes widening at Tara's battle stance. "Oh, gods," she whispered. "It's true, isn't it?"

Tara sheathed her sword. "Don't ever rush in on me like that."

Laraina caught her sister by the arms. "What is going on?"

"I don't know." Tara stilled herself with an effort.

Laraina released her. "I'm sorry. I just..." She hesitated, glanced at Jovan. "Have you told him?"

Tara shook her head. "Not yet. I was about to. Back to the garden?"

"No," Laraina said. "There are too many people out there now, and we can't talk here. Someone might come up here looking for me. Let's go up to the roof."

"Fine." Tara picked up her daggers, shoving one into her belt and the others into her boot sheaths. "Let's go."

They left the room and climbed the last two flights of stairs that led to the topmost floor of the tower. From there, a ladder bolted into the far wall extended upward to a trapdoor. Jovan ascended the ladder first. He threw back the bolt and shoved open the trapdoor. It fell backward onto the roof with a thump. A fragrant summer breeze swept through the opening, brushing their faces and sending whirlwinds of dust spinning across the floor. They climbed up onto the flat roof.

The bright sunlight was blinding. Tara walked to the edge and looked out over the chest-high parapet, shading her eyes against the glare. A flock of gray pigeons, disrupted by their presence, circled around the tower, then landed in the courtyard below.

Tara turned to her sister. "I would rather you told him. You know the story better than I do." She looked at Jovan. "Do you mind?"

He shook his head. "I just want to know what this is about."

Laraina repeated the story she had related to Tara earlier.

Tara closed her eyes as the shock and rage swept over her again. Memories crowded around her. She shoved them away, burying them deeply in her mind.

"Where is the key?" Jovan said.

"Here." Tara pulled the black, jeweled key from the inner pocket of her tunic. It was warm to her touch, and as her fingers slid over the smooth gray stones embedded in it, she felt strangely soothed, as if she were a babe lying in her mother's arms, the soft croon of a lullaby coaxing her to sleep... She tore her mind away from the enticing images and handed the key to Jovan. She had to force herself to let go of it.

Jovan turned the small key over and over in his hand. "I've never seen anything like it." He studied it carefully, then looked at Laraina. "You have no idea what it opens?"

Laraina shrugged. "None."

He gave the key back to Tara. She rubbed her fingers over the smooth stones and smiled to herself as the lullaby sang gently in her mind again. She let the song flow through her, so familiar, yet so mysterious. Where had she heard it before?

"Tara?" Laraina said with concern.

Tara blinked. "What?" The music dissipated, fading like a rainbow deprived of sunshine.

"You were humming."

"I was?"

"Yes. A tune I've never heard before. What was it?"

"I don't know. It came into my head when I touched the key." Tara stuck the key back in her pocket.

"I think you're right," Jovan said to Laraina. "I think the only way to find out what the key unlocks is to go —"

"To Wyndover," Tara finished for him. "I can tell you right now what that key is going to unlock — a nightmare... another one, that is." She rubbed her temples, which were beginning to ache again.

Silence fell, then Tara turned to Jovan. "You really didn't see the men who attacked me in the stable?"

"No, I didn't. What did they look like?"

"Four of them looked like peasants, except their eyes were empty, as if they had no will of their own. They were supposed to take me to some Master. Their leader was even stranger. He had a lackey's uniform and looked like a walking corpse. He said his name was Skuldrist. When he touched my shoulder, his hand was like ice and it made my arm tingle. The same thing happened later when he grabbed me around the neck."

"Well, where are these men?" Laraina demanded. "Why aren't we searching for them? Maybe they can give us some answers."

"They vanished," Tara said.

"They what?"

"They disappeared. Right in front of my eyes." Tara quickly recounted what had happened in the stable.

"How is that possible?" Laraina asked.

"I don't know. I—" Tara stopped as an icy chill of warning whipped through her. "Get away from the edge!" She propelled Laraina and Jovan toward the middle of the roof.

Two figures materialized in front of them, blocking their way to the trapdoor. Three others shimmered into being behind them. Tara and Jovan drew their blades and leaped back to back.

Tara yanked her sister close. "Stay between us! Don't let them touch you."

"But they have no weapons," Laraina cried.

"They don't need them," Tara said grimly.

Laraina slid between her sister and Jovan. She gave a strangled cry. "Oh, gods."

Jovan muttered an oath.

"What's wrong?" Tara looked back over her shoulder. The men she'd killed in the stable, or at least, the men she'd thought she had killed, were bearing down on them.

The man with the crushed windpipe lurched across the roof toward them, his lifeless eyes staring at nothing, his movements stiff and jerky. The assailant Tara had stabbed with the pitchfork staggered forward beside him. Blood still oozed from the puncture wounds that had pierced him through from belly to lower back. His lower body was covered with blood.

A breath of ice brushed Tara's cheek. She snapped her head around. Skuldrist stood in front of her, his gaunt face inches from her own, his bony arms about to grab her. She started back, tripped over her sister's leg, and fell hard.

Laraina screamed as Skuldrist's hands caught her from behind and closed around her neck.

"No!" Tara jumped to her feet and thrust her sword deep into Skuldrist's ribcage. Skuldrist ignored the blow, tightening his grip on her sister's throat. Tara pulled her sword out and, sweeping it in an arc over her head, brought the blade down hard on Skuldrist's arms. The razor-sharp blade sliced through the wasted limbs, severing them at the elbow; they fell away bloodlessly and dropped to the floor.

A blast of freezing wind buffeted them, knocking them all flat as it shook the tower.

The wind died as abruptly as it had started. The warmth of summer returned. Shivering, Tara sat up gingerly and looked about. Skuldrist and his gruesome henchmen were gone. The severed limbs had vanished with them. Jovan crouched a short distance away. He had risen to one knee, but his head was still bowed as if he had not completely recovered from the blast. Laraina lay motionless, her face starkly white against her red curls.

Tara barely heard the stomp of running feet rising through the open trapdoor of the tower as she scrambled to her sister's side. "Raina? *Raina!*"

Two of Prince Kaden's guards climbed up onto the roof.

"What in the Abyss is going on up here?" roared the prince. He pulled his tall, lean frame up through the trapdoor. Several more guards clambered up behind him.

"Raina!" Kaden rushed forward and dropped to his knees opposite Tara. He put his ear to Laraina's chest and let out a breath of relief. On his feet again, he whirled toward his men. "Tannin! Alert the infirmary. Ross, help me carry her down —"

"No! Stop!" Tara said sharply. "That won't do any good."

Tannin and Ross stopped in their tracks, surprised, then continued more slowly — one toward the trap door, one toward Laraina — both looking to Prince Kaden for confirmation.

"Get going!" Kaden ordered. He glared at Tara. "You stay out of our way."

Tara snatched up her sword, leaped over her sister, and shoved Kaden backward into Ross. She pointed her blade at Kaden's throat. "You will leave her to me."

Ross swung Kaden away from Tara's blade. The harsh rasp of metal cut through the air as the prince's guards drew their weapons.

Jovan moved behind Tara, sword in hand, guarding her back.

"Are you all right?" she asked him softly.

"Yes."

Kaden's men circled them and began to close in.

Kaden wrested himself from Ross's grip, waved them back, and strode toward Tara. "Get out of my way!"

Tara didn't move, the point of her sword still aimed at his throat. "What ails her is not an ordinary sickness. Whether you like it or not, I am the only one who can save her. Now back away and call off your men, or I'll kill you where you stand."

Ross, his sword drawn, cut in front of Kaden. "You must stay back, Your Highness. Let us handle —"

"No." Kaden stepped to the side, his eyes still on Tara. "I will not have you tainting her any further," he said fiercely.

Tara stiffened. Jovan started forward in fury, but she held him back. Her voice grew dangerously soft. "If you want her to live you will do as I say."

Their eyes held for several more heartbeats, anger, frustration, and indecision chasing each other across Kaden's face. Then his gaze wavered, and he looked down at Laraina. Ugly black bruises had formed around her neck. Her skin was chalky white. He glanced at his men, who were absorbing the scene with a mixture of confusion and wary curiosity. His face hardening with rage, the tall prince pointed to the trap door. "All of you off the roof. Now!"

The soldiers gaped at him.

"But... Your Highness..." Ross stammered.

"I said *now*!" Kaden bellowed. "And close the door behind you."

Glancing uncertainly at each other, all the guards except Ross hastened toward the trapdoor.

Ross stepped threateningly toward Tara. "I won't leave you, Your Highness."

Kaden clamped his hand over Ross's shoulder and pulled him back. "Get off the roof, now, or you're relieved of duty. Don't ask questions, just do it!"

When Ross had disappeared through the opening and pulled the trapdoor shut behind him, Tara lowered her blade.

Prince Kaden eyed her coldly. "You'd best not be lying."

Tara knelt beside her sister. "You'd best hope it's not too late to save her, or you won't make it off this roof." Setting down her sword, she drew her dagger and made a small cut along one of the bruises on Laraina's neck. Then she slashed her left palm, dropped the dagger, and placed her bleeding hand over the wound. Power seared into Laraina, burning through the coldness in her blood. Laraina shuddered and began to move sluggishly.

Tara grimaced. "Hold her still."

Kaden and Jovan knelt and steadied Laraina with firm grips.

Tara closed her eyes. Laraina was near death, her soul lost in a murky, lifeless fog. Tara felt the sweat beading on her forehead as she desperately searched for her sister's receding spirit. She sensed traces of dark magic exuding from the wound, sapping what little strength her sister had left. Splitting her focus, she walled off her mind to block any attacks by the evil presence and began to purge the deadly magic from Laraina's body. Pain choked her as if Skuldrist was throttling her own neck. She fought the pain and the panic that rose as she struggled to breathe. Then the constriction in her throat eased, and little by little, she expelled the magic and healed the damage that had been done.

Shaking, Tara opened her eyes. The bruises on her sister's neck had faded. Laraina's skin felt warm to the touch now, and pale color bloomed in her cheeks.

Laraina gave a long sigh and lay still, breathing easily. Kaden and Jovan released their holds on her.

Thanking every god she could think of, Tara sagged backward into Jovan's arms. Her head spun, threatening to empty her stomach, her blurred vision not helping the situation any. Jovan held her close against him, her hand in his. He brushed his thumb over her cheek. "Are you all right?"

"I will be." She breathed deeply and concentrated on settling her gut.

On his knees beside Laraina, Prince Kaden lifted her head into his lap and clasped her hand. "When will she wake?"

Tara shrugged and immediately regretted the movement. "I don't know. Soon."

Easing himself into a sitting position, Kaden drew Laraina's limp form up against his chest. "How did this happen?"

"We were attacked."

"By whom?"

"I don't know."

"No, of course not. You never do," Kaden said roughly. "You attract trouble worse than a dung heap attracts flies." He pointed at Laraina. "And someone else always gets hurt!"

"Be careful, Prince," Jovan warned.

"Think what you like," Tara retorted, her vision starting to clear. "I don't care. But she does. She loves you. If you break her heart, I'll —"

Laraina stirred and opened her eyes.

"Raina," Kaden whispered. He hugged her close.

"Raina?" Tara sat forward.

"What happened?" Laraina asked with a puzzled glance at the array of faces staring at her.

"You don't remember?" asked Kaden.

"I..." Her eyes met Tara's, and she grew sober quickly. "Yes, I do. The men..."

"What men?" demanded Kaden.

"They're gone," Tara answered.

"Who? Gone where?" Kaden's voice rose in exasperation.

"As I said before, I don't know who, and back where they came from, I would guess," Tara said.

"Well you're just full of information, aren't you?" the prince said in disgust.

"Leave her alone," Laraina said. "I'm not sure, but I think she just saved my life."

"It's her fault you were in that position to begin with," Kaden countered fiercely.

"Kaden, please." Laraina glared at him with reproach.

Prince Kaden lapsed into annoyed silence.

Laraina turned back to her sister. "Do you think they'll come back?"

"No."

Laraina looked doubtful. "Why not?"

"Because I won't be here."

"You're leaving?"

"Yes."

"The sooner, the better," muttered Kaden.

Laraina ignored him. "When?"

Tara met her gaze evenly. "Now."

CHAPTER 5

"Ach mechtoch dalia sol." The whispered words of healing hung in the warm air, then dissipated like wisps of smoke borne away by the breeze. No other sound disturbed the narrow, grassy ravine. The midmorning sun burned hotly. Six gray wolves and one black lay in sun and shadows, waiting.

Captain Natiere reached into a pouch and pulled out several packets of fragrant herbs and roots. He crushed the contents in a bowl and mixed them with water to form a thick paste.

Removing his shirt, Natiere scooped up a handful of the paste and rubbed it into the three-inch-long sword wound in his massive, hairy chest. It stung bitterly.

"Wolfgren, Gypsy Father, give me strength," he murmured through clenched teeth. He pulled from the pouch a vial of bright red liquid and, adding more water, mixed it with the remaining paste. Lifting the bowl to his lips, he drank the fluid mixture. The world spun and the bright sky grew dark. He choked, swallowed some more. Light and stability returned.

He wiped the bowl clean with a fistful of grass and placed it in his pouch. Then he eased his shirt back on.

"*Mion de menochan loor*," he rasped, his gravelly voice grown stronger. Out of habit, he traced the ragged scar slicing down the left side of his weathered face.

Gathering his gear, he lurched upright. The seven wolves rose and trotted to his side.

"Come, my Brothers and Sisters. The hunt begins."

Soundlessly, they left the ravine, heading west across the meadows.

*****

Tara Triannon strode down the wide sloping passageway that led to the stables, her packed saddlebags slung over her shoulder. Jovan had gone ahead to ready their horses.

"Tara, wait!" Laraina hurried to catch up with her sister. "You can't leave yet."

"Why not?"

"Because... because I'm not ready for you to leave," Laraina sputtered.

Tara stopped and turned. "Raina, I can't stay here. Every minute I'm here puts you and everyone else in danger."

Laraina halted beside her. "What about the wedding?"

"You said you didn't know if there would be one."

"I don't, but if there is, I want you to be there."

"And have you hurt by those walking corpses again? No." She gripped Laraina's arm. "You were nearly dead, sister, and I wasn't sure I was going to be able to pull you back. If my leaving will keep you safe, then I'm gone."

"What about keeping *you* safe?" Laraina demanded.

Tara started down the passageway again. "Jovan will be with me."

Laraina followed. "I'm coming, too."

"No, you're not. This is something I have to do myself."

"Why?"

"Because it is." Tara stopped again. "I need to find out why I'm having these nightmares and stop them before they kill me. I don't know who I am anymore. And even if that weren't the case, I would still want you to stay here." She closed her eyes for a moment, steeling herself for what she needed to say. "Raina, we're growing apart. We have been for some time. You've made it clear you want a home, a family, a settled life. I don't want those things. Not now, anyway."

"Laraina!" Prince Kaden ran down the passageway toward them. He caught Laraina by the shoulders. "You can't go."

Laraina jerked away from him. "That's not what you said earlier."

Kaden drew in a long breath. "I never said I didn't want you."

"Oh, I see. You want me, but not our offspring."

"I spoke in haste. I didn't mean —"

"You meant every word you said."

"Raina, please." Kaden put his hands on her shoulders again, more gently this time. "When I saw you lying there on the roof, I thought you were dead. The thought of life without you..." He cleared his throat. "I want you to stay. I need you to stay. Please."

Laraina eyed him coolly, but didn't pull away this time. "You said a great many things not easily forgiven."

"I know, and I'm sorry." He looked at Tara. "I... owe you an apology... and thanks... for many things."

"Yes, you do," Tara said, surprised by his admission, "but you can relax. She's not coming with me."

Relief poured over Kaden's face.

"Tara —" Laraina began.

"You're not."

Laraina frowned, but remained silent.

Jovan came up behind Tara from the stables. She felt his hand on her back in support.

"Ready when you are," he said.

Tara nodded. "I'm ready now." She turned to her sister. "It may be a long time before we meet again, so I just want to say..." She took a deep breath and fought back sudden tears. "...that I love you dearly, and I will never forget what you've done for me. I hope you will always look back on our adventures with pleasure and not pain." She wiped her eyes.

Laraina smiled through her tears. "I enjoyed them as much as you did, in different ways. Because of you, I've experienced more in my thirty-one years than most people experience in their lifetimes. The memories will always be precious to me."

"Be well, sister." Tara darted a glance at Jovan. "As someone once said to me, choose with your heart and not your head. But if you don't stay, leave word where you are going, and when this is over I will find you." She ignored Kaden's dark look.

"Oh, sister!" Laraina threw her arms around Tara and hugged her tight.

Tara returned the embrace. They laughed and cried and hugged each other for what seemed an eternity, and then it seemed like it had only been a moment that passed too quickly.

Laraina reluctantly drew away. "Take care, dear sister. I will miss you terribly."

"And I you." Tara backed toward the stable, Jovan beside her. "Goodbye."

Laraina raised her hand in a weak wave. "Stay out of trouble."

Kaden cupped Laraina's shoulders again and stood close behind her, as if to make certain she wouldn't run after Tara.

Tara flashed her sister a wicked grin. "Getting into trouble is what I do best." She turned and strode into the stable without looking back.

*****

Late afternoon found Tara and Jovan riding north across the deep green pastures and rolling hills of upper Dhanarra. They had left Carilon quickly and without fanfare. Only Laraina and Prince Kaden knew of their plans.

Villages and small farms dotted the landscape. They rode past fields of ripening grain, keeping a swift pace as they guided their horses around scattered flocks of sheep and wandering herds of red-brown cattle. Off to the east, the Amberin River flowed like a shimmering ribbon, glinting in the bright sunlight.

"We should be in Wyndover in two weeks," Jovan said as they halted beside a tiny stream to let the horses drink.

"Yes, I know," Tara agreed, none too pleased with the prospect. She pulled out her water flask and took a long draught.

"Do you remember anything about the house by the lake where your sister said Tamara lived?"

"Very little. I never went there. I had no reason to. All I remember is a big patch of weeds and overgrown thorn trees. Hardly any of the house was left standing." She jammed her water flask back into her saddlebag. "The townspeople burned everything." She kicked her mount into a canter and headed across the field. Jovan followed.

Around midnight, they stopped to rest in a narrow vale sheltered by thick patches of bramble. A half-dozen short, stocky red-brown cattle shared their refuge. The cattle stood close together, placidly chewing their cuds.

Tara and Jovan dismounted, untacked the horses and, after giving them a quick rub down, tethered them and left them to graze.

Tara wrapped her cloak around her and sat on the dew-dampened ground. Healing Laraina had taken a lot out of her, and she was more tired than she wanted to admit. Sleep beckoned. How easy it would be to close her eyes and drift off. But the dream... The creature was waiting for her. She could feel it even now, reaching toward her, edging closer. As long as she stayed awake, she could keep it at bay.

The piercing howls of a wolf pack rose in the distance behind them, nearly jumping Tara to her feet. The cattle stirred, their ears flicking back and forth nervously, but they didn't run. More howls rose from farther south and east, mingling with the first and sending wild echoes across the dark.

Shivering, Tara settled back down. "Wolf howls always give me the chills."

"They're too far away to bother us."

Jovan seemed unconcerned, but Tara noticed a tenseness in his manner that hadn't been there before. She watched him narrowly as he brought one of their saddle packs over and sat down. What wasn't he telling her this time? He dug into the pack, taking out some bread and cheese and dried fruit.

"I don't remember there being so many wolves in this area," Tara said as she took her share. She looked back toward the south. She sensed something at the periphery of her reach — something familiar, yet different somehow. She couldn't quite catch what it was, but she didn't dare open her mind any further. The creature lurked too close to take the chance.

"I can keep watch if you want to sleep for a bit," Jovan said. He washed down a bite of fruit with a swig from his water flask.

Tara knew what he was asking. Did she want to face the dream now or later? "I'll wait." She dreaded the unavoidable descent into the dungeon that sleep would bring.

"You can't go without sleep forever," he said softly.

"I know, but after the last time, I'm in no hurry to go back." Tara stifled a shiver as she remembered the dead woman she'd seen in her last dream. The woman's blood-caked silver hair and terrified eyes haunted her.

Jovan swallowed another bite. "Have you ever seen anyone who looked like her? Or like you?"

"No. Have you?"

"Only in the vision from Rinpool, and that was you."

"You're certain?"

"Yes."

Her appetite gone, Tara put what was left of her portion back in the pack. She recalled what Jovan had told her — one of the few secrets he'd shared — of the visions he'd had as a youth in the prophetic waters of Rinpool. He'd seen her standing in front of a black castle in a valley surrounded by black mountains. She had looked back over her shoulder and then had touched the wall of the castle and walked through it. Tara had never seen nor heard of a black castle. Jovan had said there was a mountain range in the Eastern Frontier called the Black Mountains, but he'd never seen them and didn't know if they were the mountains from his vision.

"Did you ever hear of anyone else in Wyndover who was accused of being a witch?" Jovan asked.

Tara bristled. "No one but me."

He put his hand on her arm. "I know you don't want to talk about it, but I need to know more if I'm to be of any help to you."

"You need to know more." Tara laughed bitterly. "That's funny, coming from you." She caught herself, but not before the anger flared in his eyes. The unreadable mask slid over his face. She closed her eyes for a moment, her hand clenching. "I'm sorry. My bad temper got the better of me."

"I thought your sister was the hotheaded one," Jovan said, his voice neutral.

"Usually." Tara could feel the tension coiling through him. She covered his hand with hers. "What else do you want to know?"

He looked at her, the cold mask fading. "Do you have any good memories from Wyndover, any at all?"

Tara stared across the darkened valley, considering. The cattle chewed contentedly. Some of them lay down, blowing loudly through their nostrils as they settled into comfortable positions. Watching them, Tara felt strangely soothed, as if their presence proved the valley a safe haven.

"I have one," she said finally, "but it's rather a long story."

"We have time."

Tara took a deep breath. "All right. On my sixteenth birthday, the Elders informed me that since I was not a child any more, I was no longer welcome in the village. Not that I had been welcome before. I had three days to get my things together and go. Laraina, of course, was free to stay, but she refused, and we made plans to leave."

"That's a *good* memory?"

"No," Tara said with a grim smile, "but I'll get to it. The next day, as we were gathering the few supplies we had been allowed, a posse from the neighboring town of Raedan rode in, looking for a 'dangerous' outlaw that had escaped from their stockade. They'd been tracking him for days but had lost him in the hills to the north. He was wounded, and they didn't think he could have gone much farther. We hadn't seen him."

"He couldn't have been hurt too badly if he made it that far," said Jovan. "Raedan is at least a week's travel from Wyndover."

Tara nodded. "The posse left to continue their search. There was something about them I didn't like. From what I'd heard, Raedan was very much like Wyndover in terms of suspicions and prejudic-es. Maybe this man was just an outcast, like me. I decided to do a little searching on my own.

"While Laraina was trying to wheedle a horse and more supplies from one of the villagers, I went off into the hills. Somehow, I knew right where he was. I found him hiding in a thicket. He was hurt as they'd said, but he was conscious, and he had a knife in his hand. He looked desperate. Then he saw me, and he said, 'Well now, if I had known you were going to be in the posse, I wouldn't have run so fast.'"

Tara chuckled. "I laughed. I couldn't help it. He was amazing. One minute he was spitting out the worst profanity I'd ever heard, and the next minute he was apologizing to me for using such lan-guage in front of a lady. He badgered me until I forgave him. Then he told me to get lost.

"Before I could decide what to do, we heard the posse coming, and he panicked. He told me to hide, as if I were somehow in dan-ger from them. Then he started to climb out of the bushes. He was going to give himself up so I could slip away unnoticed. I had the uneasy feeling he was right, but I couldn't let him do it. I started to argue with him, only to find he'd passed out. I shoved him back un-der the bushes and hid, hoping they wouldn't see the blood on the ground.

"As it was, the posse didn't come down into the ravine. They headed farther north. I checked his wounds and realized he would die without help. I couldn't let that happen." Tara smiled. "I figured he couldn't be all bad if he was willing to let himself be captured so I could escape. I was touched by the gesture. Actually, overwhelmed is more like it. No one but Laraina had ever taken any considera-tion for me before. So I healed him — not completely, but enough so that he could travel without bleeding to death. Then I bandaged his wounds and waited for him to come around."

"Who was he?"

"Blackie de Runo."

"The smuggler?"

Tara nodded. "He introduced himself as 'Blackie de Runo, pirate, smuggler, and swordsman extraordinaire.'"

"What was he doing in Raedan? I know you said you'd healed him in the past, but I assumed it was in Vaalderin or one of his more usual haunts."

"It had something to do with smuggling Cierran brandy."

"Ah, yes. Cierran brandy commands a high price."

"I took a liking to him," Tara said. "He always spoke loudly. I think it was because he was short for a man. He was barely taller than me. But he was handsome in a wicked sort of way, and he had a roguish charm... much like you do." She shot Jovan a sidelong glance. "In fact, you two are very much alike."

Jovan snorted. "Thanks a lot."

Tara laughed. "When he finally came to, he thanked me for the bandages and said he needed a boat to get back to his men. I told him I would help him with the boat if he would take Laraina and me with him. He agreed. We sneaked back into town, and then the three of us stole a boat. The townspeople came after us, but we made it to the river. Everything was one grand adventure after that." She grinned. "You wouldn't believe the messes we got into because of Blackie's big mouth. He's the only person I know who can get into trouble faster than I can."

"I'd wager that the two of you are about even," Jovan said dryly.

Tara ignored the comment. "Raina and I joined his band of smugglers and swords-for-hire and had the time of our lives. They were a good-hearted bunch, more concerned with having fun and thwarting the local patrols than anything else. Blackie taught us how to handle a sword — the basic skills and a lot of other tricks I'm sure weren't in anybody's rule book."

"Following rules was never one of his strong points."

"You know him?"

"We've met once or twice."

Tara eyed him curiously. "You'll have to tell me."

Jovan gave a brief smile. "I will, when we have more time."

"I'll hold you to that." She took another drink from her water flask. "Escaping Wyndover was the happiest moment of my life. I was finally *free*..." She trailed off into silence, then continued, her voice hard-edged. "Ironic, isn't it? The one place I swore I would never go back to is the one place that holds the key to my life. It's almost funny."

Shimmering stars had filled the blue-black sky like millions of glowing beads dropped carelessly by the gods. The moon, a sliver of brightness, hung above the fields and meadows, sparking the dew with a soft radiance that echoed the glow of winking fireflies. A chorus of crickets filled the night air with their boisterous chirping.

Jovan finished his portion and picked up the pack. "We should keep moving." He rose and went to saddle the horses.

Tara watched him, scolding herself for not helping, but she was so tired. Finally, she rose, wishing that she could sleep without losing herself in the dream.

All at once, the night sounds ceased. The red-brown cattle that had been sleeping peacefully scrambled to their feet and bolted. They didn't go far; they milled around a short distance away, their noses to the air. The horses were snorting and half-rearing, eyes wild. Jovan only just managed to hold them.

Sword in hand, Tara glanced about, the cold shock of danger banishing all thoughts of sleep. A brittle silence settled over the valley and the surrounding meadows. Even the wind ceased its low murmurings.

She hurried to Jovan's side. "Do you feel like we're being watched?" A stinging coldness brushed her face. She jumped back, startled.

"What happened?" Jovan demanded, holding the horses with difficulty.

"I don't know. It felt like something touched me." She raised her hand to her face. Her cheek was ice cold. It began to tingle. "Something did touch me." She sheathed her sword and caught her mount's reins.

Jovan cupped her cheek with his palm. He jerked his hand away as the cold bit into him.

An icy chill of warning whipped down Tara's spine. "Skuldrist! He's coming!"

They swung into the saddles, dug their heels into their horses' flanks, and galloped northward.

CHAPTER 6

All through the night they rode onward and all the next day, pushing their horses as hard as they dared. The creature relentlessly slashed at Tara's mental wall, and it was all she could do to stay in the saddle.

Some hours after nightfall, Jovan pulled up in a shadowed glen surrounded by low hills. A tiny stream choked with sedge and cattails trickled through the center of the hollow. A light wind whistled in the reeds and swayed the tall grasses. The pale moon glowed softly.

Tara lurched forward as her horse slowed to a standstill behind Jovan's, her mental wall buckling under the creature's onslaught. Darkness swirled around her, a dizzying maelstrom of blackness and pain. She slid from the saddle and fell to her knees. Strong arms lifted her, carried her away from the horses.

"Jovan," she whispered, shivering.

"I'm here, Love." He sat down and held her against him.

She smelled wet earth and stagnant marsh. He touched her brow. She reached for his hand, gripped it in both of hers. "Don't let go."

"I won't," he promised, drawing her closer.

The steady beat of his heart penetrated the shroud of blackness clogging Tara's mind. She pressed her head against his chest, straining for the sound, focusing on it until her own heart beat in rhythm. Her hands tightened on his. Then she slipped into oblivion.

*****

Shivering uncontrollably, Tara heaved herself into a sitting position. Freezing chills raced over her skin as she glanced around the familiar slime-walled hallway of the nightmare dungeon. She looked toward the closed iron door that sealed her off from the corridors beyond. Her heart sank to the floor. No red griffin lay embedded in its smooth surface.

A soft scraping sound floated through the air, drawing closer. The reek of rotting flesh filled the hallway. Tara staggered to her feet, her gut twisting in panic. She backed away from the churning darkness at the other end of the hall. Malevolence radiated from the depthless black, hatred mixed with anticipation. The creature had been waiting for her.

Tara whirled and ran for the door. She sensed the creature lunge out of the darkness behind her. She scrambled through the door and darted down the main passage. The creature dragged itself after her, shrieking its fury. She ducked her head, wincing as a stabbing pain lanced through her skull. Dodging into a side passage, she dashed through the maze of corridors, raking through cobwebs, searching for an exit, for a door that looked different. Her mind was strangely clear and alert. The hysteria that usually affected her had not taken hold. She could feel it in the background, nibbling at her sanity like a pack of diseased rats, but something was beating it down. Something that had never been there before. What was it?

She halted at one of the myriad intersections to catch her breath. She was tired but not winded. In spite of the exertion, her heart rate had barely risen above normal...

Heartbeat. Her hand flew to her chest. That was it. Her heart and Jovan's were beating as one. His strength was buoying her, keeping her sane. She closed her eyes and focused on the steady pulsing beat, the strength coursing through her, and felt a surge of hope. Whatever lay ahead, she wouldn't have to face it alone. "I love you," she whispered, and knew that he heard.

"But we've only just met," said a deep, slightly amused voice.

Tara's eyes snapped open. Not five paces away stood a man clothed in a hooded red robe. Tara leaped back and reached to her side for the weapon that wasn't there.

The man drew back his hood and raised his hands in a gesture of peace. "Do not fear, Lady Tara. I bid you welcome."

The man's voice was seductively soft and melodic. Tara regarded him warily. "You know my name."

The man smiled, a thin, mirthless smile. "Of course. You are Tara, daughter of Tamara, lost child of the Kamarians."

Tara frowned. "The who?"

"The Kamarians. The people of Kamar. They were sky Ancients — magical beings that once ruled the Black Mountains. Their powers were extraordinary. But their leaders were arrogant and foolish, and they destroyed themselves. You are the last."

He reached into his robe. Tara watched him carefully. The crimson robe he wore masked a tall, thin figure, but Tara sensed that he was lithe and strong. Long brown hair with hints of auburn flowed over his shoulders. He looked youthful; no wrinkles marred his clean-shaven face. And his eyes — a swirling mixture of steel gray and crimson — his eyes were frighteningly hypnotic.

"Have you seen one of these?" He pulled an oval pendant out of his robe.

Tara stared, transfixed. The pendant, a smooth blood-red jewel on a silver chain, glowed faintly and seemed to pulse with life. It looked just like the pendant worn by the woman in her dream, except her jewel had been black, as lifeless as she was.

"What is it?" Tara whispered.

"A Kamarian moonstone, or lifestone, as they were usually called." He rubbed his thumb over the smooth surface of the jewel. Red light flared.

Tara blinked and stepped back a pace, but she couldn't tear her eyes from the pendant. It looked familiar somehow, and yet she knew she'd never seen anything like it outside her dream. The feelings it evoked... just looking at the jewel aroused sensations inside her like those she'd felt when she'd touched the jeweled key. But more than that, she sensed power far beyond the ability to heal. Memories of people and places she'd never seen flitted through her mind, memories of a life she'd never lived. Her mind reeled. What was happening? She was falling...

An insistent pounding within her chest pulled her back from the brink. She seized it with what was left of her consciousness, concentrated on the pulsing beat — her heartbeat — until her mind cleared. The gloomy labyrinth of tunnels slowly came back into focus. She was vaguely aware of the strange man with the glowing pendant; he hadn't moved. He was watching her closely. She blinked and shook her head. The spell was broken.

"Who are you?" she demanded.

Amusement crossed his handsome features. "Forgive me. Apparently my reputation is not as great as I had thought. I am Validar Melodian."

"Melodian." Tara narrowed her eyes. "The wizard?"

"Excellent. You do know of me."

"What do you want?"

He smiled again, and Tara grew cold all over.

"I want to help you develop your powers."

"What do you know of my powers?" she asked sharply.

"A great deal." He put the pendant away. "You are remarkably strong for someone untrained."

"And if I refuse your... help?"

His strange eyes locked with hers. "Then I shall have to persuade you otherwise." He moved forward, holding her gaze. The swirling color of his eyes entranced her. She stood frozen, mesmerized. He laid his hands on her shoulders. Tara's skin crawled at his touch, but she could not break the hypnotic gaze that held her fast. The wizard bent his head. His lips closed over hers. Burning coldness seeped into her body, a heady mixture of pleasure and pain that left her numb. Her willpower drained away.

Then a sudden burst of warmth and strength seared through her veins, driving away the deathly chill. She closed her eyes and drew it in, gathered her own strength. Levering her hands against his chest, she shoved him away. The lethargy she'd felt vanished.

"That was foolish," he snarled. He stepped toward her again, uttering strange-sounding words.

Warning chills whipped down Tara's spine. Before she could react, a stunning blow delivered by an invisible hand caught her in the ribs, knocking the wind out of her. She dropped to her knees, gasping. Cold fingers probed her mind, every touch like a knife stab in her head. Her lips open in a silent scream, Tara grasped at her scattered wits. She managed to shut him out, but not before he had gathered a valuable piece of information.

"Give me the key," he said harshly.

"No," she croaked.

The wizard grasped her by the collar. "Give it to me!"

Tara screamed in agony. Then everything went black.

*****

Pain. Horrible, excruciating. Wave after wave washed over her, drowning her. She couldn't breathe. She sank deeper into the void, surrounded by darkness, cold and eternal. A faint beat echoed in the background, but every time she reached for it, the pain became unbearable. She shrank away. The darkness enfolded her, drew her in, promising an end to the pain. She closed her mind and floated toward it. Something held her back.

Let me go, she pleaded. *I can't bear it.*

No, said the familiar whisper-soft voice. *Listen to me. Follow my voice. I will ease the pain.*

I don't... have the strength... She began to drift.

Yes, you do, the voice insisted. *Tara! Love, listen to me. I will help you. Come.* The voice both soothed and compelled.

Slowly, she emerged from the darkness. The steady pulse of Jovan's heart beat against her ear.

"It's all right now, Love." Jovan cradled her in his arms. "I won't let you go."

"Thank you," she whispered and sank once more into unconsciousness.

*****

Dark winds whipped around the ruined black stone tower, shrieking like angry souls denied eternal peace. Midnight had come and gone. No moon shone through the lowering clouds, only blackness, the smothering blackness of the dead hours before dawn.

Validar Melodian muttered an impatient command, and the globe of swirling greenish light hovering above his desk brightened. The shadows that had crept over the book-lined walls and black stone floor of the windowless chamber vanished. His brows furrowing once more in concentration, the wizard carefully deciphered the last few pages of the massive leather-bound tome lying open before him.

"Nothing! Again and again, nothing!" He slammed the book shut and flung it across the room. It crashed against the bookshelves and sent an avalanche of thick tomes cascading to the floor. "A hundred volumes detailing the history of the Kamarians, yet not one mentions anything about a key."

Shoving back his chair, he stood and spoke an incantation. A gaunt man dressed in ill-fitting livery, his arms sheared off at the elbow, materialized on the other side of the desk.

"You summoned, Master?"

"Yes." Melodian glanced with distaste at the bloodless remnant of bare bone sticking through the corpse-like skin where Skuldrist's arms had been cut off, and made a mental note to reattach the limbs. "The woman, Tara, and the man traveling with her — where are they?"

"Nearing Eider Brook and the Barony border."

"They are still traveling north?"

"Yes. Shall we take them?"

The wizard considered. "No. We will wait until we are sure of their destination." He pounded his fist on the desk. "I must know what that key opens!" He strode to the bookshelves and pulled down another large volume. "Watch them. Report anything of significance to me immediately."

"Yes, Master."

The wizard uttered another incantation, and Skuldrist vanished.

Melodian dropped the tome onto his desk and began poring over the pages.

*****

When Tara woke again, the sky was black. Thick clouds hid the distant stars. She heard the soft patter of a warm summer rain. The pungent odor of wet earth and pine pitch filled the air around her.

Slipping her arms out from under the covering blankets, she levered herself up into a sitting position and bumped into low-hanging pine branches, more than would be expected at the base of a tree. Jovan must have built a shelter over her. Where was he? She tried to see out, but it was too dark.

The faint rustle of footsteps rose above the drumming of the rain. Someone was coming toward her. Her hand slid to the hilt of her dagger out of reflex.

"You're awake." Jovan knelt beside her. She could just see the outline of him in the clinging darkness. Rainwater dripped from the hood of his cloak.

"Yes." She reached out her hand to draw him into the shelter.

He removed his wet cloak, then clasped her hand tightly and sat down beside her beneath the pine boughs. He laid his other hand on her forehead. She sensed his relief at the coolness of her skin. His hand slid down, caressed her cheek. "How do you feel?"

Tara closed her eyes and let the warmth of his voice and touch flow over her, encircling her in layers of love and protection. "Fine. Where are we?"

"Nearly to Eider Brook."

"Eider Brook? But that's days from where we were."

"You've been out for three days."

Tara heard the tension in his voice. She could picture the lines of concern in his face even though she couldn't see them. "I'm sorry."

Jovan cupped her face once more, then clasped her hand again. "You have nothing to be sorry for." He reached behind him and drew forth one of the packs. "Are you hungry?"

"Starving. Why don't you sleep for a while? I'm wide awake."

"Are you sure?"

"Positive. You must be exhausted."

"A bit tired, yes."

She shifted so they could switch places, and he lay down. She tucked the blankets around him. "Sleep well." She kissed him on the cheek with a whispered, "I love you."

An hour later, the rain stopped, and the sky cleared. A half-moon glowed brightly. A few stray clouds drifted overhead, their shadows slipping over the silvered landscape like wandering spirits on an unknown journey.

Distant wolf howls echoed across the stillness, setting Tara's nerves on edge. Every time she heard the eerie sounds, she couldn't help but think of the wolf-like Captain Natiere and their climactic battle.

With an effort, she forced the Butcher out of her mind. He was dead and gone, and she had enough other things to worry about. Like a certain red-robed wizard. She knew very little about him. According to Laraina, Validar Melodian was one of the few survivors of the Wizards' War, yet how could he still be alive? He'd be over two hundred years old. He certainly hadn't looked that age. Stories she'd heard said that he'd practiced the black arts. He'd been accused of everything from cursing farmers' cattle to performing hideous sacrificial rites. She'd always dismissed the stories as ridiculous products of overactive imaginations.

Her own impressions of the wizard were hopelessly jumbled. Validar Melodian was handsome and charismatic, yet he exuded an aura of malevolence that could not be ignored. Tara found him attractive and repugnant at the same time.

She thought back to the beginning of her last dream and forced herself to relive it, moment by moment. She recalled being panicky, but still able to think clearly. Jovan's strength had sustained her and then saved her after she'd fallen under Melodian's spell. She could still feel the burning coldness of the wizard's kiss, both pleasurable and deadly, draining the life from her body. And then the pain... She shivered. The excruciating pain when he had probed her mind. What did he want from her? What exactly was his purpose? He'd said her power was strong. Did he want to steal her power, make it his own? Was that possible? And to what end? She shook her head. Too many questions. She had a feeling the answers would be frighteningly unpleasant.

It was then she remembered the pendant — the pulsing red jewel set in black stone. Melodian had called it a Kamarian moonstone, or lifestone. She had never heard of Kamarians. He'd said they were sky Ancients who had ruled the Black Mountains of the East. She'd never been to the East. The Eastern Frontier across the Cyranel Mountains was wild and lawless, or so she'd been told. Jovan was from the East. Blackie de Runo had been familiar with the Frontier, as well. He had traveled the caravan line extensively until he'd been banned for thievery.

Tara's thoughts slipped back to the dark wizard. How had Melodian known who she was? He'd said she was a descendant of the Kamarians. How did he know that, and how had he found her in the first place? He could be sensing the use of her power — but she'd used it so many times before. Why hadn't he come then? The reason must be somehow tied to her dreams. But how had he managed to tap into them? Was his the touch she'd felt after healing Prince Kaden? She rubbed her temples wearily. So many questions. She tried to recall the unfamiliar people and places she had seen in her mind when she'd looked at the pendant, but that part of her dream had grown hazy.

Thinking about the pendant reminded her of the black key. She drew the key out of her pocket. The gray stones embedded in it shimmered faintly. Was the key Kamarian made? It must be. Of course, that was assuming everything Melodian had told her was true. She rubbed her fingers over the key. The smoothness of the polished stones soothed her raw nerves. *Strange*, she thought absently. The jewels in the key were gray, but the stone in Melodian's pendant had been red. She wondered why the difference.

The faint prickling in the back of her mind that told her she was being watched grew sharper. She sat up in alarm, but the tiny valley slept soundly, and the hills and meadows beyond held no threat she could feel. Then she realized. It was the key. Whoever was watching was focusing on the key. She dropped it back into her pocket. The prickling faded. She sat back against the pine boughs. It had to be the wizard who was watching her. She wondered why he hadn't struck again, or why Skuldrist and his grisly crew hadn't reappeared to attack them.

He's waiting for something, she thought speculatively. But what? She settled into a more comfortable position and pondered the possibilities.

By daybreak, black clouds smothered the sky again. A sharp wind whistled through the brush, strong with the scent of rain. Jovan woke at first light. Tara greeted him with the news that they were being watched.

He sat up quickly, his hand on his knife. "Who? Where?"

"Don't be alarmed." She put her hand on his shoulder. "There's no danger right now." She dug a portion of bread and cheese out of the saddlebag and split it between them. "Validar Melodian is watching us. I don't know from where."

He stared at her, his expression veiled. "The wizard? Are you sure?"

Tara nodded. She had the distinct impression he'd been expecting her to name someone else. She puzzled for a moment over the implications of that thought. Who else might be watching? "Were you able to see my last dream?"

"Yes." Jovan grimaced as if with a sudden pain. Biting off a curse, he pressed the heel of his palm against his forehead. "Most of it."

Tara touched his arm. "Are you all right?" She sensed the battle within him, felt him still his rising tension.

"Yes. We will deal with the wizard."

"Along with who else?" she asked softly.

"What do you mean?"

"I got the impression you expected it to be someone else who was watching us."

"The wizard is more than enough." Jovan finished the chunk of bread she'd given him and took a long draught from his water flask.

"You know what the wizard did in the dream?"

"Yes." Jovan's eyes smoldered. "He has much to answer for."

"I think the men who attacked me in Castle Carilon were Melodian's puppets."

"That's a good possibility."

"I also think we'll be safe from them for a while. Melodian wants to know what the key unlocks, and I think he'll let us do the work, then attack afterward and try to take whatever we find. He probably assumes we know what the key opens."

"It would be easier if we did." With a glance at the brooding sky, Jovan began to pack up the gear.

"It's all so frustrating." Tara moved to help. "I have so many questions and no answers. I've never even heard of Kamarians. Have you?"

"Yes, I've heard of them," he said after a moment.

She looked at him in surprise. "You have?"

He nodded briefly. "According to the Nomads' tales, the Kamarians were sky Ancients with inborn magic powers that once lived in the Black Mountains. Some of the Eastern towns paid them tribute in return for protection." He picked up the gear and carried it over to the horses.

Tara followed. "Are they still there?"

Jovan shrugged. "I don't know. The legend says that one day the sky changed color and unnatural clouds formed like nothing that had ever been seen. Then there was a catastrophic explosion — the Cataclysm — a clash of magics, so the legends say, that devastated the land. The Black Mountains became as they are now, brittle and lifeless. The Kamarians disappeared."

"Kamarians were responsible for the Cataclysm? What happened to them?"

"No one knows." Jovan slung a saddle over his steed's back. "This all happened centuries ago... supposedly. Adventurers have tried to find them over the years, but none ever succeeded. There's no real proof Kamarians even existed — only a ruined watchtower at the edge of the Black Mountains which could have been built by anyone." He stopped, then continued, musing. "There is one strange thing. The people who went into the mountains to search for the Kamarians all came back with similar stories. They spoke of hearing the sound of a great waterfall. Some said the sound of crashing water was so loud they should have been standing right under it, but no one ever saw so much as a trickle. No trace of the Kamarians has ever been found."

"How do you know all this?" Tara demanded.

"It's a common Eastern tale."

She continued to look at him questioningly.

He remained silent, bridling his horse.

"You weren't going to tell me any of this, were you?"

Jovan met her gaze. "Yes, I was," he said quietly, "but I needed to think it through first."

Their eyes held, and Tara fought the urge to lash out at him in her frustration. Clamping her jaw down hard, she began saddling her horse.

Jovan caught her gently by the shoulders. "Tara, Love, I'm not keeping things from you by choice. You have to trust me."

She glared at him. "I'm trying, but the last thing I need right now is more secrets —"

A sudden chill snapped Tara around. The horses snorted nervously and tugged at their tethers.

"What's wrong?" Jovan asked urgently as he tried to calm them.

"I'm not sure." She drew her sword and crept along the edge of the pine grove toward a brush-strewn hill, her eyes searching the surrounding shadows. Nothing moved. Behind her, she heard Jovan draw his blade and follow. A small brown rabbit burst from the cover of the hillside, startling her so she nearly cried out. The rabbit raced along the base of the hill, scattering dew as it went. Tara watched the frightened creature until it disappeared beneath a gnarled shrub. Disgusted with herself for being so jumpy, she took a deep breath to slow her speeding heart and walked forward.

Two yellow eyes gazed at her from the bushes along the hill. Tara froze. With a soft rustling of leaves, a huge black wolf, ears flattened, teeth bared, slipped out of the brush and stood facing her not ten feet away. Whinnying in terror, the horses reared and lunged, jerking their tethers.

"Jovan," Tara called softly.

"I'm right behind you, Love." He moved up beside her. "Back away slowly."

They eased back until they stood halfway between the wolf and the frightened horses.

The wolf snarled, but did not attack. After a few moments it turned and vanished into the bushes.

Tara let out a long breath. "That was close. I wonder why it didn't attack?"

"I don't know." Jovan glanced around warily. "I just hope it doesn't have friends nearby."

She shivered. The black wolf looked very much like one of the beasts she'd seen with Captain Natiere in Relic. The wolves had knocked her down then, to keep her from interfering when Jovan had fought with Natiere, but they hadn't hurt her. Natiere had said he'd asked them not to. At the time, she'd noted the intelligence in the black wolf's eyes. Could Natiere's wolves be tracking her, perhaps seeking revenge? That didn't seem possible, yet...

A wolf howled, not far to their left, lifting the hairs on the back of Tara's neck and unnerving the horses again. An answering howl rose from somewhere off to the south. His body tense, Jovan scanned the southern landscape as if searching for something.

Tara followed his line of sight. "Do you see anything?"

"No." He headed for the horses. "We need to get moving."

Thunder grumbled through the thickening clouds. The wind grew colder. A strange sound, wild and savage, raked the southern sky — the cry of a wolf, yet different. She ground her teeth and shivered as more howls joined in, distant, but clear, coming from the south.

"What was that?" Tara asked.

"I don't know." Jovan soothed the skittish horses until they would stand quietly enough for him to finish saddling and bridling Tara's mount.

She eyed him narrowly. She'd noticed once again the sudden tension in his demeanor. Could it be just the wolves or was there more to it — something else he couldn't tell her? Vexed, she looked back to the south, sensing... something. She had the feeling something was tracking them, moving ever closer, yet she sensed no threat. Whatever it was, it seemed strangely familiar. Cautiously, she opened her mind, reaching outward.

"Don't!" Jovan said sharply.

Tara jumped, her mind snapping back in on itself, her hand flying to the hilt of her sword. She scowled. "Must you do that? As I said once before, that's a good way to get killed."

Jovan gripped her shoulders. "Love, listen to me. You must not open your mind. If you do, even the slightest bit, you will be vulnerable to both the creature and the wizard."

"But I sense something back there, following us. I can't tell what it is. It feels familiar, like I should know what or who it is, but there's something different about it..."

"Do you sense danger?"

"No."

"It's not those walking corpses?"

"No, it's not them."

"What about Laraina, or someone from the castle?"

"No." Tara shook her head, perplexed. "I can't place it. It's still a ways off."

"Good. Let's keep it that way." He let go of her, caught up the reins, and untethered his horse.

She did the same with her mount. "Do you have any idea what might be back there?"

He avoided her eyes as he swung into the saddle. "No."

Tara cursed under her breath. He was keeping secrets again. Wishing she had something to hit, she mounted her horse and urged it into a gallop.

CHAPTER 7

Black clouds hung over the marshy hollow. Thunder cracked, and the sky grew darker. Six gray wolves and one black crouched in the hollow, protected from the piercing wind. The grisly snap and crunch of bone rose into the gray morning light as they fed on the mangled carcasses of two fat sheep.

Canine footfalls approached the hollow. The wolves looked up from their meal, ears pricked forward.

The canine advanced slowly, the footfalls hesitating, then stopping as the shepherd dog came upon the waiting wolves. Lowering its head and tail, the dog sniffed the air and whined.

"Where are you, you cursed mutt?" yelled a peevish voice. Stomping footsteps and muttered profanity mingled with the rolling thunder as a large figure crashed through the brush. The shepherd, an unkempt man of middling age with his belly hanging well over his belt, stumbled into view.

He froze in his tracks. "Damnation!"

Wolves and man stared at each other for a moment, then the black wolf growled, lips curling back from sharp teeth.

The shepherd hastily backpedaled, tripped over the dog, and nearly fell. "Lousy cur! Get out of my way!" He whacked the dog in the ribs with his staff. The dog yelped and scrambled away as the shepherd rushed past and slammed into a massive figure.

The shepherd's jaw slackened as he took in the hulking giant towering over him — the broad torso, the ragged scar slashing from forehead to chin, the black eyes glittering with anger.

"If you have a complaint with my wolves, you may discuss it with me," said the Butcher.

The shepherd's mouth moved, but no sound came out. Captain Natiere wrenched the staff from his hands and snapped it in two. The shepherd staggered back and fell. Scrabbling on all fours, he tried to escape. Natiere caught him in two strides. Lifting him by the collar, Natiere dragged him over to where the mangled sheep lay and dropped him onto the carcasses.

"End of discussion." Natiere walked away.

The wolves moved in. Frantic screams rent the air.

Ignoring the cries for help, Natiere sought the abused shepherd dog and coaxed it from the bushes. The dog came forward, its head down.

"You have nothing to be ashamed of," Natiere said. "Your cousins, the wolves, take what they will. It is their way." He ran his gnarled hand over the dog's ribs and found an angry swelling. Reaching into a pouch at his belt, he pulled out a packet of sweet-smelling salve. He gently rubbed the ointment over the swollen area. Then, tearing a strip from his cloak, he wrapped it around the dog's midsection and tied it securely. He stroked the dog's head. "Return to your home now, cousin. It is not far."

The dog licked his hand, then limped away through the brush.

Natiere rose and glanced back to where the wolves were enjoying their meal. Agonized groans rose from amidst the torn carcasses of the sheep.

"Take your time," said the Wolfmaster. He looked to the north, breathed deeply the blood-tainted air. "Our quarry will wait." He sat down in the shadows to watch the storm.

*****

Tara and Jovan galloped north across the fields, covering as much ground as they could before the storm hit. Massive thunderheads lined the eastern horizon, their burgeoning tops towering high into the atmosphere. Gusty winds flattened the grasses and moaned through the scrub dotting the hillsides.

Near midmorning, the first storm struck. Thunder crashed overhead; lightning zagged between lowering clouds. Hailstones pelted down as rain poured, soaking the storm-darkened landscape. More storms ravaged the grasslands throughout the day, with only a few breaths between them. Tara and Jovan sheltered in the lee of a wooded hill until evening brought clear skies and the moon cast its silver light on the wet fields. They rode far into the night to make up for lost time.

Late the next day, they crossed Eider Brook, the rushing, tumbling shallow waterway that divided Sulledor and northwestern Dhanarra from the gently rolling grasslands of Barony. Ice cold and swift, it swept down out of the Triandol Mountains, its once crystal waters now tainted by refuse from the troll villages sprawled at its head. The weather stayed fair, with warm days and cool nights. By nightfall of the fourth day from the crossing of Eider Brook, they reached the foot of Amberin Lake.

Tara reined in her mount and stared off to the east where the moon-gilded waters of the lake funneled into a rushing torrent, the headwaters of the boisterous Amberin River. Memories of a wild boat ride flashed in her mind — the day she, Laraina, and the smuggler Blackie de Runo had escaped from an angry mob and sailed down the river, never to return. Or so she had thought. Now she was back... and so were the seething emotions. Her knuckles whitened as she gripped the reins, vitriolic memories spilling through her like acid burning into her soul. Her horse snorted and skittered sideways, upset by her mood. She pulled it up short.

Jovan moved up beside her. "Are you all right?"

"Fine," she said through clenched teeth. She forced herself to relax. "It's not much farther. Just up around the bend."

"When do you want to go in?"

"Now. The sooner we get this over with, the better."

They urged their horses forward, moving north along the edge of the lake. The night air was calm, without a breeze. The smooth water blazed silver under the brilliant moon. Crickets chirped, went still at their passage, then picked up their rousing chorus again. Bullfrogs croaked in alarm and leaped into the lake, sending ripples across the shining surface.

Tara noted every movement, every sound — the rustling of the reeds, the lap of the water, the chorus of frog and insect. Her sharpened senses drank it all in. What would she find in this reviled town? Her hand slipped to the jeweled key tucked in the inner pocket of her tunic, and she thought once more of her mother. Where would she be now if Tamara had lived? They would still have been outcasts, but they would have had each other. Not to discount Laraina — she had been a wonderful sister — but she had never understood. Tara's healing powers, her ability to sense danger, her knowing things the way she did — these talents were all foreign to Laraina. And even though Laraina had accepted them, Tara knew she'd never been comfortable with them.

Laraina had tried to be both mother and sister to Tara and she'd done the best she could, but the void was too great for her to fill. There were so many things her mother could have taught her, things she desperately needed to know. Were there other powers or talents she hadn't discovered yet? And what about the Kamarians? Were they really her ancestors? Why had they disappeared? Perhaps Tamara could have explained Tara's nightmares and helped her combat the wizard Validar Melodian. Tara clenched her fist and choked back a sob. If only her mother had lived...

Jovan's horse snorted and threw its head up, scattering Tara's thoughts. Just ahead lay the tiny weather-beaten town of her birth. Set back from the lake, the thatched clay dwellings of Wyndover huddled together along the deeply rutted wagon track that passed for a main street. Off to the left stood a small corral. The wooden bars looked like they had been recently patched. Several scruffy ponies stared at them through the railings, and a few shaggy draft horses stretched their necks over the top of the fence, their nostrils distended as they sniffed the cool air.

Tara reined her horse around to the right, keeping to the edge of the lake. Jovan followed. The penned horses whickered forlornly. Tara and Jovan skirted the lake until the bulk of the town lay behind them. A few scattered houses dotted the moon-brightened landscape, and farther on, the rutted wagon track wound like a scar through cultivated fields of ripening vegetables and grains.

They found the ruins of Tamara's cottage just north of the village on a narrow stretch of flat land backed by a low hill. Nothing remained standing. The area was wildly overgrown, in sharp contrast to the carefully tended fields. Thorn trees thick with foliage and sprinkled with small white flowers grew in masses amid the crumbled foundation, as if protecting the site from intruders.

Tara and Jovan dismounted and tied the horses. A soft hush descended, deadening all sound. The air grew thick with the smell of herbs, and Tara suddenly found it hard to breathe. Slowly, she walked toward the ruined cottage. An odd melody seeped into her mind, and she hummed it absently. She reached the wall of thorns and stopped. The leafy branches were too thickly intertwined to see what lay beyond. She parted the limbs, being careful to avoid the needlelike thorns, and a mournful wail flooded her mind. She jumped back, letting go of the branches. The piercing cry faded to a painful whisper.

Jovan caught her arm. "What happened?"

"I'm not sure. Did you hear anything?"

"No. You did?"

She nodded. "It was so sad and full of pain. It hurt."

Jovan grasped one of the branches. "I feel something, but it's very faint."

"Give me your hand." Tara clasped his other hand and touched a thorny limb. The wailing cry seared across her consciousness. Jovan's hand tightened on hers. The woeful keening filled her eyes with tears, then the sound changed. It grew intensely joyful, triumphant, softening to a tender, loving caress.

"Mother," Tara whispered. She clutched at the thorny branches, spiking her fingers and drawing blood.

Jovan caught her and drew her back, holding her firmly in his strong embrace. "She's not in there," he said gently. "It's her spirit you hear."

"Mother, why did you have to die? I needed you so much!" Tara wrenched away and ran back toward the sleeping village. "You murderers!" she shouted. "You killed her! Damn you to the Abyss!" She sank to her knees, tears burning her cheeks.

Jovan dropped down beside her and gathered her in his arms.

She sobbed bitterly. "They killed her."

"I know, Love. I'm sorry."

Tara wiped her eyes on her sleeve. After several long breaths, she drew away.

Jovan cupped her face, his thumb brushing over her wet cheek. "All right?"

She nodded and wiped her eyes again.

Jovan rose and pulled her up with him. "Do you still want to do this now? We could come back tomorrow night. Someone may have heard the shouting."

Tara straightened. "I need to do it now."

She led the way back to the thorn-covered ruins. The sweet scent of the white flowers drifted around her, and she inhaled deeply. She stopped in front of the needle-sharp barrier, hesitated, then reached out. Her hand closed over a rough branch. Tangled emotions filled her mind — love, joy, wistful longing — pictures of a mother cradling her child. Tears came again, and Tara squeezed her eyes shut to hold them back. *I love you, Mother.* The images began to fade, growing fainter with each heartbeat until they died away. Tara's eyes flew open. "No! Don't leave!" She gripped the branches desperately, but her mother's spirit was gone.

Jovan eased her away before the thorns drew more blood. "She has gone to her rest. Your coming here has released her."

Tara turned on him. "How do you know that?"

"I felt her through you. There is something here that must be passed from her to you, I don't know what. She had to stay here until it was done. Now her part is over, and your part begins."

"My part," Tara repeated softly. "Whatever that is." She pulled the black jeweled key out of her pocket. The smoke-gray stones shimmered in the moonlight. Tara rubbed her fingers over them, and the stones began to glow.

"Look at this!" Tara held the key in her open palm. "It's glowing."

"So it is." Jovan took the key and held it in his hand. The light of the jewels dimmed until only a faint glimmer remained. "But it is you who has the power." He handed the key back to her.

Tara rubbed the smooth stones, and the light flared. She started to hum again, the same odd little tune.

Jovan looked at her strangely. "What is that song?"

Tara stopped, confused. "I don't know. I didn't realize I was doing it. I keep hearing this music. It's been running through my head ever since we got here. I've never heard it before —" She broke off sharply. "The thorn trees — look at them."

The thick green foliage was shriveling, turning brown, and dropping off the trees like dead leaves in autumn. Tara grasped the darkening branches, but they'd grown brittle and broke off in her hand.

"The barrier is no longer necessary," Jovan said. "Let's see what's inside."

Snapping off the dried-up limbs, they pressed forward into the ruins. Dim light filtered through the dying canopy of leaves and branches, chasing back the shadows. The smell of herbs was strong. Tara stepped carefully around the peeling trunks, moving toward the center of the thicket. In a small open spot near the base of one of the larger thorn trees, she stopped. She closed her eyes, smiling.

"I've never heard anything so beautiful," she murmured.

"What does it sound like?"

"It's like..." She faltered. "I don't know how to describe it." Still holding the key, she took both his hands in hers. "Listen." Softly, she began to sing. The music flowed through her, touching something deep in her soul. A memory of a place she'd never seen... She stopped singing, startled. "I saw a castle made of black stone." She let go of Jovan's hands and looked down at the key. The smooth stones glowed like polished silver. She gasped. The ground under her feet was glowing as well, as if she were standing in the moon's reflection. She looked up at Jovan, speechless. He was standing just outside the two-foot circle of light, watching her, his face a mask.

She knelt and touched the silvered ground. A strange warmth rose up through her fingertips, pervading her whole being. Dropping the key back in her pocket, she pulled out her dagger and started digging. The glow faded.

She dug furiously, tearing away the soft ground, until about a foot below the surface, the tip of her dagger struck something solid. Brushing away the dirt, she found an object, hard and black. She wiped the soil from her knife and shoved it back into its sheath. Then, working more carefully, she cleared away the earth to reveal a long, slim, rectangular black box.

Jovan crouched beside her and helped her pull the box out of the hole. They set it on the ground in front of them.

Tara swept the dirt from the box and cleaned out the locking mechanism. So this was what she had come here to find — this strange box that had been buried in the earth for twenty-five years. She took the key out of her pocket once more. Tentatively, she slid her fingers over the smooth surface of the box. It was warm to the touch. Taking a deep breath, she inserted the key in the lock and turned it. A faint click sounded as the latch released. She slowly opened the black box. Inside, wrapped in black velvet, was a long, slim sword sheathed in a scabbard of simple design. Both were as black as the inside of the deepest cave.

"Blazes!" Jovan said hoarsely. "A black sword. No wonder the wizard is after you."

Tara looked at him sharply. "What's so special about a black sword? And what does it have to do with Melodian?"

"The black sword is an ancient weapon of Kamarian royalty. Only two existed. The legend said both were destroyed in the Cataclysm that killed most of the Kamarian people. They were the most powerful weapons ever known."

"Wait a minute. I thought you said the Kamarian people disappeared, not that they were dead."

"The ones that survived did disappear. There weren't many of them left."

Tara glared at him. "So you do know more. What else aren't you telling me?"

His eyes hardened. "I'm not —" He stopped, listening.

Tara became aware of the scuffing of boots outside the thicket and more running footsteps coming toward them.

"You in there," called a harsh voice. "Come out of there. Now!"

CHAPTER 8

Outside the dying barrier of thorns, a crowd was gathering. Tara squinted through the branches at the dozen glowing torches visible against the moonlit sky. An excited murmur floated in to where she and Jovan crouched amid the ruins.

"The villagers," Tara said, disgusted with herself for not hearing them sooner. "Wonderful. We'll have to fight our way out."

"Maybe not," Jovan said. "Maybe they'll let us go in peace."

"I highly doubt it." As quietly as she could, Tara lifted out the black sword and scabbard, locked the box, and pocketed the key. Jovan set the box into the hole and shoved the dirt back over it, while she attached the scabbard to the left side of her sword belt.

"I said come out!" shouted the same rough voice they'd heard moments before.

Tara fought down her emotions as they stepped to the edge of the crumbling thicket of thorns. *Be peaceful, not threatening,* she told herself forcefully. A collective gasp swept through the murmuring crowd as they emerged. About thirty men armed with swords and various farm implements had gathered around the ruins. Tara caught their widening eyes as they looked at her. A warning chill jabbed down her spine.

"The witch!" yelled a paunchy old man swathed in the black robes of the Elders, a scythe gripped in his hands. "The witch has come back from the dead!"

A frightened clamor rose above the crowd as a sea of voices repeated his cry.

Tara stepped forward, holding her hands out in front of her. "No, wait! I'm not her!"

The Elder recoiled and pointed his scythe at Jovan. "That man has raised the evil and brought it among us again. Burn them! Don't let them escape!"

The men with torches set the dying thicket ablaze. The other villagers surged forward, brandishing their weapons and trapping Tara and Jovan against the conflagration.

"So much for peace," Tara muttered. She drew both swords and sliced the air in front of her. She gasped as a blistering rush of power shot through her. Black fire erupted from the tip of the black blade. A line of charred bodies dropped to the ground. The world spun around her, and she fell.

"Tara!" Jovan cried.

The villagers screamed as they tripped over the blackened bodies. Scrambling away from the carnage, they fled back toward the village.

Tara lay on the grass, half-conscious. Fire seared through her body, as painful as if the townspeople had burned her. *The townspeople... Oh, gods, what had she done?* Her mouth tasted like ashes. She opened her eyes, but couldn't focus, her vision blurred as if she looked through rain-drenched glass. A moan escaped her dry lips.

Jovan scooped her up in his arms and carried her away from the flames. She heard the horses' frightened whinnies as they drew near where they'd tied them.

He set her down. "Tara, can you hear me?"

"Too hot... can't see," she croaked.

"The silver and blue of your eyes is swirling again." He brushed her hair back and laid his hand on her forehead. "You're burning with fever. Stay still, I'll get water."

A moment later, he helped her sit up and held a water flask to her lips. The cool water eased her parched throat. Her vision cleared, bringing into focus the bright flames consuming the remnants of the thicket. The smoke stung her eyes and nose as it swirled into the night sky.

"They burned her again," she whispered.

"No, Love, she'd already gone to her rest. No one can hurt her anymore. Can you stand?"

"I think so."

He gave her a hand up. She wobbled and he steadied her. "Here are your swords." He wrapped his cloak around the hilt of the black sword, drew it out from where he'd hooked it through his belt, and slid it into its scabbard.

"Thanks." Tara was glad he'd sheathed it himself. She wasn't sure she wanted to touch it again. With trembling fingers, she sheathed her other weapon.

Jovan lifted her in his arms and settled her on his horse.

They galloped northward, following the edge of the lake. Tara rode in front of Jovan, his arm encircling her, holding her steady. She closed her eyes and tried to block out the screams of the terrified villagers echoing in her mind. Visions of the blackened corpses flashed before her. She could still smell the burned flesh. Yes, she'd hated them, but to kill them in such a way... Nausea seethed in the pit of her stomach like witchbrew boiling in a cauldron. Bile rose in her throat.

"Stop, stop, stop!" she cried.

Jovan reined in their mount. Tara clutched the saddle as the horse jerked to a halt. Her stomach lurched. Tearing herself from Jovan's hold, she swung her leg over the horse's neck and jumped to the ground. She staggered a few steps, then fell to her knees and retched.

When her gut had quieted, she sat back on her heels. Jovan handed her a water flask. She rinsed her mouth and spat, then took a long drink.

"Are you all right?"

She looked away. "I still feel hot inside."

He touched her forehead and her cheek with the backs of his fingers. "You aren't as hot as you were."

"I don't know what happened. The power burst out of me somehow. I couldn't control it. It felt like I was burning up from the inside out." She studied the water flask in her hands, repulsed by what she'd done to the villagers. "They were right. I am a witch."

"You are no such thing," Jovan said sharply. "And it's no worse than what they would have done to you."

Tara knew it was true, but it didn't make her feel any better. "Did you know the sword would do that?"

"No."

"What if I lose control again?"

"The power within you is strong, but you are strong enough to tame it."

"What if I'm not?"

"You are. It got the better of you this time because you were caught by surprise. You weren't expecting it. You couldn't have known what the sword would do. But now you're aware of it. You have the power —"

Tara laughed bitterly. "You say I have the power. In reality, the power has me."

She broke off suddenly as a freezing chill knifed through her. She shoved Jovan aside just as a pair of bloody hands grasped for them, closed on empty air. A decaying body materialized behind the hands, groping for its missed prey. Jovan rolled away, pulling Tara with him. Four more bodies shimmered into being around them. One of them was Skuldrist. His arms had been reattached. Jovan leaped up. Sword in hand, he swung at the nearest corpse. One blow severed its neck; the rotting head thudded to the ground beside Tara. She choked down a bubble of sickness as she drew her sword.

"Stay behind me." Jovan planted his foot against the headless body tottering in front of him and shoved it backward.

Skuldrist's men attacked at once. They charged Jovan, oblivious to his hacking blade, and bore him hard to the ground.

"Jovan!" Tara ran forward.

Skuldrist seized her. She fought his grip, and they fell in a tangle of limbs. Skuldrist rolled on top of her, pinning her down. An icy tingling spread through her body, draining her strength. Somewhere behind her, she heard Jovan groan.

Jovan!

His mind touched hers, the response cold and sluggish.

No! Jovan! She struggled to hit Skuldrist with her sword, but he held her arms with a strength that belied his gaunt frame. Tara rolled her eyes back into her head and went limp. Skuldrist let go of her arms and lifted himself off her chest. She shoved him to the side and rolled out from under him. He grabbed for her. His bony hands wrapped around her ankle. She swiped at him with her blade.

A savage growl startled her. A black beast hurtled past and landed on Skuldrist, mauling him with teeth and claws. He screamed and let go of her to wrestle with the beast. Tara crawled out of the way as a snarling pack of wolves tore into Skuldrist's men and dragged them down. The men thrashed on the ground, their shrieks dwindling to gurgles beneath the wolves' onslaught.

A yelp of pain silenced the frenzied growling. The wolves ceased their ravaging and turned, heads up, ears pricked toward the source of the sound. A few yards away, the black wolf that had led the attack lay wounded. Skuldrist, his clothing torn, his wasted body covered with bloodless claw marks, stood over the injured wolf with a sharp-edged rock in his hands.

The wolf struggled to rise. Skuldrist lifted the rock over his head and brought it down hard across the wolf's back. The wolf collapsed with another yelp and lay still.

Snarling viciously, the other wolves lunged at Skuldrist. A freezing blast of hurricane wind whipped across the silvered landscape, knocking Tara flat and rolling the wolves along the ground like tumbleweeds. A moment later the wind ceased.

Gritting her teeth against the stinging cold, Tara raised her head and looked about. The wolves were getting to their feet. Frost tinged the broken grasses. Skuldrist and his mangled henchmen were gone. With a wary glance at the wolves, Tara eased herself onto her knees.

Jovan groaned. Tara crawled over to him and rolled him onto his back. She cursed under her breath. His skin was colder than hers.

"Tara..." he murmured.

"I'm here." Fear knotted her gut as she took in the numerous black bruises covering his neck and arms. She yanked the laces of his shirt apart and found more bruises covering his chest. The poisonous cold was very near to claiming him. She closed her eyes and sensed the creature from her nightmares hovering, waiting for her defenses to fall. *Oh gods, help me find the strength,* she pleaded.

A shadow fell across her, blocking the waning light of the moon. She opened her eyes. Her breath caught. Her gut turned to ice. The giant towering over her stood so close he could have touched her. Captain Natiere. The Butcher. Her eyes slid down the terrible scar on his craggy face, dropped to the broad chest her blade had pierced not so long ago. How could he be alive?

Natiere looked down at her, his expression unreadable.

A chorus of wailing howls rose into the pale predawn sky. The wolf pack had gathered around its fallen leader. Captain Natiere turned abruptly and ran toward the spot where the black wolf lay.

Nearly gasping with relief, Tara turned back to Jovan. She pulled out her dagger and sliced open her left hand. Then she made a tiny cut on the black bruise over Jovan's heart. Taking a deep breath, she bolstered her mental defenses as best she could, placed her bleeding hand over the wound, and closed her eyes.

Jovan was far away, and drifting farther. Forcing her way through murky layers of dark and cold, she reached out to him, calling his name repeatedly in her mind, pursuing him to the very core of his being. Power flared — not her own, but from somewhere deep within him. A small wellspring of power, similar to hers, yet different, responded to her touch in a burst of incandescent light. Startled, she lost her concentration. The creature ripped into her, its claws digging deep. Pain like a hatchet blow severed her healing connection. Jovan slipped away.

No! I will not lose you! Clenching her jaw against the pain, she marshaled her thoughts and focused on strengthening her battered walls. Power blazed through her veins like the blast from the black sword, burning the creature until its paralyzing grip loosened. She shot the power back into Jovan. Her magic merged with the magic inside him to form a pulsing mass of strength and life. The deadly numbing cold burned away. With an angry shriek, the creature slashed and tore at the barriers.

Fighting to hold her fraying walls, Tara came back to herself. Jovan breathed easily as if asleep, his skin warm to her touch now. The bruises were gone. She sank down onto his chest.

Jovan stirred, his body shifting beneath her. "Tara?"

She moaned and pressed her fists against her temples. "The creature... I can't keep it out."

He jerked upright and caught her shoulders. "Tara, look at me. Let me in."

Forcing down her panic, Tara focused her eyes on his and opened her mind just enough to feel his touch. Their minds joined. Power surged between them, blazing through her like hot summer sunlight. The pain in her head disappeared. Power filled her, healing her ravaged mind. The creature lost its clawhold and fell screeching back into its prison. Jovan searched her eyes, making sure she was all right. They hugged each other hard.

An anguished roar startled them, shattering the peace of the dawn.

"What in blazes —" Jovan whipped around and caught sight of Natiere. "Damn him!" Jovan jumped to his feet. His eyes swept the empty landscape. "The horses are gone."

Tara rose. "You knew he was alive, didn't you? You should have told me."

"You had enough to worry about. Let's get out of here."

"No, wait." Tara caught his arm. "He's just going to keep following us, so we might as well face him here. I have an idea. One of his wolves was injured in the fight. If I could heal it, Natiere might take it as a goodwill gesture and leave us alone."

"No."

"You have a better idea?"

"Yes. We leave. Now."

"He'll just come after us."

"So will the creature if you use your powers again."

Tara looked at Jovan squarely. "Not much of a choice, is it? There's nothing I can do about the creature." She glanced toward Natiere. "However, Blackie de Runo always told me that if I wanted to disarm an enemy, do what they least expect."

Before Jovan could stop her, she ran across the field to where the injured wolf lay. The milling wolves snarled at her, but let her pass. Easing between them, she crouched beside the wounded black wolf. Captain Natiere was on his knees across from her, near the wolf's head. The beast was still alive, but suffering greatly, its back and one of its legs broken, bone protruding through skin. The dying wolf whined softly and licked Natiere's hand as he gently placed his folded cloak under her head.

"Rest easy, Sister," he murmured. Tears poured down his scarred face. "I will end your suffering."

Tara gaped. Captain Natiere, the Butcher, was weeping. The anguish that lined his weathered face was wrenchingly genuine.

Natiere stroked the black wolf's fur, then pulled a long knife from his belt.

Tara shook off her amazement. "Captain, wait." Her voice sounded unnaturally loud against the low growling and whining of the wolves.

Natiere stopped in mid-motion. His black eyes fastened on her, as if noticing her for the first time. The snarling wolves moved closer.

Tara glanced uneasily at the surrounding wolves, noting the bloody claws, the bared teeth, the ears flattened against their skulls as they poised for attack. She felt Jovan's presence and knew he was close behind her, his sword out ready to defend her.

Taking a firm grip on her nerve, she met Natiere's unfathomable gaze and held it. "I may be able to save her. Will you let me try?"

The Captain stared at her, his expression unchanging. Tara's eyes did not waver.

"I'll need your knife." She held out her hand.

Their eyes remained locked for several more heartbeats. Tara sensed Natiere's mind brushing hers, but he did not try to force a link. Silently, he handed her the knife. He motioned with his hand, and the rest of the pack ceased growling and backed away.

Tara took the knife. Jovan moved closer and put his hand on her shoulder. Sucking in a long breath, she cut open her left palm, placed it over the black wolf's broken spine, and closed her eyes. The creature leaped on her the moment she opened her mind. She cringed and braced herself against the onslaught and the pain of the wolf's wounds. Jovan's hand tightened on her shoulder. Using his strength, she repelled the creature and locked it out of her mind. Then she channeled the power into the wolf.

The black wolf twitched and whined low in its throat. Slowly, its broken body began to knit. Tara sensed Natiere's surprise and his love for the wolf. *This just might work,* she thought. *Maybe he'll stop trying to kill us...*

As the last of the wolf's injuries healed, Tara withdrew the power. The link between her and Jovan suddenly snapped. Her mind reeled as if cut loose from an anchor during a storm. The creature lunged, latching onto her with its razor-like claws. She collapsed, screaming as pain sliced through her head. Blackness swallowed her.

*****

Jovan caught Tara in his arms and turned her face to his. Her eyes were closed, her skin starkly white. He put his ear to her chest, listening for a heartbeat, heard the frantic pounding. She was already in the nightmare.

"Curse you!" he yelled at the sky. The ancient Being had broken the connection and blocked him out. "Let me in!" The Being did not respond. He raged at the silence in his head.

Tara, listen to me. He tried to project his thoughts into her closed mind. *I'm here. Listen to me. Follow my voice.* There was no response. He wasn't getting through. "Blast it, Tara! Let me in!"

A vicious growl sounded in his ear. Hot breath blew against his cheek as the black wolf snapped at him.

"Call off your pet, Natiere," Jovan ordered without taking his eyes from Tara's face. "If I lose her I swear I'll kill every last one of you with my bare hands."

Captain Natiere had risen to his feet. "She will not harm you." He stroked the bristling wolf's fur. "Go, Sister," he murmured to the wolf. Reluctantly the wolf moved away. The rest of the pack disappeared into the shadows. Natiere turned back to Jovan. "Do what you must. We will keep watch. You will not be disturbed."

*****

Tara raced down the twisting corridor, her heart pounding, her lungs bursting. Behind her raged the beast. The harsh scraping and the uneven thudding of its movements hammered against her consciousness, driving her into a panic. The beast was so close. Its foul breath choked her. She could almost feel its dagger-sharp claws raking her back, the warm blood flowing.

She scrambled around a corner and plowed into a huge cobweb. The thick strands of web entangled her, tripped her up. The beast was on her in a second, its claws digging into her back. She screamed.

Shouted words filled the corridor, and an icy blast of wind swooshed over her, knocking the creature back against the wall.

She felt a touch on her arm, a sickening lurch as if she were falling through space, then solidity and a cold dungeon floor beneath her.

Red robes filled her vision. A hand reached down to her. She pushed herself gingerly up to her knees, gritting her teeth as she stretched the claw wounds on her back. Validar Melodian stepped closer, his hand still extended.

Ignoring his hand, Tara rose and backed away, avoiding his gaze. The creature was nowhere in sight. She could still feel it in the distance, moving toward her from wherever they had been. Somehow, Melodian had transported them to another part of the dungeon. Eyeing him obliquely, Tara wiped the dirt from her hands. "Thank you for your help. Now get out of my dream."

Melodian laughed, a sinister sound that sent chills racing over her flesh. "No. Not until you give me whatever that key unlocked — " He stopped abruptly. He was staring down at her left side.

Tara glanced down and started in surprise. The black sword hung from her belt. She hadn't noticed it before. There hadn't been time.

"A black sword," Melodian whispered in awe. He lunged forward. Tara reached for the sword. Just as her hand grasped the hilt, Melodian grabbed her by the shoulders and shook her.

"Look at me!" he shouted.

Tara looked up in spite of herself and was caught, held motionless by the swirling red-gray of his eyes.

Keeping their eyes locked, Melodian reached down. His hand closed over Tara's. Black lightning flared, jolting them both with its searing blast. Screams rocked the corridor, then faded into silence.

CHAPTER 9

Fever. Scorching hot. Black fire burned in her blood. Her heart beat wildly.

Water touched her skin. It swirled around her, blessedly cool, easing the painful throbbing, cooling the blazing heat. The steady sloshing of waves against a shore slowly worked its way into Tara's consciousness. A gentle tug of thought followed, coaxing, drawing her back.

Jovan?

I'm here, Love. The reply was like a caress, yet she sensed an undercurrent of anger.

She let her mind drift with his, trying to latch on to what had angered him, but he kept it deeply hidden. Gently, he pulled her forward.

"Tara?" Jovan's voice was soft, worried.

She opened her eyes and found herself floating in the lake. She lay on her back with only her face above water. Jovan's arms supported her. The bright midmorning sun shone in her eyes. She winced at its glare, turned away, and caught a glimpse of a familiar shoreline, several yards away, with tree-covered hills beyond.

"It's been a long time since I swam in this lake," she said.

Relief crossed Jovan's face, then apprehension. "How do you feel?"

"Fine. More or less."

"What does that mean?"

"My back hurts where the creature clawed me." She let her legs sink to the sandy bottom. Here the lake was chest deep. The water lapped against her, cooling her fevered body. Her pulse had already slowed to a more normal pace. She ducked her head underwater and came back up.

Jovan steadied her. He raised the back of her shirt. "There are no wounds." He sounded puzzled.

She sucked in a hissing breath as his fingers touched her skin. "Well, it hurts just the same." She faced him. "What happened to our link? One minute you were there in my mind, and the next you were gone. It was like you were yanked away from me, leaving a hole I couldn't fill."

Jovan's expression hardened, and she felt the anger roiling beneath the surface. "Something interfered with the connection."

"The wizard? That would explain —"

"No. Not the wizard. Explain what?"

"The wizard was in my dream. The creature caught me. I heard what must have been some kind of magical phrase, and then there was a blast of cold wind that knocked the creature off me. Melodian appeared, touched my arm, and somehow we ended up in another part of the dungeon. He tried to steal the sword, and the black fire struck both of us. That's the last thing I remember."

"You were able to take the sword with you into the dungeon?"

"Yes." She touched the scabbard to reassure herself the sword was still there. "I didn't realize it until I saw him staring at it. I was in such a panic trying to escape the creature that I hadn't noticed it. No weapons have ever come through into the dungeon before."

Jovan stared down at the water in silence.

Tara sensed the turmoil raging within him. "If it wasn't the wizard that interfered with our link, then who was it?"

Jovan looked up. "I don't know exactly. It's —" He turned away, his face livid, his mind at war with... something. She had to know what it was that sought to control him. She let her consciousness mingle with his, her touch light and unobtrusive as she searched for cracks in his mental armor, some way to see inside. She felt his defense weakening, his fury eroding his mental block, allowing her a glimpse of the violent swirl of thoughts, churning beyond the barrier he normally held tight. She caught the faintest of whispers, an ancient voice older than the ground she walked on. Icy chills raked down her spine. She gasped in surprise. Instantly, she was repelled, but not by Jovan.

"That voice... what was it?" she asked breathlessly.

"Something I can't explain right now," he said, his voice raw. "It holds all the answers but refuses to share them." He shook his fist at the sky. "I *will* solve this riddle, with or without your help." He turned back to Tara. She had the sudden urge to back away. He gripped her shoulders. "You must trust me."

"I do," she said with only a fraction of hesitation. Quicker than a knife stab his expression changed. Hurt, frustration, and bitterness flitted across his face before the mask of stone descended. His hands dropped to his sides. She floundered for something to say that would ease the hurt. She did trust him. It was just that the voice had jangled every warning nerve in her body and made Jovan suddenly seem like a stranger.

"Jovan, I'm sorry." She caught his arm before he could turn away. "I didn't mean to hurt you. That voice set off my danger sense, and it threw me. You have to tell me what it is and what it's doing to you."

"I told you I can't."

"What did it say? What does it want? I need to know!"

"I can't tell you!"

Out of the corner of her eye, Tara caught a movement at the edge of the lake. She stiffened. Two wolves, one gray and one black, had come down to the water to drink.

"The Butcher," she said, remembering. "He's still here?"

"Yes," Jovan said curtly.

Tara's eyes searched the hilly shoreline for a glimpse of their nemesis. Strange that she had not sensed his presence on waking. "Has he threatened you?"

"Not yet."

"How long have I been out?"

"A few hours."

Tara ran her fingers through her wet hair, combing it back from her face. She still sensed no impending danger. In the past, when Natiere had been near, she'd felt his presence like a murderous shadow, stalking them. But now, she sensed something different. His aura had changed to a confusing mix of impressions she couldn't quite decipher, still menacing, but in a more subtle, distant way. No wonder she hadn't recognized him as the one who'd been following them. Of course, if Jovan hadn't kept insisting Natiere was dead... She clenched her jaw, annoyed. He should have told her Natiere was alive. That was one secret he hadn't needed to keep. And she should have realized, with all the wolf howls they'd heard. She swept her gaze over the hills once more. Why had Natiere helped them? What did he want? She frowned, unable to settle on what to do next. So much depended on what Natiere did. If he still intended to torture and kill them... "I wish I knew what was on the Captain's mind."

Jovan swung his hand through the water, sending a shower of droplets off to the side. "What does it matter? Either he leaves us alone, or we kill him."

"Now how do you propose we do that with all those wolves around? It was hard enough to kill him the first time, and then he didn't stay dead." She looked back at the shore. "We need to find out if he is still a threat. The only way to do that is to talk to him."

"Talk to him? Are you mad? No one *talks* to the Butcher."

She bristled. "It's worth a try. His wolves saved our lives. I want to know why."

"That's obvious. He wants to torture us himself. And you would be foolish to believe anything he says."

"I don't think he'll lie to me."

"Why wouldn't he? How do you know he won't try to kill you on the spot?"

"He won't."

"You're certain of that? Maybe your healing of the wolf only bought you a quick death instead of a slow, torturous one."

"I don't believe that."

"Because you know him so well."

"I know him better than you think, and I'll prove it." Pushing off from the sandy bottom, she swam toward the shore. Except for the pain in her back, she felt strangely energized, not weak and nause- ated like the time before.

"Tara, wait," Jovan called after her, but she didn't stop. He would see she was right. In her previous links with Natiere, she'd glimpsed the horrific trauma that had made him the beast he was. His soul had been poisoned by the suffering he'd endured, that his family had endured before being murdered. Tormented by his past, he'd become the Butcher to claim his vengeance. He wasn't evil by na- ture. She was certain of it. The times she'd encountered him, he'd treated her with chivalrous courtesy. And even though his main purpose had been — and still might be — to kill her, she firmly believed Natiere would listen to what she had to say before taking any action. He owed her that for saving his wolf. The twisted sense of honor she'd seen in him would stay his hand. But for how long?

By the time Tara reached the shore, several wolves had gathered along the water's edge, near the black leader. Keeping a wary eye on them, she emerged from the lake. The black wolf padded up to her and nosed her palm. Tara crouched beside the wolf and stroked her soft fur, scratched her behind her ears.

"Be careful," Jovan warned as he came up behind her.

"Kelya owes you a life-debt," said Captain Natiere, appearing from around the base of a broad, wooded hill. "She will not harm you."

Tara rose as Natiere came toward her. She resisted the urge to draw her sword. Jovan drew his. He moved close and stood beside her protectively, blade lowered. The Butcher stopped about twenty feet away. The wolves gathered around him.

"Our thanks to you, Captain," said Tara boldly, "and to your wolves. You killed our enemies, instead of us." She paused. "May I ask why?"

The Captain smiled, his ragged scar wrinkling grotesquely. "You sound surprised, Lady. You should not be. The fight was one-sided. We merely evened the odds a bit."

"I see." She hesitated, disconcerted. Natiere was staring at her in a peculiar way. All at once she realized why. Soaked from her dip in the lake, her wet clothes clung to her body revealingly. She blushed, tongue-tied.

Jovan became aware of it at the same time. He swept off his cloak and draped it around Tara's shoulders, then stepped in front of her. "We have no wish to fight you, but we will if you do not go your own way and allow us to go ours without threat or hindrance."

"Perhaps our paths lie in the same direction," said Natiere.

Jovan lifted his blade in challenge. "They don't."

The Butcher smiled faintly. He stroked the head of the black wolf beside him. "One never knows where one's path will lead." His eyes moved back to Tara. "*Urani metrista elan*, Lady." He motioned to his wolves. They loped away into the hills. With a brief nod he turned and followed.

Tara stared after him, puzzling over his answers. The Gypsy words she knew — *until we meet again*. Jovan had translated the phrase for her once before. But what had he meant about not knowing where his path would lead? She'd always believed that people chose their own paths, made their own destinies, until this last adventure. Ever since the Sulledorn attack on Castle Carilon and her flight from the Butcher, she'd felt like her choices were no longer her own, like she was being driven toward some unknown end. Could it be possible that Natiere was being driven, as well?

"Perhaps my healing the wolf did make a difference," Tara said. "He didn't attack us."

"Not this time, but you can bet your last gold piece we won't be so lucky next time around."

"How do you know that? Maybe he'll feel he owes us —"

"He owes us nothing. He saved our lives, and you saved his wolf. We are even. There will be no mercy next time."

"I didn't get that sense at all. And he said the wolf owed me a life-debt."

"The wolf, maybe, but not him." Jovan sheathed his sword. "And I don't think you're considering the way he looked at you just now. He may want to do more than just kill you." Snatching up his water flask, Jovan strode away from the lake. "We need to find the horses."

Tara hesitated. She'd been trying not to think about Natiere's gaze, not because it had inspired fear, but because it was strange. His expression had startled her, not frightened her. Her instincts were telling her Natiere would not harm her, at least not yet. But that could change at any moment.

Then another thought slipped into her mind, turning her blood to ice. Captain Natiere might not harm her, but he would most certainly harm Jovan. Suddenly feeling cold, she hurried across to where Jovan stood, studying a trail of hoof prints.

"The horses went that way." Jovan indicated a path that wound northward through the hills. "Let's hope they haven't gone far." He started after them.

"There are a hundred questions I need to ask you," Tara said, catching up to him.

"And I would like to answer them. All of them," Jovan said without turning. "But I don't know what would happen if I did." His voice lowered. "The voice you heard... the Being... keeps threatening to separate us, to somehow take you away from me, if I don't follow its instructions."

"How could it do that?"

"I don't know." He swatted away a swarm of flies that rose from a pile of horse dung as they passed. "I do know it's powerful enough to block me out of your mind during your dreams, and there doesn't seem to be anything I can do about it."

"Can you tell me anything more about the Being?"

"No."

"What about the magic I felt inside you?"

"The what?" Jovan asked blankly.

"You heard me. Don't deny it. I know it's there."

Jovan was silent for several moments. "If you say it is there, it must be, but I know nothing of it," he said finally.

Tara cursed to herself and kicked a fallen branch out of her way. "Fine. I'll go to the main question — where do we go from here? You said the Kamarians lived in the Black Mountains?"

"So the stories say."

"Then I think that should be our destination. I need to find out more about them, and the sword. Everything seems to point in that direction. Even your vision from Rinpool — you said you saw me standing in front of a black castle surrounded by black mountains. Maybe it was a Kamarian castle."

"Maybe," Jovan said noncommittally.

"Do you know how to get to the mountains?"

"I know where they are. Getting to them would be a challenge. The Eastern Frontier is controlled by organized bands of thieves who are vicious enough to be blood relatives of Natiere. The Black Mountains themselves are impassable. The only entrance is a ru-ined watchtower at the edge of the mountains called Ravnaul's Keep."

"I remember you mentioning something about that before. Who is Ravnaul?"

"Ravnaul was the Gatekeeper, one of the most powerful of the Kamarians." Jovan changed direction slightly, following the horses' trail. "Some stories claim he was evil and blame him for the demise of the Kamarian race."

"What happened to him?"

"I don't know."

"And you're sure Ravnaul's Keep is the only way in?"

"Yes. The mountain cliffs along the outer edge are too treacher-ous to climb, and the rivers flowing out of the mountains are unnavigable."

Tara thought for a moment. "The wizard Melodian had what he said was a Kamarian moonstone. Does that mean he is Kamarian, too? No, wait, he can't be. He said I was the last of the Kamarians."

"All I know of Melodian is from Nomads' tales. He is said to be a dark wizard. Gor Mountain, in the Northlands, used to be his stronghold."

"Used to be? It's not anymore?"

"I don't know."

"If he's not a Kamarian, then what is he? He doesn't seem unusual in any way, except for his eyes. They're a strange red-gray. The color sort of swirls, and they become hypnotic —" She stopped short as a new thought occurred to her.

Jovan had the same thought. "The color swirls? Like yours?"

"Yes," she said slowly. "How is that possible if he's not Kamarian?"

Jovan didn't answer. He held up a hand for silence. A horse snorted somewhere off to their left, and then they heard the jingle of bridles and the stomp of hooves. Jovan pointed in the direction of the sound. Tara nodded and followed after him, treading carefully so as not to spook the animals.

They found the horses in a hollow between two hills. The skittish animals danced sideways, but didn't bolt, and Tara saw that one of them had its reins tangled in the brush. Jovan spoke soothingly as he advanced, calming the horses enough for them to get close. Tara worked on untangling the reins while he caught the loose horse. Then they checked the tack and their gear.

"It doesn't look like we lost anything," Tara said with a final tug on her mount's girth.

"Good." Jovan stowed his water flask in his saddlebag and tightened his mount's tack.

"I know nothing of the Frontier," Tara said, "and I'm not sure of the best way to get there. I do know there are two passes through the Cyranel Mountains that lead to the East, Brannen in the north and Klyder in the south, and I know we'd have to blaze a trail through Shallin Wood to get to either of them. I've been to the Gypsy Crossroads at the head of Klyder Pass, but I've never gone through."

"Brannen Pass is a dead end. It leads directly into Dharakwood, which stretches all along the eastern side of the Cyranels. If the Wood doesn't open, your only recourse is to backtrack."

"You said before that Dharakwood was the forest of impenetrable thorn trees where you found Rinpool."

"Yes. Either the branches move out of the way so you can enter, or they become more dense so you can't. Anyone who tries to force their way in gets impaled by the thorns."

"How does the Wood decide who to let in and who not to?"

Jovan shrugged. "I don't know. It's a place of ancient magic."

"Kamarian magic?"

"No, it's much older."

"Where does the magic come from? And how does it work?"

"I don't know," Jovan said again. "Dharakwood is completely silent — no animals, no birds. Nothing lives there. The branches part for you, and you have to follow the trail that's provided — and you have to do it the moment it opens. If you don't, the branches and thorns begin to seal themselves together behind you. You either move or get cut to ribbons. If we didn't get in, we would lose days backtracking through the mountains. And there's a good possibility of being captured by dwarves."

"Dwarves," Tara repeated. "Laraina said something once about dwarves living in the Cyranel Mountains. Are they that hostile?"

"That depends on who you are and what you're doing in the mountains. Jared and I stayed in the dwarven city of Aldontris for a short time while I recovered from the knife wound. Dharakwood had driven us out near one of their outposts. We did not leave on the best of terms."

"I remember the story of how you were attacked by bandits, but I don't remember anything about dwarves. What angered them?"

Jovan smiled grimly. "My brother tried to steal something."

"I see." She dampened her curiosity, knowing thoughts of his dead brother still brought him great pain.

Jovan mounted his horse. "Klyder Pass would be the safer route. It comes out below the southern end of Dharakwood."

"But Klyder Pass is weeks from here." Tara swung aboard her own mount. She formed a mental map. "Unless we use the river. We could pick up a boat in Cierra and sail down the Colin River. It's fast, and it would save us a lot of time."

"The Colin flows into the Nournan, which flows directly through the Bog."

"Well, we can't use the Amberin River because of the Falls," Tara argued. "I don't care to test my luck going over them again. And portaging around them is difficult."

Anger darkened Jovan's eyes. "You would prefer the Bog? Your dream demon lives in that Bog. Until we find a way to defeat it, I'd think that would be the last place you'd want to go."

"Well, our choices are a bit limited here," Tara snapped. "Brannen Pass seems the best route to me. I know Shallin Wood is not easy to travel through, but we should be able to get there within three weeks."

Jovan said nothing, his expression shuttered.

Tara watched him, letting the silence build. He didn't want to go back into Dharakwood. That much was obvious, but was it because he feared Rinpool, or something else? "How long would it take to go overland to Klyder Pass?" she asked finally.

"A few weeks — a moon's turn and half again."

"That's twice as long."

"Not if Dharakwood doesn't open."

"Maybe it will."

"Maybe it won't."

"Why don't you want to go back in there?" she demanded.

He looked away. "No, I will *not!*" he said vehemently. He faced her again, his fury barely in check. "I have my reasons."

Tara clamped down on her temper, vexation and guilt at provoking him warring within her. Fighting with both her and the voice in his head was tearing him apart. She urged her horse toward his. "I'm sorry. I keep letting my frustration get the better of me." She took a deep, calming breath. "Why don't we go to Cierra? It's right on the river, halfway between here and the mountains. We can get more supplies and decide where to go from there."

Their eyes held for a long space.

"All right," Jovan said, his voice and expression tightly controlled.

They rode out of the hollow and headed northeast, following the edge of the lake.

*****

Validar Melodian stumbled down the shadowy staircase, the circular steps leading him into the depths of the cavern beneath the ruined black tower. The stench of burned flesh pervaded the cold damp air. His crimson robe, scorched and tattered, clung to his blistered body. His right arm was a blackened stump.

He staggered to a halt on a narrow landing that led to a featureless door of translucent black stone. Beads of sweat dripped down his face, glistening in the silver glow that magically lit the cavern.

The pendant hanging from the chain around his neck was almost completely black; only a faint pulse of red showed through. He leaned against the wall to catch his breath and nearly fell. Pulling himself upright, he touched the door and it slid open, disappearing into the rock. Wheezing harshly, the wizard stepped through the door.

The room was wedge-shaped, rounded on one side and unnaturally warm. Silver light glowed eerily, reflected by the glassy surfaces of the floor and ceiling. Shelves, cluttered with books and other objects, lined the walls. More books, papers, and other paraphernalia covered a small table. Set into the stone floor was a long, rectangular trough filled with a black jelly-like substance. The thick ooze teemed with tiny silver-white worms.

Grunting in pain, the wizard moved toward the trough. The door slid shut behind him. A scream escaped his lips as he awkwardly peeled off his blackened robe. Discarding the burned garment, he climbed into the trough, easing himself into the black ooze. The tiny worms slithered over his charred body, eating away the dead skin. The mucous they left behind slowly healed him, while the black jelly cooled and soothed.

Validar Melodian gritted his teeth. The horrible crawling sensation of the worms was almost worse than the pain of his burns. She would pay for this. He scooped up a handful of the black ooze, wriggling with the silvery worms. "I wonder what she would say if she knew what had really happened to her precious Kamarian ancestors." He chuckled, coughed, then erupted into croaking laughter as the squirming glop dripped through his fingers and fell back into the trough.

CHAPTER 10

Tara and Jovan set a fast pace, following the curving edge of Amberin Lake northeast, riding through the night when the moon allowed. Captain Natiere and his wolf pack had not reappeared, though Tara knew they were still near. She could feel their presence keenly, like menacing shadows slipping over the verdant hills, black harbingers of death. Yet as much as they unnerved her, the knowledge of their presence brought an inexplicable sense of security. They had come to her rescue once; perhaps they would do so again if need be. She had the feeling she was going to need all the help she could get.

By midafternoon of the third day they reached the unnamed river that spilled with a cold rush into Amberin Lake, its headwaters deep in the northernmost reaches of the Triandol Mountains. They crossed without incident and pressed onward to the east, riding through the heart of Barony's horse country. The closely cropped hills and pastures made traveling easy. Numerous herds of the swift, strong horses for which Barony breeders were famous grazed on the open land. The horses raced away, kicking up their heels as Tara and Jovan rode past.

To Tara, the days passed like a blur. They stopped in the town of Brynnd to barter for fresh horses, then rode on again, slowing only long enough to eat or snatch a few hours' sleep. She knew the wolf pack still followed, though the only outward sign of their presence was the infrequent sound of a terrified whinny cut short.

A blinding rainstorm finally drove them to seek shelter. Night had fallen, and the land lay cloaked in shrouds of blackness. Lightning jagged amid crashes of thunder, lighting the sky with its brilliance. Bending their heads against the storm, Tara and Jovan galloped to one of the many large open-ended stables that had been built across the grasslands to provide shelter for the roaming herds.

They jumped from their saddles and hurried their mounts into the building. Constructed of wood, with a stone base and thatched roof, the structure reeked of damp horse. But the dirt floor was relatively dry, though strewn with straw and droppings.

A dark bay stallion snorted and shook his mane as they entered. Five or six horses milled around behind him — mares, Tara guessed. Jovan's chestnut gelding snorted and arched his neck. The bay screamed a challenge. The chestnut's ears flattened as he squealed an answer. Jovan jerked the chestnut's bridle and yelled at the bay. Then he drew his sword and slapped the bay's hindquarters with the flat of the blade. The bay jumped and kicked, but Jovan had backed out of range, forcing the chestnut farther into the stable. Tara kept a firm grip on her skittish mare, holding her well back. With another scream, the bay rounded up his mares, his ears still pinned back as he nipped their flanks and drove them out into the rain.

Tara and Jovan soothed their mounts and led them to the back of the stable, where they tied them to two of the iron rings that lined the wall.

"I'll see to the horses." Jovan began stripping the tack from the mounts.

Tara kicked together a pile of straw mixed with dried horse droppings. "This should burn." She cleared a wide circle around the pile to keep the fire from spreading, then dug the flint and tinderbox from the saddlebag. Soon she had a small blaze going. The smoke swirled upward into the peak of the vented roof. She tossed more straw into the flames, wrinkling her nose at the smell of the burnt dung.

She watched Jovan surreptitiously as she tended the fire. He'd said little since their argument over which path they should take to the Black Mountains. When he had spoken, his voice had been cool, devoid of emotion, his manner remote and impassive as a mountain cliff. His mind remained tightly closed. She knew he was still angry — with her, with the voice in his head that commanded him against his will, with the choices they were being forced to make. His rage and frustration clouded his aura like smoke from a forest fire. She tried to quell her own frustration at his refusal to answer her questions, but couldn't. It irked her that he wouldn't share his knowledge, even though her life might depend on it. How could he not tell her what she needed to know?

There has to be a reason, her conscience chided. With an effort, she forced aside her irritation and considered. What would keep him from telling her? She thought a few moments, and then it hit her. *Consequence.* Something bad enough to keep him silent. But wouldn't he have said if that were the case? *Maybe he couldn't.* A chill of foreboding slithered down her spine. What if there *was* some terrible consequence if he spoke of something the Being didn't want known? His life might be in as much danger as hers. Gods, why hadn't she thought about it this way before? Worry for him snatched her breath. How was she going to find out? He was so angry with her, he probably wouldn't tell her even if he could.

She needed to get him talking again. She needed to find the right words to repair the damage she'd done with her impatient questions, but she wasn't sure what to say. Relationships had never been her strong suit. While growing up in Wyndover, the mutual hatred between her and the townspeople had allowed her to speak her mind without caring about hurt feelings. She'd never had to worry about bruised egos with Blackie de Runo and his band, either. Her only close relationships had been with Laraina and Dominic, and she realized with chagrin that she hadn't always thought to curb her tongue with them.

What about Myles? her conscience prodded. A handsome face lodged in her mind, grinning at her with a devil-may-care smile. She scowled at the thought of her former love, the only other person she'd let inside her guard. She had to admit she hadn't been particularly tactful with him, either. But then, he'd been so careless and unheeding of the dangers surrounding the different mercenary jobs they'd taken. If she hadn't insisted that they adhere to her rules and her plans, they would have been dead many times over. She ground her teeth. Myles had craved adventure as much as she, but all he'd really cared about was money. He'd betrayed her — turned her, Laraina, and Dominic in for a bounty and left them to die in an enemy dungeon. "Sorry, my love," he had said. "All bets are off. Catch you in the next life." She'd sworn then that she would trust no man again, and woe to Myles if she ever found him. She would cut out his lying heart and feed it to the crows.

She closed her eyes and tried to banish the image of his smile and the agitation it aroused, but that was impossible. There were too many painful remembrances knotted tightly together, like long-clenched fists with cramped fingers that would no longer open. She had never faced the hurt, the humiliation, the loss she'd felt at his betrayal. She'd swept it into her mental closet and locked the door.

She took a deep breath. None of it mattered. Myles was long gone and she was glad of it. She'd been true to her word and had kept all men at sword's length, until she'd met Jovan. He alone had broken down her defenses and brought her back from the edge of the lonely precipice she'd been walking. She loved him and wanted him beside her. But at this rate, how long would he still want her?

Never doubt me, he had said. The remembered words sifted through her mind like a steadfast ray of light.

Never doubt me. She felt the words planted firmly in her mind by the familiar whisper-soft voice. Her head flew up, and she saw Jovan watching her over his mount's back, the curry cloth in his hand pausing over its withers. He had finally opened the mental link between them. With an inward cry of gladness, she surged into the connection, letting it fill her whole being like the warmth of the summer sun.

Tossing the cloth onto the tack pile, Jovan ducked under the horse's neck and came toward her. She met him halfway. He swept her into a tight embrace.

"I'm sorry," they said simultaneously.

Jovan's lips closed over hers with a deep, warm kiss. Tara leaned into him, reveling in the heat that sizzled through her, right to her toes. Gods, how she'd missed his touch. With all that had happened, there hadn't been time to share much more than a handclasp. They'd either been riding, fighting with their enemies, fighting with each other, or sleeping from exhaustion.

Jovan drew back a bit. He caressed her face. "I don't know what's going to happen now. I've refused to do something the Being wants done. It may kill me, or worse. So from now on, all bets are off —"

Tara stiffened. She turned and stood frozen with her back to him, her hand covering her face as she fought the chaotic tumult of feelings loosed by those few simple words. *All bets are off.*

She felt Jovan's hands on her shoulders, tension curling his fingers into a hard grip. "What's wrong?"

Tara took several deep breaths before facing him. "It's nothing. Something you said reminded me of something... unpleasant." She stopped as icy fingers of warning crawled down her spine. The pounding of hoofbeats rose above the drumming of the rain. She gripped his arm. "The bay is coming back." She hesitated, goose pimples shivering over her skin.

"What is it?"

"I don't know. Something else..."

Jovan drew his sword and strode to the front of the stable. Tara threw some straw and dung onto the fire to provide more light, then joined him, sword in hand. They pressed back against the wall and stared into the darkness, seeing nothing through the wind-driven rain. Their mounts snorted and stamped, shaking their manes as they tugged at their ropes.

The ground shook as the bay and his mares pounded up to the stable. Tara and Jovan shouted and waved their swords. The bay stallion skidded to a stop in front of them. With a wild whinny, it reared up. They dodged its striking hooves and brandished their swords again. The mares rushed into the stable, shouldering between them, lashing out with teeth and hooves.

"Jovan!" Tara lost sight of him beyond the crush of horseflesh. Their mounts whinnied and half-reared, still tied fast. The mares ignored the tethered horses and came right at Tara, their rain-darkened coats glistening in the firelight, their eyes glittering an eerie red, as if they were possessed by some demonic force. Tara leaped sideways, drawing them away from the fire. The mares turned as one and followed. She saw movement on the back of one of the mares — a figure that had been riding low over the mare's neck had suddenly sat upright. *Skuldrist!* Warning chills swept over her like an icy deluge. The mares surrounded her, squeezing close and trapping her between them. One of them bit her hand, and she dropped her sword with a cry. Skuldrist caught her around the waist and lifted her. Numbing cold shot through her body.

She fought against him as he pulled her up onto the red-eyed beast he was riding. "Let... go... of... me!" She swung her fist backward, past her head, repeatedly driving the back of her knuckles into Skuldrist's face. He recoiled but did not loosen his grip. The mares galloped out of the stable into the darkness, taking Tara with them. Rain pelted her, whipped by a wind so strong it stole her breath.

The primal howling of a wolf pack cut through the storm. Skuldrist's horse reared and kicked at a black wolf slashing at its heels. Tara threw her weight sideways, and she and Skuldrist crashed to the ground. Gasping from the impact, she pulled her knife and stabbed him in the eye. With a frightening grin, he sat up, yanked out the knife, and tossed it aside. She backed away quickly, reaching for her sword to cut his limbs off again, then remembered she'd dropped it back in the stable when the horse bit her. Skuldrist rose. Shoving back her drenched hair, she glanced toward the stable. A rearing horse blocked her path. She only had one weapon left. Skuldrist charged. She hesitated an instant, then whipped out the black sword and swung it in front of her. Power seared through her veins. Black fire shot outward. The flames struck Skuldrist squarely in the chest, burning through him and beyond. He shrieked as the fire engulfed him, reducing him in seconds to a blackened skeleton, ash and bone whisked away by the wind. The maddened horses stumbled and collapsed, the red light fading from their eyes.

Tara sank to her knees, staggered by the dizzying rush of power still smoldering within. She sheathed the black sword and pressed the heels of her palms against her closed lids, fighting for control. The creature from her nightmare tore at her, gouging her mental wall in a frenzied attack. She beat against it with equal frenzy, panic driving her like a whiplash. With a screech of fury, the creature lost its hold and dropped away, locked once more in its prison. The power ebbed slowly, reluctantly, coiling inside her like a beast eager to spring forth again.

The rain beating down on her eased to a soft drizzle, then stopped. The wind ceased, leaving in its wake a watery silence, cold and eerie. Thunder boomed in the distance as the storm swept off to the west.

Shaking, Tara opened her eyes and tried to focus. She needed to find Jovan, to see if he'd been hurt by the horses. Visions of him lying trampled filled her mind.

Cursing her blurred vision, she lurched to her feet and looked around. "Jovan?"

"Tara!" She heard approaching footsteps, and then he pulled her into his arms. "Are you all right?"

"I'm fine. What about you?" She slid her hands over his arms and chest, searching for wounds. "I was afraid you'd been trampled." She gave a sharp intake of breath as her fingers touched warm wetness.

His hand closed over hers. "It's nothing. A flesh wound."

"Are there others?"

"Only bruises. Nothing serious."

She drew back. "Curse it all, I need to see."

He cupped her chin and turned her face to his. "The color of your eyes is still swirling."

A warm body pressed against her leg. Startled, she looked down and saw the fuzzy image of the black wolf standing beside her. She dropped to one knee and threw her arms around the wolf's neck. "Thank you," she whispered. As she stroked the wolf's fur, she touched rough patches and smelled the acrid odor of singed hair. Cold fear washed over her as she suddenly realized others might have been hurt by the sword's blast.

A massive figure appeared, surrounded by ghostly gray shapes. "Are you hurt, Lady?"

A strange feeling crept over Tara at the genuine concern in the rough voice.

"No, Captain. I'm fine." She rose. Jovan moved up beside her, tense and silent, his blade drawn again. She squinted at Natiere, her vision beginning to clear. "You and your wolves?"

"They are uninjured, as am I." A twist of a smile flitted across his scarred face. "The Kamarian sword is quite a weapon."

Tara stared. "How did you know —?"

She was interrupted by the black wolf as it jumped up, put its paws against her chest, and licked her face. Then the wolf trotted over to stand beside Natiere.

"Kelya is acknowledging her payment of her life-debt," said the Captain. "All is even. We start anew." He backed away and faded into the night, followed by the wolves.

Tara turned to Jovan. "How did he know?"

Jovan shrugged impatiently. "It's not important."

"Skuldrist was controlling the horses," Tara said. "I had to use the black sword. It destroyed him."

"So the wizard will have to find a new puppet." Jovan stared off in the direction Natiere had gone.

"I suppose so," Tara said, only half listening, her thoughts occupied in pondering Natiere's tone of voice when he'd asked if she was all right.

A weak snort broke the silence as the bay stallion lifted its head and struggled to its feet, its eyes no longer glowing. The horse staggered a bit, as if dazed. The mares began to stir and heave themselves up. They milled around for a moment, then trotted away.

The gray light of approaching dawn revealed two horses still down, both badly burned. One appeared to have died outright from the sword's blast. The other's throat was slit.

"The Captain must have done it to ease its suffering," Tara said, guilt burning through her at the deaths she had caused.

Jovan sheathed his sword. "Since when is the Butcher concerned about easing someone's suffering?"

"He was going to kill the wolf rather than let her suffer," Tara said, surprising herself by the quickness of her response in defending Captain Natiere.

"He was going to kill us, too, in Relic — a fact you seem willing to ignore."

"I'm not ignoring it. It's just that I have this feeling about him —"

"So I see." Jovan's voice had grown cold as a wintry sea.

"Now what is that supposed to mean?" Tara demanded.

Jovan caught her by the arms. "Natiere is a vicious killer. He tortures people. That's what he does. I don't want to see that happen to you." He released her abruptly and stalked toward the stable.

Tara ran after him and planted herself in front of him so he had to stop. "He killed those people because they tortured and murdered his family. And yes, I know he's killed others, but he's not a bloodthirsty beast —"

"And you're certain enough of that to bet your life?"

She hesitated. Was she?

"I'm not." Jovan stepped around her and headed into the stable.

Tara cursed and ground her heel into the dirt. She'd done it again. Just when they had gotten back on friendly terms, she'd picked another fight. She ran her hands through her hair and took a deep breath. Jovan was right, she knew. She needed to be cautious. There was too much at stake for her to gamble and lose, and yet... She looked back toward where she had last seen Natiere. The man behind the scarred visage piqued her curiosity. His concern for her had surprised her. Could the blighted soul she'd touched with her mind during their earlier duel be redeemed? Or had the blight gone too deep and poisoned his soul beyond recall?

You would be my redemption and my downfall. She remembered Natiere's words, telling her what some Gypsy warlock had told him many years past. He'd said the Gypsy had shown her to him in a dream. She didn't know how that was possible, but then Jovan had seen her in the vision from Rinpool, long before they'd ever met. Somehow, their fates were intertwined — all three of them — whether for good or evil, she couldn't begin to guess.

She looked around once more. Mist, rising from the rain-drenched earth, obscured the grasslands like curtains of smoke, shifting in the faint breeze. She shivered as the dampness touched her skin. Pockets of fog burgeoned in the valleys and spilled outward into the meadows, swallowing grass and brush and stone. Guardedly, she opened her mind until she could sense Natiere. He was still near. She felt an answering touch. Startled, she took an involuntary step backward and closed her mind before a connection could be established. What was she doing? She had to be out of her mind. She turned and headed back to the stable.

She found Jovan saddling their horses. The mounts were skittish, but unharmed. He had stomped out the fire, spreading the ashes apart to be certain no burning embers remained. She went up to him and put her arms around him. He returned the embrace, crushing her close. They held each other for a long while, then slowly drew apart.

Tara spoke first. "I'm sorry." She ran her hand over her face. "Gods, it seems like that's all I say to you lately."

His mouth quirked upward in a strained smile. "I should be saying it to you even more." He squeezed her hand, then turned and untied the horses.

Tara grasped her mount's reins. They led their horses out of the stable, mounted, and cantered away to the east.

CHAPTER 11

Several hours later, the rain started again. Tara and Jovan rode through it for a while, the grasslands sliding past in bleary shades of misty gray. Tara spotted another stable and signaled Jovan. He nodded, and they rode toward it, their horses quickening their pace as they neared the shelter.

Ducking low over their mounts' necks, they rode inside. To Tara's relief, the stable was empty. They dismounted and tied their horses in a dry corner. Tara gathered straw and wood she'd found piled along the side and built a fire, while Jovan took care of the horses. She was soaked to the skin and desperately in need of sleep, but instead of being cold, she felt strangely warm. Was she coming down with a fever, she wondered, or was her higher body temperature the result of the black blade's fire? She didn't feel sick. At least using the sword hadn't nauseated her this time.

She laid her cloak out to dry and then sat beside the fire. Her muscles ached from the constant riding. It seemed like days since they'd had any real sleep.

The fire crackled and snapped. She jumped and realized she'd started to doze off. She shook herself awake. As much as she wanted to sleep, she dreaded what would happen when she did. *The dream.*

She shivered. What would she find this time? Had Validar Melodian been affected by the sword's blast in her last dream? And what had happened to the creature? She knew she would find out the moment sleep overtook her.

Jovan brought the saddlebags over, set his cloak out beside hers, and sat next to her.

"Do I feel warm to you?" she asked as she rebandaged the cut on his arm from his fight with Skuldrist's horses.

He touched her forehead and frowned. "You feel feverish again."

"I'm not sure that's what it is."

"What do you mean?"

"I think it might be caused by the power of the sword. The black fire. I think it somehow raised my body temperature."

"Are you ill?"

"No. I just feel warm from the inside out." She stretched and winced, her back muscles still sore where the creature had clawed her in her last dream.

Jovan's frown darkened. "Your back still hurts?"

"Yes, though it's not as bad." She shifted to a more comfortable position. "And you saw no claw marks?"

"None."

"It doesn't make sense. The pain is definitely there, but apparently the wounds are not. Does that mean if I were to die in the dream, I would really be dead?"

He cupped her face and brushed his thumb over her cheek. "That's not something I want to think about." He kissed her forehead, then turned and reached for his saddlebag. He pulled out some bread and dried fruit, splitting it between them.

They ate silently, then Tara spoke. "I've been thinking about why you can't answer my questions. Is there some consequence if you do? Tell me no if I'm wrong. Don't say anything if I'm right."

Their eyes met. Jovan said nothing.

Dread curled in the pit of Tara's stomach. "So I'm right. Is the Being able to hurt you somehow?"

Jovan looked away and remained silent.

"Can it hurt you physically?"

"No."

Tara felt his mind touch hers wordlessly, and she understood. "Mental pain? Oh, gods." She squeezed his arm. "I'm sorry. I don't know why I didn't think of it sooner. I was just so frustrated..."

"I know."

Her hand slid down to clasp his. "You said you refused to do something the Being wanted done. Has it struck back at you in any way?"

"No. In fact, it has been strangely silent."

"Does the thing you refused have anything to do with why you don't want to go back into Dharakwood?"

Jovan didn't reply.

"All right. From what you've told me, the only significant thing in Dharakwood is Rinpool." At his continued silence, she went on. "The Being wants us to go to Rinpool?"

More silence.

"Why don't you want to do that? If I were to look in Rinpool, I might see something that would help solve this mystery."

"No. It wouldn't be worth the cost."

"Cost?"

He met her eyes, his own haunted. "The visions are not free." He looked away again. "So I have learned over the years."

"I don't understand," she said softly.

Jovan drew in a long breath and let it out slowly. Tara sensed the rise of his mental defenses, and when he finally spoke, tension edged his words, as if he anticipated being struck down at any moment. "In order to see the visions, one must either drink the waters of Rinpool or absorb them in some other way, as I did through my wound. Once touched by the power of Rinpool, you become a pawn of this god-like Being, driven by its will or whim. Your life is no longer your own."

"The Being came from Rinpool?"

"Ever since the waters healed me, I've heard whispers in my mind, demanding that I do things..." His gaze drifted to the fire. "And if I refuse, it inflicts mental torture on me."

Tara held her breath, fearing the Being would retaliate for Jovan's sharing of his secret. She clasped his hand in both of hers and reached out mentally. *If it attacks you, let me in. Maybe together we can block it out.*

No.

"Why not?"

"I won't subject you to the pain."

"How is it any different than you helping me when the creature from my dream attacks?"

"I can give you strength without feeling the pain that you feel."

"And you don't think I can do that for you?"

"I don't know and I don't intend to find out."

She pounded the floor. "Why do you have to be so stubborn? I can help you."

"No."

With a growl of annoyance, she rose and stalked to the wood pile. She brought back an armload of wood, then sat and fed another piece to the fire. "You've got to stop treating me like I'm some helpless maiden. I don't need protecting."

"I can't help it. I love you. If I can spare you any pain, I will."

She opened her mouth to speak, then closed it again, the love in his eyes melting her anger. She swallowed what she'd been about to say. "It's really hard to argue with that."

He gave her a brief smile.

She shoved her hair back from her face. "The Being still hasn't struck back at you?"

"No."

"Is it safe for you to answer more questions? Can you tell me about your magic?"

"I don't know anything about it. I think it must have come from Rinpool."

"What has the Being forced you to do?"

Jovan twisted a piece of straw in his fingers. "Too many things. None of them good. I have no wish to remember them." He tossed the straw away. "Since we're asking questions, there's something I would like to know. What happened right before the horses came back? We were talking, and you looked shocked all of a sudden. You said it was nothing, that what I said reminded you of something unpleasant. What was it?"

Tara grimaced. "That's something *I'd* rather not remember."

"You told me about Wyndover. What could be worse?"

She closed her eyes for a moment. She didn't want to touch that locked mental door. But how could she be mad at him for keeping secrets if she wasn't willing to share her own? "Fine. You said once before that Dominic told you how he and Laraina and I met?"

"Yes, during a brawl in Vaalderin."

"Did he mention Myles and Xavier?"

Jovan stiffened slightly. "Yes."

"Myles and I became... more than friends." Tara gripped her emotions and tied them down firmly. "He loved me, or so he claimed, but then the moment we ran into trouble on a job, he betrayed us. Not only did he leave us all stranded, he turned us in to the local authorities, and we spent some time in a very unpleasant dungeon. He collected quite a sum of money for his efforts." Tara stared out at the rain, an endless sheet of gray driving downward, beating rhythmically on the roof. "The last words he said to me were, 'Sorry, my love. All bets are off. Catch you in the next life.'" Her eyes shifted back to the fire. "When you said some of those words, it just... it opened an old wound."

"I'm sorry."

"Don't be. It's not something you could have known." Silence fell between them like a stone wall. Tara felt the awkwardness of the moment and knew she should say something more, but her mind was growing fuzzy, and she couldn't concentrate.

A gust of wind shook the stable, scattering rain across the straw-covered floor. Tara started, shivering in spite of the warmth within. She'd gotten lost in the fire again, drawn toward sleep by the mesmerizing flames. Sensing her weariness, the creature from her dream began to tug at her mind, trying to pull her into the dungeon. Warning chills crept over her skin. She shook her head and sat up straighter.

"You need rest," Jovan said softly. He pulled blankets out of the saddlebags and wrapped one around her shoulders.

"Thanks." Tara drew the blanket closer around her. "I dread it more each time."

"So do I." His hands clenched. "It's infuriating. I can see what's happening in your dream, but I can't help you. I can't do anything. I'm useless to you."

She covered his fists with her hands and raised them to her heart. "No, you're not. It's your strength that sustains me and keeps me going. It's your voice that brings me back." She leaned forward and brushed her lips across his. "I need you." She kissed him again, felt his arms slide around her, drawing her to him. Wrapping her arms around his neck, she settled in his lap, her body pressed close to his. He deepened the kiss, pulling her closer.

"I can keep the dream away for a while," he said.

"Mmmmm, please do," she murmured.

She pulled his shirt off over his head and let her fingers play over the hard muscles of his back. His lips traced a path down her neck.

She arched against him and moaned low in her throat. "That feels so good. We need to do this more often."

He laughed and continued his trail of kisses.

She cupped his face and lifted his eyes to hers, held his gaze for a moment. "Thank you for being here — for staying with me."

He caressed her cheek. "Until my last breath, I will be with you."

Their lips met again in a tender kiss. He leaned back, drawing her with him. His mind touched hers, and she opened to him, let him flow into her like a river of molten fire. Locked in each other's arms, they made love until finally, their energy spent, they fell into an exhausted sleep.

*****

Yawning and stretching luxuriously, Tara rolled onto her back and felt cold stone beneath her. Her eyes flew open. Moldy cobwebs hung above her head. The glow from four torches flickered dimly against the slime-covered walls.

"Here we go again," she muttered as she got to her feet. She couldn't feel Jovan's mind touching hers, but she knew he was with her. She looked down and found the black sword hanging at her side. "This is more like it. All right, creature, where are you?"

Turning, she stared into the thick blackness behind her. No sound. Nothing moved. It felt empty. She looked back toward the other end of the hallway. The tall iron door stood ajar. No red griffin lay embedded in its surface. A sliver of disappointment pricked her, though she'd known it wouldn't likely be there. She glanced once more at the passage behind her and wondered where the creature was. She'd never gotten a good look at it in her past dreams. The creature had always attacked her from behind, and she'd been too intent on escaping it to really see what it looked like. Icy chills crawled down her spine, and she sensed the creature moving toward her from... somewhere. She slipped silently up to the iron door and peered into the murky corridors beyond. There was no sign of the creature, or of Melodian. She stepped through the door and started down the main passageway.

At the first intersection she paused, looking cautiously to the left and right. Door-lined corridors stretched away into the gloom. Making a quick choice, she headed into the left-hand passage. At the next intersection she turned right. Row upon row of blank-faced iron doors stretched out before her. *Why so many doors?* She turned down several more corridors, but they were all the same. She looked left and right impatiently. *This could go on forever.* She chose a door and stopped in front of it. Shudders ran through her as she remembered the corpse she'd found in the last room she'd entered. She looked up and down the passage again. Where was the creature? Why wasn't it pursuing her as it always did? She sensed its evil aura, but couldn't tell where it was. It seemed to be hovering around her, now here, now there — what was it waiting for? Did it know that this time she had a weapon? She turned back to the door, took a deep breath, and opened it.

The room beyond was the size of a royal dining hall, with a cathedral ceiling. Three of the walls were bare stone. Six glowing torches hung in black metal sconces, two on each of the three walls. A thick sheet of clear glass formed the far wall. On the other side of the glass stood an enormous banquet table, sagging under the weight of dozens of platters of food — suckling pigs, racks of beef, roasted mutton, breads, cheeses, fruits, vegetables, and wine — enough to satisfy at least a hundred people.

Tara's heart constricted. Scattered across the floor on her side of the glass barrier lay several wasted corpses. Some were sprawled with their arms outstretched, reaching toward the feast. Others slumped against the clear wall in crumpled heaps, their skeletal fingers frozen in the act of clawing the glass.

Horror welled up inside her, and she felt bile rise in her throat. Swallowing hard, she crossed the room, stopping beside the wall of glass. Cold emanated from the clear surface. She touched it and jerked away from its bitter sting.

Looking down, she studied the emaciated corpses. There were six of them, four male and two female, remarkably well preserved. All of them had silver hair of varying lengths and wore shimmery gray robes with gray leather boots. Around the neck of each corpse hung a tarnished chain with a smooth black jewel, just like the dead woman in her earlier dream had worn.

Anger surged through her. Who had done this? She rushed forward. With one mighty swing of the black sword, she shattered the glass wall. She ducked her head and covered her eyes as shards of glass rained down upon her. A blast of freezing wind from inside the smashed barrier knocked her to her knees.

The wind died away. Shaking off the effects of the penetrating cold, Tara raised her head and looked around. The room was nearly dark. One torch still burned on the left wall. The bodies lay in twisted heaps; some had been blown halfway across the room. The rancid odor of rotting food tainted the cold air. The chamber door stood wide open, blown back against the wall.

She rose and shook the glass from her hair and clothing. She felt blood dripping down her back and arms and over her fingers from countless cuts and scratches. She swiped at a trickle on her cheek and left a wet smear across her face. Ignoring the pain, she made her way carefully toward the door. Broken glass crunched under her boots as she walked. Her breath puffed outward in frosty white clouds.

The remaining torch flickered and went out. Tara froze as darkness engulfed her like a smothering sack. Her breath seized in panic. She fought the paralyzing fear, drawing strength from the steady rhythm of her heart, beating as one with Jovan's. Power flared within her, burning away the icy numbness that rooted her to the floor. Taking a firm grip on the black sword, she groped her way toward the rectangle of light that led to the corridor. She halted when she reached the door and peered out into the passage. It was empty. Leaving the door open behind her, she walked slowly down the left passageway. The torches in the passage were still burning, though not as brightly.

A freezing chill jolted her. The stink of carrion filled the corridor. She whirled and nearly lost the contents of her stomach.

The hideously deformed figure of what might once have been a man stared at her from only a few feet away. Its head was horribly lopsided, with one bulging, silver-brown eye well below where it should have been; the other eye was an empty socket. Its nose and mouth were combined in one drooling orifice, lined with rotting teeth. Bristly tufts of silver-white hair stuck out from its head in places. The bulk of its sizeable body was gnarled and hunched and covered with oozing sores. One of its twisted legs dragged along the floor in a gangrenous stump. Remnants of gray cloth clung to its bloated body.

The creature stared at the black sword, recognition burning in its eye.

Tara swung the sword just as the creature let out a horrific screech and lunged toward her. Black fire surged forth. The creature shrieked again and caught the blade in its hands, somehow absorbing the black fire. Tara suddenly felt weak, the power being sucked out of her. She pulled against it, trying to draw back, but the creature would not let go.

Jovan! she cried. She was already drawing on his strength. There wasn't much left. Seizing on one last desperate burst, she wrenched herself away and let go of the sword. The shock threw her back against the wall. Her head hit the stone with a sickening crack. Pain speared through her skull, then numbness, then nothing.

*****

Layers of blackness weighed her down. She struggled up through them, clawing her way through the suffocating folds. Velvety soft, they clung to her, enticing her to stay in the soothing dark. She resisted.

She opened her eyes and immediately became aware of a throbbing ache in the back of her head. Above her, a fly buzzed across a low, white-washed ceiling. She was lying in a bed, a rather lumpy one. She glanced about, moving her head as little as possible. The bed stood in the corner of a very small room. Dingy whitewash covered the brown-stained walls. A wooden stand with a metal pitcher and washbasin stood against the wall next to the bed. In the opposite corner sat a chamber pot around which a large spider was diligently spinning a web. A small, grimy-paned window just beyond the foot of the bed let in a bit of light.

She blinked a time or two to make certain her eyes weren't deceiving her about her surroundings. Where was she? How had she gotten here? She tried to think, but her mind refused to work. She reached up and probed the back of her head with her fingertips. Pain knifed through her head and she nearly passed out. Gritting her teeth, she pulled herself back from the edge and continued her examination. No lumps, no angry swelling, no blood. She started to frown, then stopped when the movement brought more pain. How could there be no mark? She felt like she'd been bashed over the head with a club. Several clubs. Wielded by ogres.

Gathering her strength, she threw back the covers and gingerly swung her feet to the floor. The room spun about her. Her stomach heaved. Swallowing quickly, she closed her eyes and concentrated on settling her stomach.

The sound of voices passing outside her door roused her. Very slowly, she opened her eyes again and listened, but couldn't make out any of the words. On the floor next to the bed she found her boots. Taking her time, she managed to reach them and slip them on. She straightened out her twisted and rumpled clothing as best she could and then carefully ran her fingers through her hair, combing it back away from her face.

Still sitting, she slid up the bed until she reached the washstand. Grabbing hold of it, she slowly pulled herself to her feet. Waves of dizziness and nausea rushed over her. She withstood them, barely.

She dipped her hands into the washbasin and splashed some cold water on her face. She found a tin cup beside the basin, filled it from the pitcher, and took a long draught to soothe her parched throat.

Feeling a bit steadier, she made her way along the wall to the door. Her sword belt, with sword and dagger, hung from a peg on the back of the door. Leaning against the door, she took the belt down and buckled it around her waist. She noticed an empty black scabbard. Where had it come from? No answers formed in her mind, her thoughts mired in confusion. She tried the door. It was locked from the outside.

Following the wall, she moved around the room to the window. She released the latch and threw it wide. Warm air drifted into the chamber, carrying on it the myriad scents and sounds of a city. It appeared to be late afternoon or early evening. Her window opened out on a shadowed alley. She stuck her head out and looked down, discovered she was on the second floor of whatever building she was in. The only way of escape was to jump. She leaned against the sill, putting her weight on her arms to ease the pressure on her trembling legs. That kind of a jump she wasn't ready for.

She heard the sound of a key turning in a lock, and the door opened and closed behind her. She pulled her head in and turned, gripping the window sill for support. The dagger found its way naturally into her left hand. Three men had entered the room — three of the handsomest men she had ever seen.

"Tara, you're awake," they said in joyful unison. "Are you all right?"

She shook her head, and the three men resolved themselves into one.

"Tara?" the man asked. His expression had changed to one of concern. He started toward her.

She brandished her dagger threateningly. "Keep your distance, please."

He halted in surprise. "Tara, what's wrong?"

"Why do you keep calling me that?" She watched him warily.

He stared at her, amazement and confusion chasing each other across his face. "Because that is your name."

"So you say."

The man's eyes narrowed. "If Tara isn't your name, then what is?"

She started to speak, then stopped, realizing in sudden panic that she didn't know. "That's not important," she managed to say in a somewhat steady voice. "The question is, who are you?"

"You don't know who I am?" he asked slowly.

"No, I'm sorry, I don't," she answered. Though she wished she did. He was definitely the best-looking man she'd ever seen.

"My name is Jovan Trevillion," he said, never taking his eyes from her face.

"All right, Jovan Trevillion," she said crisply. "Who are you, and why am I locked in this room?"

CHAPTER 12

Jovan stared in stunned silence, his mind refusing to accept what he was hearing. How could she not know him? He stepped toward her. "Tara —"

"Please don't." She moved into a defensive crouch. The dagger still gleamed in her hand. "I will use this if I have to."

Jovan halted again. What could possibly have happened in her dream to cause this? "I am Jovan Trevillion. You are Tara Triannon. We've been traveling together for quite some time. You were locked in here because I didn't want anyone walking in on you while you were unconscious."

Tara's brows furrowed as if in thought, then straightened. Her eyes narrowed in obvious pain. She leaned back, bracing herself against the window sill once more. "Where were we going? Where is here? And why was I unconscious?"

"We were coming here, to Cierra. We needed to decide the best way to reach the Black Mountains in the East. You were unconscious because of the dream." He watched her carefully for a reaction.

"The dream," she murmured. "I don't remember having any dream."

"I don't know why you can't remember it, but you must try. What happened to the black sword?"

"Black sword?" She glanced at the empty scabbard.

"Yes. It disappeared while you were in the dream." A thread of urgency slipped into his voice when no spark of recognition or remembrance showed in her eyes. "Where is it?"

"I don't know." Her eyes began to glaze over. She swayed, caught herself on the sill.

He darted forward. She slashed at him with the knife.

He dodged, felt the breeze as the blade whistled past his throat. Seizing her hand, he wrestled the dagger away and tossed it into a corner. She nearly fell. He caught her and swung her up into his arms. She struggled for a moment, then went limp.

"My head," she groaned, and squeezed her eyes shut.

Jovan carried her to the bed and gently laid her down. "You can trust me. I won't hurt you."

Her head sagged against the pillow, and she was lost once more in oblivion. He retrieved the dagger, then looked down at her again, at a loss. What in blazes had happened to her?

What happened in the dream? he sent outward, his anger seething through the cracks in his resolve to stay calm. The Being had completely blocked him out of Tara's last nightmare. He hadn't been able to see or hear anything that went on. He'd lent his strength, and she had drawn on that heavily, but he'd been denied anything more. If the creature had somehow gotten the sword...

He stared at the ceiling, waiting for the cold rumble of the Being's voice in his mind. Nothing. No word or echo of thought stained the silence in his head.

Answer me! he shouted soundlessly, wishing again that he had something tangible on which to focus his fury. He probed the stillness, searching for a way to connect with the Being, to wrest from its grip the answers he needed, but all he found were barriers, limitless walls of stone that closed him off from the Being's realm of knowledge.

Tara moaned softly in her sleep, her head turned to the side. He covered her with a blanket and brushed the hair from her face with the backs of his fingers. "We will get through this. I will find a way."

Outside, somewhere off in the city, a clock bonged the hour, its harsh tolling reminding him of his arrangement to meet with the shopkeeper who had promised to procure the supplies they needed to continue their journey. He hesitated, reluctant to leave Tara alone, not knowing when she would wake again or in what condition she would be in when she did. Her loss of memory worried him greatly. He wished he knew if it had been caused by injury or magic. If she would let him connect with her mentally, he might be able to help her. But unless he could get her to trust him, there was nothing he could do. He clenched his fist in frustration. If only he could have seen what had happened, both to Tara and the black sword. They had to get the sword back somehow. He cursed the Being again for its interference.

He debated his options a moment more, then made his decision. The weaselly shopkeeper wouldn't hold the supplies for him if he missed the rendezvous, and he didn't want to draw any more attention to their presence here by working out another deal with someone else. Better to go while Tara slept and chance that she would stay asleep until his return. He stuck the dagger, Tara's sword, and her boot knives in his belt. Then he closed the window and left the room, locking the door behind him.

*****

When Tara woke again, it was night. Moonlight shone through the small window at the foot of the bed, illuminating the tiny room as clearly as if it were day. Someone had closed the window, and the room had grown stuffy. The lingering odor of stale food and wine was unpleasantly strong.

She sat up slowly, taking stock of the situation. Her head still hurt, though the pain had receded to a dull ache. Upon self-examination she found no other injury. Her memory, however, had not returned.

As she climbed out of bed, she noticed her sword was missing. She searched for the dagger, but it, too, was gone. Obviously the good-looking man she'd fought with earlier did not care for a repeat performance. She kept her empty sword belt on anyway, feeling strangely naked without it. She went back to the wash basin, poured some cold water out of the pitcher, and washed her hands and face. Then she filled the cup and drained it.

Feeling braced, she tiptoed to the door and tried the latch. Still locked. Undaunted, she moved to the window. Thick black clouds covered the night sky. The light she had thought was from the moon actually emanated from a tall street lamp set at the intersection of the alley and the main street about ten yards to her right. The alley below was darkly shadowed, barely touched by the street lamp's glow. It seemed deserted, though it was impossible to tell for certain.

Tara opened the window and stood for several minutes, listening. Few sounds reached her ears — an occasional barking dog, the rolling of distant thunder. The night air was warm and damp with the promise of more rain.

Cierra, she thought, her mind working sluggishly. That was where she was, or so the man had said. What was his name again? Jovan... Jovan something. He had said her name was Tara. And there was something about a black sword. She pressed her fist to her forehead in frustration. Why couldn't she remember? She had friends in Cierra, though she wasn't sure how she knew that. She couldn't remember their names, much less how to find them. Perhaps if she explored the city a bit she might see something familiar that would spark her memory. Her left hand moved reflexively to the empty scabbard at her side. Going out into any city at night with no weapons, however, was not a smart thing to do.

She glanced around the small room, but nothing lethal remained. The only possibilities were the pitcher and wash basin. Either one could put a good-sized crack in someone's head. She winced at the thought and touched the back of her own head gingerly. It was still very sore even though there were no bumps.

Her other option was to pound on the door until someone came. But then Jovan or whoever would tell her what they wanted her to believe, true or not. If Jovan was lying to her, she would have a hard time disbelieving him, simply because she was so attracted to him. She wanted to believe everything he said, and that could be dangerous. Better to take the risk and find things out for herself than be spoon-fed false information.

She went back to the bed and pulled off the sheets. Knotting them together in a makeshift rope, she tied one end to the foot of the bed and flung the other end out the window. Emptying the contents of the pitcher into the wash basin, she looped the wide handle over her arm and made good her escape.

The short drop from the end of the sheet-rope to the dark cobbled alley below jarred her more than she expected, sending waves of pain crashing through her skull. She crouched against the wall, hiding in the shadows until the pain eased.

After a few minutes, she forced herself to rise. Booming thunder echoed among the surrounding buildings as the storm drew nearer. She slipped up to the end of the alley and peered out into the street. None of the city's inhabitants were about. The cobbled streets were fairly clean, washed down by the recent rains. The wooden buildings had been painted in a variety of colors; most were three stories high. Bright awnings that shaded the area in front of the shops during the day now lay neatly rolled up against the faces of the buildings. Decorative wooden signs hung before each edifice, proclaiming their wares to passersby.

Tara studied the darkened store fronts and silent inns — the Will-o-Wine, from which she'd just escaped, the Cockerel, the Sword and Dagger. Nothing looked familiar. Pitcher in hand, she turned to her left and made her way down the wet street.

She walked for what seemed like hours, enduring a few sprinkles, but no downpours. The wind changed, bringing cooler air and driving the rumbling storm clouds off to the west. Rubbing her arms against the chill of the night, Tara kept walking. She passed ornate houses with well-tended gardens, obviously belonging to the very rich, followed by the more modest homes of the middle class. Eventually, she reached the seedy tenements of the poor. Still no tendrils of memory uncurled.

Tired and cold, she stopped at the edge of a dirty side street to rest. She had seen only a handful of people, mostly drunks and prostitutes. A dull throbbing ache pulsed through the back of her head. She tried massaging the area but it didn't help.

She looked out at the shabby dwellings around her, dark and dreary with rotting wood and peeling paint. Garbage clogged the storm drains, creating foul-smelling puddles along the narrow streets. Drunken singing rose above the rooftops, coming from a distant street. She faded further back into the shadows. Very few street lamps lit the gloom in this part of the city. Most had burned out and no one had bothered to relight them.

As she was deciding which way to go, she became aware of a sound that had worked its way into her consciousness without her realizing it — the flow of running water. *The Bryar River,* she thought, *which flows southwest into the Amberin River. The Colin branches off from it and goes south, emptying into the Nournan.* A chill shivered through her. There was something about the Nournan she needed to remember, something dangerous. Memories darted through her consciousness, quick and elusive, teasing her with vague images before diving back down into the murk clouding her mind. She tried to catch them and pull them out where she could see them clearly, but they continued to swim just out of reach. Frustrated, she headed toward the river.

A short walk brought her to the docks. Ahead of her, not far away, she saw two men loading kegs into a longboat, with a third carrying another keg from a nearby warehouse. The boat wasn't tied in one of the usual mooring slips along the river, but rather off to the side, hidden in the shadow of a loaded barge. *Smugglers*, she knew instantly, and ducked back out of sight behind a pile of crates, wondering how she knew that. Judging from the only slightly muffled guffaws coming from the two men, Tara guessed they had sampled some of their contraband. She watched them, racking her brain, trying to grasp a wisp of memory that swiftly dissipated.

A fourth man, short and wiry with black hair, exited the warehouse and strode across to where the sniggering men were bent over a keg. He kicked one of them in the rear, sending him diving back into the boat. Laughing and pointing at his floundering cohort, the second smuggler barely managed to avoid the same fate. The black-haired man let out a stream of curses, then lowering his voice a notch, ranted at the two until they stopped laughing.

Tara shivered, suddenly growing cold all over.

"Hey, look at this — a spy," said a chuckling voice behind her.

Startled, she turned quickly. Two big men, one dark, one blond with tattooed arms, were moving in to grab her. Instinct took over. She lashed out with the metal pitcher, catching the dark one on the chin and knocking him sideways. She kicked the blond man in the belly, doubling him over, cracked him in the ear with the pitcher, then kicked him in the chin and sent him flying over backward. Just as the dark man was recovering, Tara dealt him a nasty kick in the groin that dropped him with a groan to his knees, then she whacked him over the head with the pitcher. He crumpled to the ground, clutching his bruised vitals.

Dizzied by the effort, Tara fell against the pile of crates, knocking them to the ground with a crash and toppling into the midst of them. A shower of curses that sounded vaguely familiar filled her ears, and she was hauled to her feet.

"Haedis' balls!" roared the black-haired man, who with his three cohorts had come running from the boat. "It's the Ice Queen herself. Tara, how are ya?" He hugged her, then clapped her on the back and stepped away, laughing at his own rhyme. "Tara, how are ya. Ha, ha, ha. That's good."

Tara wobbled and nearly fell again. Two of the men with him caught her arms and steadied her.

He sobered instantly. "Hey, are you all right?"

Tara pulled herself upright and focused on him. The leader of the smugglers was short for a man, only slightly taller than she was, but he was strong and wiry. He had short-clipped black hair and a short black beard that looked like it was being coaxed into a goatee. What startled her was that his face was definitely familiar.

"I know you," she said slowly, trying to force her way through the thick fog clogging her memory.

"Of course you know me," he said. "Blackie de Runo. Don't you remember? We smuggled together. I admit it was several years ago, but..." He stopped, looked at her closely. "Did one of those big behemoths do this to you? Because if they did," he glared at the two men who were just now starting to get up, "I'll hang them by their balls from the —"

"No, no," Tara interrupted, "they're not responsible. Not that I would blame them. I hit them first." She looked over at them. "I'll have to apologize."

Blackie de Runo snorted. "Don't bother. It's their own fault. They should have known better."

Tara rubbed the back of her head. "I'm not sure what's going on. I seem to have been hit over the head, and I can't remember anything. Who did you say I was?"

"Tara Triannon, the Ice Queen." He chuckled. "That's what we used to call you — either that or Troublemaker."

She smiled. "You caused more trouble than I did." She stopped as images of past adventures with Blackie and his band faded in and out of her mind. Then the fog swirled in once more. She scowled and closed her eyes. "I almost had something."

"Where's Laraina?" he asked.

"Who?"

"Your sister, Laraina." He shook his head. "Woman, you are in bad shape."

A vicious growl silenced them, froze them where they stood. A hulking shadow rose behind them. The two men with whom Tara had fought flew through the air and rolled along the dock toward the river, thrown with incredible strength. Before anyone could react, the two men on either side of Tara were wrenched away and sent tumbling after the others. The third backed hastily away. Tara stumbled, but kept her balance.

"The Butcher," Blackie de Runo said in a strangled whisper. He reached for his sword. A huge black wolf leaped at him, landing on his chest and knocking him flat. Six gray wolves surged by, surrounding the other five smugglers and trapping them against the edge of the river.

Steadying herself, Tara turned. Clad in dark leather with a dark fur-lined cloak, a giant with a ragged scar running down the left side of his face stepped toward her, a sword gripped in his gnarled hand. She backed away, maneuvering around fallen crates and spilled horse tack, scanning the area for something to use as a weapon. She had dropped the pitcher after the battle with Blackie's men, not that it would have been much use against this... this... whatever he was. She hadn't decided if he was man or beast.

The giant followed her. She wasn't sure which alarmed her more — the giant himself, or the fact that he, too, seemed familiar. She prodded her memory in vain.

"Well met, again, Lady Tara," the giant said. His black eyes gleamed with what looked like anticipation and... something else. "Where is your black sword?"

"Not where it should be," she said as she backed toward the river.

The giant gestured with his blade toward Blackie de Runo, who lay petrified, the black wolf standing with its forelegs on his chest. "Take his."

Tara hesitated only a moment before doing so. Eyeing the wolf cautiously, she slid Blackie's sword from its sheath and moved back out onto the open docks.

"Who are you and what do you want from us?" she asked as she and the giant circled each other. "We have nothing of value."

Surprise crossed the giant's scarred face. His black eyes held hers. "You don't know who I am?"

"No." She rubbed the back of her skull. "Someone, somewhere, bashed me over the head, and I can't remember anything."

The giant said nothing, continued to hold her gaze. Finally, he spoke. "I am Rylan Natiere. You owe me a duel."

"A duel." She smiled tensely. "I fear at this moment I will be a very poor dueling partner."

Natiere lunged forward, his sword thrusts quick and deadly.

Tara parried them, using every ounce of strength she possessed. Her arms and legs trembled weakly. Blackie's sword weighed heavy in her hand. She broke away from the fight, stumbled across the wharf, then stopped to regroup. Her head throbbed. She was starting to see double.

Natiere attacked again. Tara fought him off, but her reaction time was slow. Natiere drove her relentlessly backward, his blade ripping gashes in her clothing, but not touching her skin. Tara staggered and fell. Lying back on her elbows, her eyes closed, she felt the sharp point of Natiere's sword pressing against the soft flesh between her breasts. She opened her eyes and looked up at him.

"I'm sorry," she said between breaths. "I can't fight two of you."

He gave her a strange look. "Two of me?"

She nodded. She lifted her hand and pointed at him, then pointed at the empty space beside him. "I see two of you."

He stared at her wordlessly.

Tara lay back and closed her eyes again, trying to catch her breath. She felt Natiere's ambivalence and sensed he wouldn't harm her — at least, not in her present state. If he had really wanted to kill her, he could have done so easily during their brief battle. She knew, too, that her torn clothing probably didn't leave much to the imagination, but she didn't care. It was all she could do to keep from passing out.

The sound of clanking armor and running feet broke in on them from farther up the docks. Tara heard excited shouts punctuated by barking guard dogs as a squad of Cierran soldiers raced toward them.

Taking advantage of the distraction, Tara shoved Natiere's blade aside and rolled out from under it.

Natiere motioned with his hand, and the wolves returned to him. They vanished into the shadows.

Scrambling to her feet, Tara ran toward the smugglers' boat.

Blackie de Runo and his men followed. The seven of them piled into the boat, threw off the ropes, and shoved away from the docks. Rowing madly, they caught the current and escaped down the river.

*****

Jovan Trevillion turned the key in the lock and slowly opened the door. He hoped to find Tara asleep, but he would take nothing for granted. She'd attacked him once. He had no wish to fight her again. Cautiously, he eased into the small, dingy room. The bed was empty. He halted and dropped his pack, poised for defense. Where was she hiding? He scanned the room, noted the missing pitcher, then settled on the open window with the sheet draped over the sill. He stiffened in dismay. *No!*

Cursing roundly, he strode to the window and looked out onto the dank alley. Nothing moved in the narrow space, save for a few stray raindrops falling from a passing cloud. His fists clenched, his chest tightening as his mind seized on all the horrors that could befall her out in the city, injured, alone, and vulnerable. Catching his breath, he retrieved his pack, climbed down the knotted sheet, and dropped to the ground, his boots splashing in a shallow puddle. He crouched for a moment, scrutinizing the night-dark shadows behind him, before jogging to the end of the alley.

He glanced around the corner. The streets were deserted. Lightning brightened the distant sky, followed by grumbling thunder as the storm blew further westward. He breathed deeply to calm himself and reached outward with his senses, hoping she hadn't gone far. He couldn't touch her mind, but he should still be able to feel her presence. Time seemed to slow as he let his mind slip through the sleeping city. He had to find her before the creature from the dream dungeon realized her guard was down and sucked her back in. If she had another dream without knowing who she was or what was happening...

Sweat dripped down his forehead. He wiped his brow impatiently. So many people in this city... too many. He cast outward again, weaving in and out of the living auras, searching for the one soul who eluded him until — there. His head whipped around to the left — a familiar touch, cool and sharp, yet muddied with pain and uncertainty. She had gone toward the river.

He raced down the empty streets, crossing private yards and vaulting fences, taking the most direct route he could find. When he was halfway to the river, he heard distant shouts and dogs barking. Then he felt Tara slipping away from him, moving swiftly past the fringes of his reach. *No!* He stifled a curse and ran faster. The dilapidated homes of the less fortunate and the mean shacks of the poor flew by as the sound of rushing water grew. He leaped over two smelly drunks passed out in the street, rounded a corner, and stopped in the shadow of a shipbuilder's workshop. A short distance away flowed the swift Bryar River. He ducked back out of sight.

Out on the docks, deckhands were picking up bridles, saddlebags, and other tack that had spilled from a scattered pile of crates and repacking them for shipment. Cierran soldiers prowled among them, tense and alert.

Breathing hard, Jovan edged forward until he could see around the corner. He had to find out what had happened and where Tara had gone. His gut told him she'd taken to the river, sailed out of reach of his questing senses. He hoped he was wrong. The river led straight into the Bog, where the creature of her nightmares reigned.

He waited until the soldiers had moved away, then hid his pack in the shadows and hurried across the dock. He picked up a saddle and carried it over to a crate being repacked by two muscular deckhands. They paused as he approached.

"Who are you?" asked one of them, his eyes narrowing. His hand moved toward the knife at his belt.

Jovan lowered the saddle into the crate. "I'm a hand on that Dhanarran ship over there." He gestured with his head toward the line of ships moored along the river. He had seen a Dhanarran flag flying from the mast of one of them.

"The *Rivermaster*?" The man's hand hovered around his knife.

"That's the one," Jovan said, glad they hadn't asked him for that piece of information. He glanced around as if to make sure no one was listening. "If the mate asks," he said, lowering his voice, "tell him I've been here all along, will you? I had a mighty strong thirst I needed to quench, if you get my drift, so I went into the city." He glanced around again. "The mate doesn't like us fraternizing with the city folk. If he finds out, I'll be swabbing the deck for six months."

A slow grin spread over the deckhand's face, and he relaxed, his hand sliding away from his weapon. "Heh, heh. I've been in your shoes myself a few times." He clapped Jovan on the shoulder. "Me and Sully here won't let on where you been."

"Thanks. I owe you." Jovan picked up another saddle. "Say, what happened here, anyway?"

"Smugglers." The man waved his hand toward the scattered crates. "They don't usually make such a mess, though."

"Bunch of drunkards." Sully spat. "Blackie and his crew must have got to fighting over something."

"We don't know it was him," the other one said. "No one got a good look at them before they took off downriver."

"Of course, it was him, Jip. They only took the brandy. That's what they always do."

"Blackie de Runo?" Jovan asked.

"Thievin' pirate," Sully muttered. He headed over to another crate.

"What about that giant with the fur cloak Lestren claims he saw?" Jip said, following after him.

Sully stuffed a bunch of saddlebags back into the crate. "Lestren had a few too many shots of whiskey in his gut. He was doin' what our friend here was doin' and it warped that pea brain of his." Sully finished with the crate and looked around. "Hey, where'd he go?"

Jovan crouched behind the shipbuilder's workshop, thinking hard. Tara must have escaped downriver with Blackie de Runo. Maybe she'd remembered him. His hand clenched. Why should she remember Blackie and not him?

And the giant that Jip had mentioned could only be Natiere. *If you touch her, I'll kill you.* The thought arrowed outward on the spear of his anger.

The quick answering thrust surprised him.

She is not yours anymore. Natiere's gravelly whisper echoed in his mind.

Then another voice, as ancient as the Abyss, flooded his mind. *You were warned.*

CHAPTER 13

Tara woke to bright sunshine streaming in her face. The pitching and rocking of the boat had jarred her out of her slumber. She heard the rush of whitewater rapids. Disoriented, she sat up, shading her eyes against the glare. A dull ache throbbed in the back of her head.

"Hey, don't rock the boat," said a man's voice beside her.

She recoiled, gripping a thwart and the gunwale. Blackie de Runo looked at her over his shoulder from the rower's bench where he sat facing the stern. Sweat dripped down his forehead as he wrestled with the oar. "Sorry. Didn't mean to spook ya."

Holding tight to the gunwale, Tara blinked and glanced around. She was sitting crossways in the middle of the lurching boat, wedged between an oar bank and Blackie's rowing bench. A thick blanket and tarp lay beneath her to shield her from the rough dampness of the bottom. Cold spray splashed her face as the boat careened through the rapids. The longboat was double-banked with room for ten oarsmen, but only six of the seats were filled with straining men. The smugglers fought the oars, working to keep the boat away from the looming rocks that split the water like predators awaiting their prey.

"Hard to starboard!" hollered a big man in the bow, one of the two she'd clobbered with the pitcher back on the dock.

"Right or left, Brains?" Blackie yelled. "Right or left?"

"To the right!" shouted the big man's rowing partner.

Tara held her breath as the boat raced toward a jagged rock, came around to the right, and deftly swept past it.

Blackie grinned as he saw the rock receding in the distance. "Ha! That's the last one. Nice work."

With a final heave, the boat bounced out of the whitewater into a calmer part of the swift-moving river. Four of the men, including Blackie, banked their oars. The two in the stern guided the boat as it sped along with the current.

"All right, ya bunch of derelicts, you can relax now," Blackie said. He spun around and faced the fore. "Brains, how many times do I have to tell you not to use sailor talk? You know I can never remember if 'starbird' means left or right. And what do birds have to do with it anyway?"

A pained look crossed the big man's face. "It's *board*, not *bird*. Star*board*. And it means 'to the right.' Port is 'to the left.'"

Blackie snorted in disgust. "A port is where you land after a sea voyage. If you mean left or right, say left or right."

Brains shook his head. "How can a pirate not know the language of the sea?"

"I'm a smuggler, not a sailor. How far to the Nournan?"

The big man ran a hand through his blond curls and looked speculatively at the river. "With the swift current and the two portages, I would say maybe six days. That sound right to you?" He looked toward the stern.

"Six days and five or six hours," said a sinewy man with wild gray hair, who was trying to man his oar and drink from a whiskey bottle at the same time.

"Good." Blackie slapped his leg. "We're right on schedule."

Tara sat up straighter and took another look at her traveling companions. Manning an oar next to the gray-haired man in the stern was the other behemoth she'd whacked with the pitcher. He was tall and solidly built with deeply tanned skin and several long, thick strands of tightly curled black hair. On the bench in front of them lounged a slippery-looking man of maybe twenty years whose shoulder-length brown hair kept drifting into his face. *A thief*, Tara guessed, wondering again how she knew such things. The thief pulled out a knife and began whittling on a stick. Brains, the big man with the blond curls and tattooed arms, sat in the bow, staring downriver. Beside him perched a good-looking blond smuggler with a short beard and long hair pulled back in a ponytail, who looked to be in his early twenties. Her gut instinct gauged them as mostly good men — the only exception being the darker of the two behemoths. Something about him raised her hackles. He would bear watching.

"How's your head?" Blackie asked.

"Still hurts." Tara massaged the back of her head. "Where are we? And who did you say you were again?"

"Blackie de Runo. Balls, woman, you've got to get over this."

Tara stretched, feeling her spine crack and pop. "Yes, well, I'm trying. My head feels like it's full of mush."

She wished she could remember more about Blackie. His comfortable familiarity made her feel better about having jumped into a boat with a bunch of strange men, at least. He might be a smuggler, but her gut told her she could trust him.

"We're on the Colin."

"The Colin River?" Tara looked out across the wide, fast-flowing waterway. Grasslands and cultivated farmland slipped past, shades of green and gold blurring in the distance.

"Yes. It branches off from the Bryar, south of Cierra. It's shallow in places, so hardly anyone ever uses it."

"Where are we going?"

"Gypsy Crossroads. I've got an Eastern buyer willing to pay three times the going rate for these kegs."

Tara remembered the kegs she'd seen Blackie's men stow onboard. "Right. The brandy."

Blackie chuckled. "Of course, he doesn't know he's paying so much more than he might pay elsewhere, and I didn't see the need to enlighten him."

"You're still a scoundrel," Tara said. A scene in a tavern with a younger Blackie de Runo sprang into her mind. She closed her eyes and latched onto the memory before it could skitter away. "I remember something about the Gypsy Crossroads. I remember you playing cards in a tavern — the White Bull. You ran out of gold pieces and tried to pass off your rotgut as Cierran brandy to gain a new stake. You got us into a brawl, and we were thrown in the guardhouse and locked up for days."

Blackie scowled. "If you're going to remember something, why don't you remember something good?"

"I'll take any memory I can get," Tara retorted, relief streaming through her at her success in holding on to the wispy remembrance. "Maybe the rest will come back now."

"I hope so. It's kind of hard to talk old times when you don't remember any of it."

"Tell me stories of what we did. It might help." Tara's stomach growled. "You wouldn't happen to have any food around here, would you?"

"Hard biscuits and beef jerky. That's about it, but you're welcome to it." He swung to the stern. "Hey, Whittler. Some food for the lady. Pass it up here."

Whittler ceased carving long enough to lean over, grab a small sack, and toss it to Blackie. Then his knife began its rhythmical sculpting of the wood once more.

Blackie caught the sack and handed it to Tara. "Stories, eh? Let's see... where do I start?"

Tara pulled out a biscuit. "Why don't you start by telling me who's in this boat with us?"

"Oh. You haven't had a proper introduction, have you?" He jerked his thumb toward the stern. "The man with the knife is Whittler. We call him that for obvious reasons."

Whittler looked up, shook his hair back out of his face, gave a brief nod, and went back to his work.

"Behind Whittler is Gus," Blackie continued.

The tall dark man who made Tara wary touched his hand to his chest, then his forehead, and swept it outward toward her, open-palmed. *A Southlander*, Tara thought as she chewed on the biscuit. She nodded back.

"Next to Gus is Whiskey, also named for obvious reasons."

Tara looked at the gray-haired smuggler, still juggling the oar and his bottle.

Gus eyed Whiskey with disgust. "You can't steer and drink, too," he said in a deep voice, his words twisted slightly by his southern accent. "Put the bottle down, you old sop, before I throw it over the side."

"You do and you'll go over after it," Whiskey snapped, gripping the bottle tight to his chest.

Blackie ignored them and waved toward the bow. "That's Brains, with the tattoos all over his arms. The man next to him is Diamond Jack."

"Unusual names." Tara nodded to them.

They nodded back. Diamond Jack pulled a handkerchief out of his pocket to wipe the sweat from his face and a gold necklace with a dangling green gem tumbled out.

"Where'd you get that?" Blackie demanded.

Jack stuffed the necklace back into his pocket. "I found it in a bag in a desk drawer back at that warehouse, along with a couple other things. The dock master must have pinched it from one of his lady friends."

Blackie scowled. "We were supposed to be just getting the brandy."

"Well, I was looking for a bottle of brew for Whiskey when I ran across it." Jack shrugged innocently. "Somehow it ended up in my pocket."

"I can't imagine how that happened," Blackie said dryly.

Jack lay down on the open bench. "My turn for a sleep shift." He closed his eyes.

Blackie gestured toward him. "We freed him from the stocks in Norellanen a while back. He'd been caught cheating at cards with a jack of diamonds up his sleeve, hence the name."

"I see," Tara said. "Just your type."

Blackie shot her a withering look. He raised his voice. "For those of you who don't know her by reputation, this is Tara Triannon. She could whip the lot of you single-handedly. She is a very good friend of mine," his voice sharpened, "and anyone who bothers her will answer to me. Is that clear?" His tone lightened again. "Unless, of course, she kills you first."

A chorus of grunts acknowledged Blackie's warning.

Tara swallowed the last of the biscuit. "You got water?"

"What? Oh. Somewhere here." Blackie fished around between the two kegs that took up most of the space in front of his oar bank.

The other four kegs had been lodged in the ends of the boat, two fore and two aft. "Here, try this." He gave her a worn flask.

She took a long sip, choked, and spat it over the side. "That's not water." She wiped her mouth on her sleeve. "And I thought your rotgut was bad before."

Blackie snatched the flask out of her hand. "There's nothing wrong with my brew." He dug around and pulled out another flask. "Try this."

She took a small sip this time, making sure the flask contained water before drinking deeply. "That's better." She took out a piece of beef jerky and gnawed on it. "You said that I was part of your band at one time," she said between bites. "How long ago was that?"

"I don't know... eight or nine years, maybe."

"Not that I would remember, but none of these men are familiar to me like you are. What happened to the ones who traveled with you when I was there?"

"Some found better things to do. A couple of them found the wrong end of a sword. Do you remember Club? No, of course you don't. He hired on as a guard on the Frontier caravan routes."

Tara stopped in mid-motion with the beef jerky halfway to her mouth. *A guard on the Frontier caravans.* She knew someone who had been a guard on the Eastern Frontier caravan routes. He had been hurt somehow. Who was it? What had happened? She closed her eyes and concentrated, but couldn't dislodge the memory. She cursed under her breath.

"Are you all right?" Blackie asked, his hand on her shoulder.

"Yes. No. I don't know. My head hurts." She pressed the heel of her palm against her forehead. "It's all right there, just under the surface, but I can't pull it out. It's so frustrating."

"We've got smooth sailing for a while, until we hit the first portage. Why don't you get some more sleep? Might help. Not much else to do anyway." He turned suddenly toward the stern. "Whittler, I told you not to carve on the side of the boat!"

Tara finished the beef jerky, then settled back into her niche, surprised at how tired she was after having slept so many hours. The rush of the river in her ears and the steady motion of the boat lulled her toward sleep, but every time she drifted off, she felt needlelike stabs in her head like claws digging into her mind, and icy jabs prodded her awake again. Finally she gave up and, with a groan, dragged herself into an upright position. Her head ached as if a gang of her worst enemies had been beating on her. Slowly, she lifted her head and looked around, surprised to find the sky dark. Cold moonlight rode the river, illuminating their path to the south. Crisp, fresh air soothed her warm face, and she smelled the sweet scent of wild flowers and mown hay.

"Hey, you're awake," said a nearby voice.

Tara turned toward the voice, and the face of the handsomest man she'd ever seen floated before her. He looked familiar. That face... dark hair, strong jaw, and those dark eyes, so intense... where had she seen him? She tried to get her pain-clogged mind to think. The inn... that was it. He was at the inn where she'd awakened with no memory. He'd said his name was Jovan...

"Are you all right? Why are you looking at me like that?"

Tara blinked, and the image of the handsome man shifted to the narrower face, lighter-brown eyes, and goateed chin of Blackie de Runo. She saw Blackie staring at her, concern lining his face. She shook her head. "I must have been dreaming."

Blackie pressed a water flask into her hands. "If you were, it couldn't have been a good one. You've been tossing and muttering for hours. I couldn't decide whether to wake you up or not."

Tara drank from the flask. "I don't really remember."

"Surprise, surprise," Blackie muttered. He undid his cloak, folded it loosely, and stuffed it behind her to keep the gunwale from digging into her back. "Who's Jovan?"

Tara eyed him sharply. "Jovan?"

"Yes." Blackie sat back. "You said the name several times while you were asleep."

Tara looked out across the silver-bright river. Out of the corner of her eye, she could see Blackie watching her closely. "Well, I'm not exactly sure. When I came to at the inn back in Cierra, he was there. He said his name, and then he told me my name, which I couldn't remember at the time, and said we had been traveling together. I had no recollection of him or of anything that had happened before I woke up."

"What was his surname?"

Tara shrugged. "I can't remember."

"It wasn't Trevillion, was it?"

The name sounded familiar. "It might have been." She thought a moment longer, trying to recall Jovan's words. "Yes, I think it was."

"Then you did well to escape him."

"Why do you say that?"

"Because he's a crazy man, that's why."

"What do you mean?"

"I mean that the people around him tend to die, and in very unpleasant ways."

Tara thought about the man at the inn. His face came easily to her mind. He'd been happy to see her awake and then confused at her loss of memory. He'd said she could trust him and that he wouldn't hurt her. She hadn't gotten the sense that he meant her harm — just the opposite, actually. He'd seemed very concerned about her. "Tell me more — who died, and how?"

"Jovan Trevillion has been a mercenary for a long time, selling his skills to anyone who would pay." Blackie glanced at Gus and lowered his voice. "Years ago he was hired by a land-grabbing nobleman named Finian Grey to lead an invasion of the Southlands. His army sacked several cities before finally being defeated at the gates of Culhollan. Many men died on both sides. And then there was the failed coup attempt against General Caldren in Sulledor. The men with him that didn't die outright were tortured and killed by the Butcher."

"The Butcher?" That name was familiar, too. Tara tried to pull more gossamer strands of memory from the sludge in her mind, but they remained stuck fast.

"Remember the man with the wolves at the dock?"

Tara nodded.

"That was the Butcher. He cuts people's fingers and toes off and rips their guts out to make sure they die as painfully as possible. Why did he want to fight you, anyway?"

"I don't know. He said his name was Rylan Natiere."

"Yes. Captain Natiere. The Butcher. And then there was that incident in the Bog —"

"The Bog?" That, also, sounded familiar.

"Yes. The boy king of Sulledor had been kidnapped and taken into the Bog. Trevillion led a group of men into the Bog, supposedly to find his brother, who was mixed up in the kidnapping. The Bog is a nasty place, full of nasty creatures that would tear you to pieces and gnaw on your bones. Trevillion was the only one who survived."

Tara closed her eyes and thought hard. "There is something about the Bog, something I need to remember." The more she tried to pry her memories loose, the more deeply they seemed to bury themselves in her mind. She pounded the gunwale. "Why can't I remember?"

"Hey, easy there. The only thing you need to remember is to stay away from Trevillion."

Tara didn't reply. It was probably good advice. Why did it feel wrong?

CHAPTER 14

They floated on down the river, slipping silently through the moonlight like the shadow of a gull on its way to the sea. Tara tried to sleep but couldn't. Something within wouldn't let her.

An hour before dawn, the boat scraped bottom, grinding over the rocks as the river grew shallow. They climbed out and dragged the boat to shore. Blackie and his men thrashed through the surrounding clumps of brush until they found the two low-wheeled carts they had left concealed on their way upriver. They split the kegs and supplies between the two carts, and then Brains and Gus fitted harnesses around their large torsos and pulled the carts southward along the riverbank. Blackie, Whittler, Whiskey, and Diamond Jack rolled the boat over, hoisted it up onto their shoulders, and followed. Tara walked behind the carts, in front of the boat carriers. She smiled at the various patterns and animal shapes carved into the carts by Whittler's restless knife. He was quite an artist.

They walked for a couple of hours, the sun rising and getting hotter with each step, promising a scorching day. They rested in a bit of shade and ate, then set off again down the riverbank, weaving through the leafy clumps of brush that lined the edge of the river, a buffer between the rushing water and the fields of ripening grain.

Tara rubbed her eyes for the thousandth time and tried to concentrate on the path of wheel tracks in front of her. The lack of restful sleep had scrambled her thoughts and muddied her mind even more. She kept hearing whispers in her head, three different voices speaking words so faint that she couldn't understand them, and every time a bush or scrub tree loomed, she saw Jovan standing there reaching toward her. The first time she saw him, surprise had stopped her in her tracks, and the men carrying the boat had nearly run her down. Blackie had asked what the matter was, but before she could speak, Jovan had disappeared. She'd stammered something about seeing things and started off again. After the second and third times, she realized she must be hallucinating. Then a vision of the Butcher stopped her again.

Blackie yelled at his men carrying the boat, and they ground to a halt just before plowing into her. "Balls, woman, you've got to stop doing that."

Tara pointed to a tangle of berry bushes just ahead to the left. "Look over there. Do you see anything?" she asked in a low voice. As she spoke, Natiere vanished.

Blackie gestured to his men, and the four of them set the boat down. He whistled to Brains and Gus up ahead, and they halted and looked back inquiringly. Wiping his sweaty forehead on his sleeve, Blackie looked across to where she had indicated. "I see blackberry bushes, but it's too early for blackberries. What did you see?"

"He's gone now."

"Who is?"

"The Butcher."

Blackie caught her arms with both hands. "You saw the Butcher? Are you sure?" He looked back toward the bushes. His men moved close together and scanned the area around them, hands on the hilts of their swords and knives.

"No, I'm not sure." Tara dug the heels of her palms into her eyes again. "I'm not sure of anything."

Blackie gave her a flask. "Here, take a drink... and, yes, it's water," he added as Tara hesitated.

She took a long draught and gave the flask back to him. "I keep seeing things — people. I know they can't be there, but they look so real. Then they vanish."

"Who do you see?"

"Jovan, and just now, the Butcher. And I keep hearing voices, several different ones. I can't understand what they're saying, but it feels like they're trying to get inside my head. I've been blocking them out, I'm not sure how. It's getting harder and harder to do it, though."

Blackie studied her a moment, then glanced up at the cloudless sky, at the merciless sun beating down. "It's probably just sun poisoning and poor sleep. You'll feel better once we're back on the river. We've only got a short walk left. Why don't you walk under the boat? No stopping, though, because we won't be able to keep from running you over."

After a tense last look around, Blackie, Whittler, Whiskey, and Jack lifted the boat and settled it on their shoulders. Tara ducked underneath, then fell into step as they moved off after Brains and Gus.

The river deepened a mile southward, and after hiding the carts in the brush and reloading the boat, they pushed off from the shore. Whittler and Diamond Jack sat in the stern and steered the boat into the current. Tara wondered how Whittler could see anything with his brown hair perpetually in his face. Gus lay on his back on the bench in front of them with his knees bent and his well-muscled arms folded behind his head. His cloak was suspended, tent-like, from his upraised knees to his elbows, to shade him from the sun while he slept. Whiskey sat in the bow, nursing his nearly empty bottle. Brains curled up on the bench behind him and covered himself with his cloak until only his nose was showing. Blackie took up his previous position in the middle of the boat.

Tara squeezed into her niche beside him. She nibbled on the biscuit he offered, but she really wasn't hungry. She tipped her head back, closed her eyes, and tried to squelch the whispering voices in her head. They refused to be silenced. Annoyed, she focused on each of the voices, one at a time. There had to be a way to get them out of her mind. The first voice, whisper-soft, was very faint, yet it was somehow familiar, like the barest touch of a lover's hand. She wanted to reach out to it — to him — she was sure it was a man, but every time she opened her mind, even just the least little bit, the other voices crowded in around her; one smooth and enticing, yet cold and hard underneath; the other, harsh and malevolent, the embodiment of evil.

She focused for a brief moment on the evil, and in that instant the smothering blackness engulfed her. Rivers of ice swept over her skin; the shock of it sucked away her breath. She gasped. Pulling her knees up tight to her chin, she scrunched herself together and tried to muster enough strength to force the evil back. Sensing her weakness, the evil attacked, stabbing through her mental defenses as if thrusting with a sword. The world spun about her in crazy circles. She cried out, her fists squeezing against her temples.

Lady, let me help you, whispered a new voice, rough and gravelly like the grinding of broken rock. She felt a mind touch hers, urgently, but without threat. The touch was familiar, but she couldn't place it. She sensed the agony of a tortured soul, its pain and sorrow tightly suppressed. Its strength, like a wall of iron, rose from depths nearly as black as the evil that attacked her. Tendrils of subtle danger clung to the base of the iron wall like creeping vines. In desperation, she seized the offered strength, drew it in, felt it bolster her own failing strength. Power rose from deep within, startling her. The white-hot burst of intensity seared through the evil, and it fell away, its voice banished from her mind. The other voices, too, faded into obscurity. The tightness clamping her chest eased, and she could breathe again. She took a few deep breaths, filling her lungs with the sultry summer air. Her dizziness receded.

Thank you. She sent the thought outward, hoping that whoever had helped her would receive it. She shivered with a sudden chill as the tortured mind touched hers once more.

You are welcome, Lady, whispered the gravelly voice. The chill eased as the voice and touch faded from her mind.

"Tara, wake up!" Blackie shook her and gently slapped her cheek. She jerked back and opened her eyes. "Haedis' balls, woman, what... whoa!" He let go of her like she'd suddenly become a poisonous snake. "Damnation and throw me into the Abyss!" More expletives followed.

She rubbed her burning eyes, trying to clear her blurred vision. "What's wrong?"

"Your eyes," he said, keeping his distance.

"What about them?"

Blackie hesitated. "You know how your eyes are this strange silver-blue color?"

Tara shrugged. "They are?"

"You don't remem... never mind. They are, and right now, the color of your eyes is... well... whirling."

Her vision grew sharper, and she realized that all the smugglers were gaping at her. Gus made a sign to ward off evil, his face a mask of fear and revulsion.

A memory surfaced of a ring of villagers looking that same way at a much younger version of herself. The villagers' hatred of her had been palpable, and her hatred of them equally intense. She glared at the smugglers. "Stop staring at me like I'm some kind of loathsome creature."

"Hey now, just calm down," Blackie said. "There is something seriously wrong with you, and until we figure out what it is —"

"There's nothing wrong with me," Tara snapped.

"Hold your temper, woman. For your eyes to do what they were doing is not normal, and there's nothing you can say that will convince me otherwise."

"What they *were* doing? You mean they're not doing it anymore?"

"No." The boat began to drift sideways, broadside to the current. Blackie looked aft. "Whittler! Jack! Get this boat back around!" Reluctantly, they turned away and straightened the boat's course. Blackie turned back to Tara. "Now, tell me what happened."

Tara took a calming breath and did her best to describe the battle that had taken place inside her head.

Blackie listened silently. Finally, he spoke. "And you don't know what or who is causing this?"

"No, or if I do, the information is locked somewhere in here." She pointed to her head.

"What do you want to do about it?"

"I don't know what to do about it. I keep hoping my memory will return, and I'll be able to make some sense of what's going on." She rubbed her eyes again. "I did remember one thing — I saw a circle of angry people looking at me the way you were all looking at me a few minutes ago. I was a lot younger."

"You were remembering Wyndover."

"Who?"

"Not who, where. Wyndover is the town where you grew up. The townspeople hated you. They thought you were a witch."

Tara bristled. "I am not a witch!"

"I didn't say you were. I'm just telling you what I know."

"I'm sorry." Tara pounded the thwart beside her. "It's just that I really don't know what to do. It's so frustrating."

"Woman, you need help."

Tara held his gaze. "Are you willing to help me?"

Blackie smiled. "That's one thing you should remember about me — I never turn my back on my friends."

She smiled back, relief and hope stealing through her. "Thanks. I'm glad you're my friend."

Blackie squeezed her shoulder. "Get some sleep. We've got a ways to go yet."

*****

Jovan fumed silently as he guided his small canoe through the sunlit shallows to the shore of the Colin River. The creature had nearly gotten through Tara's weakened defenses. He'd felt her struggles, her searing agony as the creature stabbed through the chinks in her mental walls, and he'd known she couldn't hold out. Fear had clenched his heart so hard he could barely breathe. She was going to be mauled and consumed by the creature, and he could do nothing but sit there and curse the Being that blocked him from helping her. He'd pounded against the barrier until he was mentally bloodied, but he could not widen the pinprick hole he'd managed to create earlier. He couldn't even give her an ounce of strength to sustain her. In the midst of his fury and anguish, the Butcher's voice had slid into Tara's mind, and she had let him in. She'd used Natiere's offered strength to help her drive the creature back into its prison.

Gritting his teeth, Jovan leaped out of the canoe, his boots splashing in the ankle-deep water as he heaved the canoe up onto the shore. Natiere had done what he could not. The thought galled him, left him seething inside. Natiere wanted Tara, of that he had no doubt. And though Jovan owed him for saving her life, he would see him dead before he would let him touch her.

Jovan snatched up his supply pack and shrugged it onto his back. Then he flipped the canoe over, tipped it up on end, and bending beneath it, lifted it and settled it over his head and shoulders. He staggered a bit until he found the balancing point. The canoe was small, but awkward and heavy, and it dug into his shoulders. Shifting his burden so he could see better, he started off down the riverbank, following a path of wheel tracks and footprints that had to have been made by Blackie de Runo and his band. He couldn't make out individual prints to know for certain that Tara was still with them, but he guessed she was. Looking at the tracks in the beaten-down grass, he estimated the smugglers to be about two hours ahead of him. He stumbled and caught himself, cursing his slow pace. By the time he reached deeper water, they would be even farther ahead.

He sent his thoughts outward again, funneling them through the tiny pinhole he had chiseled through the Being's mental stone wall, but he met only blankness. Tara's mind remained closed to him. He didn't know if the Being was aware of the hole or not. He thought not. Yet he had a hard time believing there was anything this ancient god-like Being didn't know. Perhaps it was toying with him, letting him reach the fringes of Tara's mind but no farther, increasing his frustration a hundredfold. He could touch her mind, barely, but not enough to get a response. He couldn't form a connection. The Butcher himself couldn't have designed a worse torture. Tara had a brutal killer as a savior from her nightmare and a thieving scoundrel for a protector. Jovan had done business with Blackie de Runo a time or two. Blackie was an unscrupulous smuggler who was not beyond a double-cross if he thought he could get away with it. And if his schemes fell apart as they sometimes did, there was no telling how much trouble he could get Tara into.

Jovan repositioned the canoe to alleviate the growing ache in his arms and neck. Sweat dripped down his forehead, had already soaked his shirt. The canoe protected him from the sun's glare, but not from the heat of the day. Blinking the sweat from his eyes, he reached inward, his mind hovering over the small wellspring of power that pulsed in the core of his being. He didn't know where it had come from. He didn't think he'd been born with it, but suspected it had resulted from the cleansing of his wound with the magical waters of Rinpool so many years before. After he'd become aware of the power, he'd continually denied its existence. He hadn't wanted the Being that ruled Rinpool to gain any more control over him through his acceptance of the power. He'd had to use it, though, to rescue Tara from her nightmare dungeon.

And it was the power that enabled him to connect with Tara at all. Their combined power strengthened and enhanced their mental connection, allowing her to draw on his strength when she needed it. He would have to use it again — to dig deeper into it than he ever had before — if he wanted to get through to her now.

He stopped for a brief rest in a patch of shade and, kneeling, set the canoe down. He sat and stretched his aching muscles, then closed his eyes and cleared his mind. Reluctantly, he eased the cap from the well of power and felt its coolness sear through him. He focused on the pinprick hole, concentrating on widening the opening enough to force his thoughts through. With excruciating slowness, like moving one grain of sand at a time, the power ate away the barrier. He had the feeling that if he were using his power in its original form, he wouldn't be able to even scratch the barrier. But the melding of his and Tara's magic had somehow changed the essence of his power, making it stronger, strong enough to chip away at the wall. He *would* get through, no matter how long it took.

*****

Tara's eyes flew open and she bolted upright, the sound of her name echoing faintly in her mind.

"Haedis' balls!" Blackie jumped half off his bench, the boat rocking from the sudden movement. He whipped around toward her, startling her with his anxious scrutiny. "You're awake? Well, it's about bloody time." He looked at her tensely. "You're not having another whirling eye thing, are you?"

"I don't think so," Tara said, taken aback by his intensity and by the stares, both solemn and wary, from the other smugglers. "Have I been sleeping long?"

"You've been out for four days," Blackie said. "We couldn't wake you up. We thought you were dead, but we could still see you breathing, barely."

"I'm sorry. I guess my body must have been healing itself or something." She shrugged. "My head doesn't hurt anymore."

Blackie said nothing for a few moments. "What about your memory?" he finally asked.

"That's still gone," Tara said in disgust.

He eyed her silently, as if uncertain what to do next.

"Why are you looking at me like that?" Tara asked. "I'm fine."

Blackie ran his hand over his face. "It's not nor — I mean, I've never seen or heard of anyone being out that long, going without food or water, and not being... well... in bad shape."

Tara shrugged again. "I don't know. I can't explain it."

Blackie let out a long breath. The wariness and doubt in his eyes gradually eased into profound relief. "You're sure you're all right?"

She nodded. "In fact, this is the best I've felt since I woke up at that inn a few days ago — except for the lack of my memory."

One by one, the other smugglers turned away wordlessly and went back to whatever they'd been doing, their expressions unsettled.

Tara blinked in the late afternoon sunlight and took in her surroundings. Immense hardwoods interspersed with evergreens now lined the riverbank on both sides, their shadows darkening the swift-flowing river. Dense forest had replaced the wide open expanses of grain. She smelled the pungent spice of the evergreens and the musty odor of ancient timberland. "Where are we?"

"We just entered Shallin Wood. We have one more short portage coming up —"

"Where's my bottle?" yelled Whiskey, frantically pawing through the supply packs in the space behind him. He glared at Gus, who sat next to him, an expression of disdain on his face. "You hid it, didn't you?" The boat lurched as Whiskey, his gray hair flying wildly, clambered over the oar bank onto Whittler's bench. He shoved Whittler aside and tore through another pack.

"I did nothing of the sort," said Gus. "You can't row with it anyway. Now get back here and help me steer this boat. I'm not manning both oars."

Whittler had regained his seat and looked like he was about to jab Whiskey with his knife.

"Whittler, stow that knife!" Blackie roared. "Whiskey, get back to your bench, or I'll throw you overboard. Gus, if you took that bottle, I'll —"

"I didn't take it," Gus growled, as Whiskey, darting suspicious glances at Gus, climbed back to his seat.

"Then where is it?" Blackie turned to the fore. "Brains, Jack, look and see if it's up there." They fished around in the packs for a minute or two, then Jack held aloft a full bottle of red-gold whiskey. He handed it to Blackie, who passed it back to the stern. Whiskey grabbed the bottle and cradled it to himself, talking to it reverently. Then he ripped off the cover, pulled the cork out with his teeth, and drank.

Gus shook his head and muttered something in a Southland dialect.

"Now, if you three will stop acting like a bunch of alley rat children, we can have some peace." Blackie pinned Gus, Whiskey, and Whittler with a warning glare.

Gus scowled, but said nothing. Whiskey drank and rowed, oblivious to everything else. Whittler went back to his whittling as if nothing had happened.

Blackie turned back to Tara. "We're almost to the Nournan. Just beyond that bend, the river bottoms out again, and we'll have to go ashore."

"Good. I could use a bush right about now."

Blackie grinned. "I'll bet you could. You're probably hungry, too."

"Ravenous."

Blackie handed her a supply pack and a water flask. She sniffed the contents of the flask before drinking it dry. Blackie rolled his eyes. "Will you stop doing that? It's water!"

Tara smiled. "Sorry. Can't help it. I don't want to be drinking that stuff again." She pulled out some beef jerky and munched on it.

Blackie picked up another flask and took a long swig, exhaling through his mouth. "Ahhhhh. As I said before, there's nothing wrong with my brew."

Tara wrinkled her nose at the smell on his breath. "I don't know how you can drink that, but then your insides are probably so pickled it wouldn't bother you anyway."

"Good brew is an acquired taste," Blackie said loftily. "When you've tasted as many bad brews as I have, you learn to appreciate a good one." He took another swig.

"Hey, go easy with that. How are you going to keep the peace around here if you're drunk?"

"Don't worry. It takes more than a couple swallows to put me under."

Tara snorted. "I remember when a 'couple swallows' would have you howling at the moon." She stopped and closed her eyes, holding tight to a memory. "In fact, I can see you doing just that outside a tavern in Vaalderin. It was the Red Rose, I think."

"Hmmph. My brew has improved greatly since then." Blackie put the flask away. "And didn't I tell you to stop remembering bad things?"

The memory slid away, leaving her blank again. She prodded her mind, trying to force her way through what felt like thick layers of mud, but she could pry no more memories loose. She cursed under her breath.

"Remember anything else?" Blackie asked softly, watching her.

She slammed her fist on the gunwale. "No."

He covered her fist with his hand and held it. "Stop trying to force them. The memories will come when they're ready, and not before."

"I need them to come now."

He patted her hand. "Patience, woman. You obviously haven't learned any yet, have you?" He hesitated, cleared his throat. "Umm... what woke you up... back there?"

Tara noted the wariness that had crept back into his voice. She thought for a moment. "I heard someone call my name."

Blackie eyed her doubtfully. "I didn't hear anything."

"No, in my mind," Tara said. "Someone called to me in my mind. I don't know who it was."

"It wasn't that evil creature you described before?"

"No. I don't hear it now. I lost it when I woke up."

The boat slipped into the shallows, and Gus and Whiskey, with the bottle still in his hand, rowed to shore. Gus and Brains found another set of carved-up carts they had hidden just inside the line of trees, and soon they were loaded and on their way.

Tara walked in front of the boat again, the trees shading them from the sun. She sensed some vague menace haunting the deep primordial forest, but she couldn't put a name to it. As she looked around, the looming trees seemed to close in on her, heightening a disturbing sense of claustrophobia. And she couldn't shake the feeling that someone or something was watching her.

At least she wasn't having any more hallucinations. She felt refreshingly clearheaded. She thought again about the moment she'd awakened and wondered who had called to her. It wasn't the evil creature, of that she was certain, nor was it the rough voice of the man who had saved her from the creature's attack. No, she was sure it was one of the other two voices that had tried to get into her head earlier. She couldn't be sure which one, though. She had blocked it out too quickly upon awakening. She didn't dare open her mind again to find out, not after what had happened the last time.

The high-pitched howl of a wolf rose into the sky, filling the air and the trees around them and sending shivers over Tara's skin. The four carrying the boat stopped as one. Gus and Brains slowed to a halt as well, stilling the creaking of the carts. Blackie held up his hand for silence. A deeper, throatier howl joined the first, frighteningly close, the eerie sounds swelling outward to surround them until they couldn't tell from where the howls had originated.

"Boat down," Blackie whispered.

The four swung the boat to the ground and drew their weapons. Blackie handed Tara his long knife and beckoned for her and the others to follow. They gathered around the carts as Brains and Gus hastily unstrapped themselves and bared their swords. Keeping their backs to the carts, they formed a circle, waiting tensely. Silence drifted over them as the howls died away. The forest sounds had ceased; no wind rustled the tall grass along the bank. Only the steady burbling of the river broke the stillness. Tara gripped the long knife, her eyes searching the deepening shadows for any movement. Barely a dozen feet of grass and low brush separated them from the edge of the dark woods, and the shallowness of the river behind gave no protection. Whittler, close on her right, flexed his hands, tossing his knife back and forth between them. *I'll bet he's a good knife thrower*, she thought to herself.

"See anything?" Blackie asked, keeping his voice low.

Tara shook her head. "Not yet." Something moved deep within the trees. She saw a darker shape slip through the shadows, approaching between the massive boles. "In the trees, straight ahead of me," she whispered.

Blackie squinted in the semi-darkness. "Where? I don't see —" His blade came up quickly as a large black wolf appeared between the trees. The beast hovered within the edge of the forest, ears pricked forward, its golden eyes staring straight at Tara.

Tara stared back. "Hey, isn't that the same wolf we saw on the docks in Cierra?"

Blackie let out a stream of curses. "If it is, the Butcher can't be far behind." He stepped in front of Tara and, brandishing his sword, yelled at the wolf. The wolf's ears flattened, and it growled, its hackles rising.

Tara pulled him back. "Don't antagonize her."

Blackie glanced at Tara. "Her? How do you know it's a her?"

"I don't know. I just do." She paused, thinking. "Her name is Kel-ya."

"It's what?"

"Kelya," Tara repeated.

The wolf stopped growling, its ears pricked forward again. It barked twice, then turned and disappeared into the forest. After a moment, squirrels began to chitter, and the rustle of wings floated through the trees as the woodland creatures resumed their normal activities.

Blackie sheathed his sword. "Let's get out of here. Grab the boat. Brains, Gus, get the carts. Whittler, take rear guard."

Brains and Gus quickly strapped themselves to the carts again as Blackie, Whiskey, and Jack heaved the boat up. Tara hooked the long knife into her belt, ducked in behind Blackie, and grasped the gunwales to help carry the boat. Whittler stood behind them, still tossing his knife back and forth.

"All right, let's move," Blackie ordered. They set off down the riverbank at a fast pace. "And you," he said over his shoulder to Tara, "when we get back on the river, you can explain to me how you know the name of the Butcher's wolf."

Tara wished she could remember.

CHAPTER 15

It didn't take long for them to reach deeper water. They loaded the boat, stashed the carts, and shoved off. Strong, quick strokes from Brains and Diamond Jack guided them into the swift current.

"Watch the trees," Blackie ordered. "Whittler, eyes that way." He pointed to the right. "Gus, left. Whiskey, eyes front."

"Which way?" Gus asked from his position behind Whiskey in the bow.

"Port," said Brains from the stern. "He said look to the port side. Whittler is starboard."

"Here we go with the birds again," Blackie complained. "Just tell me if you see anything."

"There's a squirrel in that tree over there," Brains said, easing up on the oar as the current whisked them southward. Jack did the same.

"Brains, so help me..." Blackie looked around for something to throw at him, but couldn't find anything nonessential.

"I'm surprised you all haven't killed each other by now," Tara said from her seat behind Blackie.

Blackie turned toward her. "I want to know exactly what there is between you and the Butcher."

Tara shrugged helplessly. "I don't know. I wish I did."

"For you to know that wolf's name, you would have had to get within speaking distance of the Butcher. Most people who get that close don't live to tell about it. Yet, here you are. Balls, woman. Nobody in their right mind would get within a hundred miles of him if they could help it."

"Blackie —"

"You must have actually talked to him. Nobody *talks* to the Butcher, because he cuts their tongue out first so they can't —"

"Blackie, stop!"

Blackie fell silent. He ran his hand over his face. "There are a lot of things I'd like to do in my lifetime. Tangling with the Butcher is not one of them."

Their eyes held for several heartbeats. "Change your mind about helping me?" she asked.

"No. I meant what I said. If there is any way I can help you, I will. I'd just like to avoid Natiere while I'm doing it."

Tara let out the breath she'd been holding, suddenly realizing how afraid she'd been that he was going to abandon her.

"What about us?" said Gus. "I, too, have no wish to tangle with the Butcher."

"Nor do the rest of us," said Brains. He twisted around on the bench and faced Blackie. "I don't recall your asking for our opinions on this... situation." His gaze slid to Tara.

Tara looked back at him, then at the others. They remained silent, their eyes shifting uneasily back and forth between her and the ominous forest.

"What is your opinion, Brains?" Blackie asked, fingering the hilt of his sword.

"We don't know her as well as you do," said Brains.

"We don't know her at all," said Whiskey.

"I'm not so willing to risk my life for her as you are," Brains continued. "Not when it involves the Butcher."

"Neither am I," Gus added.

Tara could see in his eyes the fear and mistrust of things not understood. Her unseen battle with the evil creature and the resulting change in her eyes had scared and repulsed him. The others, too, judging from their similar expressions.

"And what would you suggest we do?" Blackie asked, his hand curling around the sword hilt. He looked from Brains to Gus and back again. "Throw her overboard? Leave her off in these woods, alone? Haedis' balls, what's the matter with you? Have your guts turned to mush? I thought you were better men than that." He whipped out his sword with one hand and pulled his belt knife with the other. "Anyone who tries to put her out here will have to go through me to do it."

Silence fell for the span of several breaths. Tara glanced at Blackie, surprised at how far he was willing to go to defend her. She hadn't expected such heroics. Their past friendship must have been a lot stronger than she'd thought. If she wasn't careful, though, that friendship would end here. She saw Whittler gripping his knife and knew it would take only one flick of his wrist, and either she or Blackie would be dead. She sat up slowly, her hands raised in a gesture of peace. "May I speak?"

Brains nodded.

"I know you don't know me. Right now, I don't even know myself. I would not ask you to fight anyone for me, least of all the Butcher. All I ask is that you let me ride through to Norellanen. You can go on to the Gypsy Crossroads. I will go my own way. Natiere will follow me, not you. You will be safe."

"How do you know he won't come after us, too?" asked Diamond Jack.

"He won't," Tara answered.

"How can you possibly be certain?" Brains asked. "You, who can't even remember your own name."

"I just know," Tara said. "He wants me. He has no interest in you."

"So you say," said Gus.

"So I say." Tara held his gaze evenly.

"What if he catches us?" asked Whiskey. "Those wolves of his..."

"If he confronts us, I'll face him," Tara said. "You can escape in the boat. He won't follow."

"Face the *Butcher*?" Blackie looked at her as if she were demented. "Balls, woman. I knew you had lost a few branches from your tree, but I didn't realize how many. The Butcher will torture you until you beg all the gods to let you die."

"I faced him once before," Tara said. "I can do it again."

"You faced the Butcher?" Blackie said, his eyebrows raised. "You mean back there on the docks?"

"No, somewhere else." An image flared, and she caught a brief glimpse of herself and Jovan Trevillion battling Captain Natiere before the memory whisked away, gone like a dry leaf snatched by the wind. "Jovan was with me. We fought him together."

"Jovan who?" Gus demanded.

"She doesn't remember," Blackie said quickly.

"I believe the lady can speak for herself," Brains said.

Tara caught Blackie's look and remembered what he'd said about Jovan Trevillion leading an army that had sacked the Southlands. Gus, a Southlander, would likely have no use for a friend of Trevillion's. "No," she said. "I don't remember anything else. Bits and pieces of memories jump into my head and jump out again just as fast. I can't hold them."

Gus eyed her suspiciously. "If I thought you had anything to do with a man named Jovan Trevillion, I would kill you myself."

"Why?" Tara asked. "What did he do to you?"

Gus spat over the side. "He and his army raided the town of my birth, among many others. They killed my family. One day our paths will cross, and I will return the favor."

Tara pictured the handsome man who haunted her thoughts. She couldn't imagine him doing such a thing. "I'm sorry for your loss," she said quietly. She raised her voice and looked at each of the smugglers in turn. "But as I said before, I'll hand myself over to Natiere before I endanger any of you. It is my battle, not yours."

No one spoke. Blackie followed her gaze, looking fore, then aft. "Anyone else have anything to say?"

Brains and Gus and the other smugglers exchanged looks. Whittler gave a slight shrug and turned away, resuming his watch duty. He started carving on the side of the boat, then thought better of it. Whiskey took a swig and swiveled around, eyes forward. Scowling, Gus crossed his arms over his muscled chest, but said nothing. Jack rubbed his blond beard nervously, then faced the stern, intent on manning his oar.

"We will leave things as they are. For now," Brains said. He turned his back, and he and Jack began to row in earnest, obviously wanting to put as much distance between themselves and the wolves as they could.

As Blackie sheathed his weapons, Tara drew in a long breath and let it out slowly. The crew didn't like her being there, but at least they weren't going to throw her overboard. Yet.

She touched Blackie's arm. "Thanks."

"Hey, I mean what I say." He grinned. "Hey, that's another rhyme. That's good, heh, heh." He sobered. "Just don't do anything strange."

"I'll try not to."

"And don't mention certain people," he added in a barely audible whisper. He shot a sidelong glance at Gus, who had turned away and was glowering at the swiftly passing forest.

"I won't."

Blackie bent down, picked up a pack, and pulled out a short stick. "Hey, Whittler." Whittler turned. Blackie tossed him the stick. Whittler caught it one-handed and sunk his knife into it, peeling off the bark by feel, his eyes trained once more on the trees. Blackie turned back to Tara. "Need anything?"

"You mean other than my head to work? No." She shivered, suddenly feeling cold. "You said we were near the Nournan?"

"Yes. We should hit the fork by nightfall." He paused. "Are you all right?"

"I don't know. All of a sudden I'm freezing." She shuddered and clasped her arms around herself. "I feel like there's some terrible danger ahead of us, and we're floating right into it."

"There is, and we are." Blackie pulled a blanket out from under the packs and wrapped it around her. "The Bog lies ahead. We're going right down through the middle of it. It's dangerous, but we've done it before."

"The Bog," she repeated. "I know something about the Bog. I've been there." Images and sounds flashed through her mind — spiders crawling over twisted black trees; knee-deep muck sucking at her legs; vultures with finger-length talons swooping at her; wolves, larger even than those that ran with the Butcher, attacking; screams of agony; a body mauled to pieces, a body with a familiar face... "Dominic," she whispered. Something dripped on her cheek, and she raised a shaking hand to find her face wet with tears. "Oh, gods."

Blackie slipped his arm around her shoulders. "Hey, easy. What about Dominic?"

"He's dead," she said in a trembling whisper. "He died in the Bog, on the riverbank. I was there, and so was — were some other people." She caught herself before she said Trevillion's name. "Wolves attacked us, huge ones. Dominic saved my life." Her whole body shook as the vivid memory faded.

"Balls, woman. What in the name of the Abyss were you doing in the Bog?"

"I don't know." She wiped her eyes with the edge of the blanket. "Do you remember Dominic? I know he was dear to me, but I can't remember anything about him."

"Yes, I remember him. He was tough as an old badger, but he had a soft spot for you and Raina — your sister," he added at Tara's blank look. "I can't believe you don't remember your own sister."

Tara threw her hands up in the air. "I can't remember her. I can't remember Dominic. I can't remember anything."

"Hey, calm down. Like I said before, you need to have patience. The memories are coming back. It's just going to take some time."

"I'm tired of waiting."

"Well, you don't have much choice, do you? You and Raina took up with Dominic and his two cohorts not long after you left my band. We ran into each other a few times after that."

"Dominic's cohorts — what were their names?"

Blackie turned away. "Xavier," he said after a moment. "One of them was Xavier. Can't remember the other one."

Another memory erupted with startling suddenness. A roguishly handsome face, not Jovan's, blazed into her mind with vivid clarity. Shoulder-length dark hair that curled at the ends, daring blue eyes that challenged her, a crooked smile saved for her alone. Heat rose within her, and not just in her face, as words he'd once said slid through her mind. *As long as those stars shine, I will love you.* Then his face vanished. Anger, hatred, and bitterness surged over her like a tidal wave, left her shaking again. He had hurt her somehow, and he still needed to pay for his transgression, whatever it was. She pressed her fist to her forehead. If only she could remember.

"Tara?" Blackie watched her uneasily.

She lowered her hand. "Myles. His name was Myles."

"So it was." Blackie lifted his arm from her shoulders, found his flask of brew, and took a long drink.

Tara glanced at him, surprised by his sudden coolness. Another question occurred to her. "Blackie?"

"Hmmmmm," he said around another swallow.

"Why did Raina and I leave your band?"

Blackie closed the flask and set it down by his feet. He looked at her in silence, his eyes, like shuttered windows, revealing nothing of his thoughts. "That, my dear, is something you will have to remember on your own."

Tara stared at him, perplexed. "But... why? What —?"

"Don't waste your breath, woman. I mean what I say about that, too." He looked over her head toward the bow. "Whiskey, Gus, get some sleep. You'll have the next rowing shift. The rest of you keep watching those trees."

"They haven't moved yet," Brains said from the stern.

"One more remark like that, Brains, and I'll come back there and strangle you," Blackie growled.

Something in his tone brought glances from Brains, Jack, Gus, and Whittler. Tara caught the furtive looks at Blackie and wondered if there would be another uprising. Blackie seemed oblivious to the scrutiny. The other smugglers looked at each other, then went about their business. Gus lay down and shuffled around on the bench, trying to get comfortable. Whiskey was already curled around his bottle in the fore. Brains and Jack rowed, and Whittler and Blackie kept watch.

Tara pulled the blanket more tightly around her and wondered why Blackie wouldn't answer her question. What had happened all those years ago? She had the feeling it was some kind of romantic entanglement, though she didn't remember having that kind of relationship with him. But then, she'd obviously had some kind of relationship with Jovan Trevillion, and she couldn't remember that, either. And what about this Myles? *As long as those stars shine, I will love you.* Had he really said that to her? Judging from her body's reaction, she'd had some kind of relationship with him, too. If that was so, why did she hate him now? She put her head in her hands. Why did everything have to be so confoundedly complicated?

Shoving her hair back out of her face, she raised her head and watched Blackie out of the corner of her eye. Just how close had they been? She looked at him more critically. He was attractive enough, in a roguish sort of way, but then dark-haired rogues had always been her downfall. She knew it was true, even without benefit of memory. Myles, Jovan, Blackie — they were all cut from a similar mold. She suddenly wondered if there were other such rogues in her past. She banished the thought immediately. No need to look for more trouble. Her thoughts shifted back to Blackie. If there had been intimacy between them, the situation could get extremely awkward.

"Blackie, there is something I have to know," she said softly.

"What is it?" he asked, without taking his eyes from the trees.

"Did you and I ever... did we..." She couldn't bring herself to say the words.

"No."

She exhaled in relief. "Good."

That brought him around. "Why is that good?"

"I didn't mean that it was good that we weren't together," she said hastily. "I just didn't like the idea of not being able to remember something like that. It doesn't seem like the kind of thing one could forget." She sensed she was treading in dangerous waters and jumped to another question. "What about my sister? Did you and she..."

"No." His gaze swung back to the shadowy woods.

Tara frowned. "Well, if you would just tell me something about it, it might help me remember."

"No. No more questions or answers. You should get some rest now. I'm going to need you later."

"For what?"

Blackie turned back to her, his voice low. "You used to be able to sense danger. You could feel trouble coming. It was a handy talent that kept us out of a lot of scrapes. You used to say that when danger was near, you would suddenly feel cold, like you were being doused with freezing water."

"You mean like I did earlier, when you gave me the blanket?"

"Yes. By morning, we'll be into the Bog. I'll need you to tell me if you have any more of those feelings. The Bog has many dangers, and I don't want to be fighting one and get caught by another."

"Just how dangerous is it?"

"Well, if all goes as it should, the only things we'll have to worry about are the karanaks."

"Karanaks. They sound familiar. What are they?"

"They're some sort of water lizard, but they're all teeth, and they're always hungry. They travel in groups of half a dozen or so, and they like to attack boats. Must think the boats are giant fish or something. Last time through, they chewed two of our oars to bits."

Tara saw herself in her mind's eye, swimming furiously through blood-swirled water toward a high riverbank where two people waited to pull her up onto the shore. One was Jovan Trevillion. The other was a red-haired woman — her sister, she knew. She felt a nip at her toe just as they pulled her out. The memory dimmed and was lost. "I remember them," she whispered.

"Met those, too, did you?"

"I fell into the river. They chased me. They must have fed on something, because there was blood in the water all around me. Two people pulled me out just before they got to me." She paused. "My sister has red hair."

"Yes, she does. You probably don't remember why you were in the river?"

"No. I don't know how I ended up there, or what happened after I was rescued. The memory is gone."

"You're going to have one crazy story to tell when it comes back."

"I just hope it has a good ending."

Blackie grinned. "Well, you're not dead."

"That's a good ending? That I'm not dead?"

"Well, isn't it?"

Tara thought about it. "I guess it could be worse."

"And it probably will be, knowing you."

"Thanks. That's wonderful," she said with a grimace. "You're so good at cheering people up."

"Yes, aren't I?" He squeezed her shoulder. "Get some rest."

Tara stretched to relieve cramped muscles and settled into her niche, glad, at least, that the awkwardness between them seemed to have passed. The last thing she wanted was to lose his friendship. Tired, she closed her eyes and tried to still the endless whirl of thoughts and questions churning through her mind. She took a deep breath and imagined a tornado slowly dwindling to a tiny wisp of air. Her mind cleared. Her muscles relaxed as she drifted toward sleep.

Two voices clamored faintly, vying for her attention. She tensed, her eyes snapping open to see who had spoken, before realizing the voices were in her head. She closed her eyes again and, listening intently, tried to discern the identity of the voices. One was whisper soft — the lover's touch, she called it. Cautiously, wary of the evil, she focused on it, allowing the barest of connections, but ready to sever the tie in an instant if threatened. Joy surged through the connection, enveloping her in the warmth of a thousand embraces. She heard her name whispered over and over in her mind, and the words, *I love you.* Then the voice changed, growing urgent. *Beware of the dream and the evil in the Bog. I can't break through enough to help you. Don't trust Natiere —*

The voice broke off abruptly and vanished, taking with it the warmth and the feeling of being held in a lover's arms, leaving only the echoes of the warnings it had given.

No, come back! She opened her mind further to search for the voice, but closed it again quickly, feeling the evil near. She ground her teeth. What had happened? Was the man to whom the voice belonged in trouble? Her fist clenched, and she cursed silently. She had to know. But how?

The second voice, enticing, yet, she sensed, somehow dangerous, called to her insistently. After a moment's hesitation, she focused on it and made a tentative connection. *Who are you?*

A friend, came the smooth reply.

The other voice, the one that just disappeared — do you know what happened to it... to him?

No.

Tara stifled her disappointment. *How do I know you're a friend?*

I am. You don't need to fear me. Come to me when you are trapped in the dream, and I will help you escape.

The dream. The other voice had warned her about a dream.

What do you know about the dream?

I know much. I can help you, where others cannot.

What is your name?

I am Melodian. You will be safe with me. Open to me.

Melodian. Why was that name familiar? She couldn't remember. Cold prickles goose-pimpled her skin. She heeded the warning and slammed shut her mental door, breaking the connection. She braced herself, half expecting the voice to try to force its way back into her mind, but Melodian had vanished, and she heard nothing but blessed silence.

CHAPTER 16

An hour slid by, and then another. Tara dozed, her mind weaving in and out of wakefulness. Thoughts of the man whose voice had disappeared troubled her. She wished there was some way she could find out what had happened to him, why the connection had snapped so abruptly. But whenever she eased her mind open, even a crack, to search for him, she sensed the evil creature hovering, waiting to attack.

The boat began to rock and bounce as they entered another stretch of whitewater. She gave up trying to sleep and, bracing herself on a thwart, sat up with a yawn. She shivered as cold spray misted over her. The sun had set and the sky had grown dark with rain clouds, turning the river into a churning path of gray. A brisk wind blew from the north, sweeping down the river channel like the cold breath of the gods and pushing them ahead more swiftly. The ancient trees ghosting the waterway rose on either side like black walls, their lofty branches bending and creaking in the wind. Tara gripped the thwart and the oar bank, the rush of water loud in her ears as the boat tossed through the rapids.

Blackie's shout beside her nearly jumped her out of the boat. "We're almost there. I can see it up ahead," Blackie called to Brains, in the stern.

"What did we tell you?" Brains said smugly. "Six days and just over five hours."

"Yes, you and Whiskey are geniuses. Just get us past the rock." Blackie detached his oar. "Watch your head," he said to Tara as he reached forward into the bow with his oar and poked Whiskey.

Whiskey started awake. "What? Where are we?"

Blackie refitted his oar. "We're coming up on that last rock. Can you see it?"

Whiskey wiped his sleep-bleared eyes. He gave a yelp. "Hard to port! Hard to port!"

"Whiskey!" Blackie shouted.

"Left! Left!" Whiskey grabbed an oar and rowed furiously.

They fought the current and swung the boat around. Squinting into the darkness, Tara saw the barest tip of a rounded boulder protruding above the surface, obscured by the splashing water. The boat scraped the edge of it and bumped on by into a wide, smooth waterway.

"Can I see it," Whiskey grumbled. "It was right under my bloomin' nose. Poke me sooner next time."

"I'll poke you right out of the boat, if you don't stop complaining," Blackie said. "Go back to sleep."

Tara looked at Blackie and shook her head. "Is anything ever easy with you?"

Blackie snorted. "Ha. You're one to talk. Since when is anything easy with you? And aren't you supposed to be asleep?"

Tara rubbed her eyes. "I couldn't sleep. Is this the Nournan?" She studied the steely gray ribbon of water beneath them. The Nournan River was wider and deeper than the Colin, with a much slower current. Brains and Jack continued to row, moving them along swiftly.

"Yes. We shouldn't run into any karanaks until morning, but you never know. If you're going to be awake, you might as well watch for them."

She peered into the thickening darkness. "I'm not sure I could see them if they were there. How big are they?"

"Oh, they're about the size of Brains, I'd say." Blackie jerked his head toward the big man in the stern.

Brains grunted. "So now I'm a measuring stick."

Tara looked at Brains, gauging his size. He easily topped six feet and was very solidly built. "How do you fight them?"

"Any way we can," said Jack.

"Swords, knives, oars," Blackie said. "Gus beat one over the head with his boot once."

"Wonderful." Tara glanced at the lowering sky. "What do you do if it rains?"

"Get wet," said Brains.

Blackie ignored him. "Usually we go ashore and camp in the woods until the rain stops, but I'm not sure I want to do that now."

"Because of Natiere?" Tara asked.

Blackie nodded. "We have no way of knowing how close he is."

Tara lowered her voice. "If I can sense danger, I should know when he's near."

Blackie shook his head. "I don't want to give him the chance to get near. We stay on the boat."

"But won't a heavy rain swamp the boat?"

"If it rains that hard, we'll bail."

"And get *really* wet," said Brains.

"Brains!" Blackie found a small knot of wood and heaved it at him, hitting him in the back of the shoulder. Whittler tried to catch the tiny piece of wood as it bounced off Brains' shoulder, but it flew too far away and landed with a splooch in the water. Whittler glared at Blackie and motioned with his hands.

Blackie flung his arm out in a gesture of impatience. "Would I have thrown it if it was something you could carve on? Think, man."

They stared at each other for a moment, then Whittler's expression softened. He gestured briefly before turning back to his watch, sparing only one look of longing toward the spot where the nub of wood had sunk.

Watching the movement of Whittler's hands and fingers, Tara suddenly realized she'd never heard him say anything. She whispered to Blackie. "Can he speak?" She gave a slight nod in Whittler's direction.

"No," Blackie said quietly. "He had his tongue cut out about five years ago by your friend the Butcher."

Tara grew cold again. "Natiere did that? Why?"

"Whittler was hungry. He stole some food from one of General Caldren's camps. The Butcher is the General's executioner, in case you don't remember."

"Was. He's not anymore."

"He's not?"

"No. General Caldren is dead."

"He's dead?" Blackie stared at her. "When did this happen?"

Tara raked her hand through her hair, trying to dig out more memories. Nothing came. "Not long ago, I think."

"Don't tell me you had a hand in that, too."

Tara shrugged. "I don't know."

Blackie shook his head. "I've been in the Frontier too long."

"I thought you were barred from going East by the caravanners," Tara said, surprised she remembered that detail.

Blackie scowled. "Do you think I told them I was there? And how many times do I have to tell you to stop remembering bad things?"

"Maybe there weren't any good things," Tara snapped, and immediately regretted it.

Blackie gave her an odd look. "Well, I guess that depends on who you ask."

She held his gaze. "I'm asking you. And I didn't mean..." She swore softly and looked away. "It seems like all I do lately is say the wrong thing."

He put his hand on her shoulder. "I know you didn't mean it. And yes, there were good things. Many of them. Don't you think otherwise."

She put her hand over his and squeezed. "Thanks."

He returned the squeeze, then pulled his hand away. She felt the awkwardness beginning to build again and hastily changed the subject. "Tell me more about Whittler."

"Not much to tell. They would have cut off his hands for stealing, except they wanted him for slave labor, so they cut out his tongue instead. He eventually escaped. I ran across him in Vaalderin. He was half-dead from illness at the time, but he could throw a knife better than anyone I've ever seen. He's a good thief, too."

"So you took him in."

"Too many useful talents to pass up."

"So that's two rescues to your credit — Whittler and Jack. Or three if you count me." She smiled. "And I thought you were a scoundrel."

"Don't paint me any other color than black, woman. My actions are all self-serving, and I have a reputation to maintain."

Tara grinned. "Don't worry. No one will ever hear anything good about you from me."

Blackie gave a short laugh. "And I'm sure you'll take great pleasure in that."

"I will."

He shifted around and lay down on the bench, his head near hers. "If you're going to be awake, I'm going to sleep. You can keep watch for a while." He turned his head toward her and whispered, "I don't think they'll bother you, but if they do, squeeze my hand to wake me." His hand dipped over the side of the bench and clasped hers loosely. Then he straightened his head, closed his eyes, and was soon snoring softly.

She looked at their clasped hands and wondered why he had wanted her to warn him this way. She knew the answer immediately. The body's first reaction to any threat would be to tense the muscles for fight or flight. If someone were to put a knife to her throat or otherwise prevent her from moving or speaking, her initial reaction would awaken him. She frowned. She was sure they had held hands this way before, somewhere, sometime in the past...

A cold tingling crept up the back of her neck. She turned quickly and caught Gus watching her, his hand resting on the hilt of his belt knife, a hostile expression on his face. She had thought him asleep on the bench.

"Is there a problem?" Blackie asked.

Startled, Tara spun around and saw Blackie beside her, sitting upright, bared knife in one hand, his other hand gripping hers. Blackie stared Gus down.

Gus scowled. "No." He rolled onto his side, facing away from them.

Without a word, Blackie lay back down on the bench. He gave her hand a quick squeeze and shut his eyes once more.

As Tara watched him dropping back into sleep, a memory spewed forth, dizzying her. She was lying beside Blackie on hard ground, surrounded by high cliffs and scrub brush, her hand loosely clasped with his. Beneath her covering blanket, her left shoulder was throbbing with the sharp pain of a recent wound. She was keeping watch in the night, so he could rest. They were running from... someone. She couldn't remember who. In the memory, she had suddenly sensed danger, but before she could utter a word, Blackie was on his feet with drawn blade, warned by the tension in her hand. He single-handedly fought off a half-dozen thugs to keep her safe. *Where were the rest of Blackie's men?* she wondered as the memory started to fade. *And where was my sister? Why were the two of us alone in the mountains?* The memory blurred around the edges, then fragmented and sank back into the morass of her mind. She pounded her thigh with her fist.

"What's wrong?" Blackie whispered, half rising, his hand hovering over his belt knife.

"Sorry, I didn't mean to wake you. I was just remembering something — or rather, part of something."

"What? Tell me."

"You and I were alone in the mountains. It was dark." She rubbed her left shoulder. "I was hurt. We were doing this same thing with the hands while you slept. Some men attacked us. You wounded half of them and sent the other half to the Abyss."

Blackie was silent. He lay back and stared upward at the glowering sky.

"What happened? Where were we? Where was everyone else — your men, my sister?"

"It was a long time ago," Blackie said softly. "It's not important now."

"It is to me." She let go of his hand. "Why can't you just tell me what I need to know?"

He turned toward her. "Different people remember things differently. When you remember, you'll know."

"That doesn't help me now —" She stopped as pieces of memories suddenly flashed through her mind, like shards of broken glass mirroring a jumbled series of unrelated events, one minute there, the next minute gone. She closed her eyes and dug the heels of her palms into her closed lids. "Stop!" she whispered, trying to catch the flying images before they disappeared altogether. "I need to see!"

Blackie swung around, caught her gently by the wrists, and pulled her hands away from her eyes. "Tara —"

"I'm all right. It had something to do with Laraina, didn't it? She's the reason we left."

"Your sister —"

Tara seized on another snippet of memory, and her spine straightened in shock. She gripped Blackie's hand. "She's not my sister." Her voice trembled in disbelief, and she felt again the crumbling of her world.

Blackie stared. "Not your sister? Then who is she?"

"I don't... we're half-sisters. We had different mothers." She squeezed her eyes shut again. Another remembrance surfaced, and she rifled through her clothing until she found a small black jeweled key.

Blackie cupped his hands around it as she held it. The smoke-gray jewels shimmered as she ran her fingers over them. "What's that?" he asked sharply.

"It's a key."

"I can see that. What does it go to, and where did you get it?"

Tara let out a long breath. Her mind had gone blank again. "I don't know. The memories... for a moment they were all there, all mixed up and mashed together. I only got the barest glimpses of things... and now they're gone again. It's so maddening." She clenched her fingers around the key. "I have no idea what it opens or where it came from. Have you ever seen anything like it?"

Blackie shook his head. "No, but it looks valuable."

"I'll wager whatever it opens is even more valuable," Gus said, sitting up and leaning closer.

The light of avarice in Gus' eyes sent warning chills crawling over Tara's skin. She stuck the key back into the inner pocket of her tunic.

"It belongs to the lady," Blackie said, pinning Gus with a glare, "and you had best remember that."

"It wouldn't do any good to steal it anyway," Whiskey said. "We don't know what it goes to."

"Someone must know," said Jack, looking over his shoulder from his seat in the stern.

Blackie snapped around. "Jack —"

Jack held up a hand for peace. "Right. Minding my own business." He went back to rowing.

Brains, who had ceased rowing, stopped him. "You and Whittler just steer for a few minutes." He turned toward the fore. "May I see it?"

Tara hesitated, glanced at Blackie. After a moment, he nodded and held out his hand. She took the key from her pocket and gave it to him. Surprise crossed his face. "It's heavy." Reaching back, he handed the key to Brains.

Brains turned it over in his hand, squinting at it in the dim light. "That's because it's made of rock, not metal." He held it up close to his face. "Solid black rock with no grain. Well-polished. Hmmmm, the gray jewels look like moonstones."

"What are moonstones?" Tara asked.

"Gems thought to be magical, empowered by the light of the moon. I've never seen a real one before, only drawings of them in the ancient historical texts in the Royal Library of the Twin Cities. They're just a myth."

"You were in the Royal Library?" Jack said, eyebrows raised. "Only the nobility are allowed in there."

"He was probably trying to steal a book," said Whiskey, snickering.

"I wasn't there to steal anything," Brains said with disgust. "I was there to learn. Some of us like to read, to acquire new knowledge."

Whiskey guffawed. "Yes, right. And I'm the King of Faragellyn."

Jack eyed Brains doubtfully. "But that would mean you were a nobleman."

"So what if I was?" Brains asked.

"I don't believe it." Whiskey took a swig from his bottle.

"Does it matter?" Tara cut in impatiently. "The myth about the jewels, Brains — what did it say?"

"An ancient race of people called Kamarians — true magical beings with inborn powers — were said to have used the stones to harness the light of the moon to enhance their own magical powers."

"Kamarians." Tara thought hard. "I've heard that name somewhere. Tell me more."

"Legends say that, long ago, the Kamarian stronghold lay in the Black Mountains of the Eastern Frontier. Then something happened, and all the Kamarians — the entire race — either disappeared or died. No one knows for certain."

"I've heard that legend, too," Blackie said.

"Black Mountains — as in black rock like that key?" Tara asked.

Brains shrugged. "Could be. I've never been to the Black Mountains." He gave the key to Blackie.

"Neither have I," said Blackie, passing the key back to Tara. He looked around at the others, but they all shook their heads.

"Black Mountains," Tara whispered, tugging at the edge of another memory. "I think I'm supposed to go there. Why?" The memory, like a loose feather, slipped from her grasp and floated away. "Why?" she repeated. She closed her hand over the key and squeezed it hard. "Damn everything to the Abyss — I need to know why!"

The jewels suddenly sparked to life, glowing with soft, silver light. With a startled cry, she dropped the key in her lap. The jewels darkened, the light extinguished like a snuffed candle. She heard Blackie cursing and gasps all around her. His hands flying in a series of protective wards, Gus backed away, rocking the boat as he crowded Whiskey in the fore. The others stared in shocked silence.

"Brains, Jack, steady the boat. Keep us straight," Blackie said in a hoarse voice. Slowly, he reached down and picked up the key. Nothing happened. The key remained dark, lifeless. "Hold out your hand," he said to Tara.

Reluctantly, she did so. He set the key on her open palm. The jewels flared, shining silver once more. She ran her thumb over the glimmering stones, and the light grew stronger.

"Balls, woman," he said softly, "what have you gotten yourself into?"

Tara shrugged helplessly. "I don't know." A strange melody, familiar and yet unfamiliar, played through her mind. "Do you hear music?"

"No," Blackie said. "Do you?"

She nodded, looking down at the key. "It's different, not like anything I've ever heard before... and yet, I feel like I *have* heard it... somewhere, recently." Cold chills eeled down her spine, and she suddenly knew she was being watched. Her head shot up, her gaze sweeping the dark forest. "Someone's watching us." She twisted around to search the trees on the other bank, but saw nothing between the great trunks but the black of night.

"All of you, man the oars," Blackie commanded. "The Butcher —"

"No, no, it's not him," Tara said quickly.

"How do you know?" Blackie asked, his oar poised over the water.

"It feels different." Her eyes were drawn back to the glowing key. "It's someone else."

"Who?"

An image of a man with flowing red robes and long auburn hair sprang into her mind, then vanished, leaving behind a sinister aura of violence and magic. A wizard — an evil one. One she had crossed paths with before, though she couldn't remember when or where. She glanced at the array of faces regarding her with wariness and suspicion and decided that this might not be a good detail to share. "I don't know."

She saw Blackie's eyes narrow. He knew she hadn't told the truth, but he didn't question her further. He probably thought she was trying to avoid saying Trevillion's name again. She let the key fall into her lap, and the silver light winked out. The sensation of being watched disappeared. The wizard was somehow seeing them through the key. "It's gone now. I don't feel it anymore."

"What's gone?" Blackie asked sharply.

"The feeling I had of being watched." Tara used the edge of the blanket to pick up the key and put it back into her inner pocket. "Maybe I imagined it."

"She's a witch," Gus spat. "I knew it. We should kill her now before she works her evil on us."

Blackie's sword was in his hand so fast Tara hardly saw him draw it. Arm outstretched, he pointed the blade straight at Gus. "If I hear another word like that from your mouth, it will be the last word you say. Do you hear me?"

Gus' face twisted with loathing as he looked from Blackie to Tara and back again. "I will not be in the same boat with her."

"Fine. Get out." Blackie gestured with his blade for Gus to jump overboard.

Gus glanced over the side, his eyes sliding from the deep water to the dark bank. "Put me ashore."

"Brains, Jack, row us to shore," Blackie said, his eyes never leaving Gus' face.

They rowed toward the shore. Whiskey, in the fore, knotted the mooring line around an iron stake. He grabbed a mallet, and juggling line, stake, mallet, and bottle, poised to jump. Brains tied the aft line to another stake. Rain broke from the black clouds, dimpling the smooth surface of the river, the large drops hissing as they melted into the water. Tara hunched her shoulders against the drenching cold. The boat nosed along the edge of the high bank. Whiskey leaped onto the shore, slipping on the wet grass as he dashed toward the trees. Pulling the rope tight, he dropped to his knees and drove the stake into the ground. Brains threw the other line onto the shore. Whiskey scrambled over to it, head bent against the rain, and pounded in the other stake, anchoring the boat.

"All right, out." Blackie pointed to the shore with his dripping sword.

"Maybe we should put you and the... ah... *lady* out," Gus sneered.

Blackie smiled grimly. "You're welcome to try." He pulled out his belt knife.

Tara caught up the long knife Blackie had given her and shifted into a crouch. She kept one eye on Whittler, wary of his knife-throwing skill.

Gus gestured angrily. "What say the rest of you? Are you going to ride with a... her?"

Through the pouring rain, Whittler, Brains, and Jack looked at Blackie and Gus, then at each other. Whittler moved first. He drove his knife deep into the wet gunwale, signifying, Tara guessed, that he wouldn't fight.

"I'm in," Brains said. "I want to know more about that key."

"Me, too," said Jack. "I smell treasure."

Blackie looked ashore. "Whiskey?"

"I'm sure as fire and damnation not staying here with him." Whiskey gestured toward Gus with the mallet.

Blackie turned back to Gus. "There's your answer. Whittler, toss one of those supply packs and a water flask up here. Make sure it's water, first."

Whittler sampled a flask, spat over the side, then picked up another one. The second flask contained water, and Whittler tossed the supplies forward to land at Gus' feet.

Blackie motioned to Gus with his sword. "Out of the boat."

"You are all fools!" Gus snarled. "Anything that comes from her will be cursed." He snatched up the supplies and climbed up onto the wet bank.

Blackie followed. "Get going."

Gus hesitated, looking southward toward the Bog, then northward behind him. With a glare at Blackie, he growled an epithet, swung the pack over his shoulder, and started trudging along the bank, back the way they had come, his feet squelching on the soggy ground.

Tara watched him, anger and doubt needling her. His words had stung like poisoned barbs, bringing back more childhood memories of the cruel villagers she had grown to hate. Uncertainty cooled her fury. What if he was right?

When Gus was several yards away, Blackie motioned to the others. "Everybody out. Do what you have to do and make it quick."

Tara clambered awkwardly out of the boat, followed by Whittler, Jack, and Brains. Blackie watched Gus as the others hurried into the edge of the woods. A few minutes later, all but Whiskey piled back into the boat, splashing in the small puddles that were gathering in the bottom. Tara sat next to Blackie on the bench in the middle. Brains and Jack climbed into the fore and Whittler took over the stern. Whiskey hammered out the stake that held the bow and tossed it back into the boat. Then he pulled out the aft stake and, holding onto mallet, stake, bottle, and line, jumped into the stern, rocking the boat only slightly as he took a seat beside Whittler.

"How does he do that?" Tara asked Blackie, who, along with the others, had been steadying the boat with his oar. "I was sure he would either drop something or break that bottle before he was through."

Blackie shrugged as he banked his oar. "Lots of practice, I would say. He's ridden the sea and its waterways for more years than I can count."

Brains, Jack, Whittler, and Whiskey guided the boat out into the current, then Brains and Jack banked their oars, letting Whittler and Whiskey propel them southward. Jack handed out some small buckets, and those not rowing bailed out the boat.

A chorus of wolf howls split the darkness behind them.

"Curse Haedis himself," Blackie fumed. "He's found us again."

A man screamed, and they heard panicked shouts of "Wait! Wait! Blackie!"

"Gus!" cried Jack. "The wolves will get him!"

"Or the Butcher will," said Brains grimly.

All eyes turned to Tara and Blackie.

"Put to shore," Tara said. "I'll —"

"No, you won't." Blackie gripped her arms and pulled her backward off the bench, setting her down into her niche behind him. "You'll stay right there and not move."

"But —"

"For once in this life, don't argue with me. Man the oars," he yelled to the others. "Turn us around."

"I can row as well as you can," Tara said. "Let me help."

"All right, you can row." Blackie strained against the oar as they swung the boat around and began rowing upriver. "But you stay *in* the boat. Agreed?"

"I hear you."

Blackie barred her from rising. "No. I said 'Agreed.' I want your word you'll stay in the boat."

"I can't give you that." Tara shoved his arm aside, climbed back onto the bench beside him, and grabbed the oar. "I said before that if we were caught, I would hand myself over to the Butcher, so the rest of you could escape. I won't go back on that promise."

"To the Abyss with your promise. You're not leaving this boat!"

"Will you stop arguing?" Brains said. "I think I see Gus up ahead."

Tara looked upriver and saw, through varying shades of blackness and rain, a dark shape running along the bank toward them, followed by several smaller dark shapes. Gus was yelling and waving at them, arms and legs pumping frantically. The wolves were gaining on him.

"Gus! Into the water!" Blackie shouted. "We'll pick you up."

"I can't swim!"

"You'd better learn fast!"

Gus looked over his shoulder at the wolves close behind him, screamed out something in his native dialect, and took a flying leap into the river. The wolves skidded to a stop at the edge of the bank and snarled down at him. Limbs flailing, he tried to swim.

Tara, Blackie, and the others bent their backs to the oars and pulled up alongside Gus just as he started to sink beneath the surface. Blackie shoved an oar down beside him, and he clutched at it, dragging himself, spluttering, back up into the air.

"Jack, Whittler, help me!" Blackie ordered. "The rest of you get on the other side. Keep the boat from tipping."

Blackie, Jack, and Whittler grasped Gus' arms and heaved him halfway into the boat. Another heave, and he was in. He lay across the bench in front of Whiskey, gasping and coughing. The growling wolves milled around on the bank, then grew still. Tara felt a chill of ice sweep through her as a giant figure stepped to the river's edge.

"Blackie," she whispered urgently.

He followed her gaze and let out a tirade of curses. "Boat around. Now. All of you, row!"

Everyone caught an oar, spun the boat around, and pulled southward with all the strength they could muster. Tara shuddered as the tortured mind that had rescued her from the creature's attack brushed hers.

Do not be afraid, Lady. I will be near.

Her eyes flew to the lone figure still standing on the riverbank, her breath catching as she suddenly realized that the rough voice that had saved her belonged to the Butcher. Stunned, she lost her grip on the oar, and it dragged in the water, the handle snapping forward and almost hitting her.

"Are you all right?" Blackie asked between breaths.

"What? Yes." She took hold of the oar once more and resumed rowing, her eyes glued to the Wolfmaster until distance stole him from sight.

CHAPTER 17

Jovan Trevillion woke to rain-misted darkness and searing pain. He recognized the throbbing in his head, the sheer agony that radiated down his spine and spread throughout his body. He'd felt it before when his actions did not coincide with what the Being demanded. Punishment had been swift and brutal. It had taken him days, then, to recover physically. He'd never recovered mentally. The knowledge that the Being could inflict such agony on him at any time haunted him. His powerlessness infuriated him.

Gripping his head with his hands, he tried to sit up, but pain lashed through his skull and he fell, groaning, back onto the wet ground. He drifted in and out of consciousness, his thoughts scattering and then coalescing around images from his past like raindrops gathering into pools of watery memories — pools spattered empty by the tramp of many boots, an army moving relentlessly southward, an army of his making...

For reasons unknown to him, the Being had wanted the ruler of a Southland kingdom removed. It had ordered Jovan to lead a massive army that would raze the Southlands and bring about the ruler's downfall. Jovan had refused and spent days curled in a fetal position, racked by the same agony he felt now, while some other general who had proved more pliable had led the attack. Eventually, the Being had ceased torturing him and had forced him to fight the Southlanders or suffer more torment. He remembered the atrocities of that war, and though he hadn't committed any himself, what he'd seen had scarred him for life.

Lucidity returned after a time, and he tried to think, to fight through the pain that shackled his mind. The Being could have killed him as easily as swatting a fly, but it hadn't. Why? Sluggishly, his mind began to work. The Being must still want him for something. He shuddered at the thought. What foul scheme would he be forced to play a hand in next? His breath hissed between clenched teeth as another stab of pain jolted him. Mentally raw and bleeding, he retreated to his innermost core. Perhaps it would have been better if the Being had squashed him. At least there would have been an end to this agony.

But no, he couldn't let his life end here. Tara still needed him. He had vowed to help her defeat the evil creature that sought to ravage her mind and use her to escape its prison. And he would not let her fall to the Butcher. His will hardened.

He dipped into his wellspring of power, then immersed himself completely, letting the healing coolness surround him. He felt Tara's essence in his blood, in the mix of their magics. He saw her face smiling at him, felt her lips touching his, breathing life into him and giving him the strength to fight the pain. He would survive this as he had everything else, bent but not broken.

When he woke again, it was still dark and raining. The pounding of the raindrops drummed a steady beat into his soaked clothing and ran down his neck in rivulets. He smelled the rich scents of wet earth, moldering leaves, and evergreens. He let out a slow breath of relief. The all-consuming pain in his head had lessened to a dull throb.

Gingerly, he uncurled his body and pushed himself into a sitting position. Shallin Wood — that's where he was. His pack and canoe lay beside him on the riverbank where he'd dropped them when the Being had slammed him out of the connection with Tara. He'd been near the end of the second portage. Turning onto his knees, he picked up his supply pack and tossed it to the edge of the forest, nearly falling over from the effort. He waited for the dizziness to recede, then grabbed the canoe, and, a few inches at a time, dragged it to the tree line. He leaned his back against a thick oak, his breath coming hard.

After a few minutes' rest, he eased himself to his feet and stood for a moment, getting his balance, trying to will away his lightheadedness. Then he bent, grasped the end of the canoe, and heaved it up against a tall pine. The low branches held the canoe up at an angle to the trunk. He retrieved his pack and, pushing aside branches sticky with pitch, sat down heavily beneath his makeshift shelter. Taking a cloth from his pack, he wiped the rain from his face. He found his water flask and drank deeply. Then he ate his fill of dried meat and biscuit.

Feeling steadier, he looked at the river through a curtain of rain and cursed the Being for putting him even further behind in his pursuit of Tara and the smugglers. They were nearing the Bog where the creature from Tara's dream lay in wait. He'd tried to warn her, but he wasn't sure she'd understood. He knew she wouldn't remember the dream. He hoped that her recent encounter with the creature would make her wary. If only she could remember...

He closed his eyes and tried to calm his anger. He had to know if the Being had closed the pinhole in the barrier. But if the Being sensed his agitation, it might slam him out again and inflict more agony. He took several deep breaths, emptying his mind. Cautiously, he probed the barrier. Hope burned through the coldness pervading his body. The hole was still there. Why hadn't the Being closed it? Was the Being taunting him?

A new, impossible thought occurred to him — could it be that the Being was unable to seal the hole? What if Tara's magic was stronger? Maybe that was why the Being had wanted him to take her to Rinpool. It sought to gain control of her powers. He mulled over the possibilities. Then he thought of something else. Why hadn't the Being punished him when he had refused to take her there? It had shut him out, instead, and apparently made Natiere her protector. Jovan clenched his jaw. He would find the answers and be her protector again if it was the last thing he did. Gripping the sticky branches, he pulled himself to his feet. Then he slid his pack onto his back, heaved the canoe up, and strode down the riverbank.

*****

Tara and the smugglers rowed hard through the blowing rain for at least an hour before Blackie allowed them, by pairs, to rest. He had set Gus to work, bailing. No one spoke to Gus, who'd said nothing beyond a gruff thanks since his rescue from the wolves.

The rain eased to a cold drizzle just before dawn, then ceased altogether, but the wind continued, sharp and gusty. Her whole body shivering, Tara banked her oar. Her arms and shoulders ached. Beside her, Blackie did the same and stretched.

Tara straightened her numb fingers. "Blackie, we have to dry out and get warm, or we're all going to die of the grippe."

Whittler sneezed and wiped his nose on his wet sleeve.

"Better to die that way than by the Butcher's knife," Blackie said grimly. He tried to flex his fingers and couldn't.

Tara caught his hands in both of hers. "Your hands are colder than mine." She massaged them gently. "What if we put to shore on the opposite bank? It's not likely he would have crossed the river. And you said we'd be in the Bog by morning. It's nearly dawn. With karanaks in the waters, he won't be swimming across now. We could build a fire."

Blackie drew his hands away and cleared his throat. "Listen to what you said, woman. This is the Bog. Another good reason to stay in the boat."

"We're only on the edge of it. And I can warn of any danger before it gets to us."

Whittler sneezed again. Blackie looked at him, then at the others, all shivering and bedraggled. "What will it be?"

"Ashore," Brains said.

"A-agreed," said Jack, his teeth chattering. He squeezed rainwater from his blond ponytail.

Whittler's nod turned into another sneeze.

"What'll we do with him?" Whiskey gestured at Gus.

"Tie him to a tree," Blackie said.

Gus straightened. "I will not be tied to a tree like a dog."

Blackie shrugged. "It's either that or we kill you."

Gus' face darkened, and he muttered more Southland epithets.

Whittler and Whiskey pulled the boat to the far shore. Whiskey jumped out and secured the mooring lines. Blackie marched Gus at sword-point to a tree about the thickness of a man's body and had Whiskey tie Gus' hands together behind the tree with one of his many sailors' knots. Gus wore an angry scowl, but didn't fight.

Blackie clapped Whiskey on the shoulder. "Watch him. If he tries to get loose, do whatever you have to do. I don't want him stealing the boat."

"Aye, Captain," Whiskey said, taking a long swig from his bottle.

Tara looked at Blackie, eyebrows raised. "So you're a captain, now?"

Blackie shrugged again. "I told you, he's a seaman." He motioned for the others to gather around him. "Brains, you and Jack get some firewood. Stay together and don't go far into the woods. Tara and I will do the same. Whittler, you stay here with Whiskey. Guard the boat. Do whatever is necessary."

Whittler sat near the boat and tossed his knife back and forth in his hands. Brains and Jack disappeared into the forest. Tara followed Blackie as he headed into the trees slightly to the north of where the others had gone. Though the grayness of dawn had scarcely touched night's hold on the forest, Tara could see a vast difference between the woodland they'd entered a day ago and this dying weald. The trees were stunted, their trunks blotched with moss and fungus. Rotting leaves and evergreen needles covered a wet, spongy floor strewn with broken branches and fallen logs. She heard no animal sounds, nor the flap of a bird's wing. The smell of decay hung in the thick, moist air like a palpable curtain — a smell that was very familiar...

"Tara?"

She heard Blackie's voice and blinked, realizing she'd stopped walking and let him get ahead of her.

He jogged back to her. "Hey, why did you stop?"

"This place." She tried unsuccessfully to stifle a shiver. "I can feel it dying. And the smell. I remember the smell from before — so thick it almost chokes you. But I can't remember why I was here."

"Never mind that now. Come with me." He caught her hand and drew her deeper into the woods.

"Where are we going?"

"Over here, where no one can hear us." Blackie stopped and looked around. Satisfied they were alone, he crouched behind a fungi-covered log, pulling Tara down with him. "I want to know who was watching us, back there on the boat, and don't tell me you don't know, because I know you do."

Tara hesitated, then met his eyes. "A wizard. An evil one. I can't remember his name or where I ran into him before. He wants something from me, but..." She shrugged.

"An evil wizard," Blackie repeated skeptically.

"Yes. I know it's hard to believe, but it's true." She turned away, debating whether or not to tell him about Natiere.

He touched her arm, and she turned back to him. "There's more, isn't there?" he asked.

"Not about the wizard."

"Then what?"

Tara hesitated again.

He gusted out a breath. "I told you before, I meant what I said about helping you. I'm not going to change my mind, but I need to know just how big a scrape you've gotten yourself into."

Tara threw her hands outward. "I don't know how big a scrape it is. It keeps getting bigger and bigger and more complicated, and there doesn't seem to be any end in sight."

"Just tell me."

She closed her eyes for a second. "All right. Do you remember when I told you about that evil creature attacking me, trying to get in my head?"

"You mean when your eyes..."

"Yes. Remember I said there was a rough voice that somehow gave me strength and helped me defeat the creature?"

Blackie nodded.

"That voice belongs to Natiere."

"The Butcher?" Blackie stared at her, his expression a mix of surprise, revulsion, and doubt. "How do you know?"

"When we rescued Gus, he was standing on the riverbank, look-ing straight at me, and I heard that same voice in my mind again. I knew it was him." Tara frowned. "Will you stop looking at me like that?"

"Sorry." He tried to change his expression. "You're telling me you heard the *Butcher's* voice in your mind?"

"Yes."

"What did he say?"

"He said not to be afraid, and that he would be near."

"Not to be afraid?" Blackie gave a mirthless laugh. "That would be funny if it weren't so ridiculous. How could you not be afraid with him around?" Blackie rose and paced a few steps, punctuating each footfall with curses. "That means he'll keep following us. We need to get back on the boat and row harder to stay ahead of him." He headed back toward the river.

"Blackie, wait." Tara caught his arm. "I know you'll think I've lost my mind, but I'm not sure I want to be that far away from him."

"Woman, your mind is long gone if you think that."

"Just listen to me," Tara said. "There's something evil in the Bog. I can feel it. I'm afraid it might be that creature. Last time, Natiere's voice was the only thing that saved me. He gave me strength, I don't know how. If it attacks me again, and he's not there, I don't know what will happen." She paused. "And that scares me."

Their eyes held for several heartbeats. Then Blackie raked his hand through his hair and let out another long breath. "Well, I'm not going to go looking for him."

"Neither am I," Tara said. "I just don't think we need to worry that much about outrunning him."

"Maybe you don't, but the rest of us might. Whatever his plans are for you, I'm sure they don't include us."

"What do you mean, 'plans for me'?"

"He's after you for some reason. He must have something in mind. And you'd better consider that whatever he does have planned won't likely be any more pleasant than fighting with that evil whatever-it-is." Blackie picked up some deadwood and headed toward where they had moored the boat. "We'd better get back before Gus convinces them to leave without us."

Chilled by that thought, Tara hurriedly gathered an armload of wood and followed.

Just before they reached the riverbank, they heard startled cries from Jack and Whiskey and panicked shouts from Gus. They raced forward the last few steps and burst out onto the bank. Brains, Jack, and Whiskey had started a fire near the edge of the forest and were frantically kicking dirt and moss over the burning wood to dampen the rising, wind-whipped flames. Gus, still tied to a nearby tree, struggled to free himself, while alternately cursing and demanding to be untied. Whittler still guarded the boat.

"Brainless buffoons! What are you trying to do? Set the woods on fire?" Blackie dropped his armload of branches and ran to help subdue the flames.

"Yes, we thought a forest fire would be just the thing to dry us out," Brains retorted, swatting at a spark that landed on his pant leg.

Working together, the four smugglers fought to tame the fire. Tara dumped the wood she'd been carrying, raced to the boat, and grabbed the bailing buckets. She was ready to throw water on the flames if necessary, but Blackie and the others had managed to get the fire under control. Tara crossed to where they stood sweaty and panting.

"Are you all right?" she asked, looking from one to the other.

Brains nodded. His eyebrows and the blond curls on his forehead were singed, but he appeared otherwise unscathed.

"Fine," Whiskey grunted around the mouth of his bottle.

"Toasted, but not burnt," Jack said cheerily.

"Which one of you idiots is going to tell me what happened?" Blackie said.

Whiskey shrugged. "We built a fire." He took another drink and headed for the boat.

Blackie looked at Brains. "Have anything to add?"

Brains considered. "No, not really." He followed after Whiskey, who was lifting wet blankets and gear from the boat.

"Jack?" growled Blackie.

Jack gave a half shrug, an expression of innocence on his boyishly handsome face. "No, I —"

Blackie lunged forward and collared him. "Jack!"

"It was Brains' idea," Jack said hastily.

"What was?" Blackie demanded.

"To use your brew."

"*My brew?* For what?"

"Well, the wood was wet, and it wouldn't burn very well," Jack said, "so we threw on some pine needles we found, and that helped, and then Brains suggested pouring some of your brew on it." He grinned. "It worked great."

Blackie released Jack. "Brains!"

Brains walked past with an armload of gear. "We built the fire near the woods, so we could use the branches to hang our things out to dry. As Jack said, the wet wood wouldn't burn well. Hence, the use of your brew."

Blackie stalked after him. "You wasted my good brew —"

"Better that it burn in the fire, than burn in your gut. Do you have any idea what that stuff is doing to your innards? Be glad that we care enough about you to save you from yourself." Brains walked back toward the boat.

Blackie stared after him, dumbfounded.

Tara laughed and clapped her hand over her mouth.

"What's so funny?" Blackie growled.

"Nothing at all." She hastened to help Whiskey spread a blanket over some tree limbs.

When they had everything laid out to dry and had set the boat upside down on the shore to drain, they sat around the fire and ate. The sun rose, lightening the deep purple of the sky to lavender and pale pink. The wind died down, and in the encroaching silence, Tara heard all around her the faintest of whispers, like slow inhales and exhales, as if the forest itself were breathing. She stopped chewing and listened, sensing again a dark presence in the wood watching, waiting for her to come closer, to walk into a snare like an unsuspecting animal. Evil dwelled here, somewhere in this vast forest. She could feel it. She scanned the woodland depths grown lighter now with the coming day. South — the presence lay to the south. And so did the Bog. Her eyes followed the southward path of the river, its satiny surface mirroring the mauve of the dawn sky amid the shadows of the overhanging trees. Such idyllic beauty flowing into such evil. The river would carry her to her death...

"No," she said aloud, startling herself.

All eyes fell on her.

"No, what?" Blackie, sitting next to her, asked guardedly.

Tara cleared her throat. "Sorry. I was just thinking."

"Yes. About what?" Blackie persisted.

"About the Bog and what lies ahead." Tara pushed back a strand of drying hair. "I wish I could remember more about it."

Blackie relaxed a bit. "If I were you, I'd be happy to forget it. Besides, there's nothing to worry about. We're not going into the Bog, we're going to just float down through it. Simple."

"As long as the karanaks don't eat us," Whiskey grumbled.

"Are you going to let me have some food?" Gus called.

"You can eat when we get back on the boat," Blackie said.

Gus frowned, but didn't ask again.

Jack held up a brooch with a large blue sapphire against the sky and watched the sunlight sparkle through it.

"That must be one of the 'other things' you found in the desk drawer?" Blackie asked.

Jack gazed at the brooch, his eyes sparkling almost as much as the sapphire. "Have you ever seen such a beautiful gem?"

"Speaking of gems," Brains said to Tara. He sat across from her, on the other side of Blackie and Whittler. "Now that it's daylight, may I see that key again?"

Tara took out the key and tossed it to him. He caught it and held it up to the light, examining it closely. "They still look like moonstones." He fingered the jewels. "Hey, what's this?" He dug around the teeth of the key with his fingernail. "It looks like dirt packed in here."

"Dirt? Let me see," Tara said. Brains tossed it back to her, and she caught it in the hem of her tunic. Holding the head of the key with the fabric, she studied the shaft and teeth. She saw the tiny specks of dirt Brains had noticed. "You're right. It does look like dirt."

"Maybe it was buried at one time," Jack said.

Tara felt a memory rising. She closed her eyes, concentrating. "No, not the key. The key wasn't buried, something else was. I remember digging somewhere — Wyndover. We were in Wyndover."

"We?" Blackie asked.

"What?" Tara blinked, only half listening, distracted by the memory she couldn't quite tease from the murk.

"You said 'we were in Wyndover.' Who were you with — Laraina?"

"Um... no, I don't think so." She slid her eyes toward Gus and back to Blackie. "I'm not sure who it was." She saw by the subtle shift of Blackie's expression that he understood. "I can't remember why we were there or what we were doing." She pressed her palm against her forehead. "Why were we digging?"

"What were you digging up, is the more interesting question," Jack said, leaning forward in his eagerness.

"Shhh!" Blackie said. "Let her think."

Tara struggled with the memory, feeling like she was playing tug-of-war. A piece of the remembrance broke off and sailed through her mind before disappearing, along with the rest of the memory. "I saw something long and flat and black, then a burst of fire and blinding light."

"What could be long and flat and black?" Jack asked, his brows furrowed in thought.

"Sorry. I couldn't tell what it was." Tara slipped the key into her pocket.

They finished eating and warmed themselves by the fire, letting the smoky heat dry their wet clothes. Whittler resumed carving on a thick, short stick, carefully shaping the legs of some animal. Jack and Whiskey collected more wood and added it to the blaze. The damp wood hissed, burning feebly as moisture oozed out of it.

"I'll be back in a minute," Blackie said, rising. He strode off into the woods.

Brains watched him go, then scooped up a flask hidden under his leg and poured a small amount into the fire. The flames billowed upward with a burst of intense heat. Tara leaned back, shielding her face until the fire settled down into a warm glow. Brains stuffed the flask back under his leg just as Blackie returned from the forest.

Blackie walked to where he'd been sitting, took one look at the fire, and scowled. "You did it again, didn't you?"

Brains shrugged. "Do you want to dry out, or not?"

Blackie sat, muttering under his breath.

Whittler sneezed and Blackie glanced at him, then looked more closely. "What is that you're carving?"

Whittler held up the piece of wood on which he'd been working.

Brains grunted. "It's a karanak."

Blackie cuffed Whittler on the shoulder. "Why in the name of the Abyss would you carve one of those? Why don't you carve something nice, like a bluebird or something?"

Whittler gestured, his fingers moving in sign.

Blackie raised his eyebrows. "You did? When? I didn't see it."

Whittler's fingers twitched in answer.

Blackie sat back. "Who did you give it to?"

Whittler blushed, his signed answer short.

"Oh, that girl in Norellanen." Blackie grinned. "She was a beauty."

Whittler went back to his whittling, his face hidden behind his hair.

Blackie chuckled, then grew sober. He turned to Tara. "How close is the Butcher? Can you tell?"

"I can feel him, but he's not that close," Tara answered.

"What do you mean, 'feel him'?" Brains asked.

Tara hesitated, saw the others watching her. "I can usually sense when danger is near, so when Natiere is close I can feel his presence. I'm not sure how."

"Useful talent," Brains said into the ensuing silence. He looked at Blackie. "So that's how you got away with so much back then."

"Yes, well, it helped." Blackie glanced up at the sky, now a soft blue with a few meandering clouds of puffy white. "We'll stay a little longer, then head back onto the river. The sun will be over the trees soon and will dry us out better than this fire."

Whittler gestured with the wooden karanak and dropped it into Blackie's hand.

"Done with it, eh?" Using his thumb and forefinger, Blackie lifted it by its long tail. "I can't believe you carved a karanak."

"May I see it?" Tara asked.

Blackie plopped it in her lap. "There it is. Pray you never get any closer to one." He stood and went to retrieve one of the packs.

Tara examined the carving, studying the lizard-like body, short, squat legs, and long snout. "This is amazing. Just look at this detail. It's perfect — right down to the teeth and claws." She held it by the tail, as Blackie had. "If I didn't know better, I'd swear it was alive." Blackie sat down again with the pack. "Here." She handed it to him. "Take it before it starts gnawing on me."

Blackie took it with a grimace. "You think I want it?" He opened the pack and set the wooden karanak inside. Then he fished around and pulled out another stick, which he gave to Whittler. Whittler began carving with relish.

"Are there more in there?" Tara asked.

Blackie set the pack in front of her. "See for yourself."

Tara looked at Whittler. "May I?"

He nodded and went back to his work.

Tara reached in and drew out several carved pieces: a cavorting horse with mane and tail rippling; a mountain hawk in full flight, each feather exquisitely rendered; a fox with ears pricked forward, its bushy tail streaming out behind; a fawn with wobbly legs. "These are beautiful," she breathed. "They're so lifelike." She pulled out a large spider with spindly legs. She bit back a cry and managed not to drop it. "Are you sure this isn't real?"

"Is it moving?" Blackie asked.

"Well, no." Tara turned it over in her hand. "At least, not on its own."

"Good. Though it wouldn't be the first time we've had spiders in our gear."

Tara looked the spider over again. "Raina would love this," she said wryly.

Blackie guffawed. "Wouldn't she now. Hey, you remembered something."

"What?"

"That your sister hates spiders."

Tara thought a moment. "I guess I did."

Blackie clapped her on the back. "It's coming back. Didn't I tell you it would?"

"Yes, you did." Tara placed the spider and the other carved animals back into the pack. "You have an incredible talent," she said to Whittler.

Whittler gave her a half smile and a nod of thanks before disappearing behind his hair again.

The temperature rose with the sun, banishing the soggy chill of the rain-swept night. By the time they had put out the fire, finished loading the gear, and started the boat heading south, Tara's clothes were damp with sweat instead of rain. Brains and Jack rowed in a rhythmic beat, moving the boat swiftly down the wide river. Whittler and Whiskey slept in the fore while Blackie watched Gus eat in silence. As the sun baked its warmth into her bones, Tara felt her eyes growing heavy. She tried to stay awake for Blackie's sake and help keep an eye on Gus. None of them had been able to sleep the night before amidst the pouring rain, and she knew Blackie was as tired as she was, but the gentle sway of the boat worked against her.

"Go ahead and sleep," Blackie said. "I'll wake you in a couple of hours and we'll switch."

Tara nodded, her mind already drifting, her eyelids drooping shut.

Tara. The whisper-soft voice floated faintly through her consciousness. *Love, I am coming. I will be with you soon.*

She smiled, her mind opening of its own accord to touch the tendril of thought reaching out to her. *You are all right.* Her joyful revelation brought echoes of joy from the man behind the voice. For a brief moment their thoughts entwined, and she saw the face of Jovan Trevillion. *It's you?*

Yes. Listen to me. The creature from your dream is imprisoned in the Bog. It is trying to escape through you. You must not let it. If it attacks you, I will help if I can, but don't count on it. If you get caught in the dream dungeon, look for the black sword. You must find it and bring it back out with you.

A sharp chill of warning arrowed down Tara's spine. She panicked and started to break the connection, flinging up mental barriers to ward off the creature's assault.

No! Don't shut me out! Jovan urged, the whisper-soft voice grown desperate.

The evil creature dug at the walls Tara had erected, gouging chunks from them like a beast clawing through flesh. Through a haze of pain, she seized on Jovan's voice and let their minds touch once more. A glimmer of strength squeezed through the connection. She grasped it, raised her own power, and felt a euphoric rush as their powers fused and thrust outward, driving the creature back. Together, they rammed it back into its prison.

Relief poured through her. The connection dissolved like mist in the morning sun. Jovan's presence faded from her mind, but not his face.

"Thank you, Jovan," she whispered, and slept.

CHAPTER 18

The jerk of the boat as it plowed bow-first into the riverbank jarred Tara awake.

"Hey, easy with that," Blackie called to the stern.

"Sorry. I thought I saw something moving in the water," Tara heard Diamond Jack reply.

"Did you?" Blackie's head whipped around as he scanned the river.

"I don't know," Jack said. "I don't see anything now."

Tara rubbed the sleep from her eyes and sat up. "Blackie, you were supposed to wake me long before this..." She stared at the dead black trees lining the waterway. Heavy swags of moss and spiderweb draped the twisted, leafless branches, dragging them down until their tips touched the ground. A thick yellow mist swirled through the grayness between the trunks, its noxious odor triggering a burst of fragmented memories.

"Stop complaining," Blackie said. "Be glad I let you sleep."

Overwhelmed by the flurry of images, Tara barely noticed that Blackie's tone had grown cool. She closed her eyes and succeeded in snagging a few pieces of her lost memory before all went blank again.

Blackie gripped her shoulder. "Tara?"

She opened her eyes. "I remember spiders dropping all around us, and huge vultures eating them in midair. The vultures attacked us. And I remember a pond full of writhing vines that tried to pull us under. And there was a girl — I can't remember her name — she was dying. I saved her somehow. I don't know what I did."

Blackie sat back. "You still don't know why you were in the Bog?"

"No."

"Well, I'm going to take Gus on shore, then you can go do your business. We'll turn our backs. Don't go past the tree line." He stood and, with sword out, gestured for Gus to precede him onto the riverbank. Gus picked up a small shovel and climbed out.

Tara frowned as Blackie's distant demeanor finally sank in. Why was he being that way? What had happened?

When he and Gus returned, she tried to catch his eye, but he avoided her gaze and jerked his thumb toward the shore. She climbed out of the boat, feeling vulnerable. They could so easily row off without her. Whiskey was still on the bank, tending the mooring lines, his back turned. The others all sat in the boat, looking away from her. Brains and Jack were now in the bow, hunkering down to sleep, while Whittler sat in the stern, carving on a stick as he watched the river.

She moved up toward the tree line and hurriedly did what she had to do. As she started toward the boat, she suddenly felt bone cold. A vicious growl stopped her. She spun around, her eyes searching the rotting trees. Five pairs of golden eyes stared at her from between the blackened boles.

"Back on the boat, now!" Blackie shouted.

Tara ran. Whiskey loosed the mooring lines. She and Whiskey leaped into the boat at the same time. Blackie caught and steadied her, then let go and grabbed an oar. Tara looked back at the shore and saw five huge black beasts racing toward them across the short span of riverbank. She scrambled onto the bench beside Blackie and took up the other oar. All of them rowed, their backs and arms straining as they dug the oars into the water and pulled away from the shore. The beasts didn't slow as they neared the edge, their muscles bunching for the leap across to the boat.

"Yell, scream! Make noise!" Tara cried. She shouted at the beasts. The others did the same. Brains kicked a metal pan. The cacophony echoed down the river corridor and into the distance. The wolves' ears pricked forward, finger-length claws digging into the bank as they slid to a stop at the brink of the river. One of them slipped over the edge and fell in. Dark brown logs rose from beneath the surface, logs with legs and teeth.

"Oh, gods," Tara whispered.

The wolf yelped as the karanaks tore into it. Blood spilled into the river, flowing around the boat. Sickened by the carnage, Tara rowed numbly along with the others, forcing the boat away from the scarlet waters. Another memory sprang into her mind, frighteningly clear. She saw a Bog wolf leaping at her, jaws snapping in her face, and Dominic tackling the beast, rolling over and over on the ground with it. The wolf mauled him, ripped away his life and breath. She'd stabbed the wolf to get it off him, but then the wolf had attacked her, and they'd both fallen into the river. That wolf, too, had been consumed by karanaks. She had escaped, but Dominic... Tears filled her eyes again, and she brushed her sleeve across her face to wipe them away.

"Hey, what's that for?" Concern replaced the coolness in Blackie's voice.

She blinked away more brimming tears. "I keep remembering Dominic. It was a wolf like one of those that killed him."

"That was a wolf?" Jack said. "I've never seen one that big."

"It's a Bog wolf," Tara said.

"How do you know that?" Brains asked. "And how did you know that making a lot of noise would stop them?"

"It worked once before."

"So you really have been in the Bog," Brains said.

"Yes, once. You didn't believe me?"

"Well, as far as I've heard, no one that's gone into the Bog has come out again," Brains said, "except for Jovan Trevillion."

Gus snarled, an angry, guttural sound. "Do not mention that name in my presence or I'll —"

Blackie's sword rasped from its scabbard, and he held it at Gus' throat. "Or you'll what? Whiskey, tie his hands behind his back again."

"You'll be sorry," Gus snapped as Whiskey stopped rowing long enough to do as he was bidden. "All of you."

Blackie pressed the point of his blade against Gus' neck. "My good nature is wearing thin. Threaten any of us again and I'll dump you overboard."

Gus glared at him defiantly, but said no more. Blackie sheathed his weapon and went back to rowing.

"You do know him, don't you," Brains said to Tara.

"Brains," growled Blackie.

"I just want the truth," Brains said. "Did he do what Gus says he did?"

Tara thought of the man behind the whisper-soft voice — the ruggedly handsome face, those dark eyes — the man who had just come to her rescue. The binding of his strength with hers had given her such a euphoric rush. Warmth rose from deep inside and spread through her limbs as if she'd been warmed by the sun from within. He'd said he loved her, and she'd trusted him enough to let him into her mind. He couldn't have done such a thing... could he? Or was her trust a misguided result of her attraction to him? A cool niggling of unease crept up the back of her neck. There was something wrong about him, some danger that swirled around her sense of him, lurking in the background — what was it? She fumed inwardly. Why couldn't she remember?

"I can't believe that he did," she said finally.

"But you don't know."

"Not for certain," she admitted, "but I don't think he should be condemned without hearing his side of the story."

"Agreed," said Brains, "but I also don't think Gus should be condemned for hating a man he thinks murdered his family."

"I don't care how Gus feels about Trevillion," Blackie said. "Love him or hate him — it's nothing to me. But I do care how he feels about the people in this boat — including Tara. If you threaten my friends, you threaten me, and that I will not tolerate."

The slapping of an oar on water spun their heads toward the stern. Whittler pointed to his right. Several thick, brown logs floated in the water.

"Karanaks!" Whiskey hollered.

Tara saw their undulating tails as the long-snouted lizards swam toward them.

Blackie bent his back to the oar. "Row faster!"

Brains let out a yell. "They're in front of us, too!" He grabbed the frying pan he'd kicked earlier and whacked the snout of a karanak that snapped at him.

"Keep rowing!" Blackie ordered.

"I can't," Brains panted. "This thing keeps trying to climb in the boat." He struck the hissing lizard repeatedly with knife and skillet. Jack half rose from the bench and stabbed at another one with his sword. The boat jerked as a karanak rammed it from underneath, and Jack nearly fell out.

"Everybody stay down!" Blackie jabbed his blade into the tail of one as it swam by.

Gus' head swiveled as he watched the karanaks circling the boat. "Cut me loose! Cut me loose!"

"Hold still." Blackie leaned forward and sliced the rope with his knife.

Gus ripped out an oar and clouted a karanak that had launched itself up and hooked its leg over the gunwale. Tara impaled it with Blackie's long knife, then fell back onto the bench as the boat rocked from another slam from below and turned sideways, pushed by the slow current.

Blackie struggled to bring the boat around. "Somebody help me straighten the boat!"

"I've got it!" Tara caught the dragging opposite oar and swept it forward. Working together, they got the boat back in line.

Whiskey cried out as a karanak leaped at him. He just managed to pull his arm out of the way of its snapping jaws. With a yell, he plunged his knife into its snout. The lizard jerked away and fell back into the water, taking Whiskey's knife with it. The karanak whipped its head back and forth, but the knife was stuck deep and wouldn't come out. Another karanak lunged at Whiskey. He started to swing his bottle, thought better of it, snatched up the mallet, and pounded the lizard over the head. Whittler stabbed it with his much-bloodied knife, and the karanak dropped away, hissing.

"Hey, look! They're starting to attack each other." Jack pointed at a group of three or four karanaks that were twisting around each other, biting and clawing.

"They smell the blood from the ones we've wounded," Blackie said.

A crimson stain spread into the water around them. The other karanaks left the boat and, in a frenzy of teeth, ripped the wounded karanaks to pieces and devoured them.

"Everybody row," Blackie commanded. "I don't want to be dessert."

Gus refitted his oar and they all rowed, stretching themselves to the limit, putting the blood-crazed karanaks far behind them.

They rowed in shifts for the rest of the day, the boat gliding swiftly down the wide, glassy river. Tara had taken over Blackie's spot, rowing while he slept in her niche. She kept her eye on Gus, who sat opposite on the bench in front of her, but Gus rowed sullenly, his gaze locked on the waters behind them. No one spoke, all senses trained on the Bog and the river.

Afternoon melted into evening. Soaked with sweat from the heat of the day, Tara swiped her sleeve across her dripping forehead and leaned on the oar, holding it up out of the water while she caught her breath. Hours of rowing had cramped her muscles, left them sore and aching. She picked up the two flasks near her feet, sniffing the stoppers before taking a long drink of warm, stale water. "Ugh." Tara wrinkled her nose at the taste.

Blackie stirred behind her. "Hand the other one over here, if you're not going to drink it."

"Hey, you're awake." She handed him his flask of brew. "This water isn't much better than that." She made a face as she took another swallow.

"It's hard to keep water cold in this heat." He gestured with the flask. "That's why you should drink this."

"No, thanks." Tara smiled. "I'm not that desperate."

"You ready to switch places?"

Tara grimaced. "More than ready." She banked the oar and slid across the bench to give Blackie room to climb out of the niche and back onto his seat. Icy prickles raked her skin as Gus shot her a hateful glance over his shoulder before turning to glower once more at the river. Blackie caught the look as well. Tara stilled her rising temper and raised a finger to her lips, silencing Blackie's angry words.

"It's all right," she whispered as she rearranged the blankets and sank into the niche behind him.

"No, it's not," Blackie said in a low voice.

"It is for now. I don't want to aggravate the situation."

Blackie cursed under his breath and turned away, looking fore and aft. "All right, who rested last?"

"We did," said Whiskey from the stern.

Blackie turned to the fore. "Brains, you and Jack sleep for a couple of hours, and then we'll switch again."

"Love to." Brains banked his oar and stretched.

"I'll beat you to it." Diamond Jack scrambled over the oar bank and curled up on the empty bench.

Brains tossed a blanket over him. "Asleep yet?"

"Thanks. Yes." Jack snuggled into the blanket.

Brains grunted. "Good thing you didn't wager any money or you'd have lost it."

"I would not," Jack retorted, his voice muffled in the blanket. "I bet you ten gold pieces I'll be asleep before you are."

"Done." Brains scrunched onto the fore bench with another blanket and snored loudly.

Jack sat up with an indignant scowl. "How am I supposed to sleep with all that racket?"

The snoring noise turned into a snigger. "That's your problem," Brains said. "I could conk you over the head, if that would help, but then I'd lose the bet."

"You're so kind," Jack grumbled and lay down again.

Tara poked Blackie with the flask of brew she'd dug out from under her. "Here, take this." She shook her head. "I still can't believe this crew managed to get all the way upriver from Norellanen to Cierra without someone going overboard."

"But we all get along so well. Can't you tell?" Blackie grinned. "Another rhyme. Heh, heh, that's good. Hey, maybe I should go back to the Twin Cities and write poetry for the nobles. Then Brains could read my work along with his historic books in the library."

A snorted guffaw erupted from the fore, along with snickers and chortles from both fore and aft.

"Hey, you're still awake. I win," Jack declared.

Brains was laughing too hard to reply.

"Why is that funny?" Blackie demanded. "I can write fine poetry."

"I'm sure you can," Tara said, unable to keep the smile from her face. "Just please don't read it to me."

"Why not?"

"Because I —" A barrage of anguished memories struck her, ripping open old wounds. "Dominic," she whispered.

"Dominic?" Blackie frowned. "What about him?"

"I feel him." Tara clambered out of her niche and onto the bench beside Blackie, her eyes sweeping the darkened riverbank, the black trees, and the even blacker depths between them. "I've been here, I know it. Put to shore. I need to get to shore."

"To shore? After what happened last time? Haedis' balls, woman. You may be crazy, but I'm not."

"Over there." She pointed to a spot downstream on the west bank of the river. "Just for a few minutes. It might help me remember something."

"It only took a few minutes for those wolves to find us before. What makes you think they won't find us now?"

Tara gripped his arm. "I need to get over there. If you don't pull to shore, I'll swim over."

"Good. Let her," Gus muttered.

Blackie jabbed his finger at Gus. "You be quiet."

Tara looked over the gunwale, searching for karanaks.

Blackie grasped her shoulders. "And what are you going to do — swim back?" He flung his hand toward the south flow of the river. "After we're how far downstream?"

Tara said nothing, her eyes holding his.

"Woman, you are insane." Blackie raked his hand through his hair. "And I must have squirrels in my tree." He faced aft. "Whiskey, Whittler, shore!" He pointed to the area Tara had indicated.

Whiskey and Whittler exchanged glances, then guided the boat toward the shore. Brains and Jack sat up, all traces of humor gone. Gus lifted his oar out of the water and fiddled with the fittings as he banked it.

As the boat slid alongside the eroded shoreline, Tara and Whiskey jumped onto the riverbank. Whiskey drove in the mooring lines, while Tara ran across the wide span of tall grass toward the trees. Blackie stepped onto the bank and hovered near the boat.

Tara halted halfway between the river and the edge of the Bog. "We fought here with the wolves." She turned in a slow circle. "Laraina was with me, and Dominic, and Jo—" She caught herself. "And there was another man. What was his name?" She put her hand to her forehead as the memory of the battle stuttered through her mind in scattered bits, some clear, some hazy. "Prince Kaden... and his cousin, Aurelia — that was the girl I saved."

"Prince Kaden of Dhanarra?" Blackie asked, moving closer.

Tara nodded. "Natiere was after us. That's why we were in the Bog. We were trying to lose him." She frowned. "There was another reason, too... I can't remember." She walked a few steps northward and knelt. "Dominic is buried here." Parting the grass, she pressed her hands against the firm, cool sod, her heart rending again at the loss.

Whiskey yelled, and Tara caught a flurry of motion out of the corner of her eye. She jerked upright as Blackie whirled, cursed, and ran toward the boat. Gus and Whittler were grappling in the stern. Tara raced after Blackie.

Gus backhanded Whittler across the jaw. Whittler fell backward over the oar bank. Gus reached for him, but his hand closed on air as Whittler tumbled into the water. Brains lunged toward Gus, with Jack right behind him. Balancing in the rocking boat, Gus snatched up the oar he'd covertly detached and struck Brains in the belly, shoving him backward into Jack. They both sprawled in the bow. Gus dropped the oar onto the boat and slashed the aft mooring line. The stern began to drift away from the shore. With a yell, Whiskey sprang across into the boat and tackled Gus. They wrestled for a few moments in the lurching boat. Just before she reached the bow, Tara saw Whiskey fall over the side into the river. Brains recovered his feet, grabbed the loose oar, and whacked Gus over the head. Gus fell across the aft bench with a grunt and lay still.

Blackie dove into the dark water and swam across to where Whittler floated, unconscious. He flung his arm around Whittler's chest and dragged him back toward the boat, now broadside to the river, the bow still moored to the bank. Tara scrambled into the bow as Brains reached to pull Whiskey back into the boat. Whiskey screamed, his hands scrabbling on the gunwale as karanaks surfaced around him, tearing at his legs. Tara stabbed them with the long knife as Brains caught Whiskey's hands and heaved him over the side. Blood poured from Whiskey's mangled legs. Tara grabbed a blanket and wrapped it tightly around his legs to try to stem the bleeding.

"Brains!" Jack cried from the stern.

Brains climbed aft to help as Blackie, with Whittler in tow, reached the boat. As Blackie shifted his grip to lift Whittler up, a karanak latched onto Whittler's arm and hand. Blackie yelled and fell back. Jack snagged Whittler before the karanak could yank him out of Blackie's grip. Unable to reach with his sword, Brains beat the lizard furiously over the head with the oar until it let go. Then he and Jack hauled Whittler and Blackie into the boat. Whittler coughed and retched, groaning.

"Tara, cut the line!" Blackie gasped.

Tara sliced the bow line. Loosed from its mooring, the boat slid around backward, buffeted by the karanaks.

"They're going to keel us over!" On his knees in the rocking boat, Brains swung his oar at a karanak and missed as it dove beneath the surface.

"Here, we'll throw Gus overboard." Blackie grasped the legs of the unconscious Southlander. "That'll keep them busy."

Brains and Jack hesitated.

"Blackie, no!" Tara cried.

Blackie swung around. "No? After what he did?"

"No one deserves that. If you're going to kill him, just do it outright."

"Woman, this is my crew, and you have nothing to say about it."

"And it wouldn't bother you to see one of your crew torn to shreds?"

"I've already seen it!" He jerked his hand at Whiskey, lying unmoving in the bow.

"I don't think Gus meant to kill anyone, just knock them out and steal the boat."

"I don't care! Whiskey is going to die because of him, and Whittler's going to lose his arm —" He launched into a tirade of curses as the boat lurched again, sluing back toward the shore. Jack cried out and sliced a gash across the side of a karanak that had leaped half into the stern. Dodging the swinging maw full of teeth, Brains levered his oar underneath the lizard and flipped it back into the water.

"Whiskey's not going to die!" Tara said, a vision suddenly clear in her mind. "I can save him — just like I saved that girl in the Bog."

"You what? How?" Blackie gripped the oar bank to keep from falling out of the boat.

She looked down at Whiskey, her limbs trembling with the realization that she did know how to save him. *Oh, gods, Gus was right. I am a witch.* She shoved the thought aside. "Somebody grab the oars and get ready to row!" She snatched a wooden bailing bucket, scooped up some blood from the pool beneath Whiskey's legs, and threw the bucket out into the middle of the river behind the boat, where it landed with a splash.

Leaving the boat, the karanaks converged on the bloody bucket. Brains and Jack, ready at the aft oars, turned the boat around and dug hard, driving the boat southward. The sound of snapping teeth and splintering wood rode back to them as the karanaks attacked the bucket.

Tara unwrapped the blood-soaked blanket from Whiskey's legs, sliced her palm with the long knife, and pressed her bleeding hand against an open gash. She closed her eyes. Pain like a hundred razor-sharp teeth tore through her legs, and she cried out, her concentration scattering. An icy jab of warning shocked her. The evil presence attacked, brutally clawing at her unguarded mind. Instinct saved her, her power bursting from the well of panic in which she was drowning. The power burned through her like wildfire, white hot and primal, searing the creature until it shrieked and let go. Walls sprouted from the depths of her mind and shot upward, blocking out the evil. Shakily, she gathered her strength and clung to the raging power, gradually gaining some semblance of control.

Whiskey moaned as the power shot into him, healing his badly torn limbs. Tara felt Blackie's presence beside her, kneeling, steadying Whiskey. The evil creature beat against her mental walls like a battering ram, searching for a weakness, the tiniest crack. The walls shook from the impact, rattling her concentration; her head ached from the pounding.

Her breath coming hard, she opened her eyes and let go of Whiskey. Blood still dripped from the cut on her palm. Whiskey's legs were whole, with only traces of pocked scars where the karanaks' teeth had gouged out chunks of flesh. She looked at Blackie, saw him through a blur like whirling mist.

He jumped back and nearly fell overboard. "Damnation, woman, how do your eyes do that?"

"I need Whittler." Her voice rasped in her throat. She felt her walls weakening, beginning to crack. Her blurred vision cleared, and she saw Whittler shaking his head, his right arm cradled tight to his chest. "Just get him up here," she croaked.

Blackie dragged Whittler to the fore and wrestled him onto the bench.

"Give me your hand," Tara said through clenched teeth.

He shrank back, terror in his eyes.

"Blackie, I need his hand," she whispered. Blackie's voice faded in and out of her hearing as he argued with Whittler. Every blow from the creature had become a wrenching pain like a knife digging into her mind, prying open her cracked walls. "I need it *now!*"

Blackie grasped Whittler's upper arm and pulled it away from his body. Whittler hissed in a breath, his face white and pinched, agony darkening his eyes.

"Oh, gods," she whispered, staring at his mutilated forearm and hand, a bloody mass of torn muscles, ligaments, tendons, and broken bones. Two fingers dangled, barely attached. "Hold him," she said to Blackie.

As gently as she could, she gathered Whittler's fingers together and flattened his hand between her palms. Then she closed her eyes, braced herself, and eased the power into him. A groan escaped her as excruciating pain slashed up her arm, and it took every particle of strength she had to keep the power steady until the spasm passed. The evil creature stabbed her relentlessly, and her walls began to buckle.

Jovan, help me! Shaking from the effort, she struggled to hold her walls long enough for Whittler's arm and hand to heal.

I'm here. Let me in!

Her heart leaped at the sound of the whisper-soft voice, faint though it was. She cracked her mind open and seized the thread of strength he forced through the barrier. The walls shuddered, but held for a few more precious seconds. Then her hands slipped away, and she caught a glimpse of Whittler, staring in wonder at his healed hand, before an icy black wave crashed over her, smashing her walls and driving the breath from her body.

CHAPTER 19

Jovan! she screamed. Her mind reeled in agony. The suffocating blackness bore her down like the weight of a mountain flattening her. She couldn't breathe.

I... can't... hold... you... Jovan cried out, his mental voice dwindling to a tortured groan.

No! Don't let go! With her last bit of strength, Tara wrapped her pain-seared mind around the thinning thread of Jovan's essence. Something snapped, and she fell in dizzying circles, landing hard.

She gasped in pain at the jarring impact and realized she could breathe again. She had escaped the blackness. Holding her throbbing head, she sat up and stared around her. Where in the name of the Abyss was she? Gone were the boat, the smugglers, the river with black trees lining its banks. The rough gray walls of a dungeon passage enclosed her. Four burning torches in bright metal sconces lit the long hallway, illuminating the blotches of yellow ooze that covered the rock walls. Hordes of spiders — black, brown, yellow, and red, some thick-bodied and hairy, some thin and spindly-legged — crawled across the low ceiling, spinning sinewy cobwebs. She ducked her head, watching them uneasily. Bits of memory teased her, then skittered away, like mice evading a cat. She knew this place, or had known it, sometime in her past, yet she sensed there was something different about it, something... She cursed her lost memory.

Freezing cold struck her as the sound of shuffling footsteps crept into the silence behind her. The stink of rotting meat filled the hall. She lurched to a crouch. Both the sound and the odor emanated from a fathomless red-black mass that glutted one end of the passage like some grisly jelly made from putrefied blood. Tara gagged, choking on bile. Staggering to her feet, she reached for her long knife. It wasn't there. She had no weapons.

A figure shuffled out of the viscous mass. Panic jammed her heart into her throat, and she bolted toward the massive iron door at the other end of the hallway.

"Stop!" commanded a broken voice, hoarse and whispery as if from disuse.

Her feet stopped, frozen to the floor, her arms windmilling as she struggled to keep her balance. Frantically, she tried to move her legs, but her feet remained glued to the stone. She looked behind her. Ripples of numbing cold cascaded over her as she watched the figure — a man — approach. Patchy silver hair framed a twisted smile in a slightly deformed face, his skin a sickly white. One silvery eye burned into her, the color swirling in a familiar way; where his other eye should have been gaped an empty hole. A floor-length gray robe folded around his thick body, hiding whatever deformity caused his hobbling gait. In his left hand, he held a long, black sword.

With a sharp intake of breath, Tara's eyes locked on the sword, and she remembered Jovan's words. *If you get caught in the dream dungeon, look for the black sword. You must find it and bring it back out with you.*

Memories of black fire shooting from the end of the blade rushed through her mind, people screaming and running away from a pile of charred bodies. She choked again, horrified, the stench of burning flesh mingling with the carrion smell. She had held that blade. She had killed those people. Was she a murderer as well as a witch?

The man with the sword walked around in front of her. "Look at me!" he rasped.

Her gaze swung to his. The hypnotic whirling in his one eye held her motionless as he stepped close. He raised his hand to within inches of her face, and she felt icy fingers creep through her mind, the coldness searing worse than any flame. The icy fingers mutated into claws, digging deep. She screamed. *Jovan!* Desperation and fear clutched her when he didn't answer. She screamed again as the claws ripped through her mind. Then anger surged, rising from a volcano deep within. "You... will not... have me!" Power erupted, blazing through the panic. Flowing through her like liquid fire, it torched the icy claws and melted them away. The man with the sword howled and stumbled back a few steps. Snarling, he renewed his attack. She heard faint unintelligible words, then an invisible blow to her gut doubled her over. Another blow slammed between her eyes. She groaned and fell backward, her vision dimming to a smattering of gray.

Use my strength, Lady. The urgent gravelly whisper forced its way into her mind. Barely conscious, she sensed power like an immovable column of rock reaching toward her. She snatched it, wrapped her arms around it, and gripped it to her, letting it bolster her strength and shield her from the onslaught. The pain eased enough for her to catch her breath and gather herself.

Just as she was about to strike back, the man with the sword ceased his attack. The sudden release of her mind left her gasping on the floor and able to move her feet again.

The man pointed at something behind her. Fury twisted his deformed features. "That is mine!"

Tara swung around. Another man stood in the passage, a man with long auburn hair, crimson robes, and swirling red-gray eyes. His right sleeve hung empty from just above the elbow. *Validar Melodian.* The wizard's name slid into her head. Where had he come from?

"It's mine now." Melodian curled his hand around the pulsing blood-red jewel hanging from a silver chain around his neck. "I want that sword."

Tara stared at the jewel, suddenly recalling her last meeting with Melodian. It had been here in this dungeon. She'd had the black sword then, and he had tried to take it from her. A blast of black fire from the sword had sent them both reeling. The flames must have destroyed his arm.

"Ha." The one-eyed man raised the black blade. "You think you can take it from me?" He spat. "You have no power. You are nothing but a yapping puppy." He took a shuffling step forward. "Now give me my bloodstone!"

Magical words whisked from his lips, and from Melodian's. The jewel around Melodian's neck glowed bright red.

Tara sprang at the one-eyed man, jabbing him in the throat with rigid fingers as she knocked him to the floor. He choked, the words of his spell lost in gasps for breath. Tara wrested the black sword from him, rolled to her feet, and leveled it at Melodian. The wizard leaped out of the way as black fire burst across the passage and exploded through the wall, leaving a large, ragged hole to the door-lined corridors beyond. Tara dashed to the hole and dove through it.

"No! Come back!"

Melodian's voice echoed around her as she escaped into a maze of spider-infested passages. Fire from the black sword burned in her blood like the blazing heat of a blacksmith's forge, healing the wounds inflicted by the one-eyed man and giving her strength. Hacking through thick webs, she dodged down the corridors, not daring to stop, afraid that Melodian would suddenly materialize in front of her the way he had appeared out of nowhere in the main hallway. Yet as formidable as he was, Tara feared the one-eyed man even more. She sensed his approach, felt the murderous fury raging within him.

Her fist clenched. She had to find a way out. She glanced at the many doors along the corridor as she passed, but her danger sense warned her not to open them.

She slid to a stop as dozens of spiders descended from the ceiling, dangling from sticky white webs. A smooth-bodied black spider with legs as long as her fingers hung an inch from her face, its jaws open, its eyes gleaming with malice and hunger. She scrambled backward, ducking as more spiders dropped around her. Swiping them out of her hair, she backtracked to the intersection, only to find her way blocked by a wall of spider-filled webs. She raised the black sword to burn through them, then thought better of it. If she used the sword's power, she would give away her location. She shuddered as she sawed through the cord-like webs, sidling past a host of dangling critters. Spiders didn't usually bother her much, but the proliferation was making her flesh creep.

She jogged a few steps, then halted. All around her loomed dense lattices of spider silk, swarming with arachnids. She had the strange feeling the spiders were trying to trap her. Her skin crawled, whether from real spiders or from her imagination, she wasn't sure.

Panic rising, she looked once more down the corridor at the many doors draped with curtains of web. She needed an exit. Dangerous or not, she would have to try the doors — if she could get to them. She slashed at the webs, cringing as spiders fell onto her and scuttled over her arms and chest. She anticipated with horror their venomous bites, but not one bit her. The one-eyed man must want her alive, or else he wanted to kill her himself.

Gritting her teeth, she flicked off the spiders she could reach, then attacked the webs again. Her blade caught in the sticky strands. She yanked it out and stumbled backward into a newly formed mass of web. Spiders crawled over her. She cried out and fought the entangling webs, jerking away from the skittering of hairy legs across her face. Gripping the black sword in both hands, she sliced sideways. Black fire engulfed the corridor, destroying the webs around her — but not the spiders. "No," she whispered, as hundreds of arachnids three times larger scrabbled out of the smoky passage and began spinning more webs at a much faster rate. It was as if the spiders had somehow absorbed the sword's energy instead of being burned by it.

Shaking off spiders, she ran through the narrowing gap of the passageway into the thinning smoke. Sweat soaked her clothes as she tested the scorched iron doors along the hallway. All were locked and showed minimal damage. She halted, at a loss. She could try blasting her way through the doors. She glanced at the over-sized spiders, some larger than her fist, twining webs from floor to ceiling around her. But would the spiders get even larger if she used the sword again? And what about her own fevered state? She already felt charbroiled on the inside. She wasn't sure she could stand much more heat.

Cold prickles stung her as a shimmer caught the corner of her eye. She saw the misty form of a man in a swirling of red robes solidifying in the intersection she had just left. She pointed the black sword at him and Melodian vanished, only to reappear as a glimmer behind her. She spun, bringing the sword around carefully, and the glimmer dissipated. The prickles of warning sharpened, and she sensed the swift approach of the one-eyed man. Vivid memories of a horribly deformed man-creature bursting through doors and attacking her, taking the sword from her, surged into her mind. She realized that the creature and the one-eyed man were the same, that somehow the man was using the sword's power to heal himself. If he found her, he would take the sword back, and there'd be no way she could stop him.

Clamping down her rising hysteria, she tried to think. Spiders surrounded her, weaving their webs ever closer, cutting off her escape. Her eyes flicked along the doors. The one-eyed man could spring out of one at any moment. A sudden thought struck her. Natiere.

Are you still there? she sent, cautiously slivering her mind open.

Yes, Lady.

The rough whisper sent cold shivers through her. *I can't get out. Can you see me?* She skipped sideways, dodging a half-dozen spiders descending toward her.

No. How did you get where you are?

I don't know. I fell through blackness. She struggled to find words to describe what had happened.

You must come out the same way.

But how? She slammed her mind shut, hastily casting up walls as the mental claws of the one-eyed man swiped at her. "How?" she demanded aloud. The claws scraped along the walls, screeching just beyond the edges of her mind. A memory flashed, a frightening image of her opening one of the doors and nearly falling into a limitless black void. "The void," she whispered, clinging to the memory. "Yes, but where is it?" She closed her eyes and, holding the sword out straight, turned in a circle, letting her intuition guide her. Halfway around, she stopped, sensing a vast, crushing emptiness. She opened her eyes and found herself pointing at an iron door, four doors down from where she stood. Between her and the door stretched a crawling, floor-to-ceiling mass of spider-laced web, several yards deep. Behind her rose another creeping wall of web.

Taking a deep breath, she waved the black sword in a narrow arc. Black fire shot down the corridor, incinerating the network of web blocking her path. Hundreds of spiders dropped to the floor, growing larger as they fell. Tara gasped as flaming heat seared through her. She lurched to the fourth door, squishing spiders under her feet with every step. A furious shriek hammered in her ears, echoing along the hallway, and the spiders began to climb up her pant legs, spinning webs around her. She cried out, panicking, the horrible crawling sensation fueling her terror. Stomping her feet and swatting at the spiders, she grabbed the door handle and found it locked. Hampered by the thick webs tangling her legs, she staggered across the hall, faced the door, and blasted it with the sword. The door blew off its hinges, spraying chunks of rock in all directions and filling the hall with the smell of burnt metal. She ducked and covered her head as small pieces of rock pelted her. Her breath coming in short gasps, she looked back through wispy smoke and dust and scattering spiders and saw the deadly blackness no longer hidden behind the door. Dizziness rocked her and she fell to one knee, so hot inside she felt as though she'd swallowed a forest fire.

Her danger sense screamed. The air in front of her shimmered and Melodian appeared, standing between her and the void.

He stepped toward her. "Drop the sword and back away, and I won't hurt you."

A door opened behind her, wafting in the odor of carrion. The one-eyed man clutched at her. She scrambled sideways.

"No!" Melodian lunged. "Give me the sword!"

Tara scooped up a handful of spiders and threw them into Melodian's face. The wizard recoiled. She dodged behind him, toward the void.

"Stop!" the one-eyed man rasped, pointing at her.

She felt the magic tugging at her will, slowing her feet, but the fire that filled her burned through the spell, freeing her. She gripped the sword tight and flung herself into the void.

A scream wrenched from her lips as she fell, dropping through viscous layers of blackness that sealed around her like tar and pressed down on her, squeezing away her breath.

Lady, take my hand! The rough, insistent voice pierced the entrapping layers, and through eyes grown dim she saw the faint image of a gnarled hand reaching toward her. She fought the restraining blackness, her fingers lifting even as her strength faded. Weathered fingers grasped hers, pulling her upward. The sticky blackness fell away.

She drew in a few ragged breaths. She felt a breeze on her hot face and heard the splash of water around her. She opened her eyes to cold moonlight. She was back on the boat, lying in the niche behind Blackie's bench.

Blackie cleared his throat. "Woman, you've got a lot more explaining to do." His gaze dipped to her side.

She looked down. Gripped in her hand was the black sword.

CHAPTER 20

Tara dropped the sword and clambered onto Blackie's bench so fast the boat rocked.

"Haedis' balls, woman!" Blackie roared above a chorus of yells. "What are ya doing?"

She frisked herself wildly. "Spiders!"

"Spiders? Where?" Blackie looked around. "I don't see any spiders."

She ran her hands over her sleeves and pant legs, then clawed her fingers through her hair.

Blackie caught her arms in a tight grip. "There are no spiders. Now calm down."

She stared at him and realized he was right. Even though she could still feel the scrabble of dozens of legs, there were no spiders on her or on the boat. She took several deep breaths, stilling herself. "There were spiders, thousands of them. Thank the gods they stayed in the dungeon."

Blackie eased his grip. "What dungeon? What are you talking about? And where did you get that sword?" He touched her cheek with the back of his hand. "Are you all right? You feel hot."

"I'm fine — and no, I'm not delirious," she added, guessing what he was thinking. "I'm hot from... because I was running through the dungeon, trying to escape." She felt all eyes on her as she took a long drink, hoping the water would cool her burning insides. It didn't help much. Setting the water flask down, she picked up the black sword. The polished blade gleamed in the moonlight. She looked at Diamond Jack, sitting next to Brains on the aft bench. Gus lay wedged in the space in front of them, hands and feet bound. He was looking away from her and muttering Southland epithets. Whiskey and Whittler sat silently in the fore. "This is what I dug up. The key unlocked the box it was in." She studied the smooth blade. "I found it in Wyndover, buried beneath the ruins of my mother's house. Laraina said my mother died when I was born. I lost the sword. I can't remember how. I think I lost my memory at the same time."

Blackie pointed at the sword. "I want to know how that sword just appeared in your hand."

"The creature that tried to get into my head earlier — well, actually, it's not a creature anymore, it's a man — he had it in the dungeon. I stole it back from him when he was distracted by the wizard."

"Wizards? Creatures? Dungeons?" Brains narrowed his eyes at Blackie. "Did you know about any of this?"

"No... er, not much," Blackie amended. "Nothing that made any sense, anyway."

Brains eyed Tara again. "Perhaps you could explain it a bit more coherently?"

Stifling her irritation at his words, Tara slipped the black sword into her empty scabbard and gathered her thoughts. "There's an evil man with one eye, a magic-user, who's been reaching out to me with his mind, trying to force his way into my thoughts. He's trapped in a dungeon hidden somewhere in the Bog. I don't know who he is or how he got there, but he's trying to escape through me somehow. I've been fighting him off, but after I healed Whittler, he broke through my mental defenses and pulled me into his dungeon."

"But you never left the boat," Brains said.

Tara shook her head. "I didn't go there literally. My mind became trapped there, and it was as if I *was* there in reality."

"Hmmmm." Brains glanced at Jack, then at Whittler and Whiskey in the bow.

Jack shrugged. Whittler's expression mirrored Brains' — thoughtful, but undecided as to the truth of her words. Whiskey looked doubtful. Blackie was scowling.

"The first time I remember seeing the one-eyed man, he looked like a horribly deformed creature that might once have been human," Tara continued. "Now he looks like a man, only slightly deformed. I think he must have used the sword's energy to restore himself."

"What do you mean, 'the sword's energy?'" Blackie asked.

Brains sat forward intently. "Then he would have to be a Kamarian."

"What?" Blackie demanded.

"Why do you say that?" Tara asked, her stomach tightening.

"The black sword is the weapon of Kamarian royalty," Brains said, excitement growing in his eyes. "Only Kamarian royalty can command its power."

Blackie slammed his fist on the bench. "Stop talking around me, or I'll throw you both overboard!"

Tara glanced at Blackie. "I'm sorry." She looked back at Brains.

"Can you use it?" Brains asked.

"No." She didn't like lying to them, but the destructive power of the sword was best kept secret.

"What does the sword do?" Jack asked.

"It blasts things to smithereens," Brains said, "according to leg-end."

Jack whistled softly.

"It's a demon sword," Gus spat. "That wi — she's cursed us all!"

Blackie glared at Gus. "You shut up, or this time, by Haedis, you *will* go overboard."

Gus scowled darkly and looked away.

Blackie turned back to Tara. "So you're telling me that this evil whoever-he-is had that sword in his dungeon, and you got it away from him."

"Yes," Tara said. She kept a wary eye on Gus. "He'd taken it from me sometime in the past."

"How did you get it from there to here?"

"I don't know."

The smugglers glanced at each other again.

"I don't know what to think," Jack said.

"None of it's possible." Whiskey touched his healed legs. "But neither is this."

Whittler nodded.

"Didn't you say there was another wizard?" Brains asked Tara.

"Validar Melodian. He wants the sword, too. He appeared in the dungeon while I was there. He and the one-eyed man were fighting over a jewel Melodian was wearing around his neck. The one-eyed man said it was his."

"You saw Melodian?" Brains' eyes gleamed. "That would mean wizards really do still exist."

"Who is this one-eyed man?" asked Blackie.

Tara shrugged.

"If he can use the sword, he must be a member of the Kamarian Royal House," Brains said. "The legends say that the Kamarians were led by King Lazarial. He was the most powerful and wielded *Liuminerii*, the magic of Light. His younger brother, Ravnaul, was nearly as strong, but he wielded *Diurkruna*, the magic of Darkness or Death. They each had a black sword — the only two in existence. It's thought that a power struggle between the king and his brother might have caused the Cataclysm that destroyed the Kamarians. The black swords were also said to have been destroyed in the Cataclysm."

"I've heard the name Ravnaul," Tara said. "It was a place... somewhere." She delved into the morass of her memory. "Ravnaul... it was some kind of tower or something..." She sat up straight. "Yes, that's it. Ravnaul's Keep — a ruined watchtower at the edge of the Black Mountains. It's the only way into the mountains." She hesitated and looked at Blackie. "I need to go there."

"And do what?" Blackie asked with an apprehensive look.

"I don't know." Tara felt sweat dripping down her back. The coolness of the night had done little to relieve her overheated state. She wished she could take a dip in the river.

"Is this wizard, Melodian, a Kamarian, too?" Blackie asked.

"No," Brains said. "From what I've read, his powers are not innate. Wizards and witches are not magical beings like the Ancients."

"What was that jewel you said they were fighting over?" Jack asked.

"Was it a moonstone?" Brains added.

Tara considered. "It was similar in shape to the stones on the black key, but it was much bigger, and it wasn't gray, it was red. The one-eyed man called it a bloodstone."

"And you said he claimed it belonged to him," Brains mused. "If it was some sort of mutated moonstone, and if he did draw power from the sword, he would have to be Kamarian."

"But he can't be. Melodian said that —" Tara stopped, startled as the memory of a previous conversation with the wizard played through her mind. Her voice grew hushed. "I remember. He said I was Tara, daughter of Tamara, lost child of the Kamarians, and that I was the last of their race."

Blackie stared at her, his eyes uneasy.

"Was that your mother's name — Tamara?" Brains asked.

Tara nodded.

"What did she look like?"

"My sister said she looked just like me. Why?"

"Another witch," Gus muttered, an expression of loathing on his face.

"What did you say?" Blackie demanded.

"Nothing." Gus growled.

"You and your mother both fit the description of Kamarians," Brains said to Tara. "According to the legends, they had silver hair and eyes. You have some blonde in your hair and blue in your eyes, but that could be from your father or some other ancestor. What about the one-eyed man — did he have the silver coloring?"

Tara thought for a minute. "Yes, he did, and his eye color swirled like mine did."

Whittler slapped the bench to get their attention, then held out his healed hand.

"So you used Kamarian magic to heal Whittler and Whiskey?" Brains translated.

"I don't know." Tara looked at Blackie. "I remember healing you once, a long time ago."

"I don't remember that."

"It was when we first met in Wyndover. You were unconscious at the time. You didn't know."

Blackie made a noncommittal noise and looked away.

"Is this why the Butcher is chasing you?" Brains asked.

"No. I can't remember why he's following me, but I'm sure it has nothing to do with this."

Diamond Jack poked Brains, and they straightened the boat, which had begun to drift sideways. Jack looked back at the others. "What now?"

Tara answered. "I'd still like to ride through to Norellanen. Then I'll leave, and you can all go your own way. Hopefully by then, I'll have regained the rest of my memory."

"Will you be having any more of these little... episodes?" Brains asked.

"Not if I can help it," Tara said.

"Hey, where's all this fog coming from?" Whiskey shifted from one side of the bench to the other, staring at the water.

Tara looked down. All around the boat, curls of mist rose from the river's dark surface. The mist swiftly thickened and expanded, engulfing the boat in a white cloud. She cried out, the others yelling and cursing as the thick white fog closed in around each of them, separating them. She tried to reach Blackie, but found she couldn't move. The cloud pressed against her on all sides, soft but firm, like cool pillows.

She forced herself to relax; she felt no threat. "Blackie, can you hear me?" she called over Gus' terrified cries.

"Yes. Are you all right?"

"I'm fine. I'm not sensing any danger, so I don't think —" She broke off, suddenly feeling the boat rise out of the water and float in midair.

"Whoa! Damn me to the Abyss!" Blackie's muffled swearing was drowned out by Gus' screams and shouts from the others.

After a moment, the floating sensation eased. The fog dissipated.

Tara gazed around her, her eyes watering in the harsh, cold breeze. The boat sat on a wide, moonlit lake, surrounded by dense forest and snow-capped mountains.

"Where are we?" breathed Jack.

"Not where we're supposed to be," Blackie muttered. He glared at Gus. "Will you be quiet, man!"

Gus ceased yelling and scrunched as low as he could in the boat, eyes wild.

"I'm not complaining," Whiskey said. "At least we got away from those damned lizards."

"How do you know there isn't something worse in there?" Blackie gestured at the water.

"We've left the Butcher behind, too," Jack said.

Tara stiffened. What if she became trapped in the dungeon again? What if she was too far away for either Natiere or Jovan to help her escape? Jovan! She remembered hearing him groan right before their fragile connection had snapped. *Jovan...* Cautiously, she reached out to him. Silence greeted her.

"Look! Up there." Brains pointed toward the mountains.

High on a ridge stood a gray stone castle, its angular walls painted in moonlight and shadow. Many towers and turrets of varying heights rose into the night sky, the tallest of them lost in the clouds. Arched windows glowed with warm light in the castle proper and in one of the towers.

Brains looked around and exhaled sharply. "I don't believe it. Do you know where we are?"

"Of course we don't," Blackie snapped. "We're not walking libraries like you are."

"Well, just look around you." Brains waved his arm outward. "See how still the water is, and how perfectly everything is reflected on the surface, in spite of the wind? This has to be Mirror Lake." He pointed to the castle again. "Which means that must be Estiarii Faelle."

"What is Estiarii Faelle?" Tara asked. "And where is it?"

"It's another place of legend — the home of the sorceress, Valina Mellarian, twin sister to Validar Melodian," Brains said. "It's somewhere in the Lost Mountains, far to the north, well beyond the end of the Cyranel Mountain range."

"Melodian has a sister?" Tara studied the castle, her heart pounding as she realized how far they'd traveled in the space of a few moments.

"Yes, and the only way to reach this place is to be summoned by her."

"Why would she want us?" Jack asked.

"Not us." Brains nodded at Tara. "Her."

"You are quite right." The disembodied female voice swirled around them, echoing slightly. "Come."

Gus shrieked and buried his head beneath his bound arms.

The boat began to glide over the water without any visible means of propulsion.

Whiskey took a large swig from his bottle. "Who said that? I heard a voice, but I didn't see any mouths moving."

"Neither did I," Jack said as he and Brains banked their oars.

Tara held tight to the gunwale, wondering how much more trouble they were about to get into. If Valina Mellarian was anything like her brother...

The boat skimmed along the surface, leaving no wake as it sped toward the castle. The cold breeze soothed Tara's hot skin, and she felt her body temperature cooling at last. She looked over the side, her hair whipped back by the wind. The moonlit water was still, the mirror image of the stars undisturbed by the boat's passage. She sucked in a sharp breath. A silver glow surrounded her reflection, like the bright edge of a storm cloud backlit by the sun.

"Blackie, look over the side." Tara slid across the bench and dropped to her knees in the niche behind him.

"Why, what's wrong?" he asked, alarmed.

"Nothing. I want to see your reflection."

Cautiously, he leaned over the gunwale. His frowning face stared back in perfect detail. "I don't see anything strange."

"Look at mine." Tara moved forward. The bright glow framed her reflection in silver light. "What does it mean?"

Blackie sat back. "You're asking me?"

Brains scooted over beside Jack. "Let me see."

The boat tipped precariously as Brains, Jack, Whiskey, and Whittler hung over the gunwale to get a better look.

"Get back on your benches before ya keel us over, ya numbskulls," Blackie ordered.

They moved back to their seats.

"Your reflection didn't glow like that when we were on the Nournan," Brains said.

"Is this thing going to stop by itself?" Whiskey asked, reaching for an oar.

The white-peaked mountains loomed, their bases sunk deep into the lake. The boat rushed toward them without slowing.

Blackie swung toward the stern. "Man the oars!"

"No, wait. Look!" Tara pointed to a black oval that appeared on the mountain directly in front of them at water level. "I think it's an opening."

"That wasn't there a minute ago," Brains said, straining forward to get a better view. "And look, it's getting wider, like some kind of door opening up."

"It'd better be, or we'll all be swimming." Whiskey clutched his bottle. "And I got no desire to go swimming."

Whittler nodded vigorously in agreement.

The black opening grew larger as they neared, swallowing them as they swept through it into a narrow waterway beneath the mountain. Then the cave mouth sealed shut, and they were propelled into a shallow basin ringed by faintly glowing stalagmites that rose twice a man's height into dark emptiness. On one side, stone stairs rose from the water's edge to a low platform. The boat whooshed up to the stairs and stopped, rocking in its own wake.

The smugglers looked at each other, but nobody made any move to disembark.

"Well, I want to know what this is about." Shrugging off her apprehension, Tara climbed out of the boat and onto the stone platform.

Brains quickly followed. He ran a wet hand through his unruly blond curls. "I want to meet this sorceress."

"What if she turns you into a squirrel?" Jack asked, as he and the others trailed them up the stairs.

"Then you and I will have much in common," Brains tossed back.

Jack laughed nervously. "Thanks a lot."

"Blackie, can I borrow your cloak?" Tara asked. "I want to hide the sword."

Blackie swept off his cloak and handed it to her.

"What do we do with Gus?" Whiskey gestured toward the boat, where the big Southlander still cowered beneath his upraised arms.

Gus lowered his arms. "I will not go."

"Should we untie him?" Brains asked.

Before Blackie could answer, dense fog formed around them, encasing them as it had before. Tara felt the brief, stomach-lurching sensation of floating, then settled on solid ground. With one hand on the hilt of the long knife she'd stuck through her belt, she waited to see where they'd landed. The fog evaporated. They found themselves in an immense round room cluttered with mechanical devices, including half a dozen huge spyglasses on tripods aimed at shuttered openings in the high ceiling. The room was lit with oil lamps hung at intervals along the walls. Moonlight poured in through countless skylights. Shivering in the chilly air, Tara scanned the room, but saw no one.

Several large tables covered with open books, metal-ball-and-wire models of constellations, compasses, and other objects stood near the spyglasses. Drawings of star formations papered the walls, amid notes on seasonal changes and other celestial phenomena.

"What are those big metal triangular things on the wooden pedestals?" Jack whispered over Gus' whimpering. The big Southlander lay curled up on the floor by Blackie's feet.

"They're astronomical quadrants and sextants," said Brains. "They're used for measuring altitudes of stars and angular distances between them."

"Right again," said the same female voice they'd heard on the lake. "Welcome to Estiarii Faelle."

A tall, thin woman approached. Her gray-streaked auburn hair hung straight to her ankles. Her face had few wrinkles, yet her deep-set green eyes held the wisdom of several lifetimes. She was clothed in a simple dark green robe, belted at the waist, and soft green leather slippers covered her feet.

"Thank you," Tara said. "I don't mean to be rude, but who are you, and why did you bring us here?"

The woman smiled, and Tara immediately felt at ease. "I am Valina Mellarian. I wish to help you, so that you, in turn, may help me."

"I will not stay in the house of a witch!" Gus struggled to free himself from the ropes that bound him.

"Why is he bound?" Valina asked.

"That's our business," Blackie said.

"Is he a criminal?"

Blackie looked down at the still struggling Gus. "He's dangerous."

Valina stepped closer to Gus. "Where would you prefer to be?"

Gus twisted away from her. "Anywhere but here."

"As you wish." The sorceress spoke some unintelligible words. The fog enveloped Gus; his scream was cut off as he disappeared.

"Where is he? Where did you send him?" Blackie demanded.

"I sent him back to the boat." Valina smiled again. "You need not fear. He is quite safe. Soon you all will join him."

"*All* of us?" Blackie glanced at Tara.

"Yes. If you would come with me?" Valina led them down a flight of circular stone stairs to another round room lit by oil lamps and moonlight. Artistic depictions of celestial bodies had been painted in vibrant colors along the stone walls and between ten tall arched windows. Savory smells wafted around the group as they followed the sorceress to a large table laden with roasted fowl and potatoes, several varieties of vegetables and fruit, blocks of cheese, and loaves of warm bread. Goblets of golden liquid waited at every place setting.

"I thought you might be hungry." With a graceful wave of her arm, she ushered them to the table. "There is much I must tell you, so you may eat while I talk."

"Thank you." Tara sat and filled her plate, relaxing in what she sensed was a safe haven.

The others took their places at the table more slowly, unsure whether to trust the sorceress' bounty.

"Go ahead and eat," Tara said to Brains and Blackie on either side of her. Diamond Jack, Whittler, and Whiskey sat across from her. She turned to Valina. "The food is delicious."

Valina acknowledged the compliment and moved to stand behind the chair at the head of the table. "Your friend in the boat — would you like him fed?"

Blackie nodded, his mouth full of roast chicken.

Valina closed her eyes and mouthed a few words.

Tara watched her curiously. She sensed no malice in this woman, only a true desire to help. Beneath it lay a painful longing, as if the sorceress had lost something precious, and every day spent without it only deepened the ache.

"Now, the words I'm about to say are not just for Tara, but for all of you," Valina began. "She, and I, will need your help to accomplish a great deed — the restoration of the Kamarian people."

CHAPTER 21

Tara gasped, stunned by Valina's words.

"I knew it," Brains said, as Jack ceased chewing and Whiskey choked on his food. Whittler thumped him on the back. "I was right about the Kamarians."

Blackie remained silent, his face inscrutable.

"You know my name," Tara said.

"I know all of your names." Valina turned to Brains. "And yes, Sir Alstyn, you were correct, once again."

All eyes fastened on Brains.

"Sir Alstyn?" Jack raised his eyebrows.

"I no longer use that name," Brains said to Valina. "Please just call me Brains."

Valina nodded. "As you choose." She drew herself up as if preparing for an unpleasant task. "For thousands of years, this world of Alltyyr was home to four races of magical beings called *Aiykshaav'n*. Each derived its power from a different element — the Bahaariku from the sea, the Niramaani from fire, the Gaians from the earth, and the Kamarians from the sky. The Kamarians drew their power from the air itself and from celestial bodies, primarily the moon."

Beside Tara, Brains leaned forward in his seat, ignoring his food.

"Over the centuries," Valina said, "the *Aiykshaav'n's* powers grew until they rivaled those of the gods, but as long as the *Aiykshaav'n* didn't challenge the gods and remained pious, the deities were tolerant. The *Aiykshaav'n* mostly lived apart from elves and dwarves, and later, humans. Many wizards and sorceresses, myself included, sought out the *Aiykshaav'n*, hoping to learn some of the secrets of their power, but unfortunately, their magic is innate and cannot be learned. However, they did have vast knowledge of their particular elements, which a few had been willing to share."

"Do the other *Aiykshaav'n* races still exist?" Brains asked.

"I don't know," Valina answered. "They've not been seen for centuries. The Kamarians lived in the great Valley of Kamar, hidden somewhere within the Black Mountains of the East. The Black Mountains are impassable, accessible only through a single entrance guarded by a watchtower."

Tara swallowed her mouthful of bread. "Ravnaul's Keep."

Valina nodded. "About three hundred years ago, the Kamarians were ruled by King Lazarial. His younger brother, Ravnaul, was the Gatekeeper. For some unknown reason, the brothers hated each other. Lazarial was proud and haughty and treated his brother as he would a worm beneath his foot. Ravnaul was as cruel as he was resentful and undermined his brother's rule at every chance. They chose opposite forms of power, *Liuminerii* and *Diurkruna*, and each strove to outdo the other in all things."

Valina pushed her hair behind her ears. "When war broke out in the Eastern Frontier, some men from a nearby village approached the keep and begged Ravnaul for protection from soldiers and vicious bandits. Ravnaul agreed, but in return, demanded that the villagers bring him seasonal tributes and worship him as a god. Perhaps he thought that this would finally put him above his brother. The villagers complied. Each season, a few chosen men would bring the tribute to Ravnaul's Keep and sacrifice an animal in worship."

Across the table from Tara, Whittler cuffed Whiskey on the arm and pointed to his own mead goblet, which was empty.

Whiskey huffed. "Well, you weren't drinking it."

Whittler cuffed him again, then realized Valina Mellarian had stopped talking, and his face reddened. He ducked his head in apology and hid behind his hair. Whiskey fingered the empty goblets wistfully.

Valina smiled and whispered a few words. Faint mist swirled around both vessels as they magically refilled. Whiskey drained his in one gulp. Whittler moved his goblet as far away as he could from Whiskey's roving hand.

"As a rule," Valina went on, "all Kamarians, except the King and Gatekeeper, were forbidden contact with other races. Ravnaul's daughters, Kelista and Erana, chafed at their confinement in the Black Mountains and longed to see the rest of the world. When the men brought their tributes, the sisters would watch from a hidden place. One young man in particular caught Erana's eye. His name was Ezraed. When he brought the spring offering, she sneaked from the tower and followed him back to his village. He was as taken with her as she was with him, and they soon began meeting in secret.

"One night, right before the time of the summer tribute, Ravnaul caught Erana leaving the keep. She refused to say where she was going, but he guessed her to be meeting one of the men who brought the offering. He locked her in the tower and swore that when they came, he would kill all of them with one blast from his black sword."

Valina's fingers curled over the back of the chair. "On the night before the arrival of the tribute, Kelista managed to free Erana from the tower, and together they stole the black sword. Erana's plan was to run away with Ezraed and leave the Black Mountains far behind, but before she did, she sent a note to King Lazarial, telling him of Ravnaul's agreement with the villagers and of Ravnaul's threat to kill them, in hopes the king would save them. The note was discovered by King Lazarial's son and heir, Zaniel, who also harbored a desire to explore the world beyond his mountain prison, as he called it. He read the note and then, along with six like-minded youths, he escaped with Kelista, Erana, and Ezraed and disappeared into the Frontier."

"How do you know so much of this story?" Tara asked, after another swallow of mead.

"You will see very soon." Valina bowed her head for a moment before continuing.

"When King Lazarial read the note, he was incensed at Ravnaul for forcing the villagers to treat him as a god. Fearing retribution from the gods themselves, he went to confront his brother, only to find Ravnaul gone in search of his daughters. It was then he discovered that his son, Zaniel, was also missing. Erana had not said a word about Ezraed in her note, so King Lazarial assumed Erana and Zaniel were lovers and had run away together. This made him even more angry. He sent out his warriors to bring them back and to arrest Ravnaul for deserting his post.

"On the same night that Erana and the others escaped, I was hiding outside Ravnaul's Keep, and I witnessed their flight toward the village."

Jack dropped his fork. "But that would make you three hundred years old."

"Three hundred eighteen, to be exact." Valina smiled faintly. "I've always been fascinated by the stars. I wanted to learn more about the vastness of space and the universe, but Ravnaul would not teach me and repeatedly refused me entrance to the mountains. I was sure that if I could only reach the Kamarian city, I would find someone who would be willing to share knowledge of the sky. So I waited in secret for the tribute to arrive, hoping the offering and sacrificial ceremony would sufficiently distract Ravnaul and allow me to sneak into the keep.

"But when I saw the Kamarians escaping, it seemed that the gods were finally smiling on me. I followed them to the village, where they met Ezraed. Then I introduced myself. I said I would take them far from there if, in return, they taught me about the stars. They agreed, and I transported them here."

Her voice softened. "The next four months were the most wonderful of my life. We taught each other many things. Zaniel, especially, taught me much..." A faint flush rose in her cheeks, and her eyes darkened with sorrow. She cleared her throat. "We traveled everywhere, as far as my magic would reach. I didn't know it at the time, but as long as they didn't use their powers, they couldn't be traced."

Valina's knuckles whitened as she gripped the chair. "Then one autumn day, one of the girls tripped and fell down some stairs and broke her arm. Erana healed her. The next night, Ravnaul arrived on the back of a giant roc. His dark powers were so strong that he easily gained entrance to the castle. I couldn't stop him. He shouted an incantation, and with one swoop of his arm, seven of the Kamarians, including his daughter Kelista, vanished, leaving Zaniel, Erana, and Ezraed. Ravnaul then got a good look at Erana, realized she was with child, and went berserk. He attacked Zaniel and started choking him.

"At that moment, King Lazarial's warriors flew in on more giant rocs. Ravnaul threw Zaniel aside and attacked the warriors. Their battle destroyed half the castle. Ezraed was killed protecting Erana from one of their magical blasts. I, too, was hit by a blast and was nearly knocked unconscious. Under cover of the smoke, I used my remaining strength to transport Erana and the black sword out of the castle. In my weakened state, I couldn't send them far. Zaniel tried to come to my aid, but the warriors snatched him and flew off. Ravnaul, seeing Erana gone, went after the warriors. He must have thought they'd taken her. Days afterward, a frightening cataclysm wasted the Black Mountains, and the Kamarian people were gone."

"Were they destroyed?" Tara pushed away her half-empty plate, her appetite lost.

"No one knows. As soon as I recovered from Ravnaul's attack, I returned to the Black Mountains to find out what had happened. Ravnaul's Keep was a shattered ruin. I searched the mountains for weeks, but found no trace of the Kamarians. All I did find was a sound."

"A sound?" Tara asked.

"Yes. I heard the sound of a thundering cataract, yet I saw no water anywhere. I knew it had to be the Echoing Falls that flows from Sherre Lake, a fathomless body of water hidden deep in the mountains. Zaniel had told me about it, told me how he used to swim in it." Sadness etched Valina's face. "I never found it."

Tara thought hard. "Someone told me that story — recently, I think — about the waterfall no one can find. I can't remember who said it or what the circumstances were. Is this waterfall important?"

Valina nodded. "You cannot find the Valley of Kamar without first finding the waterfall, but I don't know how the two are connected."

"What happened to Erana?" Brains asked.

"I don't know. I tried to find her with my mirror, but I couldn't locate her. I thought she must have died before her baby was born, ending the Kamarian race." The sorceress turned to Tara. "But your appearance has given me hope. Every day for the past three hundred years I have begged the gods to forgive the Kamarians and let them return to this world."

Icy prickles shivered over Tara's skin. "How do you know they can? What if they're all dead?"

"I believe they are still alive — somewhere, in some form." Valina lifted a silver chain around her neck, pulling from beneath the collar of her robe a large oval pendant of gray stone.

"A moonstone," Brains whispered in awe.

Tara caught her breath. It looked just like the stones she'd seen around the necks of the corpses in the dream dungeon.

"This belonged to Zaniel." Valina caressed the smooth stone. "It is his lifestone. He gave it to me when he pledged his love, right before he was taken. If he were dead, it would be black, but as you can see, it is still gray, though it has no pulse or shimmer of light as it did when he was here. It appears to be dormant." She came around to Tara's side. "Would you touch it? Please?"

The sorceress' beseeching gaze tore at Tara's soul. Tara looked down at the stone cupped protectively in Valina's trembling hands. Hesitantly, Tara slid her fingers over the stone. The faintest of glimmers shone deep within the jewel; the solid gray color within began to swirl sluggishly like drifting smoke.

With a cry, Valina clasped the stone to her heart. "He is alive. I knew it. After all these many, many years, he is still alive." She caught Tara's shoulders, her eyes desperate. "You must save him. You are the only one who can."

Tara returned her gaze doubtfully. "How?"

Valina released her and paced the room. "I don't know, but the fact that you are here means it must be possible. Let me think."

Tara watched her, deliberately avoiding the eyes of Blackie and the others. She needed time to figure out how she felt about all this before worrying about what they were thinking.

"You must go to the Black Mountains." Valina returned from the far end of the room. "You will find Echoing Falls, where I could not. I know you will. Hopefully, from there, the answer will be made clear to you."

Tara held up her hand to stop the sorceress' pacing. "Before we embark on any wild quests, I have a few questions you might be able to answer."

"I will gladly answer anything I can," Valina said.

"About your brother," Tara began.

"Validar?" Valina looked surprised.

"Yes. I need to know how I can defeat him." Tara described the wizard's part in her last dream.

"You have the black sword?" Valina asked in a hushed voice. "May I see it?"

Tara pulled back her cloak and drew the weapon.

The sorceress gasped. "Ravnaul's sword." Her hand flew to her mouth. "You said the one-eyed man in your dream used the power of the sword to heal himself, and that he claimed ownership of the jewel my brother wore. That can only mean — oh gods!" She caught the back of the chair again to steady herself. "The one-eyed man must be Ravnaul himself!"

Brains half rose from his seat, reaching toward her. "Are you all right?"

Valina straightened. "Yes, yes, I'm fine," she said as Brains sat back down. "I just wasn't prepared for such a shock. I had assumed Ravnaul was dead. I shudder to think such evil still lives." She faced

Tara. "You must not give in to him. He must not escape." She began pacing again. "The evil in him will have grown like it has in my brother. My brother and I have not spoken since he chose to follow the dark path of *Diurkruna* more than a century ago. How he came to have Ravnaul's bloodstone, I know not."

"Why is it called a 'bloodstone'?" Tara asked.

"When you pledge to follow *Diurkruna*, you must make your pledge in blood."

"So how can I defeat him?"

"Use the power inside you. You are Erana's descendant — you *must* be. You look so much like her. There's no other explanation. You must have inherited something of her power, and of Ravnaul's, since she was his daughter."

Tara sat silently for a few moments, overwhelmed by the sorceress' revelations. She — Kamarian royalty? The idea was too mind-boggling to contemplate. "I can heal others, and I can sense danger, nothing more." But she knew the moment she said the words, that they weren't entirely true. She *had* wielded the black sword. She could command its power.

Valina halted before her. "I sense much more than that in you. You have great strength. You must discover the power within yourself, for that is the only way you can defeat my brother and Ravnaul and bring back the Kamarians."

"But what about you?" Tara argued. "Aren't you as strong they are?"

"I am no match for Ravnaul. As to my brother, we used to hold equal power, but if Validar has somehow tapped into the power of Ravnaul's bloodstone... I don't know. I fear he is lost," she said sadly, "his goodness eaten away by the dark magic."

Brains inclined his head toward the sorceress. "I mean no offense, but even knowing what little I do about the Kamarian legends, I would find this a hard story to swallow, if I had not witnessed Tara healing Whiskey and Whittler, and then seen that sword appear out of nowhere."

Tara stole a glance around the table. Jack and Whittler were nodding. Whiskey was eyeing Blackie's half-full goblet, and Blackie had assumed a poker face.

"The story is true," Valina said. "I swear it on everything I hold sacred."

"I don't know what to think," Tara said slowly. "I know I have to stop the one-eyed man from attacking my mind. If I don't, I'll be dead. If what you say is true, then it looks like I have no choice but to go to the Black Mountains."

"I can send you there immediately." The sorceress whispered a few words. Thick, white fog rose up from the floor, muffling the smugglers' protests. Whiskey snatched Blackie's goblet just as the fog enclosed him and the others.

"No, wait! I have one more question." Tara leaped aside before the fog could seal around her.

The smugglers vanished.

"Where did you send them?" Tara asked anxiously.

"Only to the boat," Valina said.

"Oh, good. I doubt they want to go with me."

Valina looked worried. "But you'll need them. You can't do this alone."

"Won't you help?"

"Yes, of course. I'll do all I can, but I must do so from here. As I said, I am three hundred and eighteen years old. The magic of this castle keeps me young. If I leave here for very long, I will begin to show my true age and soon die."

"Oh, I see," Tara said sympathetically. "I'm sorry."

Valina gave her a wistful smile. "It's not so bad. What did you wish to ask me?"

"You mentioned something about a mirror you used to try to locate Erana."

"Yes. It is a scrimoire, a scrying mirror."

"There are two men who have been helping me fight against the one-eyed man. If not for them, I wouldn't have survived this long. Can you find them, to see that they're all right, and then send them to the same place you send me, or well, not to the exact spot, but close by?"

"I can try. Come with me." Valina hurried toward the circular stairs.

Tara followed. She doubted Blackie and the other smugglers would be pleased with her request, but she had to know what had happened to Jovan. And as frightening as Natiere was, she needed him near in case she got trapped in the dream dungeon again.

The sorceress led the way up the stairs and back to the cluttered room in which Tara had arrived. On reaching the far side of the chamber, she stopped before a thin, six-foot-tall, unevenly round object covered with a dark velvet cloth.

"I'll need to know what these men look like," Valina said as she pulled the cloth away and laid it over a neighboring spyglass.

Tara stared in surprise. The mirror looked like nothing she'd ever seen before. The irregularly shaped glass sat in a silver framework etched with the figures of trees and mountains, and it reflected not the sorceress or the objects in the room, but a sky full of stars. Tara suddenly realized that the mirror was a miniature of Mirror Lake.

"Take my hands." Valina caught Tara's hands and held them against the sides of her own head. "Picture one of them in your mind."

Jovan's face, smiling at her, filled Tara's thoughts. "His name is Jovan Trevillion."

"Now the other one."

With an effort, Tara shifted her thoughts to the Wolfmaster, envisioning him on the dock in Cierra when he'd said she owed him a duel. "He is Rylan Natiere. He travels with a pack of wolves."

The sorceress let go of Tara's hands. "Where are they?"

"I don't know for certain, but they were both following me, so I would guess somewhere along the west bank of the Nournan River in the Bog."

"All right. I'll look for Jovan Trevillion first." Valina faced the mirror and spoke the enchantment. The stars in the glass began to shift, then the mirror clouded, obscuring the reflection of the night sky. A perplexed frown crossed Valina's face. "That's strange." She repeated the magical words, with the same result. "I don't understand. That's never happened before."

The sorceress stood on her tiptoes and looked out through the opening where the spyglass perched, aimed at the lake. Tara did the same. Far below, the surface of the lake reflected a cloudy sky, instead of the clear, starry darkness above.

"How strange," Valina murmured. She turned back to the mirror. "I'll try Rylan Natiere." She spoke the words again. The star-filled sky reappeared in the mirror. The stars shifted, then blurred to reveal an image of Natiere running swiftly along the bank of the Nournan, accompanied by his wolves.

"Is that him?" Valina asked.

Tara nodded. She went back to the spyglass and peered out. The lake reflected the star positions she'd seen in the mirror.

The sorceress looked at the Wolfmaster, then at Tara. "Are you sure you want him near you?"

"Yes, but not too close."

"The other man — Trevillion. Where was he in relation to Natiere?"

Tara stepped back to the mirror. "Farther north along the river, I think, but again, I don't know for sure." Tara frowned as she watched Natiere progressing along the river bank. There was something odd about the scene, but she couldn't figure out what bothered her.

Valina tried once more to locate Trevillion, but found only obscurity. "Something is blocking my mirror. I don't know how."

"How did you find me?" Tara asked. "You didn't know what I looked like."

Valina smiled. "I found you by accident." She put her hand on the spyglass next to her. "I was using this spyglass, and a gust of wind came though the opening and blew the cloth off the mirror. As I picked up the cloth, I remembered with sadness the last time I'd used the mirror — centuries ago, when I had tried unsuccessfully to locate Erana. Her face was in my mind. I looked at the mirror as I went to cover it back up, the stars shifted, and your image appeared. I was so shocked, I think I fainted. I woke on the floor, and after finding you again in the mirror, I brought you here."

"When you searched for Erana all that time ago, did the mirror cloud over like it did when you looked for Jovan?"

"No. The mirror stayed clear. The stars in it didn't move. All I could think of was that Erana had either died or had somehow changed her looks so the mirror didn't recognize her. Perhaps she thought Ravnaul might use the mirror to find her."

Valina spoke to the mirror, and Natiere appeared once again in the glass.

Tara looked more closely at the image, studying Natiere's movement along the west side of the river. She froze, realizing what was wrong with the scene. Natiere was running north. He'd been following her southward, but for some reason had changed direction. Could he know — could he have somehow sensed that she'd been transported to the far north? With the strange mental connection they shared, she didn't doubt that it was possible.

What frightened her was the thought of his running into Jovan. Jovan hadn't answered when she'd tried to reach him. She sensed he was still alive, but if he'd been hurt when their mental link snapped... Her gut instinct told her that Natiere would kill Trevillion if he found him.

Valina touched her arm. "My dear, are you all right?"

Tara started. "What? Yes... no — I'm worried about Jovan. Natiere is now heading north. He and Jovan are enemies, and if Natiere finds him, I'm afraid he'll kill him."

"Jovan means much to you," the sorceress said with a knowing smile.

Tara blushed. "Well, I..."

Valina patted her on the shoulder. "Never mind. You don't need to explain. I will find him and send him to you."

"No," Tara said quickly. "Not *to* me, just near me," she added at the sorceress' surprised look. Until she discovered why Trevillion shivered her danger sense, she wanted a little distance between them. One touch or one look from his dark eyes, and she knew she'd be lost.

"As you wish," Valina said. "But if Natiere is that dangerous, are you truly certain you want him near you?"

Tara took a deep breath and nodded. "I need him. I have no choice. And please send his wolves with him."

"Very well." Valina stepped back. "I will send you to your friends, before they try to storm my castle in search of you. If you need me, concentrate on my name, and I will hear you. Good luck, and may the gods bless and watch over you!"

"Thank you!" Tara called as the fog enclosed her and floated her away.

CHAPTER 22

When the fog melted, Tara found herself on the low platform in the cave. Blackie and the other smugglers, including an unbound Gus, sat in the boat looking at her. Judging from their expressions, she'd interrupted a heated discussion.

Blackie looked relieved. "I thought we were going to have to come after you. What happened?"

Tara smiled, warmed by his concern. She wondered which side the others had been on — for or against rescuing her. "I wanted to ask Valina about something she said." She took Blackie's hand and stepped into the boat, noticing several stuffed sacks wedged in between the oar banks and the kegs of brandy. "What are those?"

"Supplies," Brains said. "The Lady was very generous."

"Couldn't she have waited a few days before shipping us off to whatever infernal place we're supposed to be going?" Whiskey grumbled.

"The Black Mountains," said Brains.

"I will *not* go there!" Gus stated flatly. "The Black Mountains are cursed."

Brains rolled his eyes. "You've already said that a dozen times."

"A long snooze would have been nice," Whiskey muttered. "And some more of that mead. Hey!" Whiskey's eyes brightened. "If we're not going to the Gypsy Crossroads to sell the brandy, we can drink it instead."

"Nobody touches those kegs!" Blackie said.

"Not to worry, Whiskey." Diamond Jack pulled a tall, slender bottle out of a sack. "She gave us ten bottles of —"

"Gimme that!"

Tara slid out of the way as Whiskey shot by her and snatched the bottle of golden liquid from Jack's hand. She had never seen anyone move from stern to bow so fast.

Gus spat Southland epithets as Whiskey clambered across his seat.

"Whiskey, stow it!" Blackie ordered.

White fog flowed up out of the water and enveloped the boat. Tara heard muffled cries from Gus as the firm softness pressed against them and held them in place. The boat rose quickly and seemed to hover in the air.

Icy prickles of warning stung Tara's skin. "Blackie, something's wrong."

"What —" A chorus of yells drowned out Blackie's voice as the boat rocked sideways, then gave a shuddering jerk and went still. The fog thinned into tatters of mist that faded in the predawn light.

Jack spoke first. "I don't see any mountains."

Tara looked up at the tall trees that ringed the small woodland clearing in which they'd landed. The boat lay in the middle of the clearing, jammed up against some rocks. "This place looks familiar."

"It should," Blackie said. "We've camped here more times than I can count."

"Why did we end up here?" Brains asked.

"Who cares?" Whiskey said. "Better here than there."

Whittler nodded.

"Where are we?" Tara asked impatiently.

Brains rose and stepped out of the boat. "About a mile from Gypsy Crossroads."

Tara stared at him. "Gypsy Crossroads? But..." She suddenly remembered sitting around a campfire in this very spot with Laraina and Blackie and his former gang of smugglers. They'd been cooking pheasants caught from the forest and celebrating... something. "The pheasants were good," she said, half to herself.

"Pheasants?" Blackie said.

"I remember eating pheasants here with my sister and you and the old crew. We were celebrating, but I can't think why."

"We were celebrating another successful brandy run." Blackie gave her a wicked grin. "Which is exactly what we'll be doing tomorrow at this time."

"What do you mean?" Tara asked.

Blackie waved his arms at the kegs on either side of him. "I told you I had a buyer who would pay royally for this brandy. It's an opportunity I can't pass up."

"Sounds good to me," said Jack.

"I could use a good party," Whiskey said as he, Jack, and Whittler climbed out of the boat and followed Brains toward the woods. Whiskey broke into a run. "Man, I got to go."

"That's what you get for drinking so much mead," Jack called after him.

"I want my share of the money," Gus said. "Then we part ways."

"Fine." Blackie rubbed his hands together as if anticipating a good time.

Gus leaped from the boat and strode away, leaving them alone.

Tara looked at Blackie uncertainly. She had the distinct feeling there was more wrong here than just their landing in the wrong place. "Blackie, I don't think this is a good idea."

"Why not?" He rose and stretched.

"I can sense disaster approaching."

Blackie stepped up on the gunwale and jumped to the ground. "Woman, the disaster you feel has nothing to do with the brandy. It has everything to do with that sword." He pointed toward the scabbard hanging at her side. "I have to agree with Gus — that thing is cursed. Everything about the Kamar-whatever-they're-called is cursed, if you believe the witch's story."

Tara narrowed her eyes. "She is a sorceress, and they're called Kamarians, and I may be one of them. So you're saying that I'm cursed, as well?"

"Well, aren't you?" Blackie came around to her side of the boat. "You're having nightmares about evil wizards trying to kill you, you're carrying a sword that supposedly belonged to some ancient magical madman who destroyed an entire race of people, and if that weren't enough, you're being chased by the Butcher. If that's not cursed, I don't know what is."

Tara looked at him wordlessly. He had a point. "Why don't you believe her?" she asked finally.

Blackie glanced away. "I don't know whether I believe her or not. But if what she said was true, you'd be able to use the sword, and you said you can't, so you can't be who she thinks you are. Traipsing off into the Black Mountains would be a waste of everybody's time, and it would be dangerous, too. I'm glad we landed here." He patted a keg of brandy. "We can make a small fortune off this stuff." He nodded toward the woods where the others had disappeared. "I'm not going to deny them their share of the spoils.

They deserve it after all they've been through. This was supposed to be just another brandy run."

"Blackie, I lied. I can use the sword. And it does exactly what Brains said it did."

"Then why did you say —"

"Because I didn't want them to know."

Blackie turned away, cursing. They saw Brains and Jack and the others leaving the woods and coming toward them. Blackie jerked his head toward the forest. "Go do your business. We'll talk about this tomorrow, *after* we've sold the brandy." He headed across the clearing.

With a bad feeling curdling her stomach, Tara left the boat and hurried toward the trees. Why had they landed here instead of the Black Mountains? She concentrated hard. *Valina!*

Yes, Tara, I hear you. The dulcet voice of the sorceress crystallized in her mind. *Is something wrong?*

We were transported to the Gypsy Crossroads, not the Black Mountains.

Surprise, then worry, colored the sorceress' thoughts. *I don't understand how that happened. I will try to discover who or what is interfering with my magic as soon as I retrieve the two men you asked me to find. I will send them to you there and hope they arrive as planned. Let me know if you need help.* Valina's voice faded like a sigh on the night wind.

Snippets of conversations oozed from the depths of Tara's mind. She recognized Jovan Trevillion's voice.

Something interfered with our connection and prevented me from entering your dream until it was almost too late.

The voice you heard... the Being... powerful enough to block me out of your mind during your dreams. It holds all the answers but refuses to share them.

The stream of words dwindled to silence, leaving Tara with an uneasy chill. What was this Being? What answers did it hold, and to what questions? Could this Being be interfering with Valina's magic? Just how powerful was it?

Tara stomped into the woods. Great. Just what she needed. Another enemy.

*****

Captain Natiere closed his eyes and reached outward with his mind. Lady Tara was back. He had been so close, then she'd vanished. Somehow, she'd been spirited away to the far north. He'd been able to sense her presence only on the barest fringes of his mind. For two hours he'd jogged along the narrow bank of the Nournan, retracing his steps, until her presence had suddenly become full and strong in his mind again. She was now southeast of him.

A yip from one of his wolves snapped him back into himself. He turned sharply, black eyes searching the predawn gray. His wolf pack had gathered some ten yards upriver and was milling around a large, dark shape that lay near the river's edge. He covered the distance in ten long strides. The wolves moved aside as he approached, revealing the body of a man sprawled face down in the grass. Natiere knelt, his lip curling as he rolled the man onto his back. He'd known who it was before he'd seen the man's face. Jovan Trevillion. Dark emotions chased through Natiere's mind as he searched for a pulse. He cursed to himself as he felt the beat of lifeblood beneath his fingertips. A quick glance showed no obvious injuries.

Natiere laughed. "I can change that." He drew his knife, black thoughts urging him to action. He would rid himself of his rival, the man who had everything he did not — a handsome face, an unblighted soul, and the Lady Tara's heart. Natiere raised the knife high. One stab would be enough to end Trevillion's life.

The memory of the cool touch of Tara's mind in his stayed Natiere's hand. The rush of her calm strength swept over him again, and he saw her strange eyes full of compassion. His hand slowly lowered to his side. If she discovered he'd killed Trevillion, she would hate him forever. Never again would she willingly enter his mind, or allow him to enter hers, not even to save her life. His reason to live would be gone. He jammed his knife into its sheath. Why couldn't Trevillion have fallen into the river?

Natiere glanced around. There had to be a way to dispose of Trevillion that would leave him blameless. Natiere considered shoving him into the water for the karanaks, but quickly abandoned the idea. If he had any hand in Trevillion's demise, he knew Tara would sense it.

Kelya shouldered against him, whining low in her throat as she tugged his cloak with her teeth. He saw that the other wolves had moved close. They growled and whined, ears flicking back and forth, their eyes never leaving the line of black trees.

A wolfen shadow eased out of the trees, emerging from the Bog's silent depths, ears flat, teeth bared. Three more followed, their golden eyes locked on Natiere and his wolves.

Natiere rose and slowly backed away.

The leader snarled, treading closer. Kelya crouched in front of the Wolfmaster and growled, baring her teeth.

"No, Kelya," Natiere said softly. He ran his hand over the bristling hair on her back. "This is perfect." He raised his voice and pointed at Trevillion. "Your meal is there, my Brothers and Sisters. Feast well."

The Bog wolf's ears pricked forward at Natiere's words. Ten feet away, the massive beast stopped and studied him. The other three moved up beside their leader, sniffing the air.

"We are sorry for trespassing on your territory, but we had no choice. Thank you for your tolerance. We will leave now." With a gesture, Natiere sent his wolf pack trotting southward along the river bank. He followed, keeping one eye on the Bog wolves. The huge beasts turned away and loped toward Trevillion.

Thick white fog rose from the ground, surrounding Natiere and his wolves, who yelped as they were swallowed by the cloud.

"What —?" The fog closed over his head and held him motionless. He sensed a strong magic, the likes of which he hadn't felt since his days with the Gypsies. He'd been a boy then, broken and traumatized. Wolfgren, the Gypsy warlock who'd saved his life, had possessed such power.

Natiere felt himself rising into the air; he floated for a moment, then settled on solid ground. The fog dissolved, releasing him. His wolves pressed against his legs and nosed his hands. He stroked their heads, murmuring soothing words as he took in his surroundings. A wide, dark lake stretched out before him, bounded by ancient evergreens and even older mountains. A cold wind buffeted him, but the surface of the lake remained still, reflecting the pale sky and fading stars with mirror-like perfection.

"It can't be," he whispered. His eyes found the massive stone castle rising high out of the mountains. "Estiarii Faelle is a myth." He stepped to the edge of the lake to get a better view of the castle. His wolves prowled the water's edge.

"It is quite real," said a feminine voice.

Natiere spun about, but saw no one. "Who are you?"

"I am Valina Mellarian of Estiarii Faelle." The voice seemed to emanate from the water.

Natiere looked down and stiffened, his eyes drawn to the reflections of eight wolves, six gray and two black. He glanced at the seven wolves beside him, then looked back at the water, seeing again the mirror images of eight wolves, his own face strangely absent.

"Ah, you must have magic in your soul." Surprise shifted the tone of Valina Mellarian's voice. "The mirror shows your true self."

"What do you mean?" Natiere asked.

"Look closer, and you will see."

Natiere knelt and studied the reflections of the two black wolves. They looked very similar, except that one's eyes were yellow, the other's black as a raven's wing. A long, ragged scar marred the face of the wolf with the black eyes. Natiere straightened in shock. "Are you saying I am a wolf?"

"In your soul, yes, or it would not be so reflected." The sorceress' voice grew cooler. "But that is not important now. Tara Triannon requested that I send both you and Jovan Trevillion to her location. She said she needed the two of you to help her survive her nightmares. In spite of your animosity toward each other, I hope, for Tara's sake, that you and Jovan refrain from harming each other. If this proves too difficult for either of you, know that I will intervene."

Natiere's eyes narrowed. "And what is the Lady Tara to you?"

"She has a vital task to perform, a race of people to save. She is the only one who can restore the Kamarians to their place in this land."

Natiere looked at the castle. "Show yourself. I grow weary of speaking to the lake."

An image coalesced just beneath the surface of the water — the reflection of a tall, thin woman dressed in green with gray-streaked auburn hair that draped to her ankles. The image shimmered next to the reflection of the scarred wolf.

Natiere turned quickly, but the space beside him was empty. "Where are you?"

The watery arms of the reflection spread wide. "I am here."

"Are you afraid to show yourself in person?"

The sorceress' voice grew several degrees colder. "I am stronger than you think, and this reflection is the most that you will get."

"You are not Kamarian. You don't have their coloring. Why is it so important to you that they be brought back?"

"My reasons are my business. It is Tara's destiny to follow this path — to either restore the Kamarian people or succumb to the evil that attacks her mind. That evil will destroy mankind, as it did the Kamarians. You must help her —"

"Don't tell me what I must do. My interest in the Lady Tara has nothing to do with Kamarians or magic-users, evil or otherwise."

"Your refusal to help will condemn her."

"I will do as I choose," Natiere snarled, "and as for Trevillion, if he gets in my way, I will remove him."

"As you tried to do with the Bog wolves? That I cannot allow."

So she had rescued Trevillion, curse her. Natiere gathered his inner calm. Arguing was pointless. He needed to end this conversation and get back to the southeast. The sorceress sought to use Tara for her own ends. He was certain of it, and that he would not allow. Once he found Tara, her fate would be in his hands, and his alone. "Do not interfere in my pursuit of the Lady Tara. To quote a reclusive sorceress, 'I am stronger than you think,' and I don't take kindly to anyone meddling in my affairs."

The sorceress' watery eyes blazed. "How dare you threaten me! Your powers are nothing compared to mine."

"Don't be so sure. But as it stands, I want Lady Tara alive and will do whatever is necessary to keep her so — for the time being. I will not say the same for Trevillion. If he wishes to live, he will stay away from her and from me."

"That's not good enough."

"It is the most you will get. Now send me and my wolves back, for I am the only one who can keep her alive if the evil strikes at her mind."

Valina Mellarian's reflection regarded him coldly. "I will return you, but only because Tara specifically requested it. Heed my words: I have discovered many nasty places in my travels. If you threaten Tara or Jovan, you will be discovering them, too."

The reflection vanished. The lake mirrored the rose and lavender of dawn's light. Wisps of fog curled up from the ground, unaffected by the wind as they swallowed Natiere and his wolves. He spoke calming words, reassuring his companions that they would be on solid ground again soon.

As the cloud bore them skyward, Natiere had a sudden anguished thought that Valina Mellarian might scatter his wolves to the corners of the world to repay his impertinence. Angering a powerful sorceress was not the most prudent course of action, he knew, but her condescension had provoked him. She had shown him a false reflection of himself to confuse him, and then had scolded him as if he were an errant school boy. Well, he would find the Lady Tara and, one way or another, take her away from the others. And if Valina Mellarian interfered, she would discover the true strength of his magic.

Natiere's feet touched the ground, and the fog freed him. Seven wolves rushed up to him, barking happily. Relief stole through him as he scratched their ears and stroked their soft fur. "Where are we this time?" He glanced around in the pale morning light. He recognized the Trader's Trail as it wound through the dense forest of Shallin Wood. He was a day's journey from Gypsy Crossroads. Tara was at the Crossroads. He could feel it.

He called to his wolves and started down the trail. Anticipation lengthened his stride. "We'll have her by nightfall. Come, let us run!"

*****

Jovan...

The unfamiliar voice echoed softly in his mind, the tone muffled as though someone called to him through a barrier of thick blankets.

Jovan Trevillion... you must wake...

It was a woman's voice, urging him out of his stupor. Tentatively, he probed the edges of the mental cocoon into which he'd sealed himself.

Tara needs you...

Tara... yes... he must get to her. Where was she? He emerged from his inner sanctuary and braced himself for another onslaught of pain. None came.

Yes... wake...

Cautiously, he sat up. He looked around in surprise. Tall evergreens surrounded him, the air heavy with mist and the scent of pine and hemlock. What forest was this? And how had he gotten here? Last he knew, he'd been on the bank of the Nournan River, heading south through the Bog.

Come... The voice tugged urgently at his mind.

He rose, eyes searching for the source of the summons. Through the trees, off to his right, a mirror-like body of water reflected the first pale rays of the sun. The voice seemed to be pulling him in that direction.

Fingering the hilt of his sword, he wended through massive trunks to the water's edge. A cold wind whipped his hair back from his face as he stared in disbelief at the glass-smooth lake, the looming, snow-topped mountains, the high-walled castle built into the rock. Estiarii Faelle — could it be that the legend was real?

A figure appeared beneath the surface of the lake — a tall, thin woman in green, with long, auburn hair. Startled, he took a step forward to pull her out of the water, then realized it was only a reflection. But a reflection of whom? No one stood near him.

Then his own reflection caught his eye.

"What in blazes...?" A deep blue glow, tinged with silver, rimmed his watery shape.

The image of the green-robed woman gasped. "What are you?"

Jovan's eyes flicked to the woman's reflection, and he wondered how a form without substance could speak. "What do you mean?" he asked.

"Your reflection — it has the color of the gods around it, except for the silver. But how could you have silver? You're not Kamarian."

"No, I'm not. Who are you?"

"I am Valina Mellarian of Estiarii Faelle. You are Jovan Trevillion, are you not?"

Jovan's eyes narrowed. Valina Mellarian, legendary sorceress and mistress of Estiarii Faelle. The last thing he needed was another magic-user to complicate the already tangled mess he was in. "I am Trevillion. Why did you bring me here?"

"Tara Triannon asked that I find you and send you to her, but I wanted to speak with you first."

"You've seen Tara? Is she all right?" He tried to keep his voice neutral to hide the depth of his anxiety.

"Yes, and she is fine."

She'd escaped the dungeon. Intense relief surged through him, and for a moment, he couldn't speak. "Has her memory returned?"

"I don't know." The sorceress sounded surprised. "I didn't realize she had lost it. She said that you and Rylan Natiere were mutual enemies. When I found you, Natiere was about to kill you, or rather let the Bog wolves do the deed for him. I saved your life."

Jovan gritted his teeth. If what the sorceress said was true, he was in her debt. Damn Natiere. The next time they met, it would be he who did the killing. "Then I must thank you."

"You may thank me by not harming Natiere if your paths should cross."

"I will make no such promise."

"Tara said she needed both of you to help her survive. If you care about her, you will do as I ask."

"Don't patronize me. You have no idea of my feelings for Tara. She is my lifeblood, and I will save her without Natiere's 'help.'"

"And if you can't?"

"I will."

The sorceress threw her hands upward. "You are every bit as mule-headed as he was."

Jovan tensed. "Natiere was here?"

"Yes, briefly. I sent him to Tara, as she requested."

"Then send me there. Quickly."

"I thought you might want food and rest —"

"No. Send me now."

The sorceress crossed her arms over her chest. "Not until I know why you have blue around your reflection."

"I don't know why. It's not important. I need to get to Tara as quickly as possible."

"It *is* important. Only those with inborn magic — magic in their souls — have a glow. Three hundred years ago, I begged the gods to restore the Kamarian people, after they'd been destroyed in the Cataclysm. The great god Azakai, ruler of all the gods, appeared to me as a shimmering figure in the clouds. His reflection was blue-rimmed, like yours. The highest power — how do you have it?"

"I said I don't know."

"Well, think. Have you ever had any contact with the gods?"

"No."

"With magic of any kind?"

The word "no" was on the tip of Jovan's tongue, but he did not speak it. He had no intention of discussing his relationship with Tara, but something else had come to mind — Rinpool. Perhaps Valina Mellarian could give him some answers.

"I was wounded many years ago by a poisoned blade. The waters of Rinpool healed me. Since then, my life has been controlled by an invisible Being that communicates mentally and forces me to do its bidding. I believe the Being is powerful enough to be a god."

The sorceress' brows furrowed in thought. "That's an excellent possibility. There is an old legend that says when one of the gods commits an abominable transgression, the god is banished by Azakai from their world to this world and forced to do penance for as long as the great ruler sees fit. Rinpool is a place of immeasurable power, and it's even more ancient than the *Aiykshaav'n*. It could easily be a place of exile."

"Who are the *Aiykshaav'n*?"

"Ancient magical beings — the Kamarians are *Aiykshaav'n*. When the figure of Azakai appeared to me, he said the Kamarians must serve their punishment before there could be any thought of redemption. He did not say that there was no chance of their being redeemed, which is why I've beseeched the gods every day for their return, hoping... always hoping. Perhaps now they are finally being forgiven. Perhaps this Being that plagues you is also getting its chance for redemption, by shepherding Tara on her journey to restore the Kamarians. She must defeat Ravnaul and fulfill her destiny."

"Ravnaul?"

"Yes. The Kamarian King Lazarial's brother. He is the evil one trapped in the dungeon, trying to escape through Tara's mind. If she can defeat him, the Kamarians will be saved. I'm sure of it!"

"And how can she do that?"

"I don't know. I tried to send her to the Black Mountains to find the Kamarian city, but something interfered with my magic, and she ended up at the Gypsy Crossroads. Perhaps it is your Being that is interfering. But why?"

"I don't know why, but it's very likely. The Being wanted me to take Tara to Rinpool, and I refused. Since then, it has separated us and blocked me from helping her. Gypsy Crossroads isn't far from Dharakwood."

The sorceress' reflection nodded. "Yes, Dharakwood — the magical forest of thorns that surrounds Rinpool. Why did you refuse to take her there?"

"I did not want her to suffer my fate."

The sorceress spread her arms wide. "But if restoring the Kamarians redeems this Being and frees it from exile, wouldn't you then be free of it, too?"

Jovan felt his tension rising, tying knots in his gut. "I don't trust the Being. I think it wants to control Tara's power, to use her in some way. I won't let that happen."

"Why would it do that? Why would it need to?"

"I don't know — maybe it wants revenge for being exiled. When Tara healed me, her magic blended with the magic from Rinpool to form a new, more powerful magic. Magic that was strong enough to chip a hole through the barrier the Being placed between Tara and me. But I am only the vessel for this magic; it's not mine, and I can barely wield it. If Tara herself were to drink the waters of Rinpool, the resulting power might defeat even the gods. And the Being would control it, and Tara. Who knows what it would make her do."

The sorceress looked worried. "I suppose that might be possible. At the height of their powers, the Kamarians rivaled the gods, and King Lazarial and Ravnaul were the strongest. And you cannot use this new power yourself?"

"Whenever I do try to use the power to help Tara, the Being severs our connection and inflicts mental torture on me, which is why I was unconscious when you found me." Jovan stopped, suddenly wondering why the Being was allowing him to discuss all this with Valina. If his theory, wild as it seemed, about the Being seeking revenge was correct, why wouldn't the Being want it kept secret?

The scornful laugh of the Being filled his mind. *You puny humans have no idea of your insignificance. It matters not what you know, as you, too, will soon be locked away...* The ancient voice faded to a whisper and blew away in the wind, leaving Jovan with a foreboding that chilled him to the core.

"...the combining of Tara's healing power with the magic of Rinpool in you would explain the silver in your reflection," the sorceress was saying. "If the Being really is a god, its power could have easily infused your soul, and Tara is in love with you, so her magic would have touched your soul —"

"I need to find her," Jovan cut in. "You need to send me to her now."

Valina Mellarian eyed him for a moment, then raised her hands. "As you wish."

The thick fog swept up around him. "Stay away from Natiere," he heard the sorceress say as he was lifted into the air. He counted the seconds as he hovered blindly, encased in the cloud, impatient to be back on the ground. He yearned to see Tara, to hold her again, if she would let him. He hoped the rest of her memory had returned.

Something snagged the cloud that enclosed him. A sudden jerk yanked him sideways, and he felt like a trout hooked by a fisherman and cast up onto the riverbank. His feet hit the ground hard. The fog disintegrated, and he found himself on the brink of a cliff, the toes of his boots hanging over open air. Far below, mountain hawks soared among misty crags, their dark wings catching the rising thermals.

With a shout, Jovan jumped back from the edge. Heart pounding, he looked around. Something must have interfered with Valina Mellarian's magic again. He was nowhere near Gypsy Crossroads. Jagged rocks lay scattered across the wide ledge on which he'd landed. Behind him, another cliff rose into the morning sun. A large door, engraved with runes, stood open in the cliff face, leading into the mountain. Pathways spread outward, hugging the cliff as they curled around the rocks and descended from the ledge.

With a sinking feeling, Jovan recognized his surroundings. He'd landed at the entrance to the dwarven city of Aldontris, deep in the Cyranel Mountains. He heard the heavy tread of booted feet on both sides of him. Two groups of short, thick-bodied dwarves with long hair and trailing beards, axes and maces in hand, lumbered up the pathways onto the ledge.

"I knew I heard somebody up here," one of the dwarves grunted as they closed to within a few feet of Jovan.

Jovan raised his hands in a gesture of peace.

Before he could speak, a gray-haired dwarf with a scar over his right eye pushed his way to the front. "Well, now. Jovan Trevillion." The dwarf prodded Jovan in the chest with his mace. "I don't know how you got up here, but you've got a lot of balls to set foot on dwarven soil again." He glanced around. "Where's that thieving brother of yours? I claim a grievance battle. The loser goes over the cliff."

"Jared is dead, Sauldron." Jovan dropped his hands slowly, inching toward his weapons. "And I had nothing to do with —"

"A pity about your brother," Sauldron cut in. "I would have enjoyed seeing him fall. I guess I'll have to settle for you." He poked Jovan hard in the chest again with the mace, shoving him backward toward the cliff edge.

Jovan reached for his sword.

"Sauldron!" The gruff shout echoed through the mountains. The dwarves turned as one toward the open door.

Sauldron scowled. "Gralfar. What do you want?"

A slightly taller dwarf with straw-colored hair and beard and wearing a dented helm approached. "Your grievance will have to wait. King Drordin will want Trevillion brought to him — alive and in one piece."

Sauldron cursed and spat at Jovan's feet. "You will not leave these mountains alive. I swear it." He stomped across the ledge and disappeared through the door.

"Disarm him." Gralfar jerked his head toward Jovan.

Jovan stood silently as the other dwarves roughly removed his weapons.

Gralfar turned toward the door. "Come."

Mentally cursing the Being, Jovan fell in line between the two groups of dwarves and descended into the mountain.

CHAPTER 23

Tara stood with her back to the bar, watching the boisterous crowd as she listened to Blackie haggle with an Eastern trader over the price of the Cierran brandy they'd brought downriver. The scene felt so familiar. The White Bull tavern, named for the enormous long-horned white bull head mounted on the wall behind the bar, had always been Blackie's favorite place to conduct business. The other smugglers sat at a nearby table. Brains hungrily downed his third bowl of stew, while Whiskey drank, Whittler carved on the table, and Gus drummed his fingers, impatient for his share of the money. Diamond Jack had sold the jewelry he'd taken from the dock master in Cierra and, with a stern warning from Blackie not to cheat or pocket anything, had staked himself to a card game. He sat at a table toward the back with five other players, four men and a woman.

Tara's eyes lingered on the card players, and a vague uneasiness shivered through her. Two of the men were older, shaggy and unkempt. They were big and muscular and had the rough, weather-beaten look of lumberjacks. The other two men were of average size, neatly trimmed, and dressed like wealthy traders. The woman, who sat next to Jack, had flowing black hair and the earthy skin tone of a Gypsy. She wore a dark green patterned skirt and vest with a loosely laced white blouse that barely contained her voluptuous curves, much to the distraction of those at the table.

Tara glanced out the window, noting the darkening sky. Because they'd arrived at the Gypsy Crossroads ahead of schedule, it had taken Blackie most of the day to track down the trader with whom he'd made the deal. And now the Easterner was trying to pay less than the agreed-on price. She took a deep breath to calm the nervous foreboding that twitched her muscles. Disaster was approaching. Captain Natiere would be at the Crossroads soon. She sensed him drawing nearer, with a dangerous edge to his aura that hadn't been there before. She needed to get away from here and leave the others behind. She didn't want them hurt. The problem was that Blackie wouldn't let her out of his sight. He'd claimed he needed her help. He'd dragged her all over town in his search for the trader and then asked her to stand by while he made the deal. He said her presence would keep the trader honest.

She shot the trader an annoyed look and smiled inwardly at the nervousness that crept into his voice as he abruptly settled on a price.

"Heads up!" the bartender called by her ear as he slapped a tall, empty mug on the bar.

Tara leaped away as if stung by a hornet. Chuckling, the bartender pulled on a cord, which opened the mouth of the huge bull head. Dark ale poured out of the bull's mouth and swished into the perfectly placed mug with minimal splashing.

"Woman, you are way too jumpy," Blackie said, turning toward her. "I can't believe you don't remember the 'house special'."

Tara glared at the still grinning bartender. "Why would I remember that any more than anything else?" she said to Blackie. "Are you done?"

Blackie's eyes gleamed at the bag of gold clenched in his hand. "We will party well tonight!"

"Good." She gestured toward the table where the other smugglers sat. "You get things settled between you. I need to get going. I'll look you up when I come back around this way."

Blackie scowled. "Whoa, what's the hurry?"

"I told you. I'm heading for the Black Mountains."

"The mountains can wait."

"No, they can't."

Blackie's eyes narrowed, and he gripped her arm. "What aren't you telling me? It's the Butcher, isn't it?"

Tara ground her teeth in frustration. "Blackie, I appreciate you're trying to protect me, but —"

"You cheated!" an angry voice bellowed from the back of the room.

Silence slid through the tavern as all eyes turned to the card players' table. Jack and the Gypsy woman both jumped to their feet.

"I did not!" they said simultaneously.

They pointed at each other.

"It was him!"

"It was her!"

The Gypsy slapped Jack across the face, snatched up a fistful of coins from the table, and darted toward the back door.

"Thief! Get back here!" The two traders chased after her, while the lumberjacks grasped Jack by the arms.

Blackie cursed roundly and pushed his way through the crowd toward Jack. Brains, Gus, Whiskey, and Whittler rose as one and headed for Jack's table.

Tara hesitated. With everyone distracted, she could easily sneak away, but her gut was telling her the smugglers would be in serious trouble if she did. She swore under her breath and followed after Blackie.

"It wasn't me! Ow!" Jack grimaced as one of the big men holding him twisted his arm. A jack of diamonds slipped out of Jack's sleeve and floated to the floor.

"Then what do you call that?" the man said.

"There, that's proof I didn't cheat," Jack said. "The card was still up my sleeve."

Blackie came up beside him. "Jack, ya confounded idiot! What are ya trying to do?"

"Is he with you?" the other lumberjack asked Blackie.

"We'll take him and leave." Blackie reached toward Jack.

The two men pulled Jack away. "The only place he's going is the lockup."

"But I didn't cheat," Jack whined.

"But you were going to," the lumberjack said.

Brains and Gus blocked their path. "He's coming with us," Brains said.

"To the Abyss with you," the lumberjack snarled. He shoved Brains in the chest, but Brains didn't budge.

The other lumberjack swung at Gus. Gus ducked and punched him in the stomach. Then the four tackled each other, knocking over tables as they wrestled back and forth. Angry patrons leaped out of the way, shouting and swearing as their half-eaten meals plastered the floor. Blackie snagged Jack and pulled him back beside him.

"Stop! Stop!" The bartender ran over, waving his hands. "Lena!" he hollered to the barmaid. "Call the Guard —"

Whiskey whacked him over the head with his empty bottle. "We don't need no bloomin' Guard." The bartender's eyes rolled upward, and he toppled over.

"Blackie, we've got to get out of here before the Guard shows up!" Tara slugged a drunk man who was trying to join the fight.

Whittler brandished his knife, and those around him backed away.

The two traders burst through the back door, dragging the Gypsy woman between them. She wriggled and fought, spitting out Gypsy curses. Behind them swarmed a dozen guardsmen, swords bared. With swift precision, the guardsmen closed off both exits and surrounded the combatants. Brains, his fist poised to smash the lumberjack's nose, froze in mid-motion as one of the guards pressed his blade against Brains' neck. Whittler sheathed his knife, and he and Whiskey backed up against Blackie, who had a firm grip on Jack. Tara stayed close beside them as four guardsmen hauled Gus and the other lumberjack to their feet.

"Where is Curtis?" the leader of the Guard snapped. Tara noted the lieutenant's bars on his uniform. He looked unpleasantly familiar.

Lena, the barmaid, pushed aside a table and knelt next to the unconscious bartender. "He's here." She pointed an accusing finger at Whiskey. "He hit him on the head with that bottle."

Whiskey dropped the empty bottle and assumed an innocent expression.

The bottle rolled across to the lieutenant's feet. He kicked it away. "Who started this?"

Lena gestured toward Blackie and Jack. "They did." She pointed at Jack. "He was cheating at cards. He and that Gypsy woman."

"I was not —" Jack began.

Blackie elbowed him, and Jack closed his mouth.

The Gypsy woman reeled off a fresh set of curses.

One of the guardsmen slapped her, leaving a red welt on her cheek. She cursed some more and kicked at him. He pulled back to strike her again.

"Leave her," the lieutenant ordered. He indicated the lumberjacks. "What about them?"

"We did nothing wrong. We were just playing a friendly game of cards," one of the lumberjacks said.

"And they cheated and then attacked us," the other added.

The lieutenant waved his sword, and they fell silent. "I was asking her." He turned back to Lena. "Well?"

"They're telling the truth," Lena said. "It wasn't their fault."

The lieutenant eyed the lumberjacks, considering, then advanced on Blackie. "Blackie de Runo. How many times must we throw you in the lockup before you cease to cause trouble?" When Blackie said nothing, he turned away. "And as if you and your men couldn't cause enough trouble on your own," he stopped before Tara, "you've brought the Ice Queen herself along to assist you." A nasty smile crossed his face. "It's been too many years since you graced our lockup. Where's your sister? Not here? No matter. One Triannon in the guardhouse is sweet enough." He strode away. "Disarm them. If they resist, kill them."

Tara tensed. She wasn't about to give up the black sword. She felt Blackie's warning touch on her elbow.

"We'll get it back," he whispered out of the side of his mouth. "If you move, they're dead." His eyes shifted sideways toward Brains and Gus, who stood deathly still with blades at their throats.

She clenched her fists and allowed the guards to remove her weapons.

"Bring them, and the Gypsy." The lieutenant led the way out into the street.

Tara fell in line as the guardsmen escorted them down the lamplit street to the guardhouse. The crowds enjoying the Gypsy Crossroads' bustling night life scurried out of their way. Within minutes, the street was deserted. Tara heard in her mind Blackie's voice from many years ago telling her the number one rule of the Crossroads — avoid the Guard at all costs. One more small nugget of information surfaced before the memory faded: the lieutenant's name — Lucas Romaine. She knew they'd crossed swords in the past, but she couldn't remember the circumstances. She hoped she'd whipped his behind in their last encounter.

*****

Captain Natiere slipped through the crowded streets, his cloak hood and the deepening twilight masking his frightening visage. He'd left his wolf pack outside of town to hunt. There would be no shortage of prey. The wild forest surrounding Gypsy Crossroads teemed with life, as did the town itself, particularly at night.

Natiere plowed through a knot of caravanners, oblivious to their cries of indignation. Tara's aura drew him, its cool radiance like a siren's song to his damaged soul. He wanted — no, he needed — to feel again the blending of their minds. She was very close; only one or two more streets, and he would see her. He would challenge her to another duel, and when he defeated her, she would be at his mercy.

He rounded a corner and stopped. At the far end of the lamplit street he saw Tara and the smugglers surrounded by guardsmen and being escorted into the guardhouse. Just as Tara reached the threshold, she hesitated, her head turning quickly toward him. He sensed her recognition as her eyes found him in the shadows. Then she was shoved through the doorway along with the rest of the smugglers. The guardsmen followed, closing the door behind them with a solid thud.

With a bestial growl, Natiere slammed his fist through the wall of the building beside him. He barely heard the startled scream from within. This was Blackie de Runo's fault. He knew Blackie was a notorious troublemaker who'd spent time in the lockup in every town from the Eastern Frontier to the Twin Cities in the West. Natiere's mind immediately devised several especially gruesome torments for Blackie to repay him for his stupidity.

Natiere stepped back further into the shadows and considered his options. He could break into the guardhouse and free Tara. It would be quite messy, though he had no doubt of his success. The difficulty would lie in the degree of Tara's cooperation. If the smugglers decided to fight for her, she wouldn't take kindly to his killing them or threatening their lives to coerce her into leaving with him. He could rescue the whole lot of them, but that wouldn't serve his purpose. He needed to confront her alone.

With one last glance at the guardhouse, Natiere headed out of town. If Tara was true to her reputation, she would soon find a way to escape the lockup. When she did, he would be waiting.

*****

Jovan Trevillion sat on the cold earthen floor of a holding cell, his arms loosely crossed over his bent knees. Hours had passed since the dwarves had stuck him in the cell. He wished he knew how many. The small eight-by-ten-foot room with its low ceiling and windowless walls paid no heed to the passage of time. For all he knew, the dwarves intended to leave him there until his bones became one with the mountain. He thanked the gods again for the ambient amber-colored light that radiated from the fist-sized earth stones embedded in the walls. To sit for so long in darkness would have driven him mad.

He tipped his head back against the rough wall and thought about his previous stay in Aldontris. He'd been fifteen years old at the time and still weak from the poisoned knife wound he'd received during the bandit attack on the caravan he and his older brother, Jared, had been guarding. They'd escaped into Dharakwood, where the waters of Rinpool had purged the poison from Jovan's body. After seeing Rinpool's prophetic visions, they'd been forced out of Dharakwood into the foothills of the Cyranel Mountains, near a dwarven outpost. Jared had somehow persuaded the two wary dwarves stationed there to help them. Jovan recalled wondering at the time what Jared had said to convince the dwarves to abandon their usual practice of shunning outsiders. He never was able to get Jared to tell him. The dwarves had taken them in, allowing them food and shelter while his wound healed. He'd spent nearly two weeks in a sickroom bed, recovering. The dwarven healers were amazed that he'd lived. They said the knife blade had damaged his lung.

During his convalescence, he saw only a few of the dwarves — the healers who tended him, and Gralfar and Sauldron, the two dwarves from the outpost who'd let them in. It seemed King Drordin had declared the two men to be their responsibility. Jovan had forged a friendship with Gralfar, but he could never get past Sauldron's distrustful nature. Gralfar, he was sure, was the only reason he was alive right now. If not for Gralfar's intervention on the cliff, Sauldron and the other dwarves would have gladly killed him.

Steeling himself, Jovan dredged forth the memory that pained him most — Jared's betrayal. The first of many, he was forced to admit. His brother had been both father and mother to him. Jovan didn't remember his parents, and Jared had claimed to have no memory of them, either. Jared had always looked out for him and taught him survival skills and self-reliance. But in looking back, Jovan wondered how much of that stemmed from brotherly love, and how much from Jared's need for a willing accomplice for his schemes.

Jovan swallowed the raw pain and concentrated on recalling what he knew of Jared's actions during their three weeks in Aldontris. The truth was that he'd rarely seen Jared for most of that time. Jared would eat his meals with him in the sickroom, but then disappear for hours with no explanation, returning only occasionally to sleep or to talk about things he'd seen in the dwarven city. He had seemed to be trying to ingratiate himself into the dwarves' good graces by helping out where needed and expressing interest in dwarven lore and daily life. Jovan had known that only meant he was up to something.

On the last day of their stay, Jared had been particularly on edge. Jovan had tried to pry out the scheme he saw building in his brother's eyes, but Jared had refused to admit any such scheme existed. Then that night, a beaten and bloodied Jared had woken him from a sound sleep, insisting they leave immediately. He had said if the dwarves found him, they'd kill him, and they'd likely kill Jovan, too. Snatching up their few possessions, they'd left Aldontris like thieves in the night. How they managed to avoid the dwarven pursuit, Jovan didn't know. He could only guess that Jared had searched out an escape route long in advance.

When they were far from the Cyranel Mountains, Jared had finally admitted what he'd done. He'd stolen the largest of the earth stones. According to what Jared had learned from the dwarves, the earth stones had been created by earth Ancients long ago to light the mountain depths. They held great magic, and the largest stone was the dwarves' most prized possession. He'd drugged the guards in the deep of the night and had removed the gem from its setting in the throne room wall. But Sauldron had been watching him and had caught him in his thievery. Their battle had wounded Jared and left

Sauldron with the scar over his eye. Jared had fled without the stone, Sauldron's vow to kill him echoing in his ears.

Jared had shown no remorse over the attempted theft, only bitter disappointment. "I had our future in my hands," he'd said. He'd planned to sell the stone for enough gold to stake them for life. There would have been no more risking of their lives on the caravan route and no more bandit attacks. Jovan had almost been killed in the last attack. Jared had said he didn't want it to happen again.

Jovan closed his eyes for a moment, remembering how much he'd wanted to believe that Jared had done it for his benefit, when he'd known in his heart that Jared had really just wanted the money. He rubbed his hands over his face as other memories of Jared watching out for him surfaced. Perhaps he was being too hard on his brother. Maybe Jared had cared about him. He groaned inwardly. He would never know.

The cell door opened outward, and two dwarven guards filed in. Gralfar stood in the doorway and beckoned. "Come. The king is ready to see you."

Jovan rose, ducking his head against the low ceiling, and followed Gralfar out into the smooth-walled corridor. The guards took their positions, one in front, one behind him. They marched swiftly through the corridors to a landing platform, where a transport that looked like an extra-long mining cart awaited them. They climbed inside. Gralfar took the controls and guided the transport along a rail track. The transport tipped down a long hill, picking up speed. Jovan held on as the transport shot through the mountain, rounding tight corners as it dove through dark tunnels and sped across open caverns.

A few minutes later, Gralfar slowed the transport and braked it to a halt beside another platform. Jovan unclamped his fingers from the edge of the transport and climbed out. Gralfar led them through an arched doorway into a cavernous room. Gleaming coats of arms and tapestries of great dwarven battles ornamented the polished granite walls of the great hall, amidst hundreds of thousands of small glowing amber-colored stones like those that had lit his holding cell. Rank upon rank of dwarves, both male and female, lined the hall, glaring at him as he followed Gralfar toward the raised granite throne at the far end of the chamber. Jovan stared straight ahead, unsettled by the palpable hostility rising from the dwarves.

Just before they reached the dais, Gralfar held out his arm, and they stopped. The two guards moved to either side of Jovan.

Gralfar stepped forward and dropped to one knee before his king, then rose again. He swept his hand toward Jovan. "I have brought Jovan Trevillion."

King Drordin, a stout but muscular dwarf with thick dark hair, leathery skin, and fierce gray eyes, rapped the end of his jeweled scepter on the arm of his throne to still the rampant murmuring. "So I see." He gazed at Jovan with all the enmity of the crowd. "When I returned from Ilgresta a short time ago and Gralfar told me you were here, I didn't believe it. I didn't believe that a Trevillion would dare defile our mountain again. I'm surprised that those who found you let you live."

Sauldron burst from the ranks of dwarves beside him. "I wanted to kill him but Gralfar said —"

"Silence, Sauldron!" the king commanded. "You will have your say."

Sauldron narrowed his eyes at Gralfar, his expression venomous.

Jovan felt a glimmer of hope. Gralfar must have acted on his own when he stopped Sauldron from sending him over the cliff. Perhaps Jovan's bond of friendship with him was indeed still strong.

King Drordin pointed at Jovan with his scepter. "Your brother took advantage of our hospitality. He willfully deceived us, and then he tried to steal the heart of our realm."

All the dwarves looked upward at the glowing amber stone, about four times the size of a man's fist, set into the wall above the throne. Jovan looked away.

"That stone was given to our forefathers centuries ago by the earth *Aiykshaav'n* that once lived in these mountains. Its magic drew out the other stones from deep within the rock." He gestured toward the countless smaller stones glowing in the walls. "As long as it remains under the mountain, our halls will be lit by their magical light. But if it leaves the mountain, their light will go out forever, and our last tie to the Ancients and that part of our heritage will be gone." He looked around a moment in silence, letting the magnitude of such a disaster sink in. Then his eyes settled on Sauldron. "If not for the courage and intuition of Sauldron, such would have been our fate. Sauldron bested your brother and returned the stone to its proper place."

King Drordin's gaze shifted back to Jovan. "However, what we didn't know at the time was that your brother had stolen another artifact — a ring of great significance. Its red gem was formed by the Niramaani — the fire *Aiykshaav'n* — and set in gold by dwarven masters." Jovan felt the king's eyes drilling into him. "We want it back. Since you're here, you can tell us where it is."

Jovan frowned, perplexed. He thought he'd seen all of Jared's loot over the years — Jared always bragged about his acquisitions — but he couldn't recall his brother ever showing him a ring with a red gem. "I don't know of this ring. I've never seen a ring of that description in Jared's possession."

"Where is your brother now?" King Drordin asked.

"He's dead," Jovan said heavily. "He died in the Bog twelve years ago."

"I'm sorry to hear it. I would have preferred to kill him myself. What did he do with the ring?"

"I don't know. As I said, I never saw him with it. I was never a part of his thievery."

"You traveled with him, didn't you?"

"Yes. He was my only family, but that doesn't mean —"

"How did you get here? And why did you return?"

"I did not choose to come here. I was sent here by accident." Jovan hesitated. "It's a very long story."

"Make it short."

Jovan gathered his thoughts. "Three hundred years ago, the sky *Aiykshaav'n* — the Kamarians — either disappeared or were destroyed in a great Cataclysm. Perhaps you've heard the legend."

"It's a common Eastern tale. What does it have to do with you?"

"There is a woman, a descendant of the Kamarians, who is destined to bring them back to this world, but first she must defeat the evil that caused the Cataclysm in the first place. I've been helping her with her quest. We were traveling together, but we became separated. Valina Mellarian of Estiarii Faelle used her magic to send me to the Gypsy Crossroads, where the woman is now. But something interfered with her magic, and I ended up here, instead."

"Who is this woman?"

"Her name is Tara Triannon."

The king's eyebrows shot up. "Triannon? You expect us to believe that one of the Triannon sisters is a long-lost descendant of the *Aiykshaav'n?*" He burst into laughter, which spread through the dwarven ranks lining the hall.

"It's true. I swear it," Jovan said when the laughter died down.

"An oath from a Trevillion means nothing," the king spat.

Gralfar approached the dais. "My king."

"Speak."

"What if he is telling the truth? One of the Triannons is said to have silver hair and eyes, which would match the coloring of the Kamarians of legend."

"She's likely an albino," Sauldron said.

The king turned back to Jovan. "And why would this woman need your help?"

Jovan stiffened. The last thing he wanted was to lay open his relationship with Tara to the derision of the dwarven masses. "We have a unique connection through our minds, and she is able to draw strength from me in her times of need."

"Indeed." King Drordin sat back, and Jovan felt his hope ebbing at the skepticism on the king's face. "You speak of legends — Kamarians, the sorceress of Estiarii Faelle — things that make good stories, but nothing real or solid, except for a woman who is better known for her exploits as a sword-for-hire. That she could be an *Aiykshaav'n* is unlikely, to say the least." The king sat up straight. "So the question that lies before us is, what do we do with you?" The king tapped the end of his scepter on the throne arm as he thought.

Jovan took a step forward. "I beg you to let me go, so I can see Tara through to the end of her quest. Then, if it be your judgment, I will return and serve whatever punishment you see fit for Jared's actions."

"And how do I know that you would return?"

"I would give you my word."

The king scoffed. "The word of a Trevillion?"

"I am not my brother. I keep my word."

"And what of the missing ring?"

"If I knew where it was, I would give it to you."

Sauldron stepped forward, addressing first the king, then the assembled dwarves. "You said I would have my say. Well, I say he serves his punishment now. His story stinks like goat dung, and I don't believe a word of it. Once he leaves the mountain, we'll never see his thieving hide again."

The crowd roared in agreement.

"My king," Gralfar began.

King Drordin regarded him with narrowed eyes. "Perhaps you would like to share his punishment?"

Gralfar fell silent.

The king looked back at Jovan, his expression merciless. "Unless you can produce the ring, or credible information that would lead to its return, you will not be leaving our realm. I hope you enjoyed the sunrise from the cliff this morning, because it's the last one you will see for a very long time. Take him to the Pit!"

"No!" Jovan struggled, but the dwarves bore him to the ground and bound him hand and foot. Then the tide of dwarves split, and he saw, on the far wall, a three-foot-square hole. The dwarves carried him to the hole and shoved him through it, headfirst. He slid down a long, steep, smooth chute of rock into darkness. Fiery pain shot through his head and shoulder as he thudded onto a stone floor. Then the small trap door high above closed, shutting him in utter blackness.

CHAPTER 24

Led by Lieutenant Romaine and prodded forward by the guardsmen, Tara, the smugglers, and the Gypsy woman marched in single file down the damp stone stairs to the lowest level of the guardhouse. Tara wrinkled her nose at the foul smell of feces and unwashed bodies wafting toward them. At the bottom of the stairs, the passage widened into a corridor lined with prison cells that had solid walls and barred doors. Burning torches lit the dank space, and Tara saw through the doors that some of the cells were already filled. She heard low murmuring from within them, then the shuffling of many feet. Faces, some dirty and ragged, others just beginning to show the smudge of prison filth, appeared at the cell doors, silently watching them.

"Get back!" The lieutenant rapped the flat of his sword against the bars of the nearest door, sending the inmates scurrying away. He led his new prisoners to the end of the corridor. Tara glanced in the doors as they passed. Every cell boasted at least a few occupants.

"Lieutenant Romaine!" a voice called out from behind them. An out-of-breath guardsman ran up to the lieutenant and saluted. "Wolf attacks... at the edge of town... you must come!"

Tara's breath caught. Natiere.

Blackie shot her a glance, and she felt the eyes of the other smugglers on her as well.

The lieutenant scowled. "It can't be. No wolves would come near the town, there's plenty of game in the forest."

"I only know what I was told, sir," the guardsman said.

"Well, go find out what is really happening and report back," the lieutenant snapped.

Sweat formed on the guardsman's brow as he rigidly saluted. "Begging your pardon, sir, but the mayor specifically ordered me to get you —"

"Hang the mayor!" the lieutenant said with an impatient gesture. He turned greedy eyes on Tara. "I have other business."

Tara gave him an "I dare you" glare.

"Lieutenant Romaine!" another guard shouted from the bottom of the stairs. "There are wolves in the city!"

The lieutenant glanced at him in disgust. "So I've heard. I suppose I'll have to deal with it, since no one else seems able to." He strode past the line of smugglers held at bay by a half-dozen guardsmen's swords. He stopped beside Tara and reached out to touch her hair. She knocked his hand away. "It's a pity your sister isn't here," he said, unperturbed. "I much prefer redheads." His eyes slid to the Gypsy, his gaze lingering on her low neckline. "But then brunettes have their charms, as well."

The Gypsy woman tossed her head, but wisely remained silent.

He addressed his men. "Split them up. I'll be back shortly." Sheathing his sword, he followed the two guardsmen back up the stairs.

One of the guards, a ring of keys in his hand, unlocked the next-to-the-last cell on the left. He pointed at Gus and Whiskey with his sword. "You and you — in there." Gus and Whiskey filed past him into the cell. Whiskey winced as the guard slammed and locked the door behind them. The guard moved to the last cell on the left. With a swipe of his blade, he indicated Brains, Whittler, and Diamond Jack. "You three, next." Whittler gave Blackie a beseeching look before being shoved into the cell after the other two. Tara watched Whittler back out of sight into a corner. Brains followed him, and she could hear Brains speaking in low tones.

"The rest of you, in here." The guard swung open the door to the cell directly across the corridor. Tara, Blackie, and the Gypsy woman entered. Tara glanced around. The torchlight dimly illuminated half the chamber, and she saw two people sitting in the deep shadows against the back wall. They didn't move or speak, and Tara wondered if they were asleep — or dead. Though her danger sense was on edge, she didn't feel any immediate threat.

The guard locked the door, then he and the other guardsmen exited back up the stairs.

Blackie stepped to the door, followed by the Gypsy, who stayed as close to him as she could without touching him. "Brains, can you hear me?" he called softly.

"Yes," came the quiet reply.

"How's Whittler doing?"

Brains appeared at the cell door. "Not good. He needs out. *Soon.*"

Blackie cursed under his breath.

Tara moved up beside him. She kept her voice low. "What's the matter with him?"

Blackie raked his hand through his hair. "Well, for one, he gets crazy in closed-in spaces, and for two, it was in a dungeon like this where the Butcher tortured him and cut out his tongue."

"Oh, gods." Tara turned away, her mind formulating and discarding plans of escape.

Blackie caught her shoulder. "And speaking of the Butcher, you knew he was out there, didn't you."

Tara pulled away from him. "I knew he was coming. Then I saw him in the shadows just as we were taken into the guardhouse."

"That means we're better off staying in here and taking our chances with Romaine. When he comes back, we'll —"

"No." Tara drew Blackie away from the cell door, away from the Gypsy, who'd been listening avidly, and farther away from the two who sat motionless in the shadows. "We need to come up with something now, to take advantage of his diversion," she whispered.

"Whose diversion?" Blackie lowered his voice to match hers. "What are you talking about?"

"The wolf attacks. They're distracting the guards, so we can escape."

Blackie stared at her. "You're telling me that the Butcher is deliberately having his wolves attack? That's the craziest thing I've ever heard — even for you."

"I've got to get that sword back," she muttered, ignoring his comment. "I can't believe I lost it *again*." She turned on him. "I knew this would happen."

"Look, I'm sorry. Things got a little out of control."

"As they always do with you."

Blackie bristled. "I said we'd get it back, and we will. We've gotten out of worse places. We just need a plan."

"How did we get out of here last time?"

Blackie hesitated.

Tara put her hand on her hip. "Well?"

He turned away. "Your sister slept with Romaine."

"She *what*? I don't remember —" Tara stepped around in front of Blackie, so he had to face her. "Did I know about that?"

Blackie wouldn't meet her eyes. "No. Look, it was her choice, and it doesn't matter now. The past is done, and we need to come

up with a plan to get out of here. This lockup has a lot of guards, but
—"

"No, it doesn't — not now." Tara's voice rose in exasperation, aggravated by the shock she felt at her sister's action. "That's the point. They're out fighting the wolves. Now is our best chance."

Scornful laughter rose from the back corner of the cell. "Don't waste your time," said an amused male voice.

Tara and Blackie turned quickly, eyes searching the shadows. The Gypsy woman sidled up behind Blackie and stood on her tip-toes, looking over his shoulder. Tara felt a strange warmth rising through her body, set off by the oddly familiar voice. Where had she heard it before?

The two who had been sitting in the back got to their feet and came forward. "There's no escaping from here," the man said. "I've already tried, and if I can't do it, no one can. Except for maybe the Triannon sis—" He broke off, his eyes wide. "Tara?"

Tara squinted into the shadows. "Who are you?"

A dark-haired man and a blonde woman with short curly hair stepped into the light. The leather-clad woman didn't look in the least familiar, but the man — with his shoulder-length hair that curled on the ends, his bold blue eyes, his mouth that was curving into a crooked smile — she had definitely seen him before. A flash of hatred burned all ties to reason. She couldn't remember why she hated him, only that she did. She wanted him dead. With a yell, she lunged at him and grabbed him by the throat. He staggered back, his fingers trying to pry hers from around his neck. The blonde woman screamed and tried to help him, while the Gypsy chattered furiously in her native tongue.

Blackie jumped in and wrestled Tara away from the man, shoved her hard against the wall. "Haedis' balls, woman, what's the matter with you? You can't do that now. Romaine will lock you up for good."

Tara fought Blackie's grip. "Let go of me! I'm going to kill him."

"Not now!" Blackie shouldered her against the wall again. "You can kill him later, after we're out of here."

Panting, Tara ceased fighting and met Blackie's gaze. "The minute we leave."

"Fine. We'll bring him with us."

Tara held his gaze a moment longer. "Fine."

Apparently satisfied with what he saw in her eyes, Blackie let go. "Do you remember why you want to kill him?"

Tara frowned. "Does it matter?"

Blackie snorted. "Of course it matters. Where's the satisfaction of killing him if you don't know why you're doing it?"

Still rubbing his throat, the dark-haired man took a tentative step toward them. "Hey, don't I get some say in this?" He looked at Tara. "And what do you mean, you don't remember —"

Blackie whirled. "You just keep your mouth shut."

"Myles, who *are* these people?" the blonde asked as she drew him away.

The Gypsy woman strode up to Tara and gave her what sounded like a severe tongue-lashing.

Tara didn't understand a word of it. "Don't yell at me," she retorted. "It's your fault we're in here."

Blackie stepped between them, and the Gypsy lit into him, too. He yelled back at her in her own language.

Tara looked at him in surprise. "When did you learn Gypsy?"

Then they heard guardsmen running down the corridor. "Who's causing all that ruckus?"

Tara seized Blackie's arm. "Attack me!"

"What?"

Tara stifled a wild urge to laugh at his expression. "Pretend we're still fighting." She dragged him toward the door and twisted around as if struggling with him. "Let go of me, you filthy pirate!"

"Hey, you! Leave her alone!" One of the guardsmen hastily stuffed the key into the lock.

"Filthy pirate, is it?" Blackie swung her around into the wall near the door.

"Ow!" Tara glared at him. "I said *pretend*," she whispered through clenched teeth.

The cell door flew open. Tara planted her boot in Blackie's gut and shoved him back toward the two guards rushing in, swords drawn, only a few feet away. Before they could react, Blackie dropped to the floor, rolled, and drove his heels into their knee caps. Shouting in pain, they collapsed, clutching their injured knees. Keeping low, Tara bowled into the third guard coming through the cell door and knocked him into the guards behind him. She wrenched his arm around and twisted it into an unnatural angle until he yelped and dropped his sword. Brains and Jack reached through the bars of their cell door and pinned a guardsmen who had fallen against the door. He struggled, but more arms stretched through the bars and trapped his legs. Tara snatched up the dropped sword and backhanded the guard across the face with the hilt.

"Sleep tight," Brains said as he and the other hands let go, and the guardsman sagged to the floor.

Tara whirled and kicked the guard with the twisted arm in the chin before he could get up. He landed with a grunt on top of the unconscious guard.

"You, too," Brains added. Then he jumped back from the door. "Look out!"

Tara ducked as a sword blade whistled through the air where her head had just been and clanged against the bars. Dodging and slashing, she fought off the three remaining guardsmen. "Blackie! Where are you?"

"Allow me." Myles parried a blow aimed at her shoulder.

Tara faltered, caught off guard by the heat that surged through her again at the sound of his voice and the sudden flash of memories from past side-by-side battles.

"Wake up, woman!" Blackie yanked her backward and took her place, fighting beside Myles.

Tara shook her head, dizzied by the vivid memories jamming her mind. She heard the Gypsy call out something, saw her inserting the key into the lock of the cell holding Brains, Jack, and Whittler.

"Yes, that one!" Blackie said. "And the one next to it." He wounded one of the guards. "Just let 'em all out. That'll fix Romaine's knickers."

Hands snaked out from a nearby cell and snagged one of the two remaining guardsmen. Bone snapped, and the hands let him fall to the floor, his neck broken. The last guard turned and bolted back down the corridor and up the stairs.

"Quick, get him!" Blackie pulled Tara out of the way and tossed his sword to Brains as the big man burst from the cell. "Before he brings the cavalry."

Brains nodded and whipped past, along with three other prisoners who had shared the cell. Jack and a very pale Whittler caught up weapons from the fallen guardsmen and followed as the Gypsy unlocked the next cell. Gus, Whiskey, and several others poured out.

"Gus, Whiskey, stay with her." Blackie jerked his head toward the Gypsy woman.

They protected her from the stampede as she dashed from cell to cell, opening doors. Myles was long gone, and so was the blonde.

Blackie grasped Tara's arm. "Hey, are you all right? We've got to go."

She rubbed her hand over her face. The dizziness was fading, but the recollections were not. "I'm fine. Just too many memories I don't want to see."

"Sometimes amnesia's not so bad, eh?" Blackie said as he pulled her along behind the tide of dirty humanity flowing up the stairs. With Brains, Whiskey, and the Gypsy woman in front of them, Blackie and Tara raced up the stairs to the main level of the guardhouse. Four guardsmen lay on the floor, dead, overwhelmed by the flood of escaping prisoners.

Tara spotted a small room off to the side, which she guessed was Lieutenant Romaine's office. "In here!" she cried. She leaped over a fallen guard and darted in. Blackie, Whiskey, and the Gypsy followed. Gus stood watch at the door. On a table in the corner, she found a pile of weapons. She pawed through it frantically until she found her sword belt with the black scabbard and sword still attached. She closed her eyes. "Thank the gods!" She buckled it on, then grabbed a couple of extra daggers from Romaine's supply and stuffed them in her boot sheaths.

Blackie scooped up the smugglers' swords and knives. "Whiskey, here's your... what in the Abyss are you doing?"

Whiskey was yanking open all the drawers of Lieutenant Romaine's desk. "It's here somewhere, I can smell it," Whiskey muttered as he dug through the drawers. "Ha, I knew it!" He snatched up a flask of amber liquid and took a long drink.

Gus rolled his eyes. "You crazy old fool."

Blackie doled out the weapons, then he and Tara hurriedly strapped on the remaining weapons of the group as they left the room.

Outside, chaos reigned. Shouts and screams and startled cries filled the night as the released prisoners sprinted through the crowded streets, knocking aside those who didn't get out of the way fast enough. There was no sign of Brains or the other two smugglers.

Blackie led the way down the street and into an alley. He turned to the Gypsy woman. "You're free now. You'd better run before the Guard gets back."

She hesitated, then turned without a word and sped away down the alley.

"We've got to find the others." Blackie pointed in the direction the Gypsy had gone. "Gus, go that way. Check the usual places. Whiskey, head over there." He jerked his thumb in the opposite direction. "We'll take the western end —"

"Why don't I go east?" Tara cut in. "We can cover more ground."

"No — and don't waste time arguing about it. We'll go once around, and then we'll meet behind the Weary Warrior."

"Blackie!" Diamond Jack raced up. "We got that guard, but then they got Whittler," he said between breaths. "I don't know how they found us so fast. They're bringing him back here now. Brains is following them, but he doesn't dare get close for fear they'll kill Whittler on the spot."

"How many are there?" Blackie asked. "Can we take them?"

Jack shook his head. "There must be twenty-five to thirty of them, led by Romaine. He's coming back to secure the guardhouse. I heard him say he's going to torture Whittler until the rest of us surrender."

"Here they come!" Whiskey said.

Tara followed his gaze past the guardhouse and up the rapidly emptying street. Lieutenant Romaine led a large knot of guardsmen in a swift march toward the lockup. In the center of the knot, she spotted Whittler with his hands bound behind his back, two burly guards propelling him forward. He continued to struggle despite a black eye and blood dripping from his nose and lip.

"What are we going to do? There's no time." Jack's voice was desperate. "Once he's in the lockup, he's done for!"

"We fight," Blackie said, his face grim.

"Against thirty men?" Tara gestured at the quickly approaching guardsmen. "We'll all be dead."

"I won't abandon him," Blackie said heatedly. "I'll kill him myself before I let Romaine cut him up."

"So much for your reputation as a blackguard." Tara looked back at the guardsmen, her throat constricting as she realized what she had to do. Her life and the future of the Kamarians versus Whittler's and her friends' lives... She straightened. "There's one way to save him, but you'll have to be fast. Go to the alley on the other side of the guardhouse, across the street from it. Be ready to snatch Whittler. I'll provide the distraction. Hurry up — go!"

The smugglers hesitated. Blackie started to speak.

Tara threw her hands up in the air, angry with the choice she was being forced to make. "Do you want him alive or not? Get going!"

Blackie gave her an inscrutable look, then he and the others ran down the alley behind them and disappeared around the corner.

Taking a deep breath, Tara stepped out into the street just as Lieutenant Romaine and his guardsmen crossed the last few yards to the lockup. She felt power rise up inside her. Bracing herself against the mental onslaught she knew would come, she drew the black sword and swung it in a tight arc. Power surged like molten steel, an exquisite pain burning through her body. Black fire shot from the blade and exploded into the guardhouse. Splintered wood and chunks of stone spewed everywhere. Guardsmen screamed. Some fell, and the rest scattered, ducking their heads against flying debris. She hoped Whittler hadn't been hit by any of it. She'd lost sight of him in the rising cloud of dust.

She dodged back into the alley, gritting her teeth as she fought for control of the tempestuous swell of power still flooding through her. Pain ravaged her mind as Ravnaul, from his dungeon prison, viciously attacked her mental defenses, shredding her walls almost as quickly as she erected them. He'd gained an enormous amount of strength from the sword, but to her surprise, Tara discovered that she, too, had grown stronger. She felt the magic of the black sword manifesting itself in the scorching heat that raised her body temperature. She embraced the sword's fire, felt its magic melding with her own. Gathering the power around her inner being, she focused it into a single searing mental blast that splintered Ravnaul's attack and sent him crashing back into his dungeon. The pain in her head vanished. Her vision cleared. She clenched her fist in triumph.

The sound of running footsteps coming toward her roused her. She hastily sheathed the black sword and switched the sword she'd taken from the guardsman back to her left hand. She cursed to herself, wondering how many people had seen the source of the blast.

Two people dashed into the alley. Tara raised her weapon to attack, then hesitated. Myles and the blonde woman, swords drawn, slid to a stop a few arm-lengths away.

Myles held his hands in front of him. "Don't kill me." He pointed at the street. "Romaine!"

He'd barely said the name when Lieutenant Romaine and a dozen guardsmen clattered around the corner into the alley. With Myles and the blonde beside her, Tara met the attack head on. She matched Romaine blow for blow, their blades clanging in a rapid beat. She, Myles, and the blonde woman allowed their attackers to drive them backward toward the other end of the alley, leaving a trail of dead or wounded guardsmen. Then more guards appeared behind them, sealing off their escape.

"Ha!" Romaine cried. He pressed his attack, locking swords with Tara, their faces inches apart. "You're mine," he gloated.

"I'd rather kiss a pig." Tara shoved him away, their blades rasping apart. She spotted a half-full, four-foot-long wooden refuse box beside a back door in the building on her right, and a memory, sharp and clear, sprang into her mind. "Remember Dunbarton's Alley?" she shouted to Myles, as Romaine charged at her.

Myles grinned. "How could I forget?" He dropped another guard. "Adriana, watch our backs!"

Lieutenant Romaine slashed at Tara. She parried the blow, and with a twisting thrust, drove her sword into his belly.

With a cry, he fell backward, clutching his bleeding gut.

"Lieutenant!" The guards around him caught him and lowered him to the ground.

"Now!" Tara darted to the refuse box. She lifted one end, while Myles hefted the other. Adriana jumped back by the wall, out of the way. Tara and Myles swung the box outward, emptying spoiled food and garbage onto the guardsmen coming in behind them. The guards ducked, their arms going up to cover their faces. Holding the box in front of them as a shield, Tara and Myles, with Adriana protecting their backs, bowled over the guardsmen, then dropped the box and sprinted out of the alley. The guards scrambled to their feet and gave chase.

Tara, with Myles and Adriana following, raced down several streets, zigzagging in and out of buildings, leading the guardsmen away from where the smugglers would have taken Whittler, provided they'd managed to rescue him. Twenty minutes later, she stopped behind a dance hall to catch her breath. She couldn't feel the guardsmen anywhere close and knew she'd finally lost them. Myles and Adriana halted beside her. The muffled sounds of music and cheering sifted through the air.

"I haven't had that much fun in weeks," Myles said, smiling. He reached for Tara as if to hug her. "Just like old times —"

Tara leaped back. "Don't touch me!" She glared at him, fighting her attraction. It would be so easy to fall back in with him. If only she could remember why she hated him.

Myles looked hurt. "I just saved your life. The least you could do is forgive me."

Tara snorted. "What I'd like to do is kill you... but you did help me, so I won't — this time." She turned to Adriana. "I don't know you, but I appreciate your help back there. Maybe I can return the favor someday." With a brief wave, she started off down the street. The quicker she got away from them, the better.

"Hey, wait! Where are you going?" Myles jogged after her.

Tara rounded on him, her sword grazing his tunic. "That's none of your business. And if you follow me, I will kill you."

He jumped back. Tara saw Adriana watching them with her hands on her hips.

"All right, all right," Myles said. He gave Tara his most charming crooked smile. "I just thought for old times' sake —"

His smile quickened her pulse. Cursing to herself, Tara squelched her unruly emotions. "Forget it. It won't work. You and I were done a long time ago, so if you want to live, you'll stay away from me." She backed away and sped off into the darkness.

She took a circuitous route through the once-again bustling town, stopping every so often to make certain she wasn't followed.

She recalled Blackie saying earlier to meet behind the Weary Warrior and hoped that was where he had gone.

When she arrived at the inn, she found the alley behind it deserted. She considered a moment, then knocked on the back door.

A large, bald man with an eye patch opened the door. "What do you want?"

She ignored his rudeness. "I'm looking for Blackie de Runo."

He grunted. "Who isn't?"

Tara heard voices inside, and then Diamond Jack's head poked out. He motioned for her to come in. The bald man stepped back. She went inside, and he closed and locked the door behind her. The small, windowless room was chilly and dark and stuffed with an odd assortment of chairs, tables, and boxes — a storeroom.

"Where's Blackie?" Jack asked anxiously. "He's not with you?"

Tara shook her head. "No, I haven't seen him." Her eyes adjusted to the candlelit interior. She saw Gus perched on a barstool, deliberately looking away from her and making warding signs against evil, while Whiskey slouched on a crate on the opposite side of the room, drinking from a tall bottle. Whittler sat cross-legged on the floor near Whiskey with his back to the wall, his knife handle gripped in his hands. No one was looking at her. They all avoided her gaze. Even Jack, who had, at least, spoken to her, kept his distance. He hovered nervously and seemed at a loss.

Tara hesitated, unsure what to say. She hadn't thought about how the smugglers would react to her use of the black sword. There hadn't been time to think through the consequences. She faced Jack. "Where are Blackie and Brains?"

He gestured toward the door. "They're out looking for you." He gave a helpless shrug. "They told us to stay here, what with Romaine and the Butcher..."

"You don't need to worry about Lieutenant Romaine. He won't be bothering anyone, anytime soon." Tara unbuckled the extra sword belts she'd picked up from Romaine's office and set them on a table. Then she crossed the room and knelt beside Whittler. His left eye and upper lip were swollen, and his nose looked like it had been broken, though most of the blood had been wiped away. The barely-controlled wildness in his eyes troubled her. He appeared traumatized and ready to explode. She put her hand on his shoulder. He flinched, but didn't pull away from her touch. "Are you all right?"

He met her eyes. She saw the raw fear of someone who had been scared to his limits. Behind that lay an even deeper terror. She sensed, though, that it wasn't her he was afraid of. He was terrified that Blackie and Brains wouldn't return, that they would run afoul of Romaine or the Butcher. Blackie and Brains were his anchors. He needed them.

She squeezed his shoulder. "I will find them and bring them back." A glimmer of hope lit his face. She rose to her feet. A broken chair in the corner caught her eye. She tipped it over and twisted off a cracked leg, held it out to Whittler.

Surprised, he took the length of wood and set it in his lap. His fingers twitched in sign.

"He says 'thank you,'" Jack said softly.

Tara smiled at Whittler. "You're welcome."

Whittler picked up the chair leg and began carving intently, his bruised face lost behind his hair.

Tara headed for the door. "Stay here till I get back."

Jack nodded.

The large man unlocked the door and let her out into the night.

CHAPTER 25

Pulling her hood up over her head, Tara waited in the shadows. Everywhere, pockets of people talked animatedly about the night's events. She caught a few words here and there — Triannon, Romaine, wolves, explosion. Apparently everyone had heard about her battle with Lieutenant Romaine, but she couldn't tell if anyone had seen the black sword. She was glad she still had Blackie's cloak to hide her face and the sword. There were many unscrupulous traders in the Crossroads, and she knew the Kamarian weapon would be a thief magnet with the exorbitant price it would bring on the black market. Not to mention the fact there was likely a bounty on her head now.

With one last glance up and down the street, she blended into the crowd. She headed west, letting her intuition guide her. She hoped she wouldn't run into Myles again. Her situation was difficult enough without him complicating it further. Though she still found him confoundedly attractive, she wouldn't care if she never saw him again. Their affair was truly over, and even though there was still much she couldn't remember, she knew deep down her heart lay elsewhere. She thought of Jovan and felt a sudden flicker of uneasiness. Something was wrong...

A tense coldness slid over her, jarring her out of her thoughts. She sensed Natiere approaching, but she wasn't his target. "Oh, no," she whispered and broke into a run.

Off to her left, a hoarse cry of pain rose into the night. Her gut wrenched. She knew that voice. She dashed through several groups of fleeing people and raced down a deserted alley. Sword in hand, she burst into a small moonlit square and froze. In the middle of the square near a fountain, the Butcher stood holding Blackie de Runo by the throat with his feet dangling several inches off the ground. In his other hand, the Butcher held a bloody knife.

"No! Natiere, stop!" Tara ran forward. "Your battle is with me, not him!"

Natiere turned, bloodlust in his eyes.

Something moved behind the fountain. Tara stopped and sucked in a breath, watching in disbelief as a small figure rushed out from behind the fountain, leaped onto Natiere's back, and pummeled his head. Gypsy curses punctuated each blow.

"Oh, gods," Tara whispered as she recognized the Gypsy woman from the White Bull.

Snarling, Natiere tossed Blackie away, sheathed his knife, and seized the Gypsy woman. She screamed and fought like a wildcat. He pulled her off his back and threw her into the fountain. Coughing and spluttering, she floundered in the thigh-deep water.

Tara dropped into a defensive stance as Natiere's gaze locked on her once more. Shocking cold rode over her at the savage hunger in his eyes. He strode toward her, his sword rasping from its sheath.

All at once, thin trailers of mist shot up from the ground around Natiere's feet, thickening quickly into puffy, white clouds that trapped him, sealing him within.

"No!" Natiere's roar of fury echoed in the square as he vanished.

Sending fervent thanks to Valina Mellarian, Tara dashed across the square to where Blackie lay. She fell to her knees beside him. "Blackie!" His eyes were closed, his body unresponsive to her gentle shake. Blood stained his shirt in several places. She ripped the shirt apart, revealing five oozing stab wounds. "Damn you, Natiere!" She listened for a heartbeat, heard nothing. Blackie gave a shallow, rattling exhale, then stopped breathing. "Curse it all, Blackie, I'm not losing you too!"

A shadow fell across them and Brains knelt beside her. "What happened?"

"Natiere." Tara sliced her left palm on her sword, placed her hand over one of Blackie's wounds, and closed her eyes. Power surged and flowed into Blackie like liquid fire. Tara cried out, curling in on herself as the agony of five knife thrusts stabbed into her. The pain passed swiftly, and she focused inward, healing the wounds as quickly as she could. She held her mental defenses tensely, dreading Ravnaul's attack, but her nemesis remained strangely quiet. He's waiting for me to sleep, she realized, when I won't be able to escape him.

Shaking off the frightening thought, she refocused her attention on Blackie. His wounds had healed cleanly, but she sensed his life was slipping away. *Come on, Blackie, breathe.* She reached deeper, surrounding his essence with the strength of her power. *I need you to come back to me.*

Blackie took one shuddering breath, then another. She felt his heart beating again, his chest moving in and out in regular rhythm. Tears of relief dripped on her hand as she opened her eyes.

Blackie stirred and sat up. He looked confused.

Tara hugged him hard. "Blackie, I'm so sorry."

"Whoa, there." Blackie held her awkwardly. "Sorry for what? What's going on?"

Tara let go and turned quickly, sensing another presence beside her.

The Gypsy woman crouched next to Blackie. She was drenched and bruised from her fall in the fountain, but seemed otherwise unhurt. She touched Blackie's bloody shirt, then pulled a torn piece aside and ran her hand through the black hairs on his chest, searching for wounds.

He moved backward. "Hey!" Then he recognized her. "What are you doing here?"

Her Gypsy words tumbled over each other as she gestured at Tara, then pointed at his chest, her eyes full of questions.

He looked down and tensed, his expression hardening into grim anger.

"Blackie?" Tara said tentatively.

"Where is he?" Blackie's head whipped around as he searched for the Butcher.

"He's gone."

"Where?"

"I don't know. Valina sent him somewhere."

"We're getting an audience," Brains said. "We need to leave." He helped Blackie up. "Yes, you, too." Brains nodded at the Gypsy. "Let's go."

Tara saw crowds gathering along the edges of the square as she followed Blackie and the Gypsy woman across the open space. Brains brought up the rear. When they reached the line of buildings, the throng parted and let them pass unchallenged.

Tara pulled her hood up again as they hurried through quieter streets and back alleys toward the Weary Warrior. Worry tugged at her. She'd never seen that expression on Blackie's face before. Why had Natiere attacked? There'd been no need. His fight was with her alone, and she'd hoped he would honor that and not go after her friends. She wished she knew if anything had happened between Blackie and Natiere before the attack, or if the Butcher had stabbed him without warning.

She also wondered where Valina had sent him. Not that it mattered. She felt as if he'd betrayed her, even if he'd never said he wouldn't target those with her. She'd wanted to see good in him and had blinded herself to the ugly. Her eyes rested on Blackie, a few paces ahead of her. She wouldn't make that mistake again.

A sharp ache settled around her soul as she realized what she had to do. The only way to keep Blackie and the others safe was for her to leave and head for the Black Mountains on her own — which she'd planned to do anyway, she reminded herself. Traveling with the smugglers had been a temporary arrangement. She'd grown to care for them, though, in all their quirkiness, and she'd enjoyed their camaraderie. All the more reason to leave. Better to travel a lonely road than bring your friends with you and have to bury them along the way.

Blackie stopped a block away from the inn. "Anyone following?" he asked Brains.

Brains shook his head.

"Stay here." Blackie scouted the area around the inn, then motioned them forward. He knocked on the back door, and the bald man with the eye patch let them in. Whittler, Diamond Jack, and Whiskey leaped up from where they'd been sitting and surrounded them.

"Where in the Abyss have you been?" Whiskey demanded. "We been waiting half the night."

"What's she doing here?" Jack eyed the Gypsy woman with uneasiness and dislike.

Whittler stopped short, staring at Blackie's torn and bloody shirt. Whittler's gaze swung to Tara, and she knew he'd guessed what had happened.

Blackie gripped Whittler's shoulders, gently, but firmly. "Easy. It's all right. We're fine." He sat Whittler on a nearby crate and brushed Whittler's hair back from the injured side of his face. "Man, that eye looks worse."

Whittler shrugged and turned away.

Blackie pulled his shirt off and tossed it to the man with the eye patch. "Fennel, can you get rid of this and find me another one?"

Fennel caught the shirt. "I'll see what I got." He left the room.

"We need to get out of here," Blackie said. "We can —"

"Wait," Gus interrupted. He slid off the barstool and stepped forward. "Before you make any plans, I want my share of the brandy money. This is where we part company, as we agreed."

Tara took a deep breath. "That's not necessary."

All eyes turned toward her.

"This is where I take *my* leave," she continued. "I had originally asked only to ride through with you to Norellanen. We're well beyond Norellanen now. I thank you for all that you've done for me. I'll never be able to repay you, but I can't let my presence here put you in any more danger. It's time for me to go."

Something thumped against the outside wall, and a mob of angry, drunken voices passed through the alley. Then came a muffled uproar and the distant crash of breaking glass, somewhere beyond the front of the building.

Fennel stuck his head and arm through the hall door and threw a dark-colored shirt at Blackie.

"What in the Abyss is going on out there?" Blackie asked as he caught the piece of clothing.

Out of the corner of her eye, Tara saw the Gypsy staring unabashedly as Blackie drew the shirt over his head. Tara smiled inwardly.

"Some drunks started a riot," Fennel said, "and now there's a bunch of crazy mobs looting and attacking merchants. The Guard's useless without Romaine, and with the lockup flattened and him gone, every criminal in town is having a party."

"What happened to Romaine?" Blackie asked.

Fennel gestured toward Tara. "Ask her. I got to go barricade the front door. Shove something up against the back door, would ya? If you were thinking of leaving now, I wouldn't. You can stay here the rest of the night if you want, providing they don't burn the place down. Romaine was a nasty SOB, but he knew how to keep order. I'll bring you some food." He ducked out and shut the door.

Brains and Jack grabbed a heavy table and dragged it across to the door as more drunken shouts passed through the alley. They tipped the table on its side and jammed it beneath the door latch.

Blackie turned back to Tara. "What happened to Romaine?"

"We fought. He lost." She shrugged. "He was alive when I left, though he wasn't in very good shape." Had he died? She recalled their battle and his threats against her and Whittler. No, she didn't regret her actions.

Blackie tugged a draw-string bag out of his pocket and dumped a handful of gold coins onto his palm. He counted them, added two more, and then handed the coins to Gus. "Here's your share. Stay or go as you choose. Nobody else is going anywhere until morning." He looked pointedly at Tara.

Listening to the mayhem outside, she didn't feel inclined to argue. "Fine."

Fennel reentered, carrying sacks of cold meat, bread, and cheese and some bottles of ale. He blew the dust off one of the tables and set them down.

Blackie gave him a couple of gold coins. "Thanks, Fennel."

Fennel's eyes gleamed at the gold. "For another one of those, I might be able to find you some blankets."

"All right." Blackie dropped another coin into Fennel's hand. "But we get to keep them."

Fennel tossed the coins up and caught them again. "They're all yours." He left the room.

The smugglers dug into the food. Whiskey and Jack had pulled down a few chairs from a stack in one corner and spread them near the table. They both sat and devoured their meals. Gus took his portion back to the barstool and ate alone. Tara hovered around the table and picked at some small chunks of bread and cheese. She didn't have much of an appetite. She wanted desperately to communicate with Valina to find out about Natiere, and more importantly, to ask about Jovan. She sensed he was in trouble. But she wanted to speak with Valina in private, without the others knowing, so she'd have to wait until they slept.

The Gypsy woman came forward uncertainly. Blackie turned from where he and Brains had corralled Whittler to look at his injury and waved her toward the table. "Go ahead. Have something to eat." He frowned at the dark trail her wet skirts left on the floor and set down his food. "You're drenched. You must be cold. I'll see if Fennel —"

Fennel opened the door and dropped a folded pile of blankets on the floor. Blackie picked one up, shook it out, and swept it around the Gypsy's shoulders. "Fennel, do you think you could find some clothes for the lady? Hers are soaked."

"What am I, a wardrobe?" Fennel muttered as he disappeared out the door.

"What's your name?" Blackie asked the Gypsy.

She drew the blanket close around her. "Sarita."

"Well, Sarita, I'm Blackie, and this is Tara, and that's Brains, Gus, Whiskey, and Whittler, and Diamond Jack, you've already met."

She nodded to each one, regarding them as if she was expecting unfriendliness.

"Why is she here?" Jack asked.

The smugglers looked at Blackie and Brains, who looked at each other, their expressions revealing they didn't really know what part she had played.

Tara spoke. "She distracted Natiere after he attacked Blackie — jumped right up on his back and pounded his head." She turned to the Gypsy. "You've got a lot of guts."

Sarita gave her a half smile and raised her chin in proud defiance.

The others stared in silent shock.

"Blackie, what did he do to you?" Jack asked, horrified.

Grim anger flared in Blackie's eyes again, then it disappeared behind his poker face. "Nothing you need to worry about. I owe you thanks," he said to Sarita. He waved his arm toward the table. "Please eat."

Whiskey brought her a chair as she made her way to the table.

Blackie faced Tara. "And I owe you thanks, too," he said softly, though he didn't seem very happy about it.

"What happened? Why did he attack you?" she whispered.

"That's between him and me. You said the sorceress got rid of him?"

"Yes. She used those white clouds and sent him somewhere. I haven't had a chance to ask her where."

Blackie raised his eyebrows. "How would you do that?"

"I can communicate with her mentally. All I know is that he's a long ways away."

Blackie's poker face slipped, and Tara saw relief and bitterness in his eyes. "Good," he said. "That's one less worry." He thought for a moment. "How did she know?"

"She has a magical mirror she uses to find people. She must have been watching."

"Hmmmm." Blackie's eyes narrowed, and he looked none too pleased with the idea of being watched.

Tara followed him back to the table, her own thoughts mixed on the subject. She hadn't considered that Valina might be watching her on her quest. The idea was a bit disconcerting. And yet the sorceress' intervention had allowed her to save Blackie's life. That alone was worth the price of a little discomfiture.

Tara surveyed the food spread out on the table but couldn't bring herself to eat any more. Sarita had chosen some bread and meat and ate hungrily. Blackie moved around the table to the pile of crates where Whittler sat with Brains bent over him. Brains was running his fingers over Whittler's jaw.

Blackie squatted beside Whittler. "Is it broken?" he asked Brains.

Brains straightened up and nodded. "He can't open it. I don't know how he's going to eat, or how we're going to fix it."

Tara watched Whittler cradle his jaw in his hand, his body hunched, his breathing more labored than it had been when she'd seen him earlier. His eye had turned a deeper black and was swollen shut. His nose and the whole left side of his face were puffy and purplish. She took a deep breath and let it out slowly. She couldn't leave him in such pain. She slid around the table and knelt beside Whittler. "Will you let me heal you?"

Whittler looked at her with his good eye. Fear warred with hope.

Blackie put his hand on her arm. "What will happen to you if you do?"

"Hopefully nothing."

"Are you sure?"

"I'm not sure of anything." She looked up at Whittler. "Except I can't stand to see you suffer. I've already used my healing power once tonight, so this shouldn't make things any worse for me. Please let me help."

He glanced at Blackie and Brains, then nodded.

She drew her dagger. "Blackie, Brains, take his hands. You need to stay as still as you can," she said to Whittler. He stiffened nervously. She braced herself, then cut her palm and laid her hand over a scrape on Whittler's cheek, closing her eyes as the power seared through her. Forging her mental walls, she eased the power into Whittler as gently as she could. She ducked her head, clenching her teeth as the pain of Whittler's injuries slammed into her face. Then the healing began, and the pain ceased. The puffy swelling beneath her hand shrunk into firm flesh. The broken nose, cheek, and jaw bones knit quickly.

After a few minutes she withdrew the power, thanking all the gods that Ravnaul had left her alone again. She opened her eyes to see Whittler touching his face and smiling. She smiled back, suddenly feeling exhausted as the rush of power left her.

Whiskey wiped off the mouth of his bottle and held it out to her. "You look like you could use this."

"Was that as painful as it looked?" Jack asked.

Tara hesitated. "It hurts a little in the beginning, then it goes away." She took the bottle of — she wasn't sure what it was — and tipped back a long swallow. The fiery liquid burned all the way down to her stomach. Brandy — good brandy, not Cierran, but close. She wiped off the bottle and handed it back to Whiskey. "Thanks."

"It looked a whole lot more than a 'little' painful," Brains said, his expression both curious and concerned. "Just how much does it hurt when you heal someone?"

Tara felt an array of eyes on her. "It's not important," she said, rising.

Blackie blocked her path. "Yes, it is. You've healed three of us, now. We want to know."

She let out a long breath. "Fine. I feel the pain of the original injury, but it only lasts a few moments." She saw Brains glance from Blackie to her and knew he was remembering the stab wounds she'd healed.

"You mean you felt what Whittler felt when the guards were beating on him?" Jack asked, appalled.

"Well... yes, but it doesn't matter. It's the end result that counts." She patted Whittler's shoulder.

Whittler pulled something out of his pocket and slipped it into her hand.

She looked down, surprised. A three-inch-high, perfectly carved wolf rested on her palm. It was sitting forward, howling at the moon. She caught her breath. "For me? It's beautiful! Thank you." She hugged him, much to his embarrassment. Then the possible connotations of his choice of animal struck her, and she grew sober. "I have to know — why a wolf?"

Whittler shrugged and signed an answer.

"He says he never knows what's going to come out until he's into it," Blackie translated. "It just seemed like the right thing."

Tara ran her fingers over the wolf's wooden fur. She could almost feel its softness. She put her hand on Whittler's arm. "It's perfect. I love it."

He blushed and nodded, then escaped to the table to fill his hungry belly.

Fennel reappeared at the door with an armload of clothing. "I got some extra clothes from one of my barmaids." He looked at Sarita appraisingly. "She's about your size." He set the clothes on the pile of blankets.

"Thanks, Fennel," Blackie said. He grinned. "If I think of anything else, I'll let you know."

"How about another bottle?" Whiskey called out.

Fennel rolled his eyes and left.

Sarita wiped the crumbs from her hands and went to examine the clothing. Then she glanced around the room and hesitated, finding no space for privacy.

"Here, let me." Tara picked up a blanket and spread it out, holding it up with her arms wide.

Sarita said something in Gypsy, which Tara took for a "thank you," and stepped behind the makeshift curtain. She changed quickly and emerged wearing a slate blue skirt with matching laced bodice over a cream-colored long-sleeved blouse. She hung her wet clothing over some chairs to dry. Tara set the blanket back down on the pile.

"We should get some sleep," Blackie said. "We've got maybe four hours until dawn. I'll take the first watch —"

"I'll take the watch," Tara interrupted, "since I won't be sleeping anyway."

"What do you mean you won't be sleeping?" Blackie asked.

"I used the sword and my healing power. The next time I sleep, I'll end up in Ravnaul's dungeon. I'd like to put that off for a while."

Blackie cursed and ran his hand through his hair. "Well, you're going to have to sleep sometime. What then?"

Tara shrugged, hiding her apprehension. "I'll worry about that when the time comes." She stifled a yawn and sank down into a chair. Judging from how tired she was, it wouldn't be long, she thought grimly. She looked at the other smugglers. "I'm sorry I lied to you about the sword. It's just something I thought would be better kept to myself."

Jack, Whiskey, and Whittler exchanged glances, but didn't say anything.

Gus refused to meet her eyes. He turned his back and moved the barstool to the farthest corner of the room.

"I can understand why you'd want to keep it secret," Brains said. "I've never seen such a powerful weapon." He stroked his chin thoughtfully. "Is there any way we can help you with whatever happens in the dungeon?"

Surprised by the offer, Tara considered. "Thanks, but I don't think so..." She trailed off, realizing the full consequences of the night's events. Jovan was still cut off from her, and Natiere was now far away. Even if he were close by, she would not allow any contact between their minds. She would have to escape Ravnaul's dungeon on her own.

"How do you get out of this dungeon?" Brains asked.

"What? Oh... I..." She stopped, not wanting to reveal her odd mental relationship with Natiere. And she certainly didn't want to bring up Jovan with Gus still listening. "It's hard to explain."

"I'm sure it is," Brains said, "but I would like to know how it works. How does your mind go somewhere else, while your body stays here?"

She sighed. They had helped her through so much, she owed them some sort of explanation. "I don't know exactly what happens.

I fall asleep, and when I wake, it's as if I am in the dungeon, even though only my mind is truly there. Somehow, Ravnaul manages to draw me in. The only way to escape is to pass through a crushing black void that sucks the life and breath out of you. I've never been able to get through it alone. I've always needed someone with magic to help me escape."

"Who has magic?" Brains asked. "Besides Ravnaul, and Melodian, and Valina Mellarian, of course, but you just met her, so it couldn't have been her that helped you before. Who, then?"

Tara hesitated. "Natiere," she said finally.

Brains stared. "The Butcher has magic?" His eyebrows rose higher. "And he helped you?"

"Yes. I don't know where his magic comes from —"

"He has Gypsy magic," said Sarita, her voice low and heavily accented.

"What do you know about him?" Tara asked quickly, hiding her irritation with the Gypsy for not speaking the Western tongue sooner.

"When Naticre was a boy, the Gypsy warlock Wolfgren saved his life and gave him the magic of the wolf's blood, so Natiere could exact his revenge. It is common knowledge among the Gypsies."

"Revenge for what?" Jack asked.

"For the butchering of his family by bandits," Sarita answered.

Jack glanced at the other smugglers, then sat back thoughtfully.

"How does the Butcher help you?" Brains asked Tara.

"When I was trapped in the void, I heard his voice in my mind, and I was somehow able to use his strength to get out. I didn't realize until afterward that it was him." She held up her hands to stem any further questions. "I know you probably have many more things you'd like to ask, but right now I'm too tired to answer them."

Brains reluctantly swallowed whatever he'd been going to say.

Blackie tossed each of the smugglers a blanket. "There's not a lot of room, but pick a spot and get some sleep."

Sarita wrapped herself in the blanket Blackie had given her earlier and curled up in a chair. The others draped themselves over various tables and chairs or sacked out on the floor.

Blackie dropped a blanket onto Tara's lap. "Will you be all right?"

She nodded. "Thanks."

"I want your word you won't sneak out while we're asleep."

She shook out the blanket. "I won't."

He crouched next to her in the chair, at eye level. "That's not good enough. Look me in the eye and say it."

She gusted out a breath and met his gaze. "Fine. I won't. All right?"

"Fine." He stood up and then bunked down on the floor in front of the door.

As she settled the blanket around her, Tara caught Sarita glaring at her, but when she turned to look, the woman's eyes were closed.

CHAPTER 26

Rylan Natiere strode along the perimeter of the vast underground cavern he'd found himself in when Valina Mellarian's cloud trap had dissipated. Dim milky-white light from scattered patches of luminescent fungus reflected off the surface of the large pool of water in the center of the cavern, aiding his wolfen sight. The deep red of the rock walls told him he was in the Scarlet Mountains, far to the west of the Gypsy Crossroads. He was glad his wolves weren't with him in this living tomb.

A short distance along the wall he found a tunnel leading into the mountain, the passage hewn from the rock with man-made tools and shored up with rotting timbers. He cursed the sorceress for the hundredth time. She'd stuck him in an abandoned gold mine. Thousands of miles of mine shafts riddled the Scarlet Mountains, whose jagged peaks formed many spines that sprawled across the countries of Mardainn and Jendairin and stretched deep into the Southlands. From the crudeness of the cuts in the rock and the rough construction of the timber framework, he guessed he was in Jendairin. The miners there were poorer than those of Mardainn and less educated in the art of mining and stonework, barely more than slaves to the avarice of the Twin Cities' nobles.

Natiere worked his way around the edge of the cavern and discovered two more tunnels, both of similar construction to the first. He sniffed the air in each. In one, the air hung still and dead; in the other, his heightened sense of smell detected a slightly fresher staleness. He entered the passage, treading carefully to avoid pitfalls. Although his wolfen sight allowed him to see in the near dark, he wasn't taking any chances. He would not allow the sorceress any satisfaction at his expense.

He'd been so close to achieving his goal — Tara had been within his grasp. He clenched his fists. The sorceress had caught him by surprise this time. Never again. The magic imbued in him by the Gypsy warlock Wolfgren prowled through his blood like a savage beast. The sorceress would not be sending him anywhere any more. He would find his way out of this cursed mountain, and next time, the surprise would be on her.

*****

Jovan Trevillion groaned and shifted his position, trying to ease the pain in his shoulder. His hands and feet had grown numb from the ropes that bound him. It was as if the thick darkness was slowly consuming him, turning him into a ghost. In a few short hours, his body would be completely assimilated, leaving only his spirit to forever haunt this black pit, as his brother's spirit haunted the Bog.

No... can't die here... must stay alive... He berated himself for his macabre thoughts. But it was so hard to beat back the blackness that preyed on his sanity like some demonic phantom. How long had he lain here? He couldn't tell how many hours had passed since he'd been tossed into the Pit. He'd fought against his restraining bonds until he'd felt warm blood running down his fingers. He could see nothing, he could hear no sound, and all he could smell was the faint mustiness of the cold rock beneath him.

So thirsty. His mouth was so dry he could barely swallow, his body weak from lack of food and water. He felt himself slipping again toward unconsciousness.

Tara, I'm sorry. I failed you...

His weakened thoughts bounced back to him, unable to penetrate the barrier. Despairing, he numbly stared into the darkness until oblivion swallowed him.

*****

Tara Triannon sat up straighter in her chair, waiting impatiently for the last of the smugglers to fall asleep. When Whittler finally stopped twitching and Brains' breathing deepened, she took one last glance around the room and then half closed her eyes and concentrated. Cautiously, she slivered her mind open.

Jovan...

She felt nothing, no answering touch, only a cold foreboding that froze her like an icy wind. What had happened? Where was he? She had to find out.

Valina...

The sorceress answered immediately. *Tara, are you all right?*

Yes. Thank you for sending Natiere away.

I know you said you wanted him near, but I feared for you.

It's all right. Where did you send him?

Into a mine shaft deep in the Scarlet Mountains. He is searching the tunnels for a way out. Knowing his persistence, I'm sure he will discover one. When he is free, he'll come after you again. What should I do?

Nothing, yet. Valina, where is Jovan Trevillion?

I don't know. I still can't see him in the mirror. Vexation colored the sorceress' voice. *He should have caught up with you by now, unless he went astray, as you did.*

Tara's heart skipped a beat. *You mean you found him once and sent him to me? Was he all right?*

Yes. He was on the bank of the Nournan River, as you thought. I only found him because I was watching Natiere, and Natiere came upon him. Jovan was unconscious. It looked like Natiere was going to kill him, but he didn't. I'm not sure why. Then the Bog wolves came, and Natiere was going to let them kill Jovan, but I intervened. When I sent Jovan to you, he was awake and seemed well. He should have found you hours ago.

Tara cursed to herself. *He's not here, and there's something very wrong. He's in danger, I can feel it, but I can't reach him with my thoughts. I'm worried.*

I will keep trying to locate him. If you do get through to him, see if you can find out what is close to him. We might be able to work around the interference that way, though if I were to transport him, he'd likely get sent elsewhere again. It's all so frustrating.

Yes, very, Tara agreed. *Thank you again for your help.*

You're welcome. The sorceress' voice receded, a fading echo in Tara's mind.

So Jovan's whereabouts were now even more of a mystery. Where had he landed? Tara thanked the gods that Valina had rescued him from the Bog wolves. The sorceress said that Natiere had been going to kill him. Tara wondered what had stopped the Wolfmaster from striking. She pounded her thigh, angry at her own helplessness. At least Natiere wouldn't be a threat for a while. She had no doubt he would find a way out of the mines, but the Scarlet Mountains were far away from the Gypsy Crossroads. And she had no intention of waiting around for him to catch up.

She yawned, and another wave of exhaustion rolled over her. Her eyelids drooped. Icy jabs of warning startled her. She sensed Ravnaul's approach. Hastily, she flung up her mental defenses and sat rigid, awaiting his attack on her mind. Ravnaul retreated and hovered on the edge of her consciousness, a stalking beast content to wait until sleep claimed her.

Shivering, she rose, dropping her blanket in the chair. She had to move to keep herself awake. The moment she took a step, Blackie's eyes opened. His head turned toward her. He ran his hand over his face and sat up, watching her narrowly.

She crossed the room and squatted beside him. "Sorry," she whispered. "I didn't mean to wake you. I just needed to move around. It's hard to stay awake. And no, I wasn't trying to leave," she added. "I don't break promises."

He relaxed. "Did you talk to the sorceress, however it is you do it?"

She nodded. "Valina sent Natiere into a mine shaft, somewhere in the Scarlet Mountains."

Blackie smiled grimly. "Good place for him. I don't suppose it was a sealed shaft?"

"No." She sat cross-legged beside him and rubbed her eyes. "I don't know the best way to handle this. If I have the black sword with me when I sleep, it will come through into the dungeon, and I can use it against Ravnaul. But if he gets it away from me again, all is lost. I know my powers have grown stronger, but so have his, and I don't think there would be any way for me to get it back." She stifled a yawn. "I think it would be best if I give the sword to you or Brains until afterward, so there'll be no way for it to fall into Ravnaul's hands."

"No, you can't." Blackie's aversion to the sword lay plain on his face. "You'll be defenseless. How will you fight him without it?"

"I don't know. I'll just have to find a way." She shuddered at the thought of thousands of spiders crawling over her again.

"Can't the sorceress help?"

Tara shrugged. "I don't know. I didn't think to ask her. I know she said earlier she was no match for Ravnaul."

"She's supposed to be a powerful sorceress. If the Butcher was able to help you, she should be able to. She must be more powerful than he is."

"Maybe, maybe not. I have the feeling Natiere's magic is a lot stronger than anyone thinks." She shoved her hair back away from her face. "But anyway, it doesn't matter. I won't accept help from him again, not after what he did to you."

Blackie gripped her arm. "Tara, listen to me. You need to live. That's all that counts. You need to use whatever means necessary to stay alive. If that means using the Butcher to get you out of the dungeon, then use him."

Tara bristled. "You think I would trust him after —"

"You don't have to trust him, just do whatever you have to do to survive."

"I can't believe you're telling me this."

"Well, think about it. What good will you be to anyone if you're dead?"

She had no answer to that. "There has to be another way."

"I hope there is, but if there isn't, I want you to promise me you'll use him. Don't pass up your last chance because of what happened to me."

She glared at him. "I don't want to promise that."

His grip on her arm tightened. *"Promise me."*

Their eyes held for several heartbeats. Blackie's words echoed through her mind — *you need to live, that's all that counts. What good will you be if you're dead?* If she died, the Kamarians would be lost forever.

She released her anger. "All right, fine. I promise."

He held her gaze a moment longer, then let go of her arm. "You should stay with us at least until after you've slept. You can decide about the sword when the time comes. If you want one of us to take it, we will, but I don't think it's a good idea."

She caught his hand in hers and squeezed it. "Thanks, Blackie. I don't know where I'd be without you." She leaned forward and kissed him on the cheek, then rose and went back to her chair. Blackie lay down again and stared at the ceiling. She arranged her blanket, leaned back in the chair, and did the same. She had to admit, the knowledge that she could use Natiere as a last resort did ease her mind somewhat. If the sorceress was unable to help her, at least she would have some recourse to escape the void.

She was about to contact Valina Mellarian again when she realized she was being watched. She turned her head quickly and caught Sarita's eyes closing. The Gypsy had been staring daggers at her again.

Tara frowned. She knew that look of jealousy, had even felt it herself when Myles had flirted with other women in the past. She closed her eyes. That was another detail she wished she hadn't remembered. Sarita had no reason to be jealous, though. Tara didn't feel that way about Blackie. She loved him like a best friend, not a lover, and she thought he felt the same about her. A touch of unease twitched through her. Didn't he? She knew there had never been any intimacy between them. No, they were just the best of friends. She sighed. If Sarita's jealousy became a problem, she would enlighten the Gypsy about her and Blackie's relationship.

Shifting into the most uncomfortable position she could find to avoid the lure of sleep, she cleared her mind again. *Valina...*

Yes, Tara?

The sorceress' calm voice soothed her nerves. *I may need your help soon.*

How may I help you?

I need to sleep, but when I do, I'll be drawn into Ravnaul's dungeon. I haven't been able to escape the dungeon on my own. I've always needed someone with magic to help me through the void. Can I call on you, if necessary?

Of course. I will do all I can to help you.

Thank you. She paused. *You haven't found Jovan yet, have you?*

Not yet, but I will continue to look.

Thank you. Disappointment washed over her. Where was he? Frustrated, she stared into space and listened to the muffled shouts and sword clashes filling the streets in front of the inn.

Three hours later, Tara heard a knock on the hall door. The door pushed in a few inches and banged into Blackie. Blackie cursed and moved as Fennel, with a grunted apology, brought in another sack of food. He scraped what little was left of the night's meal to one side and spread out more bread, jars of strawberry and blueberry jam, and some dried fruit, with bottles of honey mead to wash it down. He tossed Whiskey a tall bottle of dark amber liquid. Slouching in a chair with his leg over the arm, Whiskey caught the bottle with his eyes barely open. The other smugglers and the Gypsy roused and stretched and converged on the table.

Even though she wasn't very hungry, Tara was glad to have an excuse to get up and walk around without having to worry about waking the others. Staying awake for that last hour had been a challenge.

"Is the town still standing?" Blackie asked Fennel around a mouthful of dried berries.

"Most of it. The Guard has managed to restore some order, but walking the streets is still risky. You'll have to watch your backs."

Blackie nodded.

Fennel looked more closely at Whittler. "Didn't you have a black eye?"

Whittler gestured with his hands and turned away.

"He says he heals quickly," Blackie said.

"Hmmmmm." Fennel glanced at Whittler with a puzzled frown, then shook his head and left the room.

Tara caught Gus' glance of abhorrence, his fingers twitching his warding signs. He muttered something in a Southland dialect and took his breakfast back to the far corner. Cold anger rose within her. She had the power to save lives, and yet in his ignorance and fear, he would condemn her for it, just like the villagers she'd grown up with.

She felt a touch on her arm and turned to find Whittler beside her, holding out a slice of bread slathered with strawberry jam. Surprised, she smiled and took the bread, her anger dissolving. At least not everyone hated her. "Thanks," she said softly.

He nodded with an embarrassed smile and went to get his own meal.

Sarita stepped up beside Tara and spoke in a low voice full of amusement. "You'd better watch your step. The dark one over there," she nodded at Gus, "just cursed you."

Blackie moved close and whispered, "You understood him? What did he say?"

She looked at Tara. "He said, 'May the gods strike down the evil and leave your bones to bleach in the sun.'"

Tara grimaced. "Wonderful." She half expected Blackie to storm over and confront Gus, but Blackie had caught the scent of opportunity.

"Do you know other languages?" he asked Sarita.

"I know many. I am a Gypsy, I travel all over. I trade with everyone." She tossed her head. "I learned to speak many tongues, so I would not get cheated. Men think that because I am a woman, I can be easily fooled and taken advantage of. They talk their trickery among themselves in their own language, thinking I don't under-stand their words." She laughed. "But they soon discover it is not wise to double-cross Sarita." She flashed Blackie a wickedly flirta-tious smile and went back to the table for more food.

Tara watched Blackie covertly as he slowly began eating again. She caught his speculative glances at the Gypsy and knew he was already scheming about ways to use this latest talent he'd found. She smiled to herself. *Good. He's hooked.*

After they'd finished eating, they packed up the rest of the food and their blankets. Tension sharpened the air as Brains and Jack dragged the heavy table away from the back door. Tara wondered what Gus would do — would he leave as he'd declared earlier, or would he stay, since she had said she'd be leaving? The others, too, seemed to be waiting for both of them to reveal their intentions.

Gus shouldered his share of the supplies. He inclined his head and pressed his fingers to his chest, then to his forehead, then dipped his hand outward toward the smugglers, palm up. "I bid you farewell."

Brains and Diamond Jack nodded.

"Farewell," Blackie said stiffly.

The others remained silent.

Gus strode to the door and exited.

Tara sensed a collective exhale from the smugglers and knew she wasn't the only one who wasn't sorry to see him go. She knew she should be relieved, but instead she felt uneasiness like a feathery nervousness in her gut. She had the distinct feeling she hadn't seen the last of him, and that the results would not be pleasant when they crossed paths again.

Blackie turned to Sarita. "If you tell us where your home is, we'll see that you get there."

"I have no home," she said.

"What about your clan?"

She spat. "My clan is —" She lapsed into a Gypsy tirade. "They cast me out because I traded with the Shokani, a rival Gypsy clan. But I say, what difference does it make? When the caravanners and Westerners are tight with their gold, you trade where you can."

"Well, where do you live?" Blackie asked.

She tossed her head. "I said, I have no home. I want to travel with you."

Blackie raked his hand through his hair, nonplussed. "You can't," he said finally.

"Why not?" Sarita gestured toward Tara. "Because of her? She said she was leaving."

"I am," Tara said.

"But not until you sleep," Blackie said with a glance at Tara.

"But she's had hours to sleep." Sarita threw her hands up. "You make no sense."

"It doesn't matter," Blackie said. "You can't come with us right now."

"Why not?" Tara asked. "You're down a man. And you already know she's resourceful, and she's got guts." Despite Sarita's adversarial manner, Tara found herself liking the Gypsy — her bold brassiness, her fortitude, and her willingness to follow her own path, rather than be dictated to by the Gypsy clan elders. And no one could question her loyalty to Blackie after her actions in the town square. Her presence would be good for him, and good for Tara, too, if Blackie was beginning to think of Tara as more than a friend. The last thing she wanted to do was break his heart.

"Because we never know where we're going to end up with you," Blackie said to Tara. "I don't want to put her in that much danger." He faced Sarita. "When we're done with this thing with her," he nodded at Tara, "we'll come back for you."

"Don't we get to vote on this?" Jack asked. He didn't seem pleased with the idea of the Gypsy joining their band.

The hall door slid open, and Fennel's head appeared. His expression silenced them. "I got guards out front." He jerked his head at Tara. "They're looking for her, but they'll take the rest of you if they see you. Beat it out of here, quick!"

Tara, Sarita, and the smugglers snatched up the food and blankets they'd packed and headed for the back door. Blackie went out first, then motioned for the others to follow. Keeping a sharp watch, they wove through the streets, avoiding the Guard and knots of drunken looters. They reached the edge of town without incident and continued on into the surrounding forest.

Blackie led them back to the campsite in the clearing. The boat still lay jammed up against the pile of rocks. They tossed their gear into the boat, then checked to make sure the supplies Valina Mellarian had given them were still hidden where they had stashed them.

Blackie cleared his throat. "You'll have to excuse us," he said to Tara and Sarita. "We have some things to discuss."

Tara nodded and went back to the boat. Sarita followed reluctantly. Tara sat on a flat rock, her eyes lingering on Blackie and his men as they talked near the trees. She was really going to miss them.

Sarita paced restlessly, then sat down next to Tara.

Tara felt the Gypsy's eyes burning into her. She turned. "Well?"

"What are you?" Sarita asked.

Tara looked away. "I'm just like you or anyone else, except I have a gift."

"You healed them with your touch. How?"

"I don't know exactly. As I said, it's a gift. I was born with it."

Sarita uttered a Gypsy exclamation. "You have the magic of the Ancient Ones?" She made warding signs similar to those Gus had made.

Tara rolled her eyes. "Not you, too." She faced Sarita. "My magic is not going to hurt you. It's not so much different from the Gypsy magic you spoke of earlier."

Sarita digested this for a moment, then gestured toward the smugglers. "What about him?"

Tara knew who she meant. "What about him?"

"You're hurting him."

"What do you mean?" Tara asked, irritation needling her.

Sarita tossed her head. "You are heartless. You are one of those..." She spat out what Tara guessed were particularly unflattering Gypsy phrases.

"If you're going to curse me out," Tara interrupted, "at least do it in a language I can understand."

"He's in love with you, and you treat him like —"

"He's not in love with me," Tara snapped. "He can't be," she added more softly, her eyes finding Blackie across the grove.

Sarita stood, her hands on her hips. "Are you blind? Can you not see that he loves you?" She scoffed. "But you do not love him."

"No... yes... I mean I do, but not in that way. I love him as one would a best friend, but I'm not *in* love with him. My heart belongs to someone else."

"Then you should leave now, before you hurt him anymore."

"I just need his help for one more thing, then I will leave."

"Good." Sarita lifted her chin. "And you won't need to worry. I will make him forget you." She caught up her skirt and walked across the grove to meet the smugglers, who had finished their discussion and were coming back toward the boat.

Tara fought back sudden tears as a pang of loneliness pierced her soul. She swiped her sleeve across her eyes and stood resolutely. *I hope you make him forget the hurt*, she thought, *but please don't make him forget me.*

"Well, well. Look who's sharing our campsite."

Tara whirled at the familiar voice, her heart leaping, then sinking.

Myles and the blonde woman, Adriana, had left the woods and were walking toward her. They reached the boat at the same time as the smugglers.

Myles stayed well back out of sword's range, and Tara saw the wariness in his deep blue eyes. "Just like old times, eh?" he said with a disarming smile.

Blackie moved between him and Tara. "What do you want?"

Myles shook his head. "Blackie, why must you always bark at me like some nasty dog wanting to bite my head off? The town was a bit too wild for us last night, so we camped here. We just went in for some breakfast, and now we've come back. There's no crime in that."

Tara watched him closely. There was something in his eyes that bothered her, some scheme he'd hatched. What was he up to? The blonde was in on it too, judging from the nervous glances she kept throwing in every direction, particularly at Tara.

"Well, this is our spot, so go find another." Blackie jerked his thumb toward the woods.

"Your spot, eh? So that's your boat?" Myles looked at it appraisingly. "How'd you get it there? The nearest waterway is leagues from here."

"We flew it here. Now be on your way." Blackie's hand settled on the hilt of his sword. "Or do we have to help you?"

Wary of opening her mind very far, Tara let her senses drift through the human auras around her. Warning chills raced down her spine. Many auras surrounded her, many more than there should have been.

She spun in a circle, sensing danger all around her. Anger filled her. Now she did have a reason to kill him. "Blackie, the Guard is coming! They're surrounding us."

Blackie cursed, and with the look he threw Myles, she knew if Myles had been a little closer, he would have been dead.

"It wasn't me, I swear it!" Myles protested, but his reaction of surprise at the ambush couldn't erase the guilt she saw his eyes.

"Into the woods! Stay in pairs." Blackie drew his sword, and they bolted into the forest.

Myles and Adriana ran for the woods, too, but angled away from the smugglers. Tara chased after them, her hatred of Myles blinding her to all else. Blackie's voice, shouting for her to stay close, barely registered in her mind as she dashed between the trees. This time she would kill that lying skunk.

A few yards into the forest, the Guard met them with bare blades and fierce shouts. Tara dodged a sword thrust, jumped in close, and elbowed the guardsman hard across the jaw. With a grunt, he staggered sideways. She shoved him headfirst into a tree. Evading another blow, she cut down two more guardsmen, then ducked through the undergrowth and raced after Myles. She heard more guardsmen crashing through the brush after her, but she quickly outdistanced them.

She hadn't gone far when she saw Myles ahead of her, jogging through the trees. Where was Adriana? She couldn't see the blonde anywhere. Myles was running at half speed, and Tara had the odd feeling he wanted her to catch him. Well, she would be more than happy to oblige.

Ignoring the warning chills that raked her skin, she darted forward. "Myles!"

He slowed to a halt and turned, his hands held out in front of him. "Look, I'm unarmed. I just want to talk to you."

Tara stopped a few feet away. "Draw your sword, you lying snake. This time I *will* kill you."

"Tara, wait. I know you're mad, but just listen —"

"Listen to what — to you explaining why you turned us in to the Guard? I already know why. The glint of gold in your eye speaks volumes. Now draw your sword."

"No, Tara, not you. I wanted you to follow me, so you wouldn't get caught. It's true I don't care if Blackie and his band are taken. Blackie always hated me. Earning a little gold at his expense is fair payback." Myles took a step toward her, his blue eyes intense. "You don't need them anyway. You can come with me. We had something magical once. We were an unstoppable team. Adriana is only a friend, nothing more — nothing like you and I were." He took another step. *"Come with me."*

For a fraction of a second, Tara considered his offer, let his insistent, almost pleading, voice beguile her. Then she held him up beside Jovan in her mind's eye, and Myles withered in comparison, like a blighted fruit shriveling in the bright glare of the desert sun. The spell of his voice lost its lure. She had no desire to go with him; whatever hold he'd had over her in the past was gone.

"No, Myles," she said coldly. "We're done. Draw your sword, or I'll kill you outright."

An icy jab of warning startled her. She whirled, but not quickly enough. Something bashed her over the head. Blackness swirled around her as she hit the ground. She felt rough hands at her waist, vaguely heard the sound of voices arguing as she fought to stay afloat in the sea of thickening tar.

No! she screamed inwardly as Ravnaul's claws sank into the edge of her mind and dragged her inexorably downward. Ignited by her panic, power exploded in her mind, flaring outward in a blinding flash of fire that shattered Ravnaul's hold on her and left her gasping for breath. Frantically, she struggled through her semi-consciousness haze, but it was like trying to swim through quicksand. She couldn't see, and the only sound she heard was the clash of swords, fading in and out of her mind. She felt herself slipping into unconsciousness.

A splash of cold water on her face shocked her awake. She sputtered as full awareness returned, along with an aching knot on the back of her head. Slowly, she wiped the water out of her eyes and sat up. "What hit me?"

Someone knelt beside her. "Are you all right?"

She focused on the face hovering in front of her. She recognized the curling dark hair, the crooked half smile, the bold blue eyes now filled with uncertainty. Anger burned through her dizziness. "You!" She punched him in the nose. He fell back with a cry. She rose unsteadily. "You've got a lot of gall to show your face to me again after what you did."

Myles held his bleeding nose. "It wasn't my idea, I swear it. It was Adriana's. I didn't know she was going to —"

"What are you talking about?" Tara picked up the sword she'd dropped and noticed three men in guard uniforms lying, dead or unconscious, on the ground around her. Where had they come from? She faced Myles again, feeling like her brain had a cog out of place. "You turned me, Raina, and Dominic in to the Nightwatch and left us to rot in the Lord Marshal's dungeon." She stopped, her breath catching in her throat as the cog snapped into gear. "I remember," she whispered. Her voice rose to a shout. "I remember!" She gave a wild laugh and spun around. "Everything!" She laughed again, then turned on Myles and poked him in the chest with her blade.

"Ow!" He scrambled to his feet and backed away, looking at her as if she were a lunatic.

"Curse you, Myles, you've done it again."

"Done what?" he asked warily.

"Just when I'm about to kill you, you do something to help me." With a wince, she felt the lump on her head. Between the roaring pain and the memories flooding her mind, it was hard to think straight. An intense longing to see Jovan overwhelmed her. She swayed on her feet. Oh, gods, where was he? She nearly tripped over one of the prone guards. She caught herself and straightened. The Guard — Blackie — what had happened to the smugglers? Then she noticed something else — the black sword, sword belt and all, was gone.

She cursed roundly. "Not again!" She skewered Myles with a glare as she advanced on him. "Where is it?"

He raised his blade defensively. "That's what I was trying to tell you — it wasn't my idea. I had nothing to do with it. I didn't know Adriana wanted to steal it —"

Tara let out a furious growl. "She's going to be one sorry woman when I find her."

"Look, I'm sorry. I'll help you find her. I'll help you get the sword back."

Tara pointed at him with her blade. "You'll do nothing of the sort. You've caused me enough trouble." She looked past him, in the direction Adriana had likely gone, then looked at the downed guardsmen. Every second, the black sword was moving further away, yet she couldn't desert Blackie and the others with no word. And they'd been outnumbered — what if the Guard had captured them? She should have stayed with them and not let her anger get the better of her.

Uttering another curse, she left Myles standing where he was and jogged back toward the clearing. She wanted to go faster, but too much speed jarred her aching head and made her nauseous.

"Tara, wait!" Myles caught up with her and matched her pace. "Stop! Please. There's something I have to say to you."

Tara stopped, not because he asked, but because she was about to throw up. She leaned against a tree and took deep breaths, trying to settle her stomach.

Myles moved closer and held out his hand to touch her, then let it fall. "Do you remember what I said to you, all those years ago?"

Tara eyed him evenly. "Yes. You said, 'Sorry, my love. All bets are off. Catch you in the next life.'"

Myles winced. "No, I mean before that. I said, 'As long as those stars shine, I will love you.' Do you remember?"

Tara looked away. "Yes, you loved me so much, you left me stranded in a dungeon and made a huge profit from the bounty on my head."

"You have to understand. I thought you were going to die. Dominic had the fever. You and Raina were exposed to it. I couldn't bear to watch you suffer from that horrid disease."

"Dominic lived. I never caught the disease and neither did Raina. You just didn't want to catch it yourself. You couldn't get away from me fast enough."

Myles pounded his fist against the tree. "That's not true! I meant those words. I loved you."

"Well, if you were so in love with me, why didn't you ever try to find me? How many years has it been? You had to have known I was alive."

Myles gave a bitter laugh and gestured to the sword in Tara's hand. "You would have killed me."

Tara studied the blade. He had a point.

He raked his hand through his hair. "I can't count the times I wanted to search you out, but I knew you'd never believe me or trust me again." He moved closer. "But I never stopped loving you."

Tara swallowed, her stomach calmer. "I'm sorry, Myles, but I don't love you anymore."

He read her eyes. "There's someone else, isn't there."

"Yes."

He took a step back, a repulsed expression on his face. "Not... not Blackie..."

Tara smiled faintly. "No, not Blackie. But if I had to choose between the two of you, I'd choose him in a heartbeat. He's ten times the man you'll ever be." She pushed away from the tree. "Goodbye, Myles." Moving as swiftly as her head would allow, she made her way back through the woods toward where she'd last seen the smugglers. This time, Myles didn't follow.

CHAPTER 27

Tara found the smugglers still battling the Guard. Blackie, Brains, and Whittler had formed a triangle, with Sarita between them. Several guardsmen littered the ground around them, and the smugglers were holding their own. She couldn't see Whiskey or Diamond Jack.

Keeping low, she crept through the underbrush until she spotted the other two smugglers. Jack and Whiskey fought back to back, using the trees to their advantage, but even so, the eight guardsmen surrounding them were wearing them down. She saw blood on Jack's sleeve, and Whiskey was panting like he'd run a ten-mile race.

The guardsmen pressed their attack. Jack stumbled backward into Whiskey, who tripped over a root and fell. Tara snatched a dagger out of her boot, sprang from the brush, and flung it at the guard who was about to run Jack through. The dagger caught the guard in the chest, and he toppled over backward. Jack recovered his footing, surprise and gratitude on his face as he glanced around, searching for the source of the dagger.

Whiskey had curled his body around his brandy bottle, and he cradled it against his stomach as he rolled nimbly to his feet, sword poised in his other hand. A guard stabbed at Whiskey's gut, and the sharp crack of breaking glass rang out above the clash of swordplay as the point of the guard's blade shattered the bottle. Whiskey roared as the red-gold liquid soaked into the ground at his feet. Yelling like a madman, he slashed at the guards in front of him with the fury of a starving bear denied its favorite meal.

Then Tara leaped into the fray, and within minutes, the few guards left standing fled back toward the Crossroads.

Fighting her dizziness, Tara retrieved her dagger. Jack thanked her with a brief salute, and they dashed back through the trees.

They found nine guards still battling Blackie and the others. Tara wounded two of them. Jack and Whiskey downed two more. The Guard leader shouted for a retreat, and the rest of the Guard withdrew on the run, heading back toward the town.

Brains leaned on a tree and caught his breath. "Well, that was fun."

Jack sank down with his back against the tree. "You call that fun?"

Blackie sheathed his blade. "Anyone hurt?"

Whittler shook his head.

"A few scratches, nothing serious," Brains said.

"They smashed my bottle of brandy!" Whiskey said indignantly. "Half a bottle wasted — soaked right into the ground."

"That'll make for some happy worms," Brains commented.

Whiskey scowled at him.

Blackie patted Whiskey on the shoulder. "We'll get you another one."

Jack tipped his head toward his left arm. "Just a flesh wound."

Sarita bent down and ripped some strips of fabric from her petticoat. "I'll take care of it." She crossed to where Jack sat, gently tore back his sleeve, and began to clean away the blood.

He started to object, but at a glare from Blackie, he fell silent and accepted her ministrations.

Blackie's glare shifted to Tara. "Haedis' balls, woman, why in the Abyss did you go running off like that?" He strode toward her. "Didn't you hear me telling you to stay close?"

Blackie's words echoed in her throbbing head, and she felt dizzy again as she undid a sword belt from one of the fallen guards and buckled it around her waist. "I heard you, but I had a score to settle."

He stopped before her with his hands on his hips. "Did you settle it?"

She sheathed her borrowed sword. "No."

"He got away?"

"Not exactly." Her vision grayed, and she would have fallen if Brains hadn't caught her. He lowered her to the ground. She sat cross-legged with her head down and ran her hand gingerly over the welt on the back of her head.

Blackie knelt beside her. "What's wrong?"

"That blonde wench bashed me over the head." Tara looked up. "Blackie, she took the sword. I have to get it back. Again."

Blackie cursed. "Why didn't you go after her?"

"And leave you all at the mercy of the Guard? Some friend I'd be. But there is one piece of good news in all this."

"What's that?" he asked skeptically.

"I remember."

"Remember what?"

"Everything. The whack on the head brought my memory back."

Blackie stared at her, his expression unfathomable. "Well, then, I guess you finally know what you're doing." He rose.

Tara shot him a puzzled glance. That wasn't the reaction she'd expected. He didn't seem happy at all that her memories had returned.

He and Brains gave her a hand up. Brains kept a hold on her elbow to steady her.

"We need to get our stuff and go before the Guard comes back," Blackie said. He turned to Tara. "We'll find your sword."

Whiskey led the way back to the stash. By the time the others reached the cache of supplies, he'd already dug out one of the bottles Valina Mellarian had given them and had tipped it back with a look of utter bliss on his face. Brains and Jack retrieved the food and blankets they'd dropped into the boat earlier. The smugglers packed what they could easily carry and hid the rest.

Tara shivered as a sudden chill skated up and down her spine. She turned quickly, eyes raking the forest. "Blackie!" she whispered. She sucked in a breath as she spotted a large black wolf slinking through the undergrowth toward her. It was Kelya.

Blackie's sword was in his hand before she finished saying his name. "I see it." He thrust Sarita behind him, and the smugglers drew their weapons and closed ranks.

More wolves slipped through the brush like gray shadows, and Tara caught glimpses of yellow-gold eyes and bared teeth.

Kelya stepped through a patch of tall ferns and stopped about four yards away, her yellow eyes fastened on Tara. She growled low in her throat, then barked.

"Curse his foul hide! I thought we were rid of him." Blackie looked around as if expecting the Butcher to materialize between the trees.

Tara put her hand on his arm. "He's not here." She saw the wolf's flattened ears flick forward at the sound of her voice, then flatten again, and she suddenly realized why the wolf had sought her out. "She's looking for him. She thinks we're responsible for his disappearance."

Blackie's eyebrow arched. "How do you know that?"

"I can sense it."

The wolf's lips curled back in a snarl. She took a step toward them, the hair bristling along her back.

The smugglers braced for attack.

Tara hesitated. She hated Natiere for what he'd done to Blackie, but she couldn't help feeling sorry for the wolf. "Kelya, wait." Tara moved forward, her hands held out in front of her.

"Tara —" Blackie started to follow her.

She waved him back. "Stay there."

The black wolf watched her, her ears flicking back and forth.

"I know where he is." Tara advanced slowly. "He's not hurt, but he is far from here." She knelt a few steps away from the wolf and held out her hand. "If you will trust me, I'll try to have you sent to him."

Kelya whined and came forward, nosed Tara's palm.

Six gray wolves eased from the undergrowth and stood close together, silently watching them.

Tara ruffled the black wolf's fur and marveled again at the intelligence in her eyes. Somehow she knew the wolf understood what she was saying. She sensed the wolf's distress, her loneliness and anxiety, and felt an answering pang in her own heart — the pain of being separated from one you loved. She closed her eyes. *Valina...*

Yes, Ta — The sorceress gasped. *That's Natiere's wolf. How could he have come back so quickly? Are you all right?*

Yes, yes, I'm fine, Tara said, *and no, he hasn't come back. Valina, I need two things, if possible.*

Of course. The sorceress regained her composure. *What can I do?*

Can you see Natiere? Is he anywhere near an entrance to the mine?

He is getting close to one, Valina said after a moment.

Could you send his wolves to the entrance nearest where he will come out? They miss him.

They — Really? How extraordinary. Yes, I can send them there, she said, her voice thoughtful. *What else do you need?*

Can you find this woman and tell me where she is? Tara pictured Adriana in her mind.

Let me look. Valina gave a little shriek. *She has Ravnaul's sword!*

Yes, I know. She stole it. Where is she?

She's in a tent on the east side of the Gypsy Crossroads. She's talking to a man who is dressed like a wealthy merchant, a caravanner. The sorceress' voice caught. *She must be trying to sell it.*

A sense of urgency twisted Tara's gut. *Can you show me in your mind?*

An image of the merchant, along with the tent and its location, burned into Tara's memory. *Thank you. And don't worry. I'll get the sword back.*

I know you will, Valina said, though she couldn't quite hide the concern in her voice. *I will send the wolves now.*

Thank you. Tara patted the wolf. "You will see him soon. Don't be afraid." She laughed as Kelya licked her face. "You're welcome." She rose and stepped back a few paces.

Mist swirled around the wolves, thickened into dense clouds, and vanished. The wolves were gone.

Tara heard audible sighs of relief as she hurried back to where the smugglers stood sheathing their blades.

"I can't believe you're friendly with that wolf," Blackie said.

Tara smiled. "I saved her life once, and she saved mine."

"That would be a story worth hearing," Brains said as he slung his pack over his shoulder.

"I'll tell you sometime, but right now, I've got to find that cursed sword."

"She's probably taken it to the caravanners," Blackie said. "They'd pay the best price."

"Yes, and I know exactly where she went." Tara led the way at a jog, out of the woods and across the clearing.

Blackie kept pace with her, the others following behind. "How do you know —" Comprehension slid across his face. "Oh. Right. Never mind." He looked uncomfortable.

"You don't need to feel that way," Tara said as they entered the forest again. "Valina isn't watching all the time." If she had been, she wouldn't have been startled by the wolves or the missing sword.

Keeping to the woods, they circled around to the east until they found the caravanners' encampment. Dozens of colorful tents of varying sizes, their flags tossing in the breeze, had been set up in a wide, semi-cleared area. A few trees had been left standing to shade the tents of the wealthiest merchants from the heat of the late summer sun. A three-strand rope fence surrounded the encampment, and hired mercenaries bristling with weapons patrolled the perimeter. At the entrance, a stout, middle-aged man with a round face and double chin sat at a table, asking visitors their business in a bored voice.

Tara crouched in the undergrowth, surveying the busy camp. Merchants and traders from both the East and West hawked their wares and haggled over prices. Lackeys and pages ran every which way, delivering goods and messages. The mercenaries fingered their weapons and glowered at everyone.

"Which tent?" Blackie whispered.

"On the left, toward the back, underneath that tree over there." Tara pointed to a tall hardwood with a spreading canopy of yellow-green leaves.

"Let's go then." Blackie started to rise.

Tara pulled him back down. "You can't go in there. They'll arrest you on sight."

"No, they won't. I haven't done anything lately."

Tara raised her eyebrows. "Lately?" She shook her head. "The caravanners have long memories. Besides, we can't all go in there together. It would draw too much attention."

"So we'll go in one at a time," Blackie argued.

"No." She patted Blackie on the arm. "I'll be fine." She rose and stood for a moment, waiting for the dizziness to fade.

Blackie rose to his feet beside her and crossed his arms over his chest. "You're not going in there alone. You look like you're about to pass out."

Tara took a deep breath. "Fine, but you're staying here." She turned to Brains. "Brains, may I borrow you?"

"By all means." He jumped to his feet and followed her to the camp entrance.

The man at the table glanced uninterestedly at them, then sat up and looked more closely. "Buying or selling?"

"Buying," Tara said with as pleasant a smile as she could manage with an aching head.

The man looked suspiciously at Brains.

"He's my bodyguard," Tara said.

Brains gave the man an icy stare.

The man's gaze shifted back to Tara. "Since when does a Triannon need a bodyguard?"

Tara smiled again, pleased with her reputation. "My sister is busy. I wanted someone to watch my back. You never know what kind of trouble you might run into in this town."

The man grunted. "Rumor has it that you've already run into quite a bit of trouble in this town." He signed a pass and handed it to her. "However, the caravan pays no heed to town trouble, as long as the trouble doesn't spill over here, if you catch my meaning."

Tara nodded. "Yes. Thank you. I understand."

She and Brains left the table and hurried through the crowd.

"Did you know him?" Brains asked.

"No, I've never met him."

"I'll bet you have many stories worth hearing," Brains said.

Tara laughed. "I'll bet you do, too, Sir Alstyn."

Brains grinned. "Perhaps we can work out a trade — your stories for mine."

"It's a deal."

As they approached their destination, a crack like thunder shook the encampment, and they heard an agonized scream from inside the tent.

Brains stopped in midstride. "What was that?"

"I don't know." Tara raced to the tent with Brains close behind her.

Two lackeys burst through the tent opening and darted away like frightened deer, calling for the mercenaries.

Tara and Brains dashed inside. On a blackened rug in the middle of the richly appointed space lay a charred body. The stench of burnt flesh and incense clogged the air.

A man in a dark silk robe and jeweled headwrap stood staring down at the corpse. He jerked his head up. "How dare you enter my tent! Who are you? What are you doing here?"

Tara approached the body. "Sorry. Tara Triannon. Retrieving stolen property."

The caravanner stepped back a pace, eyeing Brains, who had drawn his blade. "I command you to leave my tent at once."

"As soon as I have my sword." Tara knelt beside the burnt remains of Adriana.

"What happened to her?" Brains asked.

Tara slid the half-drawn blade back into its scabbard. "Apparently, she tried to draw the sword." The black sword and scabbard were undamaged.

"That sword is mine," the caravanner said. "I just bought it."

Tara slipped the scabbard onto the sword belt she'd taken from the guardsman. "You couldn't have bought it from her, because it wasn't hers to sell. The sword belongs to me, and I have no intention of selling it." Tara picked up a bag of gold pieces from next to Adriana's body and tossed it to him. "You can keep your money."

He caught the bag. "I want that sword!"

A commotion outside the tent brought them around. Tara heard Blackie cursing. She felt a sinking in the pit of her stomach. Why couldn't he have stayed in the woods? She drew her sword and backed up beside Brains. Two fierce-looking mercenaries shoved Blackie and Diamond Jack through the tent opening and followed them in, bare blades in hand. One mercenary held Blackie's and Jack's sword belts in his other hand.

The eyes of all four of them focused on the burnt corpse. Jack turned away, his face pale. Relief softened Blackie's grim expression as he realized Tara and Brains were unhurt. He caught Jack's arm and slid toward them while the mercenaries were distracted. Tara and Brains moved forward quickly and stepped in front of the smugglers, swords ready.

"Remove these people at once!" the caravanner commanded the mercenaries. He eyed Blackie, recognition flitting across his face. "Take them away and make certain they don't return — ever."

The mercenaries tossed the smugglers' sword belts aside and advanced warily. "Drop your weapons," one of them said.

Brains snorted. "Not likely."

The caravanner let out a shrill whistle.

Tara heard the sound of many running footsteps approaching the tent. Two more mercenaries strode inside, and she could see others behind them.

Tara swept the black sword from its scabbard.

The mercenaries halted as the caravanner cringed.

Tara pointed the black sword at the caravanner. "Unless you want to end up like her," she gestured toward Adriana's corpse, "you will tell these... gentlemen... and the other mercenaries outside to grant us safe passage from the encampment."

The caravanner straightened. "Why weren't you burned, like her?"

"Because the sword is mine."

Fear and fury twisted the caravanner's face. His eyes flicked from Tara to the sword and back again. She could almost see the wheels turning in his mind as he tried to figure out a way to regain the upper hand and take possession of the black sword.

Tara narrowed her eyes. "So be it." She stepped toward him, the sword aimed at his head.

He backed away, eyes widening. "No!" He gestured at the mercenaries. "Let them go."

The mercenaries reluctantly sheathed their weapons and stepped back.

Tara glanced at the tent opening and noted the gathering crowd outside. Chills goose-pimpled her skin. She slipped behind the merchant and pressed the point of her blade against his back. "I'm sorry, my lord caravanner, but I don't trust you. I'm afraid you'll have to come with us." In a swift motion, she sheathed the black sword and drew her dagger. She prodded him in the back with it. "Let's go."

He started to turn around. "How dare you!"

She grasped his shoulder and faced him forward, the point of her dagger digging into his spine. "Save your bluster. We won't harm you unless someone tries to harm us. Now move."

Blackie and Jack retrieved their weapons. Tara gestured for the mercenaries to leave, then marched the caravanner out of the tent, the smugglers close behind her.

Blinking in the bright sunlight, Tara watched as the mercenaries cleared a path through the curious onlookers to the back of the encampment. Tara hurried the caravanner along the short distance to the rope fence. As soon as the smugglers had climbed through, she released him and slipped through the fence.

They ran into the woods, back to where they had left Whiskey, Whittler, and Sarita. The three plied them with questions, but they waved them away for later as they sped away from the Gypsy Crossroads.

The group headed east toward Klyder Pass, which wound through the Cyranel Mountains into the Eastern Frontier. After two hours' travel through the forest with no sign of pursuit, they stopped in a small glade to eat. Tara sat back against a tree and let Brains field the others' questions. The ebbing of her adrenaline rush had left her exhausted. Her head still ached, but at least her dizziness was gone. Her body seemed to be healing itself more quickly than usual, and she wondered if it was due to her absorption of the black sword's power after destroying the guardhouse. Ravnaul had used the magic of the sword to restore his ruined body, so it made sense that she might be able to do the same.

The thought of Ravnaul chilled her. She could feel him prowling in the shadows of her mind as she fought her need for sleep. The warmth of the sun and the buzz of the smugglers' conversation were lulling her into a stupor. She forced her eyes open. Before she slept, she had to decide what to do with the black sword — keep it and take it with her into the dream dungeon, or give it to Blackie for safekeeping.

She let out a long breath, her eyes filling with sudden tears. Gods, she wished Jovan was with her. She longed to lay her head on his chest and hear the sound of his heartbeat, feel his arms around her again. His strength had sustained her so many times during her nightmares. She thought of how he'd once used the magic of the ruby ring she'd found to transform into a griffin and rescue her from the dream. He'd always been able to get her out, until the Being had blocked their connection as effectively as if a mountain had sprung up between them. Jovan's isolation had become so absolute that even the great sorceress of Estiarii Faelle couldn't find him. And yet — Tara latched on to a shred of hope — he'd gotten through to her, albeit faintly, more than once since they'd been separated. There had to be a way to get through to him.

With great effort, she cleared her mind and gathered her power. Focusing what strength she could muster, she sent a single thought arrowing outward on a desperate wave of energy. *Jovan...*

She heard no words, but felt a weak stirring in their connection, like a breath of wind barely strong enough to bend a blade of grass.

Jovan! she called again. *Please answer*, she begged silently.

Tara... The sound was so faint, she sensed more than heard it.

Joy and anxiety twisted knots in her gut. *Tell me where you are, and I'll find you.*

In the jumble of despairing thoughts that followed, she could make out only one word: dwarves.

Dwarves, she thought. The dwarves lived in the Cyranel Mountains — the mountains that loomed a very short distance to the east of where she sat. Jovan and his brother had stayed in the dwarven city of Aldontris many years before, while he'd recovered from a knife wound. He'd told her they hadn't left on good terms. Could that be where he'd been sent?

Are you in Aldontris? she asked, and held her breath.

Yes. His thoughts became incoherent again. She tried to decipher them — something about a stolen jewel and a pit. He'd said before that Jared had tried to steal something from the dwarves. Was Jovan being punished for his brother's transgressions? She didn't know how large Aldontris was, but if the city was sizable, it could take forever to locate him.

Show me a landmark. What's near you?

She caught the brief image of a dwarf with straw-colored hair and beard and a dented helm. Then Jovan's thoughts faded, the connection drifting into dark emptiness.

She clenched her fists. Curse it all, she'd lost him. He was alive, but weak. She had to get to him quickly. She leaped up, startling the smugglers into silence. "Blackie, I need to talk to you." She pulled him to his feet and dragged him into the woods, far enough away so the others couldn't hear. "Blackie, I..." She stopped, suddenly realizing she didn't know how to say what she needed to without hurting him.

"Just spit it out," Blackie said, his expression guarded.

She took a deep breath. "I know where Jovan is. He's being held by the dwarves in Aldontris. It's a very long story. I need to find him and get him out. I-I love him. I'm sorry." She ran her hand through her hair and turned away, fighting tears again.

He turned her around to face him. "Don't ever apologize for being in love. Love is the most wonderful thing in the world. It's what *makes* life — love of family, friends. There's nothing more important."

Tara smiled through her tears and gave him a quick hug. "Blackie, you are amazing. You're so much more to me than a friend.

We've shared so much — so many adventures. You rescued me from Wyndover. You treated me like a human being and not some sort of freak. I had some of the best times of my life running with your band. And now that my memory's back, I can honestly say there were no bad times." She squeezed his hand, then let go. "You saved me more times than I can count. Call yourself a blackguard if you want, but I know what kind of man you are. You will always be special to me."

She held his gaze a moment longer, then his eyes wavered, and he studied the ground at his feet. She sensed he wanted to speak, but couldn't find the words.

"You don't have to say anything," she said softly. "I know that you care, and if either of us ever needs anything, the other will be there. I already know that's true for you, and I promise it will be true for me." She smiled and quoted him. "'I never turn my back on my friends.'"

He cleared his throat and met her eyes again. "So — what's your plan?"

"I'm going to ask Valina to send me there."

"To Aldontris? How do you know you'll get there? How do you know you won't end up somewhere you don't want to be?"

She wiped her eyes with her sleeve. "I don't, but I have to try."

"And then what?"

"I'll come back here with him. I hope. I still have to face the dream."

"You won't need us, then, to watch your back," Blackie said in a neutral voice. "You'll have him."

"I *will* need you. I don't have time to explain everything, but Jovan's mind is sometimes controlled by this ancient, very powerful Being —"

Blackie's eyebrows shot up. "Another one?"

Tara bit down on the urge to laugh at the insanity of it all. "Yes, another one. I don't know what this one is. Jovan got his magic from it. It has something to do with Rinpool. Do you know of Rinpool?"

"I've heard of it."

"Jovan's used his magic to help me escape the nightmare dungeon in the past, but then this Being somehow broke our mental connection, and he's been locked out for a while now. I'm almost certain that it's the Being who's interfering with Valina's transport magic." Tara took a breath and tried to get her tired mind to focus. "The point is that I do need you to keep watch while I'm asleep. I don't know what condition Jovan will be in, or if he'll be able to help me or not, and I still haven't decided what to do with the sword —"

Blackie held up his hands. "All right. Stop. You don't need to worry about that now. We'll stash our stuff, and your sorceress can send us — wherever." He started back toward the others.

"We? Blackie, wait." She stopped him. "I want you all to stay here. I'll go."

He put his hands on his hips. "You're going into a city full of hostile dwarves by yourself?"

"Yes. I don't know what'll happen, and I don't want anyone else getting hurt."

"What was that you just said about when one of us needed help, the other would be there?"

"I know what I said, but I didn't mean now." Tara gestured toward the smugglers. "I can't keep asking them to risk their lives for me."

"Fine. I'll ask 'em." Blackie strode back to the campsite.

Tara stared after him. "Blackie, you are amazing," she whispered, and followed.

All eyes were on Blackie as he stopped before the other smugglers. Blackie jerked his thumb at Tara. "She's going to have the sorceress send her to the dwarven city of Aldontris to rescue Jovan Trevillion. I'm going with her. Anyone else in?"

Brains was on his feet in an instant. "I'm in. I've never seen a dwarven city, or even a dwarf, for that matter."

Whittler rose a little more slowly. He looked apprehensive, but resolute.

"This is rather sudden," Jack said. "What does Trevillion have to do with all this? And what's he doing with the dwarves?"

Tara opened her mouth to speak, then closed it again, unable to form a quick explanation.

"There's no time to explain," Blackie said. "If you want to stay here, that's fine. You and Whiskey can stay with Sarita."

"No." Sarita stood. She shot a smoldering glance at Tara, then her eyes settled on Blackie. She raised her chin. "If you're going, I'm going."

Blackie frowned. "You should —"

Tara elbowed him surreptitiously, and he stopped, throwing her a look of surprise.

Whiskey heaved himself to his feet. "Beats sittin' here doin' nothing, I guess."

Jack shrugged and got up. "I bet they dig up a lot of jewels in those tunnels."

"Just don't steal one," Tara said quickly. "That's what got him in trouble with the dwarves in the first place."

"Trevillion stole something from them?" Brains asked.

Tara shook her head. "No, his brother did, or tried to, a long time ago, and I think Jovan is paying the price for it." She looked at each of the smugglers, her heart swelling with gratitude. "I don't know how I'll ever repay you for all your help."

Brains grinned. "We'll think of a way."

She smiled.

"I wonder what they drink down there," Whiskey mused, as he and the other smugglers hid their packs in a dense thicket.

"Everybody stand close and link arms and hands," Blackie said. "That way, if we get sent to the wrong place like last time, we'll hopefully all end up in the same wrong place."

They linked arms and clasped hands. With Blackie's firm grip on her left hand, and Whittler's nervous one on her right, Tara closed her eyes. She squeezed Whittler's hand reassuringly.

Valina... Tara couldn't keep the excitement out of her mental voice.

I'm here, Tara. What's happened?

I've found Jovan, sort of. He's in the dwarven city of Aldontris in the Cyranel Mountains. I managed to communicate with him briefly. He seemed hurt and weak, but he sent me this image of a dwarf. Can you find him — the dwarf, I mean — and send us there? She shared the dwarf's image with the sorceress.

Let's see if I can find him... Yes, that's him! The sorceress' voice rang with triumph. *He's walking in a tunnel, deep beneath the mountain. There's no one near him at the moment. Are you ready? I'll do my best to get you there.*

Yes. Thank you!

You're most welcome, my dear.

"All right, hold on," Tara said aloud.

Wisps of white mist swirled up around them, burgeoning into thick white clouds that firmly enclosed them. Tara held tight to the hands holding hers and prayed to all the gods they would land in the right place.

CHAPTER 28

Tara held her breath and counted the seconds as they hovered, weightless. A chill of warning eeled down her spine, and she felt a sharp tug sideways.

Valina! she cried.

I feel it, the sorceress said anxiously. *Concentrate on the dwarf. Use your power — help me break the pull!*

Tara released her power, felt it shoot through her like a bolt of fire. Anger at the Being fueled the flame. *I will find him,* she vowed, gritting her teeth as she fought the Being's pull. Concentrating all her thoughts and energy on the dwarf, she willed herself to go there. She felt a scream building inside her as the Being's power warred against hers and Valina's, tearing her apart. Blinded by pain, she lost control. Black fire exploded outward through her mind. Something snapped; the tug-of-war ceased. She heard Valina scream. A furious roar deafened her as the Being recoiled. She was flung through space as if fired by a slingshot, then dashed to the ground.

Dazed and disoriented, she heard an unfamiliar gruff voice utter a startled exclamation. A stream of curses from Blackie followed. Shaking off her pain and dizziness, she opened her eyes. Everything was a blur. She felt movement beside her and heard Blackie cursing again.

"Damnation, woman, I hate it when your eyes do that."

She squeezed her eyes shut and pressed the heels of her palms against them. *Valina?* Nothing. No answer. Worry choked her. What had happened to the sorceress?

Tara felt Blackie's hands on her arms as he sat her up against a wall and gave her a gentle shake. "Hey, stay with us here."

Her dizziness ebbing, she opened her eyes again. Blackie came into focus.

"All right?" he asked.

"I think so, but I can't reach Valina. I'm afraid she might have been hurt."

"You mean we're stranded?"

"At least until I can get through to her."

"Great. What in the Abyss happened?"

"The Being I told you about earlier — it tried to send us elsewhere." She glanced around, relieved to see the other smugglers and Sarita standing nearby. In between them, she glimpsed the smooth wall of a wide tunnel lit with fist-sized amber stones that Diamond Jack was examining with interest. "Where are we?"

"Believe it or not, I think we're where we're supposed to be." Blackie stood and gave her a hand up. She leaned on his arm and clenched her teeth against the pain in her head.

"Who are you, and how did you get in here?" demanded the same gruff voice she'd heard before.

Held at bay against the wall by Brains' sword was the straw-haired dwarf with the dented helm she'd seen through her connection with Jovan. She could have shouted for joy. Jovan was close. She could sense his nearness like shivery tingles all over her skin.

Steadying herself, she stepped closer to the dwarf. "I am Tara Triannon. I'm looking for a man named Jovan Trevillion. I know he's here. I can feel it. He sent me your image with his thoughts. Will you take us to him?"

The dwarf stared at her, stunned. "Everything he said was true," he whispered. "I knew it."

"What's your name?" Tara asked. "Are you his friend?"

"Gralfar, and yes, I am his friend." His expression grew grim. "His only friend among the dwarves."

Tara gestured for Brains to lower his weapon. "Take us to him. Please."

"I can't. He's in the Pit."

Tara remembered that word from Jovan's jumble of thoughts. "What is the Pit?"

Gralfar's face grew grimmer still. "It's a black hole in the mountain that King Drordin uses as a prison. Only he can open it."

"You must take us there now."

Gralfar's hand waved outward in a gesture of helpless frustration. "It won't do any good. It can't be opened. I've tried."

Tara eyed him steadily. "I can open it."

The dwarf gave her a doubtful look, then turned and led the way down the tunnel. "Follow me."

They passed through several deserted tunnels before reaching an immense cavern of tombs with pillars carved in the likenesses of dwarven kings, its walls depicting hundreds of years of dwarven history. Brains and Whittler exclaimed in delight over the exquisite carvings, leaving them regretfully as the group moved on. Finally, they arrived at a tunnel that ended in a blank wall.

"Where's the door?" Tara demanded.

Gralfar pointed at the smooth wall. "You're looking at it. I'm telling you, only King Drordin knows how to open it."

Tara narrowed her eyes. "How big is this pit, and is Jovan near the door?"

"The Pit is vast," Gralfar said. "Jovan was sent down the throne room chute, which empties on the far side, so no, he's not likely to be near the door."

"Good." Tara drew the black sword. "Stand back." She waited until the others were far down the tunnel, then held the sword level and let its power burn straight to her soul. The sword's power blazed through her, energizing her. She lashed outward with her mind, and black fire struck the wall, blasting a hole large enough for a horse and rider to fit through. She closed her eyes against the cloud of dust and ducked her head as a spray of pebbles spattered her. Then she sheathed the sword and climbed through the rubble to the edge of the gaping hole.

The pit beyond was pitch black. No amber jewels lit these walls.

"Jovan!" Tara called. She listened intently, but heard nothing, not even an echo. It was as if the blackness smothered everything within it. "I need light!" She whirled on the dwarf, who had come running up with Blackie and the others, a look of incredulity on his face. "Do you have a torch, or can you take those gems out of the walls?"

Gralfar shook his head. "No, neither."

She cursed under her breath and looked back at the pit. She could go in blindly, but who knew how long it would take before she managed to stumble over him, lying unconscious somewhere on the floor? And time was one thing they didn't have. She knew it wouldn't take the dwarves long to find them, now that she'd announced her presence.

She gusted out a breath. "Is there anything in there I should know about — creatures, pitfalls, anything like that?" She wasn't sensing any immediate danger.

"Not that I know of," Gralfar said.

"All right." She took a step onto the floor of the pit. The blackness was so thick, it swallowed her whole. Hit with a sudden idea, she dug the jeweled key out of her inner pocket. The moment her fingers closed over it, light from the moonstones blazed forth.

Gralfar gasped.

"Of course," Brains said. "The key. Good thinking."

Tara spread her fingers apart and held the key high, illuminating a two-foot circle around her. Then she opened her mind just enough to sense Jovan's weak aura. Moving carefully, she picked her way through broken rocks and debris and crossed the floor of the pit. She counted her steps — fifty... sixty. She stopped and turned in a circle. Curse it all, where was he? She moved diagonally forward to her left, then back to her right.

The worn edge of something caught the light — the toe of a boot. With a soft cry, Tara dropped down beside him. "Jovan!" He lay on his side, his eyes closed, his arms twisted behind him, his breathing slow and even. She brushed his hair back, her fingers tracing his darkly stubbled cheek. *Jovan!* Still no response. She sliced through the ropes that bound his hands and feet and eased him onto his back. Then she cut a small gash on her left palm and placed it over the raw wound on his wrist where the rope had torn through his skin. Her power flowed into him, healing his injuries and restoring his wellbeing, and hers. Yearning for his touch, she slipped deeper, her magic binding with his again, their souls joining in a familiar euphoric rush that swept her into ecstasy.

He woke and sat up, his fingers twining with hers. The look in his eyes took her breath away. Then they were on their feet and in each other's arms. She had so many things she needed to say, but she couldn't stop kissing him. He didn't seem to mind.

"I can't believe you're here," he whispered at last, his hand caressing her face. "And your memory?"

"It's back." She kissed him again. "Gods, I've missed you. I'm so sorry for what happened."

"It wasn't your fault." He drew her close.

Blackie's voice finally separated them. "Hurry it up in there! We've got company."

"Who's that?" Jovan looked toward the voice.

"Blackie de Runo." Tara seized Jovan's hand. "Come on." Using the light from the jeweled key, she led the way back to the opening in the pit wall.

Blackie and the smugglers stood with weapons drawn, Sarita behind them, their backs to the pit door. Filling the ten-foot-wide tunnel facing them were at least two dozen dwarves armed with maces and double-bladed axes. Gralfar stood in the intervening space, a hand raised toward each group of combatants as if he could push them apart.

A gray-haired dwarf with a scar over his right eye advanced toward Gralfar, mace gripped in his hands. "Get out of the way, Gralfar, or you will share their fate."

Tara paused just inside the pit opening and pocketed the key. *Valina?* Still no answer. Swallowing her worry, Tara drew the black sword.

Jovan caught her arm. "You got the sword back."

"Yes." She quirked a smile. "Several times — I'll explain later."

They stepped out of the pit. Tara caught Blackie's glance and gave a quick shake of her head. There would be no magical rescue. A grim expression settled over his face, and he tightened his grip on his sword.

"Sauldron!" Jovan moved past the smugglers. "Leave Gralfar out of this."

Sauldron halted as Tara and Jovan stepped up beside Gralfar. Several emotions played across Sauldron's scarred face — surprise and wariness as his eyes slid over Tara with her black sword, hatred when his gaze reached Jovan.

"I should have killed you on the cliff," Sauldron spat. He looked at Tara. "And what is a sell-sword doing with a weapon of *Aiykshaa-v'n* royalty? Tell me, who did you steal it from?"

Tara felt Jovan stiffen beside her, and she touched his arm to still his anger. She gave Sauldron a faint smile. "It was a gift from my late mother. And since you know what it is, you must also know of its power." She swept her free hand back toward the hole in the pit wall. "As you can see, I am fully capable of wielding it, but I would be more than happy to provide another demonstration, if you so require." She pointed the blade at his chest.

His eyes narrowed. "What do you want?"

"I wish to speak with your king."

Sauldron grunted a laugh. "The likes of you addressing our king? I wouldn't waste his time."

"Either you take us to him," Tara said, her voice cold as an arctic gale, "or I'll destroy as many tunnels — and dwarves that get in my way — as it takes for him to come to us."

An ugly expression crossed Sauldron's face. He glanced at the hole in the pit wall as if weighing her threat. With a snarl, he stalked back to the dwarves blocking the tunnel and shoved his way through them. "Bring them!" he ordered.

The dwarves backed against the tunnel walls, forming a path down the middle between them. A rugged dwarf with long dark hair and a braided beard pointed toward the tunnel with his axe.

Tara shook her head. "No. You first. We'll follow."

The dwarves exchanged looks, their expressions hardening. Silently, they turned and marched up the tunnel.

Jovan put his hand on Gralfar's shoulder. "Thank you, my friend. I owe you my life — again."

Gralfar inclined his head. "I felt you were innocent."

"What will this cost you?" Jovan asked.

"I don't know," Gralfar said grimly.

Tara waved the smugglers in close. "Stay near, but give me room, in case there's an ambush." Taking the lead, she followed the dwarves and Gralfar through the tunnel.

The dwarves led them back through the twisting tunnels and the cavern of tombs, past the place where they'd first arrived, and on into a wider tunnel laced with side passages.

Tara slowed as icy prickles rode up the back of her neck.

"What's wrong?" Jovan asked.

"Ambush!" Tara motioned to the others. "Get down!"

They dropped to the floor.

Tara held the black sword out straight and turned in a swift circle. There — the side tunnel on the left they were about to pass. She released a bolt of power, sending black fire into the ceiling just inside the passage opening. Shattered rock rained down, collapsing the entrance to the side tunnel. Startled by the explosion, the dwarves leading them ran back. Anger burned in their eyes as they surveyed the damage.

"The next time you try to ambush us," Tara said coolly, "I won't be so careful with my aim."

Bristling with hostility, the dwarves strode back down the main tunnel.

"How did you know?" Gralfar asked Tara, as they started after the dwarves.

"It's a talent I have," she answered.

They walked on through a long series of ever-widening upward tunnels until they came to a large platform with a half-dozen transport carts and rail tracks leading in several directions. With a wave of their weapons, the dwarves indicated the two transports at the front.

"We're supposed to ride in those?" Tara asked doubtfully.

"They're a wild ride, but they're safe enough," Jovan said, "as long as you hold on."

Tara frowned. "I don't like the idea of splitting up, but it doesn't look like we have much choice." She turned to Gralfar. "Can you drive those things?"

"The transports? Yes," he answered.

"Good. Would you drive the second one? I want to be sure everyone ends up in the same place."

He nodded. "As you wish." He climbed into the second transport, along with Blackie, Sarita, Whiskey, and Whittler.

Tara, Jovan, Brains, and Diamond Jack got into the first transport and stood behind the rugged dwarf with the braided beard, who was impatiently waiting for them. The other dwarves piled into the remaining transports.

As the transport began its swift descent along the rails, Tara leaned back against Jovan, savoring the feel of his solid presence. Their hands touched as they gripped the edge of the cart. His lips brushed her hair, his body heat warming her through.

In front of them, Brains shifted from one side to the other, looking down at the wheels and studying the transport workings with fascination. "This is ingenious."

"What is?" Jack asked. He clung to the cart as it flew around a corner.

"These transports are propelled by gravity and the natural forces of motion. See how the tracks cant — the varying up-and-down slopes and spirals — that, along with this mechanism underneath —
"

"Stop moving around!" growled the dwarf driver. "You're throwing us off balance."

Brains stood still. "Sorry. It's just so impressive. Some of the Twin Cities' nobles who own mines have been trying for years to invent this kind of propulsion system, but they always failed. Tell me, did you use —"

Tara lost the rest of Brains' words as the transport roared down a sharp descent before spiraling upward into another tunnel. The dwarf apparently heard, though, and to Tara's surprise, he answered Brains' question. They exchanged a few more questions and answers over the whine of the wheels, the dwarf's voice conveying pride and grudging respect.

Finally, the transport ground to a halt at a high, wide platform. The transport driven by Gralfar slowed and stopped behind them, followed by the carts carrying the other dwarves.

Tara climbed out and flexed her fingers. She'd clenched the edge of the cart for so long, they'd grown stiff. Jovan and the smugglers gathered beside her. The dwarves surrounded them, but kept their distance. Tara noticed that Sauldron wasn't with them.

Gralfar led the way through an arched opening into an enormous room. Countless amber stones lit the walls of the great hall, glowing like miniature suns between sweeps of tapestries and heraldic trappings, suffusing the room with warm light. Jack stared at the gems, his eyes wide. Brains could barely contain his excitement. His gaze wandered over the walls, absorbing everything. Blackie, Sarita, Whiskey, and Whittler glanced around cautiously. The hall was empty, save for five dwarves at the far end of the chamber — the king on his granite throne, and four others, two on either side at the bottom of the short stairs leading up to the dais.

Several arched openings led in and out of the hall, and Tara scanned them as she passed, wary of another ambush. She and the others, accompanied by the contingent of dwarves, followed Gralfar to within a few feet of the dais. As they neared the throne, her gaze was drawn to the large amber stone glowing radiantly above it. She felt a flicker of anguish pierce Jovan's heart. She turned and saw him look away from the stone. She glanced back at it. Was that what his brother had tried to steal?

Gralfar motioned for the group to halt. He dropped to one knee, then rose. "My king." He swept his hand toward Tara. "Tara Triannon has requested an audience."

King Drordin ignored the group and addressed Gralfar. Tara could feel the hostility rolling off him. "How did Tara Triannon get in here without passing one of our outposts? And how is it that this man," he pointed at Jovan with his scepter, "stands before me again, after being condemned to the Pit?"

"My king," Gralfar implored, "everything Jovan Trevillion said earlier is true. Tara Triannon has a black sword of *Aiykshaav'n* royalty. I saw her wield it. She is a true *Aiykshaav'n*."

The king's eyes narrowed, and he looked coldly at Tara. "That doesn't answer my questions."

Tara held his gaze evenly. "Then allow me." She took a step forward. "I asked the sorceress Valina Mellarian of Estiarii Faelle to send my friends and me here with her magic, so we could rescue Jovan. I need his help on my quest to bring the Kamarians — the sky *Aiykshaav'n* — back to this world. Valina sent us to Gralfar after Jovan mentally shared his image with me. Gralfar then took us to Jovan, and I released him from the Pit with the sword."

"Legends and bedtime tales again," the king scoffed. "If that is the case, why are you still here? Why did you not magic your way out again?"

"There were complications in the process. We'll have to leave your realm the conventional way."

The king sat back. "And what makes you think I'll allow you to do that?"

Tara drew the black sword and held it upright. "If you don't, I'll blast my way out."

King Drordin eyed the sword warily, his recognition of its power clear. His expression slid to grudging acceptance.

Tara smiled inwardly. She'd won the round. She had drawn the sword without consequence, and the king could not deny her claim to her birthright.

But the battle wasn't over. Icy prickles danced over her skin as the great hall began to fill with dwarves. The smugglers fingered their weapons nervously. Tara raised her voice, so she could be heard throughout the hall. "I have no quarrel with you, other than your treatment of Jovan Trevillion. He is not responsible for his brother's actions and should not be punished for them."

"Says you!" A dirt-smeared Sauldron pushed his way through the growing crowd. He looked like he'd been buried in a pile of rubble. "But who are you to say what dwarves should or should not do?"

"It is not for me to say," Tara declared above the murmuring of the other dwarves, "nor is it for you. You are not the king."

Sauldron stopped a few steps away from Tara. "Someone must pay for Jared's treachery."

"Jared has already paid," Tara said, "and he's still paying. His spirit haunts the Bog, trapped for eternity where he died. He will never find his place, for good or bad, in the afterlife. He will never know peace." Her voice softened as she felt Jovan's sorrow in her mind. "And Jovan suffers because of this, as well." She raised her voice again. "The guilty one has been punished in a way far more brutal than you would have done. Even death at your hands would have been less harsh. Can you not forgive and forget?"

Sauldron stepped toward her. "No!"

Tara's hand dropped, leveling the sword at his chest. Jovan started forward, as if to move between them. She caught his arm, and he subsided.

"Sauldron!" King Drordin's shout silenced the crowd.

Sauldron snarled and stepped back.

Tara slid her hand down Jovan's arm and curled her fingers around his. The smugglers behind them slowly sheathed their half-drawn weapons.

"You've made your point," King Drordin said. "But there's still the matter of the stolen ring."

Tara frowned. "What ring?"

"A gold ring with a red gem that the dwarves say Jared stole," Jovan said. "I know nothing of it. I never saw a ring like that in Jared's possession."

"Can you tell me more of this ring?" Tara asked the king.

"It was crafted by the dwarves and the fire *Aiykshaav'n* over three hundred years ago to honor the first High King, chosen to rule the Western Kingdoms after the defeat of the Eastern invaders. The fire gem holds magic for those who can use such things."

Tara sucked in a breath and turned to Jovan. "The ring with the red griffin."

Jovan looked surprised, as if he'd forgotten about the ring he'd used to transform into a griffin. Then his expression grew doubtful. "But you found that ring in your dream dungeon. Jared didn't have it."

"But what if he did? What if he had it with him in the Bog when he died, and it sank through the quicksand and ended up in the dungeon — magic drawn to magic somehow?"

"Where is this ring?" King Drordin demanded. "I must see it."

Tara and Jovan both hesitated. What if it was the right ring? Returning it to the dwarves would buy Jovan's freedom, but at what cost? They might still need its magic to defeat Ravnaul. Their eyes met in silent agreement. Jovan would show him the ring, but they would not relinquish it, not until Tara's quest was over. She would just have to get Jovan out another way.

Jovan pulled the ring from his pocket and held it in his palm. The murmurings of the crowd rose.

The dwarven king leaped to his feet. "Bring it to me!"

Tara and Jovan crossed to the stairs leading up to the dais. Jovan ascended the steps while Tara waited at the bottom, not wanting to get too far away from the smugglers. Jovan reached the throne and held out his hand. The ring's red stone glittered, as if responding to the earth stones' magical light.

King Drordin stepped closer and uttered an exclamation. "The stone of kings!" He raised his fist in triumph and addressed the crowd. "The fire gem has returned to our realm at last!" He reached for the ring.

Jovan closed his fingers over it. "I'm sorry, I can't give it to you yet. We may need its magic to survive our quest."

Fury lined the king's face. "Give me the ring!"

Jovan jumped off the dais, landing beside Tara. They backed up quickly to where the smugglers stood with their hands on their swords again.

"I swear I will give the ring back to you after our quest is finished," Jovan said.

"You will give it to me *now!*" King Drordin waved his scepter, and the dwarves surrounding them raised their weapons and advanced.

Tara aimed the black sword and black fire shot outward, smashing the stairs leading up to the throne. The dwarves leaped out of the way as broken rocks flew through the air and scattered across the floor.

"Call off the attack," Tara said, "or that stone will be next." She pointed the black sword at the large amber gem above the throne.

King Drordin raised his scepter, halting the dwarves' advance. Uneasy grumbling filled the hall. Ignoring the cloud of dust still sifting through the air, the dwarven king moved to the edge of the dais. "That ring belongs to the dwarves."

"And we will return it," Tara said, "as soon as we can. I give you my word."

The king snorted. "Beneath that power, you are still a sellsword. Your word is no better than his." He gestured at Jovan.

"I am many things," Tara said coldly, "but I am not a liar, nor a breaker of promises, and neither is Jovan. If we say we'll bring the ring back, we will. We have only honorable intentions."

"What do men know of honor?" the king sneered. "When the Easterners invaded the Western Kingdoms, the Western kings begged for our help to repel them. Against our better judgment, we formed an alliance. Together, and at great cost, we defeated the Easterners. The Western kings hailed us and called us friends. In honor of our great alliance, we helped build a wondrous castle at Crystalir for their newly chosen High King, who would rule the West in peace. We even forged this ring as a gift to the new High King.

"But soon after, the High King fell from a parapet and died. My forefather, who witnessed the event, said he was pushed, murdered by his own power-hungry son. But it was my forefather's word against the son's, and no man would believe him. The son became the new ruler, and he blamed the dwarves for his father's death. He broke the alliance and gave us nothing — no payment of any kind for our work, nothing to compensate us for our great losses in battle. We took back the ring and quit the world of men."

"I'm sorry for your ill-treatment at the hands of men," Tara said, "but you have to believe that not all men are dishonorable. You can't condemn an entire race for the actions of a few." She'd learned that lesson well.

The king's eyebrows lifted skeptically, his gaze shifting to Jovan. "I have not seen anything of men that would make me think differently."

Tara took a step forward. "Then let us be the first to prove to you that men — and women — can act with honor. But if this is not enough to persuade you to let us leave in peace with the ring, consider that my quest is not for the world of men, but for the Ancients — the *Aiykshaav'n*. I am the last descendant of the sky *Aiykshaav'n* who once lived in the Black Mountains of the East. The Kamarians were lost in the great Cataclysm three centuries ago. I seek to bring them back to this world."

"And what if you do not survive this supposed quest?" the king asked.

"Alive or dead, we will find a way to get the ring back to you," Tara said.

"I say the ring stays here!" Sauldron burst out. "If they won't hand it over, we'll take it."

The muttering from the dwarves surrounding them sharpened, and icy fingers curled down Tara's spine. She cursed to herself as she realized they weren't likely to escape without a fight. She aimed the sword at Sauldron. "I have no wish to shed dwarven blood, but I will if I have to, and believe me, I can kill many before you can kill a few."

King Drordin raised his scepter high once more, silencing the dwarves. He eyed Tara shrewdly, considering. "There is one way I will allow you to leave with the ring."

"And what is that?" Tara asked, keeping one eye on Sauldron.

"You must leave one of your group here as a hostage. If you do not return with the ring in a reasonable amount of time, he or she," he nodded at Sarita, "will die."

"No," Tara and Jovan said at the same time.

"I will serve as hostage," Gralfar said, sinking to one knee before the king.

"No," Jovan said again.

King Drordin regarded Gralfar narrowly. "Your life is already hanging by a thread. It was your soft-heartedness that brought this trouble to us in the first place."

Tara? The weak voice of Valina Mellarian crept into her mind.

Tara stiffened and fought to keep the surprise off her face. *Valina? Are you all right?*

I-I think so.

A quick glance around showed that most of the dwarves' attention was focused on Gralfar and the dwarven king. *Can you get us out of here? The dwarf, too?*

I don't know. I'll try. I'll need your help.

All right. On my signal. Tara slipped her hand behind her back and waved it surreptitiously to get Blackie's attention.

"What?" he whispered.

She moved her finger around in a circle and then pointed upward.

"Now?"

She turned enough to catch his eye and gave a barely perceptible nod. He edged closer to the other smugglers and joined hands with Whittler and Sarita. The others caught on quickly and followed suit.

Jovan, she thought, her mental voice urgent.

Yes, Love?

The whisper-soft voice sent warm shivers through her. *Grab Gralfar, then take my hand. Valina's going to try to get us out of here.*

King Drordin faced Tara and Jovan. "If you will not consent to a hostage, the ring will remain here."

Jovan lunged to the side, seized Gralfar, and pulled him back to where the smugglers stood in a tight group. Tara caught his hand and linked her other arm around Blackie's, squeezing them all in close.

Now, Valina!

White mist shot up around them, thickening quickly into dense clouds. Tara heard startled gasps from the dwarves and a yell from Gralfar. With all her strength, she concentrated on the Black Mountains. A swift yank sideways threw her off balance. *No! Valina!*

I-I can't stop it!

Tara felt the sorceress' power weakening, then fading altogether. *Valina!* There was no reply. Tara cried out as a sharp pain jabbed through her skull, shattering her concentration. They jerked to the side again, then hit the ground.

Tara sat up slowly, holding her aching head. She heard a round of curses, this time from Jovan. She looked about. As her eyes cleared she saw an impenetrable tangle of trees with long, talon-like thorns surrounding the small clearing in which they'd landed.

"Don't touch the water!" Jovan said sharply to someone behind her. He knelt beside her. "Are you all right?"

"My head hurts." She let him help her up. "Where are... oh, no." The smugglers had stepped aside and given her a glimpse of a small pool of water hemmed in by gray stone. At the far end of the pool, rising from the water, stood a waist-high obelisk, veiled in shadow. They had landed at Rinpool.

CHAPTER 29

"So the Being found a way to get me here anyway." Tara stared at the mysterious pool of dark water. The oblique rays of moonlight shining down into the silent clearing had not yet touched it. She walked toward the pool.

Jovan caught her by the shoulders. "Don't get too close."

The pool was unevenly shaped, roughly four feet wide by five feet long. No moss or algae marred the stone border, and only a few wisps of grass grew along the edge. The obelisk was made of the same gray stone as the border. A series of runes had been carved into the side facing them. Crowning the apex of the obelisk was a filigreed, hollowed-out rock, cut and shaped in an intricate pattern of curves and whorls that flowed in never-ending circles.

"Is this what I think it is?" Blackie asked. Sarita stood beside him, her hand curled around his elbow. Whiskey, Whittler, and Diamond Jack crowded close behind them. Gralfar stood off to the side, staring at the pool as if in shock.

"It's Rinpool," Brains said in awe. He stepped carefully around the edge of the pool toward the obelisk. "I've seen rough drawings of it, but nothing that showed these details." He studied the runes. "This is incredible."

"Do you know what the runes say?" Jovan asked.

Tara felt the tension snaking through his body.

"I can't be certain," Brains answered. "I've never seen runes quite like these. They're similar, in a way, to ancient elvish." He drew his sword and pointed to a few of the runes in the first line. "Change the shapes a bit, and this would say 'eye of the gods'." He indicated a series of runes below it. "This would be something about the moon. It looks like 'moonlight gift, daylight curse,' or something like that." He shrugged. "It doesn't make a lot of sense."

"It makes perfect sense," Jovan said grimly.

"How so?" Brains asked.

"In order to receive the 'moonlight gift' — visions of the future revealed when the moon shines directly on the pool — one must drink the water of Rinpool or somehow absorb the water into one's body." Jovan rubbed the spot by his right collarbone where Tara knew the poisoned knife wound from long ago had been healed by Rinpool's magic. "But once you taste the water, you become a slave to the Being that rules this place."

"What Being?"

"An ancient Being with god-like powers. Valina Mellarian spoke of a legend that said when a god commits a terrible transgression, the great god Azakai banishes the transgressor and imprisons that god on this world to do penance. I think that's what Rinpool is. A prison of the gods."

"You mean the Being — that voice in your head — really is a god?" Tara asked. She remembered eavesdropping on one of Jovan's mental arguments with the Being and hearing, for a brief moment, its harsh, otherworldly voice.

"Yes. I'm sure of it," Jovan said.

"That's a legend I've never heard," Brains said slowly. He gestured toward Tara. "What did she mean, 'voice in your head'?"

Jovan hesitated, then let out a long breath. "When I was fifteen, I was wounded and ended up here. The circumstances of how and why are not important. My brother, Jared, was with me. I drank from the pool, and the water healed what should have been a death wound. I saw visions of the future, which I'm also not going to discuss, and then we were driven out of Dharakwood near a dwarven outpost, where we met Gralfar," Jovan nodded at the dwarf, "and Sauldron.

"After we left the dwarves, I began hearing a voice in my head. This ancient Being explained the price I must pay for taking the waters of Rinpool. From time to time, the Being would order me to do something, and if I didn't do it, the Being would inflict mental pain on me. From then on, my life has been controlled by this Being. Either I did what it wanted, or I endured mental torment so excruciating as to drive me mad."

Brains stared at him with horrified comprehension. "The invasion of the Southlands, and Shalimar... and —"

"All things I was forced to do by the Being." Jovan's face was a mask of stone.

Tara reached for his hand and held it tightly. The others remained silent.

"Well," Brains ran his hand through his blond curls. "I guess the most important question is, why are we here now?"

Tara turned to Jovan. "The Being wanted you to bring me here earlier. Do you know why?"

"I believe the Being wants you to drink the water, and then it will control you and your powers."

"If it's a god, why would it need my powers?"

"To gain revenge for its banishment. At the height of their strength, the Kamarians' powers rivaled the gods. You have inherited power from one of the strongest of the Kamarians, and every time you use the black sword, your power grows. My magic comes from Rinpool, from the Being itself. When you healed me, our magics combined within me, into an even more powerful magic, strong enough to put a hole through the wall the Being set between us. That's what the Being wants — to take your power and combine it with its own. With power like that, the Being could challenge and possibly even defeat the great god Azakai."

"That's crazy," Tara whispered, stunned. She looked down at the still water. The idea that the problem of her nightmares had mushroomed into a battle of the gods was insane, unbelievable. And yet, what if it were true?

"If this Being already controls you, why does it need her?" Blackie asked Jovan. "It sounds like you already have the power it wants."

"The power I have is acquired, not innate. I am not a magical being by birth, therefore my power is barely a fraction of what the Being could command if it combined Tara's power with its own."

"I think you may be right about this being a prison," Brains said. He had squatted near the edge of the pool and was studying the runes once more. "Again, using ancient elvish, these last few lines on the bottom say something about being bound by the gods' decree."

"Maybe I should drink the water," Tara said. "If the combination of our magics is stronger than the Being's power, adding that power to my magic should make me stronger than the Being. Perhaps I could defeat it."

"No. You can't take that risk," Jovan said.

"Is there any way out of here, other than the way we came in?" Blackie asked.

"Not unless a path opens in the thorn trees." Jovan glanced around at the encircling wall of thorns. "And that doesn't appear likely."

All eyes shifted to the tightly woven trees.

Blackie turned back to Tara. "And the sorceress can't get us out?"

"She's not answering again." Tara leaned against Jovan as a wave of tiredness rolled over her. The energizing effect of the black sword was wearing off. She rubbed her eyes and forced herself to remain upright.

Jovan slipped his arm around her in support. "How long has it been since you slept?"

Tara shrugged. "I don't know. A day or two. I've been putting it off. I don't want to face the dream." She rested her head on his shoulder.

Jovan frowned. "I know you healed me in the pit."

"Yes, and I've healed others, too... and I've used the sword a few times."

"And you haven't been pulled into the dream?"

"Ravnaul tried once, but I fought him off. I can feel him hovering near the back of my mind, but he appears to be waiting until I sleep." Which she'd be doing soon if she didn't get moving. With an effort, she straightened and took a step toward the smooth pool of water. "What do we do about this?"

"You're not touching the water," Jovan said flatly.

"Well, we can't just sit here forever." Her gaze slid back to the thorn trees surrounding them. "What do you think would happen if I blasted the trees with the sword?"

His gaze followed hers. "I don't know."

Tara turned sharply at the odd tone in his voice. The bitter resignation on his face scared her. "The Being will strike back at you, won't it — to force me to do its will," she said.

Jovan looked away and said nothing.

Tara looked at the smugglers. "Anyone have any ideas?"

Blackie and the others looked at each other silently, then shook their heads.

"I wish I did," Brains said.

"I'm sorry I can't be of any help to you here," said Gralfar. He seemed to have recovered from the shock of leaving Aldontris.

Tara ground her teeth. She shook her fist and railed at the pool. "I won't do it! Do you hear me? I won't be your pawn!"

Jovan cried out and dropped to one knee, his head in his hands.

"Jovan!" Tara knelt beside him.

He groaned and collapsed.

"Jovan!" She tried to reach him mentally and couldn't get through. He'd shut her out to keep her from sharing the pain that consumed his mind. She gripped his shoulder, her other hand slipping to his face. "Let me in!" He groaned again and curled into a ball. She tried to force her way into his mind but couldn't crack his mental walls.

"Is there anything we can do?" Brains asked as he and Blackie came up beside them.

"Help me up." Tara caught their hands, and they pulled her to her feet. She stumbled to the edge of the pool and glared at the dark water. "Curse you!" Metal rasped as she drew forth the black sword. "You want my power? Well, here it is!" Holding the sword point downward, with both hands wrapped around the hilt, she raised the sword high and stabbed down through the water, driving the blade into the stone base of the pool.

A resounding crack like a thundershock rattled the air, and the ground shook as the floor of the pool fractured. The waters of Rinpool drained out through the web of cracks. A roar of pain blew through the clearing like a hurricane, knocking the smugglers and Gralfar off their feet.

Anchored by the sword, Tara leaned hard into the wind as she fought to control the conflagration of power that threatened to burst right through her skin. With a roar of her own, she wrested the sword from the stone floor and slashed sideways. The part of the blade that had been submerged in the water shimmered with faint blue light. "Stay down!" she yelled to the others as blue-black fire surged across the open space and smashed into the trees, torching them into an inferno. She gasped as the heat from the sword's power, more intense than she'd ever experienced, seared her from the inside out. She didn't dare absorb the flames that blazed through her body. She could feel the Being's essence permeating them.

The wind died as the Being's roar twisted into an eerie moan that made the hair on the back of her neck stand on end. The trees writhed as they shriveled in the fire. Tara pressed her advantage and blasted the trees behind those already burning. If she could keep it up, she could blaze a path out of here. She moved as close to the convulsing trees as she could without getting singed and sent another shot of the blue-black fire deeper into Dharakwood. The flames spread quickly. The thorn trees crackled and withered amidst the agonized groans of the Being.

Tara fell to one knee, panting, close to passing out. She saw that the skin of her hands had reddened, grown dry and cracked from the fire within. Her face, too, felt rough and papery.

Jovan and Blackie appeared on either side of her, reaching out to her.

"No, don't touch me!" she said quickly, and they stepped back. Her eyes sought Jovan's. "It let you go? Are you all right?"

Jovan gave a brief humorless smile. "Yes. The Being has other concerns at the moment. Are *you* all right?"

"I'll be fine." She heaved herself to her feet, hope surging through the volcanic heat in her veins. "Just a few more blasts..." She walked stiffly forward into the skeletal remains of the burning swath of Dharakwood, stepping over blackened stumps, the ground so hot it scalded her feet right through her boots. When she reached the wall of flames, she took a deep, trembling breath, gathered her strength, and let loose another wave of blue-black fire. The flames hissed like a thousand snakes, then roared as they fed on another deep cut of twisting trees. The Being moaned.

Tara cried out and fell to her knees again on the smoldering ground. Curls of smoke rose from her body through holes burned in her clothes from the heat of her skin. Her breath rasped in her parched throat. She felt Jovan's presence beside her. She could barely see him, her vision blurred by her use of the power. Her head spun from exhaustion and from the inferno within. She gasped as an icy stab of warning jolted her. Her hands flew to her temples. "No, no, *no!*" She frantically tried to shore up her mental defenses, but she couldn't get her whirling mind to focus. "No!" she screamed again as Ravnaul smashed her walls and sank his claws into her mind.

"Tara!" Jovan gripped her hand.

"Help me," she whispered, then the smothering crush of the void swallowed her.

*****

Tara groaned as her body thudded onto the stone floor. She smelled the foulness of carrion, heard the approach of uneven footsteps.

"Welcome back to my dungeon." Ravnaul's hoarse voice slithered through her torn mind. "And you've brought the black sword back to me, as well. How thoughtful." He released her mind as he walked toward her.

Tara squinted at him, her vision clearing. She tried to push herself off the floor, but her blistered arms wouldn't hold her weight. She collapsed onto her back, gripping the sword in her left hand. Thousands of spiders covered the walls and ceiling, encasing the corridor in sticky white webs. A massive spider, its smooth black body at least two feet long, had spun a web over the hole she'd blasted in the wall with the sword in her last dream. The monstrous arachnid hung in the center of the web, awaiting its prey. She shuddered, cursing her weakness. Her body still smoked. The sword's fire blazed through her blood, but she dared not let it fuse with her own magic.

Ravnaul looked down at her. "Can't handle the fire? I thought you were stronger than that." He reached down and wrenched the sword from her hand. He held it out before him in triumph.

Tara saw him frown and look at the blade more closely. A horrible thought struck her. Earlier, Ravnaul had used the sword's energy to partially restore himself. The black blade still glimmered with blue light. If he used that energy again now, would he absorb the Being's power? Who would be in control — the Being or Ravnaul? Neither possibility was good.

"What have you done to my sword?" Ravnaul demanded.

The harsh shriek of a bird of prey filled the corridor, and with a whistle of wings, a large red blur whooshed past Tara and thudded into Ravnaul, its talons digging into his arms and chest as it slammed him to the floor. The black sword scraped across the stone, clawed out of Ravnaul's grip by the red griffin.

Jovan! Joy and relief surged through her, giving her strength. Avoiding the falling spiders knocked loose by the force of the griffin's wings, Tara rolled to her hands and knees and crawled toward the sword. Her hand closed over the hilt. *Got it!* She turned to aim it at Ravnaul, who still lay on the floor, stunned and bleeding.

The griffin lifted off him, its head turning toward her. Jovan's voice filled her mind. *Behind you!*

Tara whirled to find the giant spider scrabbling up beside her. She swung the black blade around, too late. The spider sank its fangs into her sword arm. She hissed in a breath at the stabbing pain, her arm deadening as poison ripped through her veins.

Then the griffin's claws snatched the spider away and crushed it. Tara fell back, her strength sapped by the poison coursing through her. The griffin shimmered and blurred, shifting into human form. Jovan scooped her up in his arms. Her stomach lurched as the world spun around her. Her numb fingers lost their grip on the sword.

No, wait! she cried in her mind.

The world straightened, and she found herself lying in a dark field of tall grass, Jovan kneeling beside her, tying a tourniquet on her swollen arm. She smelled smoke, saw Dharakwood burning in the distance. Moonlight shone on the anxious faces surrounding her — Blackie, the smugglers, Sarita, and Gralfar. She looked down at her empty hand. Dismay knotted her stomach.

"No," she whispered.

"Tara — the poison — can you stop it? Can you clear it out?" Jovan's voice was urgent.

"I lost the sword."

"I don't care about the sword. Can you cure the poison?"

"I don't know. It's..." The faces around her grew fuzzy. Her whole body felt numb. Even the burning pain of the black sword's fire dulled beneath the poison's paralysis.

"Tara!"

She heard his voice as though he spoke through thick glass. She barely felt his fingers holding her arms in a tight grip. Her limbs refused to move. Panic seized her. She couldn't breathe. She needed more strength. And there was only one way to get it. Fighting for one last deep breath, she let the blue-black flames into her soul. The black fire, colored with the Being's essence, merged with her own wellspring of magic. She screamed as a burst of power exploded through her body, purging the poison.

"Tara?" Jovan lifted her head against his shoulder.

Her eyes met his, and lucidity returned for a moment. "Sorry," she whispered. "I didn't... have a choice." She closed her eyes, and unconsciousness claimed her.

*****

Rylan Natiere pried a small boulder out of the pile of rubble blocking the mine shaft and flung it away with a vile curse. *Sorceress,* he fumed, *you had best hope we don't meet again.* He dug out another rock and threw it into the tunnel behind him. Tara had nearly died, and he had been too far away to do anything about it. With helpless horror, he'd sensed her life slipping away. Fear and frustration still clenched his chest. Only once before had he known such fear —as a child, when bandits had tortured him, slaughtered his family, and left him for dead.

He shoved more rocks aside, focusing on his anger to help quell his other emotions. The strength of his fear had both tantalized and infuriated him. He'd met many people in his travels, but he'd never cared whether any of them lived or died... except her. Just thinking about Tara made him feel alive. The touch of her mind was like rain on his arid soul, nourishing and coaxing forth his lost humanity to bloom again within him as a desert flower blossoms after a storm. But his need to feel her touch had become his weakness. His life was now tied to hers, and his helplessness, his inability to save her, had ignited a fearsome rage — against the sorceress for sending him out of reach; against Jovan Trevillion — who, thanks to the sorceress, was probably with her — for his failure to prevent whatever trauma had almost cost her life; against those worthless smugglers...

Remembrances of his encounter with Blackie de Runo filled him with chagrin. Tara likely wouldn't have accepted his help even if he had been able to offer it. He hurled a stone down the tunnel with all his might. He should not have allowed himself to be provoked. As much as he despised Blackie de Runo and had owed him a good thrashing for getting Tara thrown in the lockup, a moment of vengeance was not worth losing the fragile trust he'd sensed in her. If he'd broken it...

With one last heave, Natiere pushed forward a rock atop the rubble and sent it crashing down the other side of the pile, opening a hole almost large enough for him to crawl through into the tunnel beyond. Fresh, cool air full of night scents poured in. He breathed deeply and smelled... wolf. A familiar bark startled him. The face of a black wolf appeared in the hole, whining and pawing furiously at the loose rock.

"Kelya," he whispered. "How...?"

Kelya barked again, lost her footing, and slid out of sight.

"Kelya!" Natiere thrust aside some more stones and forced his way through the hole. One black wolf and six gray yipped at him as he clambered down to the tunnel floor. Just beyond the impatient wolves lay the mine entrance, open and flooded with moonlight. He knelt in the midst of his pack and hugged them as they pressed against him and licked his face.

"My Sisters and Brothers, I've missed you, too," he said with a laugh. "But how did you get here?" He cupped the black wolf's jowls and looked into her yellow eyes. She uttered a series of soft barks and whimpers. He released her, stunned, and stared off into the moonlit distance. "Could it be she has forgiven me? Or was she merely taking pity on you?"

Not daring to hope, he rose and headed out of the mine. "Come, we must move swiftly!"

CHAPTER 30

The buzz of soft voices brought Tara back to consciousness. She kept her eyes closed, letting her mind rise to full awareness, listening as the sound of light footsteps faded and a door quietly opened and shut. Nearby, a chair creaked, and she heard a long exhale. She sensed Jovan's presence, his aura weary and tense. Then memories of Rinpool and Ravnaul and their last ordeal rushed into her mind. She snapped her eyes open and sat up, finding herself in a bed in a small, round room. Someone had dressed her in a green sleeping gown.

"Jovan?"

Startled, Jovan looked up from where he was sitting with his elbows on his knees and his head in his hands. "Tara?" Hope colored his strained voice and softened the lines of his haggard face. He looked like he hadn't slept in a week. He sprang from the chair to the edge of the bed and embraced her. "Gods, I thought you were gone this time."

She held him tight and choked back a sob, happy that he was there with her and not still lost somewhere far away. They eased back, each lifting a hand to caress the other's face, smiling at their singular thoughts. Then their lips met in a fervent kiss.

"How are you feeling?" Jovan asked after a few moments.

"Fine, but what about you? You look like you could use some sleep."

He gave her a tired smile. "I'm fine, now that you're awake."

"Truly?"

"Truly."

She touched the ruby ring he wore, her fingers tracing the jeweled griffin. "I had a feeling we'd need this again."

"I'm just glad I was able to use it this time."

"Has the Being plagued you since..."

"No."

"What about Blackie and the others? Where are they? Are they all right?"

"They're here, and yes, they're fine."

"Thank the gods." She hesitated, puzzled by the subtle rise in tension and the slight coolness in Jovan's voice when he spoke of the smugglers. "Is there a problem with them?"

"No."

She frowned inwardly. There was a problem somewhere, she could tell, but she knew from his expression that questioning him further would be pointless. She glanced around the chamber, taking in the tapestry-covered walls, the sparse furniture, the small fire crackling in the grate, and the tall, narrow window with a view of rose-tinted clouds. "Where are we?"

"Estiarii Faelle. We've been here four days. Valina's been tending you."

Tara turned sharply. "Then she's all right?"

"Yes. She's weak, but she was able to bring us here without any trouble."

Tara sent up another silent prayer of thanks. "I've been really worried about her."

"Not nearly as worried as she's been about you." Jovan clasped Tara's hands. "Are you sure you're all right?"

Tara smiled and leaned forward, kissing him after every few words. "You're here... we're alive... what more could I need?"

He brushed her hair back and slid his thumb over her lips, concern tightening his brows. "That doesn't exactly answer my question."

She took a deep breath and sat back, uneasiness stealing through her. "Well, I don't really know, exactly. I haven't had time to think about what happened." She looked down at herself and noted that her skin had healed. She was no longer red and blistered.

"What did happen? And what did you mean, right before you passed out, when you said you were sorry, you had no choice?"

Tara ran a hand through her tangled hair. "Well, you didn't want me to touch the water, and I didn't, but the sword did. I got so angry at what the Being was doing to you that I stabbed the sword into the bottom of the pool, and all the water ran out."

"I know. They told me."

"Did they tell you that the part of the sword that was in the water turned bluish, and that the fire that came out of it had a bluish tint to it?"

"No." Jovan cursed. "Bluish tint. The color of the gods."

"What do you mean?"

"Something Valina said earlier. The blade is contaminated." Jovan pounded the bed. "Blast that infernal Being." He paced to the window and back. "You used the sword. Did the Being's power mix with yours?"

"Not at first, but then I had to let it in. It was the only way to cure the poison." Tara took his hands as he sat back down on the bed. "That's what I meant when I said I had no choice. It was either absorb the sword's fire or die."

Jovan cursed again.

Tara squeezed his hands. "I would have had to do it anyway."

"Why?"

"Because Ravnaul has the sword, and if he uses its power to fully restore himself, the Being's power will merge with his. I don't know who will be in control, but I've no hope of defeating either of them without that same blend of power."

"But what if —"

Tara held her finger to his lips. "We'll worry about the what-ifs when they happen."

The door opened, and a much thinner Valina Mellarian walked into the room. Her eyes widened, and she rushed to the bed. "Tara, you're awake! Thank the gods!"

Jovan rose and stepped back. Tara embraced Valina gently, troubled by the sorceress' frailty.

"I was so worried about you," they said simultaneously.

Valina laughed. "You needn't worry about me. With a little rest, I'll be bright as the sunrise again."

Tara smiled. "That's good to hear. Thank you for everything you've done for us. You've risked so much."

"There is no risk I wouldn't take to help you in your quest," Valina said, sobering. "Not just because of Zaniel, but because of who you are, as well. You are strong, caring, courageous, and determined, and I know you'll succeed."

"Thank you," Tara said quietly.

Valina nodded. "Your friends are down in the dining hall, having breakfast. I know they'll be excited to see you, if you feel strong enough to join them. Are you hungry?"

Tara's stomach grumbled. "Apparently." She grinned.

"Would you rather eat here and rest?"

"No, I'll go down. I feel fine."

"There are fresh clothes and a place to wash up in the room below this one. I'll go prepare more food. Just come down when you're ready." Valina turned and left the room.

Tara slid to the edge of the bed.

"Are you sure you're well enough to be up and about?" Jovan asked.

"I'm fine." She rose and stepped into his arms. "I love you." Her lips sought his. Many moments later, she let her head drift to his chest and listened to his heartbeat, heard words of love breathed against her hair, and wished she could stay forever in the circle of his arms. But then her stomach growled again, and she stirred. She took his hand and led the way out of the room.

After she'd washed and dressed, they descended the circular stone stairs to the dining hall. The smugglers' conversations ceased the moment they entered.

"Hey," Brains said with a grin, as he and the other smugglers leaped up and came forward. Brains gave her a bear hug. "It's about time you decided to join us."

"Haedis' balls, woman, don't ever do that again," Blackie said, his voice oddly gruff. He hugged her loosely, and Tara felt Jovan stiffen. Then Blackie stepped back and kept his distance as she hugged Whittler, Jack, and Whiskey. Sarita and Gralfar had risen and come around the table. She smiled and nodded to them. The Gypsy glowered and gave her only a brief, unsmiling nod in return, but the dwarf seemed relieved and glad to see her. They all sat down again as Valina entered and magically transported more bread, fruit, and cold meats onto the table. Tara sat between Jovan and Whiskey, with Brains and Jack across from her, while Sarita and Blackie sat to Jack's left. On the other side of Whiskey, Whittler protected his glass of mead and gestured for Gralfar, on his right, to do the same. Tara glanced at Blackie furtively, sensing in him a tension echoing from Jovan. So that's where the problem lay. The other smugglers seemed on edge as well.

"Tara, we have so many questions for you," Valina said, "but I know you need to eat, so are there any questions you'd like to ask us first?"

Tara swallowed her bite. "Yes. How did we escape Rinpool, and what happened after I passed out?"

The smugglers glanced at Blackie, who remained silent.

"The fire from the sword burned all the way through Dharakwood and into the grasslands of Rone Valley," Brains said. "It might still be burning, for all we know. We carried the two of you out, you both came to, and then you passed out again." Brains nodded at Tara. "Not long after that, Valina brought us here."

"Yes," Valina said. "I regained consciousness and was able to muster just enough strength for the transport. If the Being had interfered again, I wouldn't have been able to do it."

"Is there any way of knowing what happened to the Being?" Tara asked. "I heard moans like it was in pain when the thorn trees were burning, but then I fell into the dream and lost all sense of what was happening."

"I fear you may have freed it," Valina said. "It may be weakened from your attack on the pool and the forest to which it was bound, but there's no way to know for certain."

Cold foreboding shivered through Tara as she drained her mead glass. She was surprised Whiskey had left it alone. He must've thought she'd need a good bracer.

"If the other gods imprisoned this Being once, couldn't they lock it away again?" Brains asked.

Valina lifted her hands in a helpless gesture. "Who knows? We don't even know for certain the Being is a god. It's all speculation."

Tara looked at Jovan. "You mentioned that Valina had said something about blue being the color of the gods." She turned back to the sorceress. "What did you mean, and how do you know this?"

"When the great god Azakai spoke to me centuries ago, his reflection in Mirror Lake was edged in blue," Valina explained, "as yours is silver from your Kamarian heritage. Jovan's reflection has a mixture of both blue and silver — blue from the magic of Rinpool and silver from you. That is what led me to believe Rinpool might be a prison of the gods, but it's still just a theory."

"No. It's true, I'm sure of it," Tara said. "The part of the black sword that touched the water of Rinpool had a bluish tint, and I could sense the Being's power in it. That power is now in me. I had to absorb it in order to cure the poison from the spider bite."

Valina gasped. "Do you mean you have the power of the gods?"

The power of the gods. Tara lost what she'd been about to say. She hadn't had a chance to think about the ramifications of what she'd done. How could anyone have that kind of power? The enormity of the possibility dumbfounded her. "I-I don't know. I don't feel any different. And I'm not sure how I would use that power, if I did have it. Except for my healing magic and danger sense, my power has only manifested itself through the black sword. Without that, I have no means of releasing the power, no conduit to channel it through."

"And Jovan said that Ravnaul has the sword," Valina said worriedly.

"Yes. When the spider bit me, my arm went numb, and I dropped it." Tara shook her head in disgust. "If I just could have held onto it a moment longer..."

"Don't waste your energy over might-have-beens." Valina drew herself up in her chair. "What's done is done, and I can't thank the gods enough that you are still with us. We'll find a way to get the sword back and destroy Ravnaul before he can escape and wreak havoc on the world."

"Yes, but he has the sword," Tara persisted. "He will restore himself to full power, if he hasn't already, and he'll have the Being's power on top of that."

"Ah, but will he?" Valina's eyes narrowed as she thought. "If our theory of the Being wanting revenge on the other gods is true, then the Being will want to control that power as much as Ravnaul will. Their power struggle may give us the time we need."

"Time for what?" Tara asked.

"There's more than one way to kill a Kamarian." Valina leaned forward. "Has Ravnaul touched your mind since you've awakened?"

Tara shook her head. "No."

"What about the Being?"

"No. How else do you kill a Kamarian?"

"By destroying his lifestone, or in this case, his bloodstone."

"Validar Melodian has Ravnaul's bloodstone," Tara said. "I'd nearly forgotten about him. He wasn't in the dungeon in my last dream. Ravnaul didn't have the stone, so it must still be in Melodian's possession. Do you know where he is?"

"No, and I can't locate him with the mirror. His powers are too strong."

"Then how will we find him?" Tara asked. A thought seized her. "Wait — he has communicated with me mentally before. Maybe I can reach out to him, find him that way."

"No, it's too dangerous," Jovan said.

"Well, we have to find him some way," Tara said.

Valina stood. "I don't know how much time we'll have, so this is what I propose. I'll send you to the Black Mountains first. I still feel in my heart that finding the city of Kamar is most important. Whatever you find there should help you in your battles against Ravnaul and this Being. Then you can search out Melodian and..." She faltered for a moment, then recovered. "And do what you must."

"Will destroying the bloodstone destroy him as well?" Tara asked.

"I fear so," Valina said softly. "He must have bound himself to it in some way to use its powers."

"I'm sorry," Tara said. "I know he is your brother."

"No." Valina shook her head sadly. "He ceased to be my brother when he chose the dark path of *Diurkruna*." She straightened. "I'll ready some supplies for you all while you finish eating." She headed for the stairs.

"Valina, wait." Tara rose. "We only need supplies for myself and Jovan." Her eyes swept over the smugglers, her hands upraised to stem any protests. "No, don't say it. You have risked your lives for me too many times already. As soon as Valina has fully recovered, she can send you wherever you want to go." Tara turned back to Valina. "Can't you?"

Valina looked concerned. "Well... yes, but—"

"And couldn't Gralfar stay here until we get back?"

"Of course, but —"

"Good. That's settled then. I'll help you prepare." She crossed the room without looking back and followed a hesitant Valina up the stairs, Jovan close behind her.

The sorceress led them to a large room and opened closets full of clothes. "These belonged to Zaniel and Erana and the others who came back with me from Kamar, so long ago. I'm sure you can find something that will fit." Valina frowned worriedly. "Tara, I really think you should —"

"Please don't say it," Tara interrupted. "I've already lost someone dear to me." Dominic's face slipped through her mind. "I don't want to lose anyone else." She picked up a pack and set it on a table. "I'll get the clothes. Jovan, why don't you help Valina with the food? We can leave that much more quickly."

Jovan nodded and left with the sorceress.

Tara pulled an extra set of clothes and a cloak for Jovan from the closets, folded them loosely, and stuffed them in the pack. She knew she'd left the dining hall rather abruptly, but as Valina had said, time was short, and they needed to act swiftly. She dreaded saying goodbye to the smugglers. Her journey would likely be less difficult if she allowed them to come with her — that is, assuming they would even want to continue on. But the thought of any of them dying was more than she could bear. She set a second pack on the table and chose some clothing and a cloak for herself. The tension in her gut as she packed told her she might not be making the right decision where the smugglers were concerned, but she quashed her misgivings. She would figure out something. At least this way, they'd be alive.

"So, that's it?" said a voice from the doorway.

She whirled. Blackie stepped into the room. She'd been so embroiled in her thoughts, she hadn't heard him approach.

He lifted Jovan's backpack, then set it back down on the table. "You're just going to dump us and leave?"

"Blackie, I'm not dumping you, I'm trying to keep you alive."

"What about keeping you alive?"

"We'll manage." She laced shut the second backpack.

"And what happens when you both end up in that dream place of yours?"

"Like I said, we'll manage."

Blackie pulled the pack away from her. "Tara, listen to me. You were both out cold. You would have died in the fire if we hadn't been there to carry you out. If we don't go with you, there won't be anyone to get you out of trouble if it happens again."

"Valina can transport us if she has to."

"You can't count on her. If that whatever-it-is interferes with her again, you're dead."

"Blackie, I can't let you do it. I've lost Dominic, I almost lost you. I couldn't bear it if anything happened to you — to any of you. You're not going."

"Damnation, woman, how do you think we'll feel if something happens to *you?* We *are* going — at least, I am — and you've got nothing to say about it."

"Oh, so you're going whether I like it or not?"

"Yes, so I don't want to hear any more arguments."

Tara snatched the pack out of his hands and slammed it on the table. "You are the most stubborn, pig-headed, infuriating person —
"

"Are you done yelling at me? 'Cause I've got to go get ready. Hey, that rhymes." He grinned.

Tara threw a pair of leggings at him. "It does not, and no, I'm not done yelling at you. I —" She stopped as Brains appeared in the doorway.

"You're going to have to yell at me, too." Brains stepped inside and leaned against the wall by the door.

"And us," said Diamond Jack. He, Whittler, and Whiskey entered the room and stood beside Brains.

Tara glared at them in consternation. "You have to stay here."

"Are you kidding?" Brains said. "And pass up the chance to see a real *Aiykshaav'n* city and maybe even meet one of the Ancients?"

Whittler nodded vigorously.

"Imagine the treasures they must have," Jack said.

Whittler nodded again.

"And the drink," Whiskey added. "I'll bet it's even better than this." He swallowed the contents of his mead glass in one gulp.

Whittler kept nodding.

Tara shoved her hair back, not sure whether to scream, cry, or laugh. What had she done to deserve such friends? "You're all impossible," she said finally.

Blackie grinned. "You may as well admit defeat, woman. You're not leaving without us."

She smiled, unable to help herself. "Curse you, Blackie." She hugged him impulsively. "Thank you," she whispered. He hugged her back, a real hug this time, not his usual loose, awkward embrace. Surprised, she stepped back, then froze when she saw Jovan standing in the doorway.

"Valina would like you to come to the observatory and speak with her," Jovan said to Tara, his expression shuttered, "as soon as you're done here."

Cursing to herself, Tara moved away from Blackie. "I'll be down in a minute."

Jovan nodded and left, his footsteps fading down the stairs.

Tara ran her hand over her face. Great. How did she keep getting herself into these situations?

Blackie cleared his throat. "Sorry. I know what you said earlier, and I didn't mean it to look like... I was just... well... back at Rinpool, I thought you were... I mean, it didn't look like you were going to... oh, damn it to the Abyss." He raked his hand through his hair. "It's just that you've always been... kind of special to me, too, and if there's any way I can prevent anything like that from happening again, I want to be there to do it."

"*We* want to be there," added Brains, softly.

Tara squeezed Blackie's arm. "Thank you," she said over the lump in her throat. "All of you." She looked at the smugglers. "With friends like you, how can I lose?"

CHAPTER 31

"You wanted to talk to me?" Tara wended through the cluttered tables and astronomical equipment toward Valina Mellarian, who was pulling the velvet cloth from the scrimoire. Tara glanced around, but saw no one else in the room. She'd hoped Jovan would be there. She needed to straighten things out between them before the situation got out of hand.

"Yes. I have something for you." Valina laid the cloth on a table and lifted a silver chain from around her neck.

Tara recognized the smoky oval stone dangling from the end of the chain. "Zaniel's lifestone."

"Yes. I want you to take it with you." Valina held it out to her.

Tara took a step backward. "Oh, no, I can't. What if something happened to it? I don't want to be responsible for his life, too."

"Please, you must." Valina took Tara's hand and placed the stone on her palm. "I feel you will need it." The sorceress closed the ends of Tara's fingers around the stone. "I'm certain it's the right thing to do, and I trust you to keep it safe."

"But I don't trust me," Tara protested. She watched the gray smoke within the stone begin to stir from her touch. "I have too many powerful enemies. It would be much safer here." She tried to give the lifestone back to Valina.

The sorceress refused to take it. "No. It's time for Zaniel's stone to be returned to him. He is the eldest child of the Kamarian king. If King Lazarial didn't survive the Cataclysm, Zaniel must assume the throne. He'll need the power of the stone to rebuild his kingdom."

"How do you know I'll find him?"

"I don't, but I'll keep praying you will."

Reluctantly, Tara slipped the chain over her head, settling the jewel beneath her shirt. Footsteps echoed in the stairwell, and Tara felt a nervous tightening in her stomach as Jovan made his way toward them, his mind closed to her, his expression unreadable. The smugglers, Sarita, and Gralfar tramped down the stairs behind him. Jovan stopped beside Tara, but made no move to touch her. As the others formed a silent half-circle around them, Tara clasped Jovan's hand and sidled closer until her arm rested against his.

"I wanted to show this to you." Valina swept her arm toward the scrimoire. "This is what is left of Ravnaul's Keep, at the edge of the Black Mountains." The late morning clouds reflecting in the mirror shifted, and a tall, grim mountain range appeared — an endless panorama of black summits with sharp, snowless points spearing the sky.

Tara shivered with foreboding. She caught Jovan's glance of concern as he squeezed her hand, but she couldn't explain what she felt, her emotions a confused mix of anticipation and apprehension.

The image in the mirror swooped down to the base of a craggy peak, where a single ragged tower of black stone stood, as if grown out of the mountain. The top of the tower had been destroyed, leaving it open to the elements. All around it, the collapsed fortress lay in ruins.

Tara studied the broken tower, frowning at the smooth translucence of its round wall. "It looks like it's made of glass. The whole mountain looks that way — like it was formed from some kind of obsidian. Are there volcanoes?"

"No," Valina answered. "The Black Mountains used to be solid stone like any mountains — strong and vibrant, full of plants and wildlife. But then the Cataclysm changed the very fiber of the rock, leaving the mountains as you see them now — brittle and silent, dead." The sorceress pointed to an open archway in the tower, its door hanging by one ornate hinge. "This is the only way in. Unfortunately, after three hundred years, I can't remember what was inside the tower. There were tunnels leading back into the mountain, but I can't recall how to get to them, nor can I remember the path I followed." She sighed in disgust. "You'll have to discover the way yourselves." She turned to Tara. "Or perhaps when you get there, what I see will jog my memory."

Tara nodded.

"Now," Valina said briskly, "I need to know who is going."

"We are," Tara said, lifting her and Jovan's clasped hands.

"So are we." Brains indicated the rest of the smugglers.

Valina looked relieved. "All of you?"

Sarita moved closer to Blackie and wrapped her arm around his. "All of us."

Tara held her breath for a moment, but Blackie didn't argue.

"What about you, master dwarf?" Valina asked.

"If there are tunnels, you'll need a dwarf. I'm going too," Gralfar said.

"Are you sure you want to do this, Gralfar?" Jovan asked.

"It's better than spending all day picking my teeth with my axe. There's not much to do around here — no offense, Sorceress," he added quickly, with an apologetic nod to Valina.

"None taken. Very well." Valina closed her eyes, mouthed some words, and, amid whorls of mist, their filled backpacks materialized on the floor in front of her.

The group picked up their packs and slung them over their shoulders.

"Before we go, I just need a minute," Tara said. She squeezed Jovan's hand. "Come with me." She drew him toward the stairs. "We'll be right back." She led Jovan up the stairs and into an empty room. Then she kicked the door shut, backed him against the wall, and pressed close. "Never doubt me," she said fiercely, and kissed him. His arms slid around her as hers curled around his neck, and she lost herself in the kiss.

After a few moments, she stepped back. "I love you, Jovan. I'll keep saying it and saying it and saying it until you believe me."

He traced his fingers over her cheek. "I do believe you."

"Good." She drew his fingers to her lips and kissed them, then clasped his hand again. "You have to understand. I love Blackie, too, but in a different way. He's family. I'm *in* love with you, and that's not going to change. And he knows that." She searched Jovan's eyes. "Do we have that straight now?"

He smiled. "As an arrow flies."

She smiled back. They shared one last kiss, then hurried back to the observatory. As they came down the stairs, the smugglers suddenly developed an intense interest in whatever astronomical contraption stood next to them, except for Whiskey, who had eyes only for his bottle of mead. Sarita regarded them appraisingly. Tara gritted her teeth, wishing she knew how to erase the awkwardness that kept rearing up like an unwanted guest. Why must relationships be so confoundedly complicated?

"All right, let's go," she said, as she and Jovan picked up their packs. She turned to Valina. "Are you sure you have the strength to send us all?"

"I'll do my best." Valina took a deep breath. "Move in close, please."

Tara and the others crowded together and linked arms. The thick, white fog swirled up from the floor, firmly enclosing them. Tara's stomach lurched as they rose into the air. She concentrated on the ruined black tower they'd seen in the mirror. If they didn't get there this time...

They drifted in a restless stream of air for several heartbeats, then landed gently on solid ground. The fog thinned, melting into a cold mist that hung like veils of spider web in a narrow mountain pass barely touched by the sun.

Shivering from memories of her last encounter with spiders, Tara swiped at the mist with her hand. Feathery tendrils of white whirled in front of her, then formed into a tremulous mesh of lines. "I don't remember seeing this in the mirror."

"Can anyone see the tower?" Brains asked.

A chorus of no's answered him.

"It's this way." Tara drew the sword she'd taken from the guard back in Gypsy Crossroads and moved forward through the mist. Weapons drawn, the others followed, with Brains keeping rear guard. She could sense the black tower just ahead on her left. She stifled another shiver. The mountains reeked of horror and death. And it didn't help that the surrounding mist truly resembled spider webs. She felt like she was back in her dream dungeon.

She froze. What if the dream dungeon was sifting through to this world? What if Ravnaul had found a means of escape through the Being? She was near his keep, and his powers might be even stronger here.

Jovan stopped beside her. "What's wrong?"

"Do you see how the mist is shaped like spider webs?" she asked tensely. "It's just like my dream dungeon — a ghost version of it. I fear Ravnaul is very close to escaping. We have to hurry and get through into the mountains."

Whiskey let out a yell and pointed to his right.

Spectral spiders as big as frying pans scuttled along the mist webs, moving swiftly toward them.

Blackie sliced his blade through three of them. The mist spiders dissipated, then reformed and scrabbled closer. "Curse me to the Abyss!" he sputtered as he backed away.

"Follow me!" Tara ran toward the tower, plowing through the mist, dodging around chunks of stone from the fallen fortress. She heard the pounding footsteps of the others close behind her. She didn't know if the ghost spiders could hurt them or not, but she didn't care to find out.

Just ahead, the black tower loomed, cold and lifeless as a mausoleum. Tara's eyes flitted up the smooth black walls, rising thirty feet in the air, jagged edges silhouetted against a strip of pale sky. It was much more imposing than the vision she'd seen in the mirror. Quivers of anticipation and dread goose-pimpled her skin. What would she find here — answers to the mystery of the Kamarians, or more death and destruction?

She shoved aside the half-hung door and entered the tower. A quick glance showed her it was empty, save for a staircase against the far wall that went nowhere and a waist-high stone cylinder in the center, filled with water. "Everyone inside!"

They dashed into the tower. Jovan and Brains wrenched the door shut as best they could.

"They may come over the top," Jovan said, moving close to Tara.

Tara shot nervous glances upward as she scanned the tower's darkly shadowed interior. The circular chamber was about twenty feet across. The stone staircase spiraled upward, with small, arched windows spaced evenly along its length.

"I wonder where that led," Brains mused, as he and the others spread out to search the chamber.

"Who knows?" Tara said. She crossed to the well in the center of the room. About six feet in diameter, the well was filled with water that reflected the black translucence of the stone from which the well was crafted. She could see nothing in its depths, and yet... She closed her eyes. Something called to her in vague whispers, something alien and yet familiar at the same time, awakening something inside her. Images crowded into her mind of people she'd never seen, places she'd never been, as if she were recalling someone else's memories.

"Tara?"

She jumped at the sound of Jovan's voice.

He cupped her shoulders. "Are you all right?"

Tara, I remember now, Valina said in Tara's mind. *There's a door into the mountain beneath the —*

"Hey, there's a door over here," Diamond Jack burst out. He poked his head out from under the staircase. "And it's not locked."

Yes, that's it, Valina said excitedly.

Everyone except Tara and Jovan hastened toward the door Jack had found.

"No, wait." Tara rubbed her forehead, trying to still the chaos in her mind. "Yes, I'm all right," she said to Jovan. "There's something here." She looked down into the water again. "I can sense people — spirits maybe — I don't know who they are." She circled the well, studying the smooth rock, looking for — she wasn't sure what. Seeing nothing obvious, she knelt and ran her hands down the side.

Small silver symbols glowed to life, ringing the edge of the well. She pulled her hands back in surprise. The symbols vanished.

Jovan touched the well. Nothing happened.

"Do it again," Brains said to Tara.

She laid her hands flat against the cool rock. The symbols reappeared, glowing brightly.

Brains traced them with his fingers. "I've never seen markings like these. Do you know what they mean?"

"No... well, maybe... sort of..." She pressed her hand to her forehead again. "Aaahhhh, stop! It's too much."

Jovan knelt beside her. "What is it?"

"It's like hundreds of people trying to get in my head all at once." The voices and images subsided, leaving one clear thought — a particular symbol...

"Spiders!" Jack pointed upward.

Ghostly spiders swarmed over the edge of the tower and crawled down the walls.

"To the door!" Whiskey cried.

"No! Everybody over here!" Keeping one hand on the side of the well, Tara slid around it until she found a symbol that looked like four crescent moons. They were back to back in opposite directions, intersecting to form a curving eight-pointed star.

Tara, are you sure? Valina asked doubtfully.

I'm sure. Tara pressed the glowing symbol and stepped back. With a grinding noise, the well began to spiral upward, as if growing out of the floor. It rose about eight feet and stopped, revealing an open archway — a door in the side of the well.

Tara heard Valina gasp.

"Hurry, get in." Tara gestured for the others to go inside.

Whittler balked, but Brains and Blackie each grabbed an arm and dragged him in. The others squeezed in after them. They just managed to fit. Then Tara backed into the small remaining space and touched the inner wall. The well spiraled downward, the archway descending into the floor moments before the creeping spiders reached it. A silvery glow like soft moonlight flooded the compartment.

"That was close," Jack said, exhaling sharply. "Do we know where we're going?"

"Do we ever?" Blackie grumbled. "Whiskey, stow that bottle somewhere else, will ya?"

"We'll find out in a minute." Tara pressed back against Jovan. He crossed his arms in front of her and held her close.

The well rumbled to a halt. Tara faced an open landing high above a narrow cavern that bristled with stalactites. Stone stairs led downward along the wall to the left.

Not sensing any danger, Tara stepped onto the landing. The muted silver glow lighting the cavern brightened. Jovan followed. He and Tara moved to the side to give the others room to come out. Blackie and Jack practically flew onto the landing, propelled by Whittler, who burst out so quickly he nearly fell off into the cavern. Brains' firm grip on his arm saved him. Panting and sweating as if he'd fought in a battle, Whittler clung to Brains' arm.

"Haedis' balls, man," Blackie said. "You've got to calm down."

"It's all right," Brains said gently. "Take a deep breath."

Tara squeezed Whittler's hand. "I'm sorry. I forgot you didn't like small spaces."

Whittler gave her a wan smile.

Tara started down the stairs. "Let's see where this goes."

They followed the curving stairs deep into the cavern until they came to another landing, where a featureless door of translucent black stone blended into the cavern wall. Tara stared at the door, overwhelmed again by the mass of souls crying out to her — such desperation in their voices. She had to help them. Taking a deep breath, she pressed her left hand against the door. The eight-pointed star symbol flashed once above her hand, and then the door slid open with a slight hiss, disappearing into the wall. Silver light bloomed, illuminating a wedge-shaped chamber, its walls lined with shelves of books, bottles, beakers, and countless other items. A desk covered with open books stood on the left side of the room. Across from the desk, on the floor near the wall, lay a pile of books that had fallen off the shelves.

Jovan's hands grazed her shoulders as he stepped up beside her, and together, they entered the chamber. The others followed. Tara frowned at the warm air brushing her skin. How was it so warm in here? The cavern had been quite cool. There were no fires in the room — maybe thermal slits in the floor? She looked down and froze, her eyes riveted on a long, rectangular trough set into the floor in the center of the room. She hadn't noticed it at first because the blackness of the substance in it matched the black stone of the floor. Hundreds of pleading voices clamored in her head, drawing her toward it. As if in slow motion, she crossed the room and dropped to her knees beside the trough.

"Oh, gods," she whispered, a horrible feeling twisting her gut as she stared at the tiny silver-white worms wriggling in the black glop. It couldn't be... *Valina!* she cried silently.

Oh, no. Tara could barely hear the sorceress' tearful whispers. *Oh, please, gods, forgive them — please don't leave them like this for eternity. Please!*

Tara felt a tear trace down her cheek. Jovan knelt and slipped his arm around her. "We'll find a way," he said softly.

Brains squatted beside her, a stunned look on his face. "Is that — I mean, are they..."

Tara wiped her sleeve across her eyes and nodded. "The Kamarian people... what's left of them. They've been here all along, cursed by the gods, trapped in this form for three hundred years."

Icy jabs of warning spurred Tara to her feet.

"Ah, I see you've met your relatives," said a smooth, faintly amused voice.

Validar Melodian stood in the doorway. His red robes were burned black in several places, and he was breathing hard, as if he had climbed a steep hill. The thinness of his body and the dark hollows under his eyes suggested he was still recovering from whatever damage Ravnaul had inflicted on him before he'd escaped the dream dungeon.

"Master Wizard," Tara said, avoiding the direct gaze of his red-gray eyes, "you're just the person I wanted to see."

Melodian's brows arched upward. "Indeed? Have you reconsidered my offer to help you develop your powers?"

"Well, that depends." Tara's mind raced. How was she going to get Ravnaul's bloodstone away from him? "I want to restore... my relatives, as you call them... to their true forms. Perhaps you can help me."

An apologetic smile crossed Melodian's face. "I'm afraid only the gods can do that. I can help you in other ways, however. Just give me the black sword, and I'll —" He stopped, his eyes on the empty scabbard at Tara's left hip. "Where is the sword?"

As Tara debated whether or not to tell him the truth, comprehension dawned on the wizard's face, along with a touch of fear. "Ravnaul has it, doesn't he? That might explain..." His hand slid to his chest and closed over an oval shape hidden beneath his robes.

Tara saw through the fabric a throbbing red glow, a pulse much faster than a normal heartbeat. Ravnaul's struggle with the Being must be affecting Melodian as well.

Frustration etched the wizard's thin features. "I need that sword." He shouted a magical phrase and flung his hand out at Tara.

Jovan snatched her out of the line of fire and spun her to the side, keeping his body between her and Melodian. A concussive force struck the wall, shattering bottles and beakers and sending books flying. Melodian groaned and stumbled to his knees.

Tara looked past Jovan, shocked to see a knife handle protruding from the wizard's chest. She recognized it at once. It belonged to Whittler.

Melodian stared in disbelief at the knife, at the dark crimson leaking around it. He pulled the knife free, let it clatter to the floor. His eyes glazed, the light in them dimming as he fell to the floor.

Tara rushed toward him. Just as she reached him, he vanished. "No!" She clenched her fists. "Curse it all, I almost had it." *Valina, where is he? Can you find him?*

I don't know. Valina's mental voice trembled. *I'll look for him.*

Tara sensed the sorceress' anguish like a wound deep in her own heart. *I'm sorry.*

It's not your fault. He chose his own path, Valina said, her voice catching as it faded.

Swearing under her breath, Tara picked up the knife. She'd been so close. She wiped the blade clean and held it out to Whittler. "Thanks. I owe you one."

The apprehension in his eyes flicked to relief, and Tara realized he'd been afraid she'd be angry with him. He took the knife and shook his head, touched his hand and face.

She smiled in understanding. He'd felt he owed her. She squeezed his shoulder. "All right, we're even."

"Where to now?" asked Brains, with a longing glance at the shelves full of books.

With a similar yearning, Tara scanned the chamber. How much of her heritage might she learn from these ancient tomes? She hungered for a chance to sit down and pore over them, to perhaps unearth a past and a family she'd never known. But a strange sense of urgency was building inside her, driven by the voices of the trapped Kamarians. They needed her help, and they needed it now. She gestured toward the shelves. "Why don't you all look around for a few minutes, while I try to communicate with..." She trailed off, her eyes on the wriggling white worms.

"Good idea," said Brains. He reached the shelves in two strides and began thumbing through one of the books.

The others dispersed throughout the room, poking through the clutter, examining objects, except for Jovan, who stayed near.

She caught his hand. "Thank you for saving me yet again," she said softly.

Jovan clasped her fingers tightly. "I don't think the wizard meant to kill you." He nodded toward the shelves, only slightly damaged from Melodian's attack. "He just wanted to knock you out, so Ravnaul could pull you back into the dungeon. Maybe he can't enter the dungeon unless you're there."

"It doesn't matter now." Tara knelt beside the trough. "He's gone who knows where, and he's taken the cursed stone with him. I only hope Valina can find him. Maybe if he's weak enough, or dead, he won't be able to hide from the mirror."

She looked into the trough and hesitated, reluctant to touch the wriggling worms, yet wanting so badly to connect with the souls she sensed within. She tried to imagine them as people and give them faces, but her mind couldn't quite make the stretch.

Taking a deep breath, she plunged her hands into the trough and scooped out some cool black jelly crawling with white worms. The squirming mass tickled her palms, and she shivered involuntarily. Then she closed her eyes and reached out with her mind. A whirlwind of raw emotions swept through her, as if the trapped souls had been holding their breath for three hundred years and had finally been allowed to exhale. Visions of the Cataclysm — the clash of magics between King Lazarial and his brother, Ravnaul, that had rent the very fabric of earth and sky — inundated her. *Oh, gods!* She cringed as the Kamarian people's horror twisted through her mind in violent shades of red, yellow, and black, punctuated with frightened shrieks and the groans of the dying. Then the colors dimmed to the muted gray of endless rain, and the sounds dwindled to the exquisitely painful silence of a tomb.

Tara shuddered at the utter hopelessness drowning the Kamarian souls. But then the gray began to shift subtly into faint shades of blue and mauve, as if the rain clouds were thinning with the dawn of hope. She could feel their deep yearning to return to the blue skies they'd not seen in three hundred years.

What do I do? she whispered mentally, shaken by the visions.

More images slipped into her mind: the rising and setting of the sun three times in swift succession; a towering cataract, its dark torrent crashing silently into a pool obscured by mist and spray; a deep, wide valley — an empty sweep of withered grass beside a lake rippling with black water. As she watched, the dead grass in the center of the valley began to shimmer in ever-widening circles, and then tall, black spires rose from the blurred ground, climbing into a sky bright with morning until an ethereal edifice of black stone filled her vision, breathtakingly beautiful with its graceful, curving lines and elegant minarets.

"A black castle," she breathed, remembering Jovan's vision from Rinpool that he'd seen as a boy, so long ago. It had to be the same one.

Perfectly carved statues of kings and queens rimmed the parapets, their faces upturned, their arms reaching upward to the sky. Of course, she thought. Sky *Aiykshaav'n*.

Jovan — the castle — can you see it? She tried to project the image into his mind. *Is it the one?*

She heard his sharp intake of breath, felt him stiffen beside her. *Yes.*

Kamarian voices tugged urgently at her thoughts, and she realized the focus of the vision had shifted from the castle to the morning sun. The sun edged higher in the sky, marking perhaps a half hour of time, then the castle sank back into the ground, disappearing within the space of a few moments, leaving behind a valley swathed in sorrow.

CHAPTER 32

Tara's hands shook as she gently set the worm-filled black jelly back into the trough. Jovan helped her to her feet.

"I have three days to find the valley where the black castle will rise." She wiped her hands on her leggings. "And then I have only a short time to get into the castle and do whatever I'm supposed to do."

"What castle?" Brains asked.

"Castle Kamar." She rubbed her temples, her mind still seething from the storm of visions. "Sometime during the morning of the fourth day, the castle will rise from the ground in the center of a valley that lies near a lake. After about half an hour, the castle will disappear again. And I had the sense that it will not reappear in my lifetime." The hopeless sorrow of the Kamarian souls haunted her. She could not fail them.

Brains stroked his chin thoughtfully. "Did they tell you how to find the castle?"

"They did show me a gigantic waterfall that made no sound."

"How can a waterfall not make any sound?" Jack asked.

"Didn't the sorceress say something about a waterfall?" Blackie asked.

Brains nodded. "Yes, she did. She called it Echoing Falls. She said you couldn't find the Valley of Kamar without first finding the falls."

Tara turned to Jovan. "You told me about the falls, once. You said the same thing Valina did — that those who had searched for the falls had heard the pounding of water, but could never find it."

"It's an Eastern legend," Jovan said.

"I've heard that legend, too," said Blackie.

"So how do we find this waterfall?" Jack asked.

"We'll have to go back up to that door under the stairs in the tower," Brains said.

"I'm not going back up there with them spiders," Whiskey said flatly.

"Maybe they're gone," Jack said.

"Maybe they're not," Whiskey retorted.

"Perhaps Valina can tell us." Tara closed her eyes. *Valina? Can you see if the ghost spiders are still in the tower?*

Yes, they are, came the worried response. *The tower is filled with them, and they're starting to look less ghostlike.*

Tara felt a clenching in her gut. They had no time to lose. "Valina says the spiders are still there. We'll have to find another way into the mountains."

"How do you know there is one?" Blackie asked. "I didn't see any other doors in the cavern or in here." He gestured toward the cluttered walls of the chamber.

"There has to be another way out," Tara said. "This is Ravnaul's fortress. He wouldn't have allowed himself to be trapped down here with only one exit." She strode out of the chamber and back up the stairs to the upper landing, examining the smooth, translucent walls and the base of the well. She found no cracks, no openings, and no other magical symbols to aid their escape. The Kamarian voices remained silent. Either they didn't know the way out, or something was preventing them from speaking.

Valina?

I don't know, Tara. I've never been where you are.

Tara descended the stairs to the lower landing where the others had collected, their searching as fruitless as hers. "And there's no way down," she muttered, peering over the landing's edge. The cavern dropped away, funneling downward into a darkness so thick and absolute it reminded her of the crushing void that led to her dream dungeon. She tensed, her throat constricting. Had something moved down there? Fleeting shadows skittered past the edges of her vision, but she couldn't tell if they were real or if her eyes were playing tricks on her. She leaned out a bit farther. If she could just get a better look...

"Hey!" Blackie's arm blocked her forward progress just as Jovan's hands gripped her shoulders and pulled her back from the edge. "Balls, woman, what are you trying to do?" Blackie demanded. "We're not jumping, if that's what you think."

She shook her head. "I think there's something down there, but I can't quite see it." She felt Jovan's heart hammering against her back as he held her to him. She hadn't meant to scare them. She just needed to see. "I want one more look, so if you hold onto me," she said over her shoulder to Jovan, "I'll —" Freezing cold engulfed her as if she'd suddenly plunged into a frigid lake. Whatever had been in the cavern depths was now up here — with them.

"Everyone back in the chamber!" She spun, trying to catch sight of the shadowy force whirling through the cavern.

"I don't see anything," Blackie said.

"Just go! Now!"

He and the others backed into the chamber, crowding the doorway.

Jovan circled with Tara, his back to hers.

She touched his arm. "Jovan —"

"I'm not leaving you."

She cursed to herself, afraid for him, yet glad of his nearness. She took a deep breath to clear her mind, and suddenly she knew what dwelled in the cavern. Ravnaul's magic. She gasped as the magic surrounded them, flowing through the air like a live thing. She could see it now — a dark red mist that whispered around her in sinuous clouds, filling the cavern with malevolence. *Diurkruna, the magic of blood and death.* She shoved Jovan away as the mist swirled around her legs and twisted up around her body in ever-tightening coils, squeezing the life out of her like a giant rock serpent crushing its prey.

"Tara!" Jovan ran forward.

"No!" she choked out, fighting the red mist. "Stay back!"

"What is that?" Blackie stopped beside Jovan, the others piling up behind them.

"I don't know," she heard Jovan say as she braced herself against the strangling pressure. He took another step toward her. "Let me help you!"

"No!" she croaked. "This is... my... battle." She gathered her power. A scream tore from her throat as her own magic blazed forth, burning the red mist away with a fiery bluish incandescence. She thrust her arms out to the side. Brilliant light spread throughout the cavern, driving back the dark magic.

"I am Tara, daughter of Tamara, descendant of Erana, daughter of Ravnaul. Royal Kamarian blood flows through me, and so does the magic of Ravnaul's own sword. You will not harm me, nor those with me. Now, show me the way out!"

A small circle of air shimmered next to Tara's outstretched left hand, and a symbol — four thin rectangles, descending like stairs —

glowed red within. She touched the glimmering symbol. It vanished, then a grinding sound shivered through the cavern. Thin slabs of rock slid out from the wall, forming a disconnected series of steps down into the depths of the cavern. The remaining whorls of red mist melted into the blackness below.

Tara's strength ebbed. The brilliant light faded as she sank to her knees.

Jovan lifted her up. "Are you all right?"

She saw him through a hazy blur. "Fine. Just tired." Her vision cleared as the others gathered around.

"That was impressive," Brains said.

She smiled faintly. "Thanks."

"Just what happened, exactly?" Blackie asked.

"Ravnaul's magic. *Diurkruna.* It tried to kill me, but I was able to defeat it. For now. It may come back. I want to be out of here before it does." She took a shaky step toward the stairs. Her strength was returning much more slowly than she would like.

Jovan kept his arm around her. "You should rest for a minute."

"No. There isn't time." She forced her trembling limbs to move. The stairs stretched downward, the stone slabs appearing oddly disembodied against the black depths of the cavern. Icy chills slithered over her skin whenever she looked at the blackness. Her dream dungeon lay beyond it, she was certain.

She remembered the dead Kamarians she'd run across in previous dreams — the woman in the bleeding room who had looked so much like her, and the six men and women she'd found starved to death in the room with the glassed-in feast. Valina had said that when Ravnaul found his runaway daughters at Estiarii Faelle, he'd uttered an incantation that had caused seven of the Kamarians there to disappear, including his daughter, Kelista. Could he have sent them into the dream dungeon? Could it be that the dream dungeon was Ravnaul's own creation? And had the gods, as punishment for his part in the Cataclysm, imprisoned him in it, in some form of poetic justice? The woman who had looked like her must have been Kelista, her however-many-times-removed great aunt. *Ravnaul murdered his own daughter.* Her mind reeled at the thought, and she stumbled on the steps.

Jovan caught her. "Love, you must rest."

"No." Shivering all over, she regained her balance. "Not until we're away from this place."

They continued down the stairs, spiraling deep into the cavern. The tarry blackness beneath them began to churn like a boiling cauldron. Fragments of red mist oozed in and out of the roiling depths, shifting ever closer, as if sensing her weakness.

As they neared the last step, she slowed, every nerve screaming for her to get away from the void. Only a few feet separated the bottom stair from the viscous black pit. She could feel its inexorable pull, like metal drawn to a magnet.

She twined her arm through Jovan's and gripped his hand. "Don't let go," she whispered.

He squeezed her fingers reassuringly. "I won't."

Sliding her left hand along the wall for support, she reached the bottom slab. And saw no door — only blank wall, smooth as black silk. Her breath stopped. Had the mist tricked her, showing her only a symbol that would get her closer to the void?

The red mist burst from the pit like a tornado, lashing out at them, feeding off her doubt. Cries and curses echoed in the cavern as those on the stairs above her shrank back against the wall.

"No!" Quelling her panic, Tara reached deep inside. She dredged up every ounce of power she could muster and flung it outward with a sweep of her arm. The dark magic recoiled. With her last bit of strength, she pressed her left hand firmly against the wall. A symbol — a square with countless pinpricks of light — blazed above her hand, and a section of the wall slid inward, revealing a dim tunnel.

"Go, quickly!" She waved the others toward the tunnel. Then exhaustion claimed her, and she crumpled.

Jovan scooped her up in his arms and darted into the tunnel after the others. The door grated shut behind them, sealing out the red mist.

*****

Rylan Natiere crossed the darkened stable and spoke soothingly to the skittish dun stallion, patting its neck and flank as he transferred the tack from the spent horse he'd taken from a merchant on the Trader's Trail. The familiar raucousness of a Gypsy Crossroads night flowed past the closed stable door. The scents of exotic foods and ales teased his hungry belly, but he would not stop to eat. Night and day he had traveled, covering countless miles. Yet he still had many more to go. Tara had reached the Black Mountains. He sensed grave danger there, an evil that had grown to monstrous proportions. He had to find her before the evil consumed her, mind and soul.

It is Tara's destiny to follow this path — to either restore the Kamarian people or succumb to the evil that attacks her mind, an evil that will escape from its prison and destroy mankind, as it did the Kamarians.

His lip curled as he recalled Valina Mellarian's words. The sorceress was using Tara, had convinced her that the Kamarian race was worth restoring. He sneered to himself. The Kamarians' abuse of their own magic had led to their downfall. Tara had no more need of them than he had for the rest of mankind. They could burn in the Abyss for all he cared.

Whatever the sorceress' plans were, he would take pleasure in disrupting them. He would steal Tara away from her misguided mission, help her drive the evil from her mind, and save her from herself. He cinched the saddle down tight, impatient to be on his way.

The stable door opened and a large shadow slipped inside, the cacophony of the nightlife blaring and then cutting off as the door latched shut behind the intruder. Natiere stepped back out of sight, cursing to himself at the delay. He reached for his knife. One swift slice across the man's neck, and he'd be on his way.

Light flared as the man opened a shuttered oil lamp and held it up. His eyes darted nervously about the stable. "Butcher! I know you are here," he said in a hoarse whisper, his words twisted by his southern accent. "I saw you come in. I wish to strike a bargain with you."

Natiere studied the man curiously from his hidden vantage point. No one had ever sought him out before. Most ran screaming at the mention of his name. The man was tall and broad, with thick black strands of hair twisting down his back. He had a sword gripped in his hand. Natiere narrowed his eyes. He'd seen this man before... yes, he was one of those worthless smugglers. What was he doing here? Had Tara and the smugglers parted company? Was she finally alone, or was Trevillion with her? A snarl burned through the quickening of his blood as his fingers tightened on his knife. He had no time to waste.

The Southlander took a wary step forward. Sweat dripped down his forehead. "You seek the witch, Tara Triannon. I seek a man by the name of Jovan Trevillion. I know they have traveled together in the past. If I find her, I'm certain I'll find him."

Natiere lowered his knife. This was an interesting development. He considered a moment, then stepped into the light. "Why do you seek Trevillion?"

The Southlander jerked around at the sound of his voice, sword and lantern grasped in shaking hands. Natiere saw terror in his eyes, overshadowed by hatred strong enough to keep the Southlander from bolting for the door.

"I wish to kill him," the man said, the venom in his voice matching the hate in his eyes. "When he and his army invaded the Southlands, they murdered my family. They took everything that was mine. I will repay him tenfold. I will take all that is his and kill everyone he cares for. And then I will take his life."

Natiere betrayed no emotion. "Why did you come to me?"

"Your tracking skills are legendary. I want to ride with you to find the witch. I swear I will not be a hindrance, and I'll pay you in gold."

Natiere weighed the man's request. Here was the perfect opportunity to eliminate his enemy while leaving himself blameless. He could hardly believe his good fortune. Yet the risk to Tara, as someone Trevillion cared for, could not be ignored. "If I allow you to accompany me, you must travel at my pace. I will not slow down if you lag behind. You will stay away from my wolves, and you will not touch Tara Triannon. If you harm her or my wolves in any way, I will spread pieces of your carcass from here to the Twin Cities."

The man's eyes widened, but he stood his ground. "Agreed."

Natiere jerked his head toward the far end of the stable. "Get a horse."

*****

"Tara!" *Tara!*

She heard Jovan's urgent call, a cord of strength to which she clung as she fought the drag of the void. Jovan carried her tightly against him, her body swaying gently as he ran down the tunnel.

I won't let you go.

She focused on his pounding heartbeat, drawing heavily on his strength as she scrambled to erect her mental walls. Icy cold trembled through her limbs. *Oh, gods!* She braced herself. Ravnaul, his magic intensified by the Being's power, attacked her with a shrieking fury. Her hands clamped to her head, and she screamed as Ravnaul's claws tore through her walls and into her mind.

Jovan groaned and stumbled to his knees. He clutched her to him. "Keep fighting," he gritted through his teeth.

She knew the Being must be attacking him, but there was nothing she could do to help him. She couldn't even help herself. She screamed until the void sucked away her breath.

A shimmering silver light blazed into her mind, forcing back the blackness and stopping her fall into the dungeon. She felt many hands lifting her, as if she had dropped from the sky into a crowd of people. Then she saw them in her mind's eye — hundreds of ghostly figures standing together with their hands raised, enveloped in a silvery luminescence. The light flooded her brain like a healing balm, soothing the pain.

Milady Tara, said a male voice she didn't recognize. *You must hurry. We will block them for as long as we can. You must reach Castle Kamar before their transformation is complete.*

Barely conscious, Tara struggled to comprehend his words. *Transformation?*

Ravnaul and Gorgrast have begun to merge, but each is fighting for control. Once they achieve their final form, they will be beyond our strength. Hurry!

Gor... who...?

Gorgrast — one of the war gods. Hurry!

Tara opened her eyes and tried to sit up. Jovan was kneeling beside her. She fell back into his arms, unable to find the strength.

"Tara," he said urgently, fear for her clinging to his words. "What happened? Are you all right?"

She nodded weakly. "Kamarians helped me. You?"

"I'm fine."

She tried to sit up again. "Need to hurry... find the castle... before..." Dizziness overcame her.

"Before what?" She heard Blackie's voice as if from a far distance. Then she blacked out.

*****

Tara drifted in and out of unconsciousness, never fully waking. Sounds floated around her: the rustle of clothing; voices — heated, arguing; the endless tramp of walking feet. In near conscious moments, she was vaguely aware of being carried. Though the feel of the arms holding her and the scent of the person carrying her differed from time to time, the gentle rocking motion always lulled her back into oblivion.

A cessation of motion finally woke her. She glanced about and found herself lying on a blanket in a small cavern that glowed with pale silver light. Another blanket covered her. All around her, the others lay bedded down, eyes closed, occasionally shifting in their sleep. Jovan lay beside her, his breathing deep. Only Diamond Jack remained awake, sitting across the way with his back against the wall, on watch.

He noticed her movement and sat up straighter. She held her finger to her lips to stop him from calling out to her. Judging from the lines of weariness on Jovan's face, he and the others needed the sleep.

She crossed to where Jack sat and dropped down beside him. "Is everyone all right? Where are we? How much time has passed?"

"Yes, except for certain people being cranky and ill-tempered; somewhere under the mountains; and I have no idea. You'll have to ask the dwarf. He's been leading us. Last I heard, he said we'd been traveling about a day and a half, but that was quite a while ago. You said we had to hurry, so this is only the second time we've stopped to rest."

"I'm sorry. I didn't mean for you to run yourselves into the ground. Why don't you get some sleep now? I'll keep watch while I eat." She was starving.

Jack shook his head. "Brains said he'd take over in a couple of hours. I'll sleep then."

"Are you sure?"

He nodded.

She tiptoed over to the pile of backpacks, picked up hers, and sat down next to Jack again. Pulling out her water flask, she took a long drink, then dug some dried meat out of the pack. "Want anything?"

"No, thanks. We just ate. We've been eating as we go."

She ate silently. So there was only a day or so left to find the valley where the castle would appear. She hoped Gralfar had been leading them in the right direction. But how could he possibly know which way was right? He'd never been in these mountains before. A knot twisted in the pit of her stomach as she looked around the cavern. Four tunnels led out of it, all filled with the same dark emptiness. And finding their way through a maze of passages apparently wasn't their only problem.

"You said certain people were ill-tempered. What happened?"

Jack hesitated. "Well, your friend there," he jutted his chin at Jovan, "refused to let anyone else carry you, and that started an argument about him slowing us down by tiring himself out more. He eventually gave in, and we've been taking turns."

"I'm really sorry. You shouldn't have had to cart me around all this way."

Jack shrugged. "You're not that heavy. And that's why we're here." He yawned and blinked sleepily.

Tara put her hand on his shoulder. "Go get some sleep. I'm wide awake. It doesn't make sense for us both to sit here."

He yawned again. "Blackie will kill me if I leave my post."

"No, he won't. Go."

Jack rubbed his face. "All right. You win." He pushed himself upright and dragged across to his bedroll. He was asleep within minutes.

She finished eating and sat listening to her companions' slow, even breathing. The smugglers had saved her once again. Jovan was strong, but no one could carry another person over such a long distance and maintain any kind of speed. The odds of their finding the Kamarian castle within the time frame would have been a lot slimmer. And what if he'd been disabled by the Being's attack? Her eyes lingered on his sleeping form and she felt her soul burn with the fierceness of her love. She realized she could not have left him to go on alone if that had happened. Her cause would have been lost. Tears filled her eyes as she thought of the Kamarian souls, doomed to their current form for eternity. She looked across at the smugglers and gratitude overwhelmed her. She wiped her eyes on her sleeve and smiled.

Then her smile faded as she remembered what they were up against. A war god. The Being was a war god, one that had committed an act terrible enough to get it banished from the gods' realm. How would they ever prevail against such an enemy? She didn't know.

Sometime later — she'd lost all sense of time underground — Brains stretched and sat up. He glanced over to where she sat, then looked back again, surprise on his face. He smiled as he came over and lowered himself down beside her. "I'm glad you finally woke up. We were wondering what would happen if we found the castle and you were still out."

Tara smiled back. "I'm sorry. I didn't intend for you all to have to carry me around."

"It wasn't a problem."

Tara sobered. "I understand from Jack that things haven't gone too smoothly."

Brains hesitated, choosing his words. "Jovan and Blackie don't like each other, to put it bluntly. They both care a great deal about you and are being... a bit overprotective." He shook his head. "I've run with Blackie for near on five years now, and I've never seen him act this way over anyone else."

"Blackie and I have a lot of history," Tara said softly, her eyes drawn to where he lay sleeping. She tipped her head back against the wall. "Gods, I don't want to hurt him."

"Just don't get yourself killed, and he'll be fine," Brains said with another smile.

Tara laughed. "That simple, eh?"

Brains grinned. "So tell me, now that you've got your memory back, how did this whole mess get started?"

"Now that is a very, very long story. It began back in the spring, when my sister, Laraina, and I were staying at Castle Carilon in Dhanarra." She felt a pang of worry as she thought of her sister. She wondered if Laraina had married Prince Kaden, or if she'd left him and was roaming around on her own somewhere. Or worse, what if Laraina had set out in search of her? The idea scared her. If Laraina ran afoul of her numerous enemies... Why hadn't she thought to ask Valina? The next time she had a minute to herself, she'd ask the sorceress to check on her sister in the scrimoire.

"What were you doing in Carilon?" Brains asked.

Tara took a deep breath, then told him about her sister being in love with the prince, their flight from the Butcher, and all their adventures leading up to the defeat of the Sulledorn-Mardainn army. Then she briefly recounted her quest with Jovan, ending with the battle with Ravnaul that had caused her amnesia. "You know the rest," she finished, taking another drink from her water flask. "Now it's your turn. What is a Twin Cities' nobleman doing running with smugglers?"

He gave a short laugh. "As you said — long story. I was born on the Dunsmore side of the Twin Cities. My family owned a gold mine deep in the Scarlet Mountains of Jendairin. They were quite powerful and liked to make sure everyone knew it. I never paid much attention to what went on, though, because I always had my nose in a book. I spent more time in the museums and the Royal Library than I did at home, even after my years in the Scholars Academy.

"Then one day, my father decided it was time I took an interest in mining. He gave me tours of the mines and showed me the business end of it. He was planning on retiring and was grooming me as his successor. I had expected my older brother to take on that role, but he had wormed his way into a position on the Dunsmore council and couldn't possibly do both, or so he said. So the 'honor' fell to me."

Brains' expression darkened. "I was shocked at the abuses I found at the mines. I didn't realize it was all driven by slave labor. And the slaves were horribly treated. Many of them died from the dangerous working conditions, resulting in the need to 'acquire' more slaves. When my father needed more workers, he would just send out his private army to kidnap men, women, and even children from mountain villages and force them to work in the mines. I couldn't believe it.

"When I officially took over the business from my father, I tried to institute some... rather radical changes. My father discovered what I was doing and put a stop to it. We had a monumental argument. He took back control of the mines. I couldn't let things continue on the way they were, so I helped all of his slaves escape and blew up the mines. My family disowned me and tried to have me killed. They said my life would be forfeit if I ever set foot in Dunsmore again."

"What did you do?"

"I ran. The thugs they'd sent after me chased me through the city and down to the river. As I was running across the docks, I saw this small boat just about to shove off. I had nowhere else to go, the thugs had cut off my escape, so I ran straight to it. It was Blackie and his band, smuggling out some Jendairin gemstones. Blackie saw the men chasing me and said, 'Need a lift?' I jumped into the boat and down the river we went."

"So Blackie rescued you, too?"

Brains nodded. "He seems to have a knack for that. It wasn't long afterward that we picked up Whittler and Jack. Whiskey was already part of the band. Blackie had saved him from a hanging. Apparently he'd been in another band of smugglers and had been caught during a raid. His cohorts abandoned him. Blackie said he knew Whiskey's sailing experience would be useful, and he was right."

How curious, Tara thought, the way the details of these seemingly unrelated events had fallen into place. She wondered again how much of life was chance and how much, if any, was predetermined. "Do you believe in Fate?"

"That's an interesting question. Why do you ask?"

"Well, with all the things that have happened, it feels like I've been driven to this point — that it wasn't an accident that I've met certain people at certain times. Like meeting Dominic unexpectedly in Vaalderin, and Jovan just happening to be there, too, when I needed a guide. And running into Blackie and all of you right after I got amnesia and needed help. And Valina, and Gralfar, and even Natiere. So many people have been in the right place at the right time to help me. And I think it goes back even further, like when I first healed Blackie back in Wyndover when I was sixteen. I think we were meant to meet."

"Is that how you met?"

Tara nodded. "And Blackie being there at each of the right moments to rescue all of you. We're all caught up in it. And I can't help feeling that our paths have been chosen for us, and they're all tangled together, and we have no choice but to follow where they lead."

"Where do you think these paths are going?"

"I think our actions are deciding the fate of the Kamarian race. If we succeed, they'll be allowed to return to this world. If we fail..." She couldn't finish the thought.

Brains turned toward her, his eyes alight with determination. "We'll just have to make certain we don't fail."

CHAPTER 33

Tara and Brains talked quietly, sharing past adventures until Gralfar roused and began waking the others. Tara crossed to Jovan's side. The moment she touched him, his eyes opened.

He sat up quickly. "You're awake."

She hugged him. "Yes, and I'm fine," she added, answering the question she knew was next on his lips.

He brushed her hair back away from her face. "You had me worried again."

"I know. I'm sorry."

He kissed her gently, then they rose and joined the others, who had gathered near the packs.

Whittler nodded and gave her a bright smile, while Whiskey saluted her with his bottle. Blackie met Tara's eyes once with a brief, searching gaze, then he turned to Sarita, who was whispering in his ear. Sarita moved closer to Blackie, her fingers curling around his. Tara noticed he didn't seem to mind the Gypsy's possessiveness.

"Ah, good." Gralfar stepped forward. "It wasn't going to do us much good to find the castle with you unconscious."

Tara smiled. "That would have been a disaster. I must thank you all for getting me this far. I know it wasn't easy, and I'll be forever in your debt." She turned back to Gralfar. "I have to ask, though. I don't doubt your skills in finding your way through mountain tunnels, and I've no wish to offend you, but how do you know we're going the right way?"

"No offense taken," Gralfar said. "It's a talent we dwarves have. We go by feel and smell and gut instinct, and we listen to the voice of the mountain."

"What voice?" Brains asked.

"All mountains speak with a language as old as their making. If you listen, you can hear it whispering all around you, giving you the answers you seek. Even this mountain, damaged and brittle as it is, has a voice."

Brains closed his eyes, as if trying to hear the mountain's whisperings.

Tara gestured toward the four tunnels leading out of the small cavern. "Which one should we take?"

"The third from the left," the dwarf said without hesitation.

Tara shook her head. "That's amazing."

Gralfar hoisted his pack. "Shall we go?"

Tara took a deep steadying breath and raised her hand in front of her. "Before we do, there's something I have to tell you all."

The others moved closer, and she saw frowns of concern at her sober tone.

"What's wrong?" Jovan asked tensely.

Tara clasped his hand. "When the Kamarians saved me, they identified the Being. They said it was Gorgrast, one of the war gods."

"That's not good," Brains said. "From what I've read, Gorgrast is the most brutal and vicious of the war gods. The accounts of his conquests are gruesome."

Jovan's frown deepened, and the others looked solemn.

"Vicious or not, I have to find some way to defeat him." Tara faced the others. "As I said before, this is my battle. If anyone wants to leave, I'll have Valina transport you back to her castle."

Blackie crossed his arms over his chest. "I'm staying."

Wordlessly, Sarita linked her arm through his.

Brains gave a nod. "I'm still in."

The other smugglers glanced at each other. Jack shrugged. "We've come this far."

Tara turned to Gralfar. "Master dwarf?"

Gralfar hitched his pack up higher onto his back. "This is the most interesting thing that's happened to me in ages. I'm staying."

Tara smiled, gratitude welling up inside her again. "You are all amazing. Thank you." She picked up her pack and swept her hand forward. "Lead on, Gralfar."

They traveled through labyrinthine tunnels for many hours, their warped reflections gliding along the smooth black translucence of the walls as they passed. The silver glow lighting the tunnels moved with them.

Finally, Tara discerned a change in the air, a freshness that chased away the smell of dust and age. The others noticed it too and quickened their pace. A short time later, they arrived at the tunnel's end — a square wall filled with tiny holes that let in air and faint light.

"Just like the symbol." Tara brushed her hand over the openings and felt cool air blowing through.

The wall slid sideways at her touch. They stepped out into a windswept canyon that stretched away into the mountains on either side of them. Directly ahead rose a sheer black cliff. The approaching dawn had faded the stars and lit the eastern sky with streaks of pale pink.

A chill wind lifted Tara's hair. She shivered. *This is it,* she thought. *The morning of the fourth day.* Somewhere in these mountains, the castle would rise from the valley floor, and she had to be there when it did. She looked left and right, tension curling through her. Which way? She closed her eyes. *Valina, are you there?*

Yes, Tara.

Does any of this look familiar to you?

No, it doesn't. I came into the mountains through a different passageway — the one under the stairs in the tower. I don't know which way you should go. Anxiety quivered her voice. *There's so little time.*

I know.

Brains cocked his head. "Do you hear that?"

"It sounds like rushing water," Jovan said.

Tara heard the sound, like a distant pounding of a torrent against the rocks.

Blackie gestured to the right. "Sounds like it's coming from that way."

"Well, then, let's go," Jack said.

They raced down the canyon, Brains, with his long strides, leading the way. Tara ran with them, a growing sense of not-quite-rightness plaguing her. The thundering of the cataract intensified with every step. Echoing Falls had to be near.

Tara stopped short, remembering her vision of the falls. Echoing Falls was silent. They were going the wrong way.

"Hold up!" Jovan called to the others as he jogged back to Tara's side. "What's wrong?"

"The vision from the Kamarians," Tara panted.

The others ran back and gathered around.

"Why'd we stop?" Blackie asked between breaths.

"In my vision, the falls made no sound," Tara said. "We need to go the other way. Come on."

They raced past the closed tunnel door and down the left branch of the canyon. The sky lightened over the surrounding mountains, marking the morning's rise. The sound of rushing water faded into stillness.

A mile north, the canyon diverged into three deep chasms, one to the west, one continuing north, and the third heading northeast. Tara halted again, hearing another sound floating faintly through her mind. Music. So familiar. Where had she heard it? Tears stung her eyes as she realized it was the melody the spirit of her mother had sung to her at the ruined cottage in Wyndover.

"Tara?" Jovan stopped beside her.

"Do any of you hear music?" she asked.

They all shook their heads.

"What does it sound like?" Jovan asked.

"The same melody I heard at my mother's cottage. I think it's coming from that way." She pointed to the northeast chasm.

With Tara in the lead, they worked their way down into the chasm. The narrow path twisted through a tight channel of stone hemmed in by soaring walls of black rock, barely wide enough for them to pass in single file. The music in Tara's mind grew stronger, a haunting mix of grief and hope.

Tara...

The weak, ragged voice of the sorceress stopped Tara in her tracks. "Valina!"

"What about her?" Jovan held his hand up to stop the others behind them. "Is something wrong?"

She touched his lips to stem his questions and closed her eyes. *Valina? What happened? Are you all right?*

Found Validar... barely alive, came the sorceress' faint voice. *Tried to bring him here... but Ravnaul used the Being's power... wrenched *him away from me. I fear... he is in the dungeon...* Valina's words crumbled away.

Valina? Valina! Dead silence. Cursing her helplessness, Tara rushed forward through the narrow chasm, the others pounding behind her. They had to find Echoing Falls *now.*

The chasm widened, then rounded out into a dead end.

Tara stared in consternation at the confining walls of black stone. "There has to be a door here somewhere." She slid her hands over the walls, searching for cracks or irregularities in the stone, hoping for the flash of another symbol.

"What happened to Valina?" Jovan asked urgently.

Tara continued along the wall to her left. "Valina found Melodian and tried to bring him to her castle, but Ravnaul was able to use the Being's — Gorgrast's — power to snatch him away. She thinks he was taken into the dungeon."

"So Ravnaul could get his bloodstone back," Brains said.

"Yes." Tara swiped her hair back out of her face. "And he'll get stronger more quickly." She touched the wall again, farther to the left.

Whittler seized Tara's arm and pulled her to a spot a few feet to the left of where she'd been standing. He pointed to a tiny shallow oddly shaped depression in the wall about chest high. She touched the depression and silver light glowed brightly beneath her fingers. The depression melted inward, deepening to a small hole.

"Is that some sort of keyhole?" Brains asked, leaning closer.

"I don't know." Tara stuck her finger into the inch-deep depression. "No key that I've ever seen would fit in here. Whatever it is, it's lumpy and about the size of a gold piece."

"And we can't get through without it?" Blackie asked.

She placed both hands over the depression and tried channeling her power into the glowing area. Nothing happened. Her hands fell to her sides. "Apparently not." She slammed the wall with the edge of her fist. "Curse it all, we have to get through."

"Maybe there was a key back in that room with all the books," Blackie said.

Tara flung her arm out impatiently. "We don't have time to go back and look."

A startled look crossed Jack's face, as if he'd just had a brainstorm. He dug something out of his pocket. "Here, try this." He held out a slender silver chain. Dangling from it was a small irregularly shaped smoke-gray jewel.

Tara took the jewel and ran her fingers over its smooth surface. Silver light blossomed, shimmering in the dim space. "Where did you get this?"

"I found it in that room, in a black box stuck between some books," he said sheepishly. "I meant to show it to you, but then the wizard appeared, and I stuffed it in my pocket out of habit and forgot about it. Sorry."

She inserted the jewel into the depression. Silver light flashed, and a section of the wall opened outward. "Yes!" she said with a grin, as the others cheered. She hugged Jack. "Bless your light-fingered, gem-loving soul!"

He laughed, still looking a bit sheepish.

Tara slipped the chain over her head, and they rushed out into a pass that curved sharply to the left between the bases of two immense mountain cliffs. They rounded the corner.

Tara gasped, barely hearing the chorus of exclamations from the others. Her feet slowed, her eyes traveling upward to an almost neck-breaking height as she stared at the sweeping cataract, its dark waters plunging soundlessly into a wide, mist-shrouded pool. The rocks under her feet vibrated from the silent pounding of the water.

"Incredible," Brains breathed. "It must be over a thousand feet high."

"Just don't tell me we have to get to the top," Blackie muttered.

"I don't know what we have to do." Tara glanced uneasily at the patch of sky overhead, where the pale shades of dawn had given way to morning's bright blue. They were running out of time. She pointed to the left. "Jovan and I will go this way around the edge of the pool. Blackie, you and Brains go the other way and see if you can spot anything — any caves, or I don't know what — and *be careful*. The rest of you stay here."

She grasped Jovan's hand and hurried along the twenty-foot-wide span of slippery rock between the surrounding cliff and the water's edge. Swirling plumes of mist and spray completely hid the pool. She couldn't see beyond to the cliff face behind the falling water without looking up quite a distance, nor could she see the water's outward flow. She guessed the pool to be a good fifty feet across and likely very deep. She shivered, not so much from the cold of her spray-drenched clothes, but from the eerie quality of the silence. She sensed an aura of life unlike any she'd ever encountered. Somewhere near prowled another living creature — friendly or not, she couldn't tell. Whatever it was, it had to be in the pool.

The span of rock narrowed with the curving of the cliff, blending into the water's edge less than halfway around the pool.

"I don't see anything," Jovan said.

"No, but there's something here." She drew him back from the edge. "I think it's in the water."

"Alive?"

She nodded. "Let's go back."

They returned to where the others waited. Blackie and Brains appeared a moment later from around the other side of the pool.

"There's nothing over there," Blackie said.

"Or if there is, it's hidden behind the mist," Brains added.

"We didn't find anything, either," Tara said. "But I think there's something in the pool — a creature. I can sense it."

"What sort of creature?" Jack asked, backing quickly away. He yelled as an enormous beast reared up out of the pool, water glistening on the silvery green scales covering its massive head and sinuous body. A sharp, bony ridge extended from the top of its head down its back, trailing down to its lower half, which remained hidden by the mist and spray.

"Um... that sort." Tara stared at the beast's six arms and clawed, webbed reptilian fingers.

"Haedis' balls!" Blackie cried. "What in the Abyss is that?"

"A sea dragon!" Whiskey yelped.

The dragon roared, drowning out the yells and Gypsy curses as Tara and the others leaped back and flattened themselves against the cliff.

"Great gods, will you look at that!" Brains said, awe overriding the fear in his voice. "How would a sea dragon get here?"

"Who cares?" Blackie said. "Let's get out of here before it eats us for breakfast!"

"No, we can't! Or rather, I can't," Tara amended. She moved around Jovan, who had put her behind him protectively. "I have to get past these falls somehow, and find the valley."

Blackie pointed at the dragon. "You're going to fight *that*? Has that power of yours completely fried your brain?"

"No one is keeping you here," Jovan said coldly to Blackie. He gestured at the path leading back toward the chasm. "There's your escape. Go."

Blackie jammed his hands on his hips. "And just how do you think *you're* going to defeat that thing?"

"Will you two stop it!" Tara snapped. "We may not have to fight it."

"What do you mean?" Jovan asked.

"It's not setting off my danger sense."

The dragon watched them intently, but didn't attack.

Tara studied the gigantic beast, overwhelmed by its sheer size. She had to do something. But what? "Maybe the Kamarians put it here to guard the entrance to their valley. If so, then maybe I can communicate with it." She took a deep breath and forced her feet to move toward the dragon.

Jovan followed. "Be careful, Love."

The dragon bent down and gripped the edge of the pool with its lowest set of hands, claws scraping the stone. A shudder slid down Tara's spine at the sound. It lowered its head to her level. Its hot, fishy breath steamed her face. She halted, eyeing the dragon's massive jaws and dagger-length teeth. Blackie was right. She had lost her mind. She reached behind her, and Jovan clasped her hand.

"I'm right here," he said.

The dragon's green reptilian eyes narrowed to slits. Its rumbling voice startled Tara as it filled her mind. *You bear the key.*

Her free hand closed over the jewel hanging from the silver chain around her neck — the key to the entrance to Echoing Falls. Light filled her hand, spilling out between her fingers. *Yes.*

The dragon raised its huge head and looked down at her. *Daughter of Kamar, what is your wish?*

Intense relief wobbled her, then excitement stole her breath. She was almost there. *We need to find the Valley of Kamar. We must get there before the black castle rises. Can you show us the way?*

I will take you there. The dragon laid its three left hands palms upward on the stone floor. *Climb on.*

Thank you. Tara turned to the others. "The dragon will take us to the valley. We have to go quickly. Climb into its hands. Hurry."

"Haedis' balls, woman," Blackie said, panic on his face. "You've not only lost all your branches, you've cut the tree down, too, if you think I'm going anywhere near that thing."

"Blackie, please. If you all don't come with me, you'll be stranded here. Valina can't help, and I don't know if I'll be able to get back here to get you out. You have to trust me."

"I'm game." Brains clapped Blackie on the shoulder. "Come on, Blackie. You don't want to wander around in these mountains forever. And just think of the story you'll have to tell when we get back to civilization."

"Like anyone would believe me," Blackie growled.

"Fat lot of stories we'll be able to tell once that dragon chews us up," Whiskey said, clutching his bottle to him.

"If the dragon was going to eat us, it would have done it already," Brains said. "Now, come on. If we don't hurry up, we'll miss the castle, and then this will have all been for nothing." He took Whittler's arm and pulled him toward the dragon's hand, Whittler vigorously shaking his head "no" the whole way.

"Well, we'll never get any kind of reward if we stay here." Jack shoved a petrified Whiskey forward. "You don't have to worry about the dragon eating you. It'd spit you out, you're so pickled."

Gralfar strode forward. "Never let it be said that any man, or woman, was braver than a dwarf." He climbed onto the hand with Tara and Jovan.

Tara caught Blackie's gaze and held it. "Please. I don't have much time."

Blackie looked at the dragon. "And I thought the Butcher was bad." He gusted out a long breath, then held his hand out to Sarita.

She pressed back against the cliff and shook her head.

He stepped toward her. "You're not staying here alone."

She gesticulated toward the dragon and shouted at him in Gypsy.

He said something back to her in her language, then in a swift, smooth motion, bent down and tipped her over his shoulder. She pounded on his back and cursed him as he carried her to one of the dragon's empty hands. He set her down on the dragon's open palm and climbed in after her, dragging Whiskey in with them. Brains and Jack wrestled Whittler into the other hand.

The dragon closed its right hands over them, tent-like, the webs between its fingers sealing together to form airtight spaces. Then, amid screams and yells from Whiskey and Sarita, the dragon sank into the pool and swam downward through the clear water in a sinuous motion.

With Jovan's hand squeezed in hers, Tara watched wide-eyed through the transparent membrane of web as they descended to the bottom of the pool and sped into a wide channel, traveling under the cliff over which Echoing Falls spilled. The walls of the channel glowed with silvery-greenish light. She saw more channels branching off in other directions and wondered what lay beyond. Schools of large fish, some a speckled brown, some rainbow-hued with silver bellies, darted away as the sea dragon approached. Seaweed in various shades of yellow, green, orange, and red undulated in the passing currents.

Ten minutes later, they began to rise, bearing up and up until finally they broke the surface of a large lake. The dragon deposited them on the edge of a wide, sunlit valley covered in stiff brown grass that crunched under their feet.

Tara faced the dragon. *Thank you for bringing us here.*

The dragon dipped its head. *Daughter of Kamar, you are welcome.* Then it dove beneath the water and was gone.

Tara looked anxiously at the sky. It was nearly midmorning.

"Are we in time?" Brains asked.

Tara glanced at him and then at the others. Whittler looked pale, Whiskey was shaking, and Sarita was furious, but other than that, they didn't seem too much the worse for wear. "I don't know." She looked at the sky again. She couldn't seem to calm her jitters.

"What do you want to do?" Jovan asked.

"I don't think there's anything we can do but wait —"

The ground trembled, sending shivery tingles up Tara's legs. The brown grass in the center of the valley began to blur in outward-rippling circles until a wide span lay glimmering and out of focus.

"Oh, gods, it's happening," she whispered, and realized she was shaking as much as the ground.

Jovan's hands closed over her shoulders, and she pressed back against him, steadying her frayed nerves with his warm strength. The haunting melody that had been whispering in the back of her mind rose in a glorious crescendo as the black castle burst from the shimmering ground, its elegant towers ascending into the cloudless sky.

"It's just like my vision," Jovan murmured.

"And mine."

The ground ceased to shake, and an expectant hush fell over the valley, full of hope and promise.

"Do you know what I would have given to see this?" Brains asked softly. "Anything... everything..."

Tara stared at the castle, hardly believing that it had appeared. Ever since she'd begun this journey of self-discovery, she'd had tiny motes of doubt floating in the dusty corners of her mind — doubts that she could really be some long-lost descendant of the Ancients, that she was truly fated to come to this place. Even after she'd used the black sword's power and drawn it within, even after she'd found and communicated with the wretched Kamarian souls, she'd still had some niggling of disbelief deep in her heart. It just couldn't be possible. Now the Kamarian castle stood before her, waiting for her to enter, needing her to defeat the evil and break the curse that had trapped the Kamarian people for three hundred years. Only she could do it. All doubt vanished. She would not fail.

Tara roused herself from the shock of the castle's rise. Her eyes swept over her companions. "I have no idea what's going to happen now. Wait for me here. Hopefully, I'll be back before the castle disappears."

"I'm going with you," Jovan said.

"And so are we." Blackie crossed his arms over his chest.

"I'm sorry, you can't," Tara said. "Only I can enter it. Don't ask me how I know. I just do. I need you to stay here by the lake. I don't want anyone caught near the castle when the ground starts to shimmer again."

Brains sighed in disappointment. "We'll be here, then."

Tara smiled. "Thanks." She embraced Jovan. "I'll be back as quickly as I can."

He cupped her face and gave her a tight smile. "Call to me if you need me."

She nodded. "I will."

She jogged across the brittle grass toward the castle. She felt more alive at that moment than she'd ever felt in her life. She slowed as the castle walls loomed above her, her eyes drawn to the statues lining the parapets with their arms extended skyward. Their faces were so detailed that they looked like living beings frozen in stone. A sharp pang twisted her heart. She wished she could have known them.

She halted before what appeared to be the front of the castle. Smooth black stone greeted her, with no visible entrance. She remembered what Jovan had said about his vision from Rinpool, where he'd seen her standing before a black castle with no door. He said she'd touched the wall and then walked through it. She looked back over her shoulder to where Jovan and the others stood near the lake, etching them into her mind. Then she turned and placed her left hand on the wall. A faint silver glow sparked beneath her palm and spread outward, forming the shape of an arching doorway. The archway blurred before her eyes. Her hand sank into the wall. Taking a deep breath, she followed her hand and stepped through.

CHAPTER 34

Tara's skin tingled as she pressed through a thick space of viscous shadow before emerging into a grand entry hall. Despite the sunlight that poured down through vast skylights in the roof high above, the spacious hall seemed dark and full of shadows, shrouded by grief. The air was cold and heavy, as if weighed down with hopeless sighs for those lost. The music in Tara's head died away.

Burdened by a sense of despair, Tara walked slowly across the black marble floor, taking in the two rows of black spiral columns on either side of her and the two huge silver chandeliers set with moonstones and yellow gems that were hanging from the stone rafters. Vividly painted and sculpted murals — breathtakingly beautiful depictions of people, historical events, and celestial phenomena — graced the upper half of the walls all the way around the room. Everything was polished and immaculate. Six closed doors lined the hall, three each to her left and right. She saw no one, heard no sound beyond her own footsteps.

In the far corners of the room, two curving staircases rose to a stone balcony supported by more columns. More closed doors lined the balcony. She wondered where they led. Beneath the balcony, in the center of the back wall, a door stood open. In the room beyond, faint movement like drifting fog caught Tara's eye.

She hurried across and peered through the door into a palatial room with more murals, ornate mirrors a full story tall, and even bigger chandeliers. On the left wall, five steps led up to a semi-circular dais. A single row of six gold thrones spanned the dais. The two in the center were larger than the others, with finely carved backs, one in the likeness of the sun, the other, the moon.

A shadow moved near the sun throne, a tall, nebulous shape. Tara could see the lines of the carved sun through the ghostlike form. She stepped into the room. The shadow swirled as if blown by a sudden gust of wind, then reformed in the shape of a tall man with shoulder-length silver hair and a full beard. He wore rich white robes, embroidered on the front with a large sun. A smooth oval stone, dead black, hung from a chain around his neck. On his head rested a gold crown encrusted with yellow gems, like those in the chandeliers.

The ghost-man stared at her, his face frozen in shock. Cautiously, Tara moved closer, and tried not to look equally stunned at seeing the spirit of one of the Ancients — one that might be her ancestor.

"Who are you?" he demanded, his voice a hoarse whisper. "How did you get into my castle?"

Tara stopped a few feet from the steps. "My name is Tara Triannon. If this is your castle, you must be King Lazarial." She gave him a deferential nod.

The ghost of King Lazarial moved to the edge of the dais. "The silver in your hair and eyes... who *are* you?"

"I am the last descendant of Erana —"

"Erana! Daughter of Ravnaul?" Anger stained the king's shadowy form red. "That arrogant, power-mad brother of mine who destroyed the Kamarian civilization and killed all its people?"

"Yes, that one," Tara said sharply, "and he's going to do it again if I don't find a way to stop him."

The king laughed, his face clothed in bitterness. "How can he destroy what has already been lost?"

Tara took a step forward. "With all due respect, Your Highness, you must listen. I don't have time to explain everything, but at this moment, Ravnaul is merging with Gorgrast, a banished war god. Once Ravnaul has fully transformed, he will break out of his prison, and not only will he prevent the remaining Kamarians from returning, he'll destroy mankind and possibly the kingdom of the gods as well!"

"What remaining Kamarians? There are none. They all died in the Cataclysm three centuries ago." He turned away, head bent. "All of them..."

"No, they are not all dead. Some still live, in an altered form. I've seen them and communicated with them. Their strength is keeping Ravnaul from attacking my mind and dragging me into his prison. I have to defeat him. I need your help."

"I tried to save them." King Lazarial crossed to his throne and sat, his hand over his eyes. "I begged the gods. I offered my life in exchange for my people, but the gods would not help me." His shoulders sagged. "Pride and jealousy condemned me. I was as much to blame as my brother. Now I am cursed, trapped in these halls forever."

"No!" Tara climbed the stairs to the dais. "I can end that curse and bring back what's left of the Kamarian race — including your son, Zaniel."

"My son." The king's bitter gaze lingered on the smaller chair beside him. "My son betrayed me. He ran off with my brother's daughter — that same daughter from whom you claim to be descended. A shameful union —"

"No, no, you're wrong. Zaniel didn't run off with Erana. Yes, they left at the same time, but not as a couple. Erana was in love with a man named Ezraed. He was the father of her unborn child. Zaniel loved another — a sorceress, Valina Mellarian. He left because he wanted freedom. He wanted to see the world beyond the Black Mountains. So did Erana and the others who went with them."

The king looked at her suspiciously. "How do you know this?"

"Valina is my friend. She told me the story of Erana and Ezraed and Zaniel, because she believes I can restore the Kamarian civilization, and because she wants me to bring back Zaniel, her love."

"It isn't possible. My children are dead. The people of Kamar are all dead!"

"Your son still lives. I can prove it." Tara knelt beside the throne and drew Zaniel's lifestone from beneath her shirt. The moment her fingers touched the stone, the smoky grayness inside began to swirl.

The king gasped. "Zaniel!" He reached out a ghostly hand. "I feel his energy." King Lazarial's hand passed right through the lifestone. His fingers curled into a fist, his expression a mixture of anguish and hope. "How did you get this?"

"Valina gave it to me. Zaniel had given it to her when he pledged his love."

The king's gaze remained fixed on the stone. "My son... alive. I would do anything — pay any cost — to have him returned." The king looked at Tara. "And you say there are others?"

Tara nodded. "Yes, many others, but I need your help to bring them back. Ravnaul and Gorgrast are merging. Very soon, they will become one. Once that happens, it will be beyond anyone's power to stop them. Especially since Ravnaul also has his black sword."

"How did Ravnaul get his sword? He didn't have it when we fought our final battle, when all was lost."

"Erana had stolen it and taken it with her when she ran away. Over the generations, it passed down to me. It's an impossibly long story, but Ravnaul pulled me into his dungeon, and I lost it. Now he has it back. I need some way to fight him."

"Come with me!" King Lazarial sprang from his throne and sped across the room to a door on the far wall, his shadowy feet making no sound. Tara had to run to keep up with him. He passed right through the closed door, and when Tara opened the door and rushed through, she found him halfway up a circular stairway. She raced up the stairs after him.

When the king reached the second landing, he vanished through another door. Tara followed, bursting through into a luxurious sitting room with plush chairs and divans, shelves filled with books, low tables carved from polished black rock, and a massive fireplace of black marble. It was the walls, though, that stopped her. They'd been painted from floor to ceiling in sweeping mountainscapes, mirroring the views from the windows with such depth and clarity that Tara could hardly tell which was real and which was art. She felt like she was standing on a plateau, surrounded by mountains and open sky, and if she moved too close to the edge, she'd fall off.

"In here," King Lazarial rasped impatiently. The upper half of him beckoned to her from a door in the side of a painted cliff. Tearing herself away from the view, she hastened to the next room — a spacious bedroom with walls and ceiling that glittered with the deep blue-black and silver of a star-filled night sky, oddly juxtaposed against the bright sun streaming through four large windows.

"Over here, in this chest." The king pointed to a long, low chest set against a wall.

Tara eased open the lid and caught her breath. Inside lay a long, slim black box, instantly familiar. "Another black sword!" She tried to open the box, but it was locked. "Where's the key?"

"Here." The king lifted another chain from around his neck. "But alas, it won't work. It is as insubstantial as I am."

Tara's fingers passed through the ghostly key. She clenched her fist. "How do I open it?"

"If you are truly destined to wield the sword, there will be a way —"

"Wait!" Tara said with a sudden thought. "Will this key work?" She snatched the black-jeweled key from her inner pocket and held it out. "I used it to open the box with Ravnaul's sword."

"Yes." The king's voice shook. "Both keys can open both boxes."

With trembling hands, Tara inserted the key into the lock and turned it. She heard a faint click. Pocketing the key once more, she lifted the lid. Inside, wrapped in black velvet, lay another black sword, identical to Ravnaul's blade.

Exhaling sharply, Tara lifted the sword free. A stinging pain shot up her arm, and she nearly dropped the sword. Grimacing, she gripped the hilt with both hands. "Why does it hurt?"

"It senses the dark power of *Diurkruna* in you." The king's eyes narrowed. "Did you wield Ravnaul's sword?"

Tara struggled to hold the blade. "Yes, several times. I had no choice."

"You must let the power of *Liuminerii* purge the dark magic from your soul."

"No, I can't! I need it!" She cried out as she fought the cleansing pain of the sword of Light's power.

"You must, or you'll be forever corrupted by its evil!"

"*Liuminerii* is not enough. You proved that three centuries ago. Only the combined strength of *Liuminerii*, *Diurkruna*, and Gorgrast's power can defeat the monster Ravnaul has become."

The ghostly king moved back a step, horrified. "You can't hold all three. It will tear you apart."

"I have to, or we're all doomed."

Tara. Jovan's urgent voice slipped into her mind. *Hurry.* She caught a frightening snatch of emotions — fear, abhorrence, desperation — before his voice vanished abruptly. And one terrifying image: the valley half-covered with spiders.

She sheathed the black sword and bolted for the door. "I have to go. My friends are in trouble!"

I'm coming, she sent as she flew down the stairs, the stinging in her limbs fading now that she was no longer holding the sword. Jovan didn't answer.

"Wait!" the king called, trailing after her. "You're not prepared. The sword has not yet accepted you."

"We'll work it out," Tara said over her shoulder. "Thank you for letting me use it!"

She raced through the throne room and entry hall and shoved her way through the wall-door, bursting out of the castle into a valley crawling with arachnids — real ones, no longer ghostly — some over four feet long.

"Oh, gods," she whispered, as the chittering creatures veered and headed straight for her.

"Tara, this way!"

Looking toward the lake, she saw Jovan beckoning. They had set fire to the dead grass, forming a low wall of flame to keep the spiders at bay long enough for her to reach the lake. Many spiders had perished in the flames, but some had made their way through. Jovan and the others stomped furiously on the smaller ones and used sword, knife, axe, and skillet to slice, skewer, and smash the larger ones as they skittered toward Tara.

Tara reached for the black sword. The fire from Ravnaul's blade of *Diurkruna* had made the spiders in the dungeon grow larger. Maybe this one, with the power of *Liuminerii*, would destroy them. She grabbed the hilt, and a painful shock blazed up her arm, numbing it. She cried out and let go.

Cursing under her breath, she drew her normal sword with her right hand and dashed toward Jovan. Behind her, the ground blurred and shook, and out of the corner of her eye, Tara saw the black castle sinking into the ground. Then Jovan caught her hand and, flanked by the others, they ran toward the lake.

She sent out a desperate call. *Dragon, we need help!*

With relief, she sensed the dragon's approach. They had almost reached the edge of the lake. If they could just hold out a few moments more...

A huge hairy spider leaped over the flames and landed in the midst of them. With yells and curses, the group scattered, scrambling away from the spider's stinger and fangs. Several more of the four-foot-long jumping spiders bounded over them to the water's edge. The dragon exploded upward beside the shore, showering everything with water. Then the giant spiders sprang onto the dragon, clinging to its wet scales with sticky webs and stabbing it with their stingers. The dragon roared in pain and snapped and swiped at the spiders, but they were too quick for it, scrabbling over its neck and arms.

"Oh, no!" Tara sprinted to the edge of the lake. "We have to save the dragon!"

"How?" Jovan asked. "We can't get to it." Then his eyes caught the black sword in Tara's scabbard. "How did you get the sword back?"

"I didn't. This is King Lazarial's sword of *Liuminerii*."

The others regrouped beside her.

"You saw the Kamarian king?" Brains asked in awe.

"I saw his ghost. His spirit is trapped in the castle. He gave me the sword. The only problem is —"

"Look out!" Jack yelled, as a stream of arachnids poured through a break in the fire wall, where the flames had been dampened by the splashing of the writhing dragon.

"Stay behind us." Jovan forced Tara back as he and the others fended off the onslaught.

With a sploosh, the dragon ducked beneath the water. The giant spiders dropped away and skimmed along the surface of the lake, following the dragon's path beneath them. Then the dragon burst out of the lake, swatted the monstrous spiders aside, and spewed forth a jet of water that cleared the lakeshore, sweeping the spider horde a hundred yards back into the valley.

Soaked to the skin, Tara shook back her wet hair and glanced at the others to make sure they were all right. "We've got to get to the dragon!"

"It wouldn't do any good," Blackie said. "Look."

Four giant jumping spiders were attacking the dragon again, driving it back underwater.

"The other spiders are coming back," Jack said, "and I don't think they liked their bath."

Chittering fiercely, the horde scrabbled toward them across the steaming ground, no longer hampered by the grass fire, which had been doused by the dragon's spray.

Tara cursed to herself. They were trapped. They couldn't swim for it. The spiders would skim across the lake and have them easily, and there were too many to hold off with their weapons.

"Hey, look! Over there!" Whiskey pointed up the shore. "Stuck in those reeds. A boat!"

Brains clapped Whiskey on the shoulder. "Good man! I never would have seen that." He eyed the oncoming spiders swarming between them and the boat. "How do we get to it?"

Another blast of water from the dragon gushed over the lakeshore, swamping the advancing spiders.

"Run for it!" Tara cried.

They raced across the wet grass toward the boat. Tara could just see the tip of the bow among the reeds.

"What if it's not seaworthy?" Jack asked.

"You'd just better hope it is," Blackie panted.

They reached the boat. Flattening the reeds, they uncovered a rowboat about two-thirds the size of the smugglers' longboat, sunk in the mud. The vessel had one set of oars and a tiller at the stern. It was made of light-colored wood, and all its surfaces had been sealed with a clear, milky, greenish substance, forming a rock-hard protective coating. A thick layer of dirt and dead reeds covered the boat's floor.

Whiskey flung out the reeds and scanned the interior. "Never seen a boat like this before. No rot, no parasites. Help me pull it out."

Whittler sliced through a half-rotted rope that moored the boat to a stake driven into the mud.

Tara shoved against the boat and gasped, sensing strong magic unlike anything she'd ever felt. Cool and effervescent, it bubbled over her skin like sea foam.

Jovan caught her shoulders. "What's wrong?"

"The boat. It's magical."

"It is?" Brains' eyes gleamed.

"Don't care as long as it floats," Whiskey said. "Now, heave!"

They dragged the boat free. Brains and Whiskey anchored the boat in the shallow water.

"Hurry up, get in!" Whiskey urged. "I don't wanna be spider food."

They crowded into the boat. Blackie manned one of the oars and sent Jack, Tara, and Jovan to the fore, and Sarita, Whittler, and Gralfar into the stern. Brains took the other oar. The spider horde skittered toward them, almost to the water's edge. With a grunt, Whiskey shoved the boat out into the lake, then swung himself into the stern and took charge of the tiller. The boat drifted sluggishly, its hull dangerously low in the water.

Blackie and Brains dug in with the oars.

"Where are we going?" Blackie asked. "I didn't see any place to land on the other side of the lake. It's all rock and mountains."

Whiskey adjusted the tiller. "Row to starboard! There's a current just ahead of us."

"Whiskey!" Blackie snapped. "How many times do I have to tell you —"

"Right! To the right!" Whiskey said.

"A current to where?" Jovan asked.

"Who cares, as long as it's away from the spiders," Whiskey said.

Tara stared at the rippling water. "How can you tell where the current is?"

Whiskey grinned. "The mountains aren't the only things that speak." He moved the tiller again and started whispering to the boat.

"Speed up the sweet talk," Blackie warned, "or those spiders are going to catch us."

Tara looked back and saw hundreds of spiders fanning out around them, gliding over the surface of the lake. The giant spiders were still attacking the dragon. Tara sensed the dragon weakening, succumbing to the spiders' poison.

Dragon, stay underwater! Save yourself!

No, Daughter of Kamar. I will keep them distracted until you are out of the lake. Farewell.

Tara clenched her fists. The dragon was sacrificing itself so they could escape, and there was nothing she could do about it.

Blackie and Brains rowed hard through the buffeting waves caused by the thrashing of the dragon. The spider horde skimmed closer.

"Where's that current?" Blackie demanded, sweat dripping down his face.

"Just ahead," Whiskey said. "There's a river streaming out of the lake — a fast one — just around the leg of that mountain." He pointed toward a promontory ten yards away. "Should pull us right along."

"I don't hear anything," Jack said. "Shouldn't we be able to hear it?"

Whiskey shrugged. "It's there."

"Wait a minute." Tara turned to Jovan. "Didn't you tell me the rivers through the Black Mountains were unnavigable?"

"So the stories say," he answered grimly.

The boat sped up, snagged by the current.

Whiskey snorted. "No such thing as an unnavigable river."

"What about Echoing Falls?" Tara grabbed the gunwale as the boat swept forward, then hurtled over a five-foot drop into a chasm of raging whitewater as startlingly silent as Echoing Falls had been.

"Whoo-hoo!" Whiskey shouted. "Hang onto your tails. This is gonna be fun!"

CHAPTER 35

Tara held on as the boat shot through a sluice of wild rapids, careening around boulders and diving half-sideways over sickening drops. Whiskey wrestled with the tiller and barked directions at Blackie and Brains on the oars as Jack called out the obstacles. Tara and Jovan did their best to anchor Jack after he was almost knocked out of the boat by whitewater crashing over them. Sarita alternately prayed and cursed, and Gralfar looked decidedly green.

"Gods help us," Jack muttered.

Tara blinked the water out of her eyes and saw a huge rock looming in the middle of the river, blocking most of the waterway. Either side would be a tight fit.

"Hard to po — I mean left, left!" Jack shouted.

"Whoa, that's a big one!" Whiskey cranked the tiller around. "On my mark, pull in the oars, then hang on."

The current whisked them toward the rock.

"Now!" Whiskey ordered.

Blackie and Brains yanked in the oars. Everyone ducked low and held on tight. Whiskey fought the tiller. The boat came around and whooshed past the rock, barely grazing its outside edge, then shot into open air and dropped ten feet, plunging back into the silently roiling river. The bow dug into the water, then nosed upward, still buoyant despite being almost swamped.

Held securely by Jovan, Tara swiped back her drenched hair. She felt like every bone in her body had been jarred out of place. "Everyone still here?" She counted nine heads, most of them either coughing, cursing, or trying to clear water out of their eyes without letting go of the boat. Gralfar was vomiting over the side. Sinking back in relief, she readjusted her hold on Jack as the boat slung through another series of stomach-tossing rapids. Her fingers ached from gripping him and the gunwale.

"I can't believe this boat is still afloat," Brains said as he wrestled with the oar.

"We need to start bailing, or it won't be," Blackie said.

Jack ducked against another surge of whitewater. "If we let go, we won't be *in* the boat!"

Tara looked down in surprise at the water sloshing around her legs. Moments ago, it had been up to her waist. "Hey, the water's going down." Within seconds, the water level in the boat dropped from their knees to their ankles. "It's like the boat's bailing itself."

"How could it do that?" Blackie asked.

"She said it was magic," Brains answered.

"An unswampable boat." Whiskey grinned. "I've died and gone to the Celestial Oceans!"

Tara bolted upright with an icy chill of warning. "We're nearing Echoing Falls!"

"Whiskey, what now?" Blackie yelled. "And don't tell me you don't know!"

Whiskey let out a whoop. "We've got a magic boat. Let's go right over and see what she'll do!"

"Whiskey!" Blackie looked ready to strangle him.

Whiskey laughed. "The river splits up ahead. It'll be a hard swing to port — left. Just do what I tell you, and we'll be fine."

Tara and the others hung on doggedly as the boat swept past two more boulders and lurched over another short drop. Then the river widened, and she could see the split Whiskey had been talking about. Divided by an outcropping, the left branch of the river funneled silently into another narrow chasm, while the right continued on to the verge of Echoing Falls, a straight edge of dark water against the cloudless blue sky.

Blackie stared at the looming precipice. "Whiskey!"

Whiskey worked the tiller. "Bring her around easy — now dig!"

Blackie and Brains rowed with all their strength.

Tara held her breath.

Bucking the rapids, the boat slipped across to the left and veered into the chasm, where another rush of whitewater swept them down the offshoot, away from the falls.

Tara closed her eyes and exhaled, silently thanking the gods for not ending her quest here. She heard similar murmurings from some of the others, along with Gralfar's retching.

"Hold on!" Whiskey said.

The boat whipped down the chasm, gaining speed. Blackie and Brains kept the boat relatively straight, while Whiskey steered them through sharp curves and descents, hollering which way to lean through the turns, his job made easier by the absence of obstacles in this branch of the river. No one else spoke. The flowing of the water itself made no noise, while the passing of the boat was merely a hissing whisper in the shadows, punctuated by occasional grunts from the rowers. The mountains rose up around them like black walls of translucent glass, hemming them in and eventually swallowing them as the river passed through a tall crack in the base of a cliff and swept them into the bowels of the ruined mountains.

They sailed for hours through the narrow silver-lit tunnel, propelled by the swiftly rushing river. No other passages branched off the waterway. Tara spent half her time looking forward into the gloom, trying to see what lay ahead, and half looking back, watching for spiders. So far, no one had seen any. A cold sense of foreboding curled in her gut. She dreaded the trial yet to come. Soon, she would have to somehow master King Lazarial's sword, combine the three powers within her — light, dark, divine — and use the resulting magic to destroy the merging form of Ravnaul and Gorgrast, preferably without destroying herself. An impossible task. Yet she could not fail. An entire race of people depended on her.

The air grew suddenly warm and humid, and they plunged out of the tunnel into a small, steamy cavern. White mist rose from its hot bubbling waters, obscuring the way ahead.

"End of the line," Whiskey said.

"I didn't think a river could just... end," Jack said, looking around.

Whiskey took a swig from his bottle. "It doesn't. It goes through a hole on the other side there, but the hole's too small for the boat."

"Where to, then?" Blackie asked.

"I don't know," Tara said. "It's hard to see through all this steam. Can you row us around the edge?"

Blackie and Brains obliged.

On the far side of the cavern, they found two open archways in the rock wall, one to the left of the river's exit and one to the right. The paths beyond were concealed by thick white fog. A large, flat rock split by the narrow waterway formed a natural landing leading up to both arches.

"There's our way out," Jack said.

"Yes, but which one?" Brains asked.

Tara studied the two openings, sensing a strong pull from the left one. "I think —"

She and Jovan cried out, hands flying to their heads at the same time. No matter how many mental walls Tara flung up, she couldn't block out the sudden sharp pain digging into her mind, and it didn't look like Jovan could, either.

Blackie gripped her arm. "What's wrong?"

"Ravnaul," she said through clenched teeth. "The Kamarians are weakening."

We can't hold him back... much longer, whispered a hoarse Kamarian voice. *Bring King Lazarial's sword to us —*

The voice cut off, and Tara reeled from the force of intense pressure that the Kamarians were only barely withstanding.

Jovan squeezed her hand. "Let me in. Use my strength."

"No. You need it." She pointed to the archways. "Left. Quickly."

Blackie and Brains rowed up to the platform and helped everyone out of the boat. The empty boat shimmered and vanished.

"Hey, where'd it go?" Whiskey asked.

"Back to the lake," Tara said, not certain how she knew. Fighting the pain in her head, she rushed toward the archways, the others right behind her. Two silver symbols appeared in midair, each hovering in front of an opening. She stopped in front of the left symbol — a tall, thin tower.

Brains jumped across the narrowed river between the two archways. "This one looks like sea waves."

Whiskey perked up. "You sure we can't go that way?"

"Sorry, not this time." Tara clasped Jovan's hand. "Everyone hold hands and stay close." She stepped forward into the thick fog filling the archway, the others crowding in after her.

The fog swirled around them, warm and damp like the steam in the cavern, smelling faintly salty. A slight feeling of displacement shivered through Tara, then she emerged into a short passageway that ended at a solid stone wall. After making sure everyone had come through, she led the way forward and pressed her left hand against the stone. With a grating hiss, a section of the wall slid to the side. Cold mountain air flowed into the passageway. They looked out onto the web-draped ruins of Ravnaul's Keep.

"Oh, gods," Tara whispered, surveying the tangled mass of web that stretched from one side of the mountain pass to the other, to the left and right of her, the sticky, rope-like strands reaching high up on the rock walls to completely ensnare the ruins and everyone in them. The shattered pieces of the thin tower pictured in the symbol lay strewn on the ground in front of them. The broken tower with the well that led to the trapped Kamarians stood off to the right, covered in strands. She couldn't see any spiders, but she could sense them approaching. She bit back a groan, holding her head in one hand as Ravnaul-Gorgrast's onslaught intensified.

Jovan grimaced and bowed his head, fists clenched.

"I need to get to that room where the Kamarians are," she ground out, gesturing to the right.

The smugglers and Gralfar hacked at the web but made little progress, their blades catching in the sticky strands instead of cutting through them.

"This stuff is like glue," Brains muttered.

"What about the king's sword?" Jovan gritted through his teeth.

"I haven't figured out how to use it yet," Tara said. "It doesn't like me."

"It *what?*" Jovan looked at her like he hadn't heard right.

"It's a sword of Light. I have the power of *Diurkruna* in me from Ravnaul's sword, and it doesn't like it. It won't let me draw it without inflicting a lot of pain."

"Well, we'd better think of something," Blackie said as he sawed through a strand of web. "This is getting us nowhere."

"Spiders!" Jack pointed at the top of the broken tower, where a wave of arachnids was flowing over the top and down the side toward them.

Brains whacked at the web. "We'll have to go back in the tunnel. Can you open it again?"

"Yes, but I don't want to go back in. I have to get to the tower." Tara touched the hilt of the king's sword. Pain shot into her fingers, and she jerked away. She cursed roundly. A strange sensation flitted through her tortured mind, and she had the distinct impression Ravnaul-Gorgrast was laughing at her. She narrowed her eyes. "All right, sword, you and I are going to come to an understanding." She whipped the black sword from its scabbard and gripped it with both hands. Pain like lightning bolts jagged up her arms, but she refused to let go. "I need your power to defeat your nemesis, and I don't have time to argue with you." She sensed the spiders moving closer.

White fire flooded her body, the power of Light purging the Darkness. She closed her eyes and fought against it. *No, no, no, no, no! You can't do that now! I need the Darkness as much as I need the Light.*

Words, like blazing sunlight, filled her. *The powers of Light and Darkness cannot both dwell in the same soul without dire consequences.*

I have no choice, she sent with grim determination.

Hands touched her shoulders from behind, holding tight. Jovan. This time, she seized the offered strength, just enough to tip the struggle in her favor. *Power of Light, search my soul... join the power already within me. When our enemy is defeated, I promise you may purge the Darkness from me, but for now, fight with me, not against me. Please...*

The pain in her arms ceased, only to be replaced by an inner agony — the clash of the Light and Darkness within — made more acute by the presence of Gorgrast's power. Tara's hand flew to her chest, and she gasped for breath.

"Tara!" Jovan said urgently. He pulled her back against the mountain, away from the spiders that were almost upon them. "Open the tunnel!"

She touched the rock, and a silver symbol that looked like rising clouds of steam flashed. The door grated open. "Get in," she croaked.

The others darted into the passage. Jovan stood behind her in the open doorway, his hands on her shoulders, holding her close against him, his breathing as ragged as hers.

Gripping the king's sword in both hands again, she swung it sideways. White fire tainted with black and streaks of blue blazed outward in a wide arc, incinerating both spiders and web. The acrid smell of burnt arachnids thickened the air. Tara swept the sword back, arcing it higher, clearing a path to the broken tower. Then the pain of the writhing powers within overcame her, and she slumped forward. Jovan caught her, then stumbled, and they both ended up on all fours, gasping. Her vision cleared and she touched his hand, her eyes asking if he was all right. He gave a brief nod, and she did the same in reply.

The smugglers helped them up.

"Are you two all right?" Brains asked anxiously.

Tara managed one more nod and a faint gesture toward the tower. The white fire raged within her, fighting with the black fire she'd absorbed from Ravnaul's blade and the divine power from Gorgrast, all of them battling for supremacy. Her insides felt like they were being ripped apart, and it was all she could do just to breathe.

Brains lifted Tara in his arms. Jack and Whittler put Jovan's arms around their shoulders and supported him between them.

"Keep your eyes open for more spiders," Blackie warned.

They wove their way through the scorched ruins toward the tower. Icy chills raked Tara's skin. Something was setting off her danger sense — something worse than the spiders, but her senses were so overloaded from the turmoil inside her that she couldn't tell what it was or where it was coming from. She glanced around warily, trying to focus. Most of the webs had been burned away. Blackened remnants dangled from the rock walls, but no spiders scrabbled along them. She wondered hazily if the arachnids had all been destroyed, or if they'd only retreated and would attack when she and the others entered the tower.

Brains stopped a short distance from the closed tower door, likely having the same thought. The others gathered around, eyes combing the surrounding rocks. Blackie gusted out a deep breath, strode to the door, and yanked it open. No spiders swarmed out. His relief was palpable.

He looked inside, then waved them forward. "It's empty."

They hurried into the tower. Brains set Tara down beside the well. She gripped the rim for support. The ring of symbols around the edge sprang to life. She touched the curving, eight-pointed star, and the well spiraled slowly upward, the grinding of its motion echoing in the stillness.

Jack and Whittler helped Jovan into the space inside the well. Tara followed. The others squeezed in after them. Tara rested her back against the wall, forcing her legs to hold her up. She caught Whittler's eye and raised her eyebrows. He was nervous and sweating, but he gave her a slight smile and nodded. She mustered a smile in return and squeezed his arm.

The well spiraled downward into the cavern. Cautiously, they stepped out onto the upper landing. A red haze had dimmed the silver glow lighting the cavern. Tendrils of dark red smoke swirled in the air, trailing the faint odor of carrion. Far below, the black pit churned violently, like a volcano about to erupt.

The pain in her head spiked, and she groaned, hearing an echoing groan from Jovan. Brains kept her from falling.

Milady... hurry... The Kamarian's taut whisper spurred her on.

Leaning heavily on Brains' arm and the cavern wall, Tara stumbled down the steps to the lower landing and opened the door to the room with the trough filled with black jelly and silver-white worms. She sank to her knees beside the trough and carefully slid the blade of the black sword into the jelly. The worms crawled over it, leaving silver trails over every inch of the blade before slipping back into the black jelly.

Our strength is yours, said a host of Kamarian voices.

Thank you. She removed the sword from the jelly. The black blade shimmered with a silver iridescence.

Then a great rumbling shook the cavern. Cold dread filled her. She caught Brains' arm, lurched to her feet, and rushed out onto the lower landing where the others stood with their backs to the wall, staring down at the seething blackness. Geysers of putrid red mist spewed forth and dispersed into the air, dimming the silver light even further.

Laughter echoed through the cavern, then two red blurs shot upward from the blackness. Rising to the top of the cavern, they landed on the upper platform, next to the well, and materialized into men. One stood tall — a good ten feet tall — with gray-robed arms raised, the black sword with its bluish tinge clasped in his hand — Ravnaul and Gorgrast, fully merged. Ravnaul's face and body had lost their deformities. Silver hair with a taint of blue spilled over his shoulders to halfway down his back, his empty eye socket his only remaining defect. Around his neck hung a pulsing red bloodstone.

The other man lay prone on the upper landing, his red robes torn, his auburn hair caked with dried blood — the wizard, Validar Melodian, alive or dead, Tara couldn't tell.

"I'm free!" Ravnaul-Gorgrast shouted with a clench of his fist. "After three hundred years." He glared down at Tara and sliced his hand sideways in a cutting motion. Tara dropped to her knees, an unbearable pain in her head. With a disdainful wave of his arm, he froze Jovan and the others where they stood.

"Ah, much better," Ravnaul-Gorgrast said in a deep, echoing voice. He looked down at Tara again with his hypnotic silver-brown eye. "Now, what shall I do with you, child of my traitorous daughter?"

Slowly and painfully, Tara rose from her knees. "You destroyed the lives of the entire Kamarian race. I won't let you do it again."

Ravnaul laughed. "*You* won't *let* me? You think that sword you hold from my pitiful brother will be enough to stop me?" He laughed again, then his expression changed in an instant from scorn to hatred. He swung the black sword and stabbed the air in Tara's direction. Blue-black fire blazed down at her.

"No!" Jovan shouted.

Tara's reflexes as a swordfighter saved her. Using Lazarial's sword as a shield, she just managed to block the bolt of fire and deflect it. The blast struck the stone ceiling above Ravnaul's head. With a resounding crack, the stone shattered. Stalactites rained down, along with chunks of rock and debris.

Ravnaul-Gorgrast shielded himself with magic. Tara ducked away from the plummeting rocks, her legs so wobbly she could barely get them to move.

The moment Ravnaul-Gorgrast's magical shield dissipated, more rocks started pelting him, from below this time, and Tara turned to see Sarita snatching up fist-sized stones and heaving them at Ravnaul-Gorgrast, striking him in the head and chest. She and the others had been freed from his hold by the distraction of the falling stalactites. The smugglers and Gralfar followed Sarita's lead and bombarded him with rocks, forcing him to reform his shield and diverting his attention long enough for Jovan to scoop Tara up in his arms and carry her back to the wall.

Leaning back against the wall, Jovan set Tara down on her feet. His breathing was labored; she sensed he was near the end of his strength. She clung to his arm to stay upright as she struggled to withstand the pain in her head. She was very near her own limits.

With an angry growl and a sweep of his arm, Ravnaul-Gorgrast cleared the landing, sending the downed rocks and Melodian's body crashing onto the lower platform. Blackie pulled Sarita out of the way and the others scattered, dodging deadly stalactites aimed to skewer them. Jovan staggered to the side, dragging Tara with him. They dove behind a boulder. The smashing of the rocks against the wall pounded in Tara's throbbing head.

A burst of blue-black fire demolished the boulder and slammed them into the wall, where they collapsed. Tara fought to stay conscious. She saw blood on Jovan's temple, and her breath caught. She struggled to her knees and felt for a pulse, started breathing again when she felt it beating weakly beneath her fingers. He opened his eyes.

"Goodbye, weak child." Ravnaul-Gorgrast laughed scornfully.

Another bolt of fire seared toward Tara and Jovan. Jovan heaved himself up and wrapped his arms around Tara's waist, infusing his remaining strength into her and igniting the warring magics within. Energized by the sudden rush of power, Tara brought up her sword and fired back. Silver-gray flames shot outward, striking the blue-black fire in midair. Blinding light flashed, and then a thunderous explosion shook the mountain to its roots.

CHAPTER 36

Flying... As if in a dream, Tara felt her body flying through the air, then she hit the ground with a jarring whump. Pain in her head and left side darkened her vision. She couldn't breathe, all the wind knocked out of her. So much pain, inside and out, that she couldn't think. Desperately sucking in air, she fought the urge to vomit. When she could breathe normally again, she moaned and curled into a ball.

Someone touched her arm and eased her onto her back.

"Tara!" *Love, can you hear me?*

The urgent words, the familiar whisper-soft voice sifted through her mind. Jovan. She opened her eyes and tried to focus on him, her mind catching some details with vivid clarity while losing others. He lay beside her, propped on his elbow, his face streaked with dirt and blood. Behind him she could see a smeared red trail where he'd dragged himself across the broken ground to reach her. He was badly hurt. She had to heal him. If she could just get her brain to work...

Jovan's voice faded in and out of her hearing. She couldn't comprehend what he was saying. He fell back weakly.

Gritting her teeth, she levered herself into a sitting position. Dizziness swayed her. Pain tore along the length of her left side, but she held firm. "Lie still. I'll try to heal you."

"No. Ravnaul... may have survived... have to destroy him."

Ravnaul. *Oh, gods!* Tara stiffened as everything came back to her. She looked around at the ruins of Ravnaul's Keep — broken rocks were strewn everywhere, the tower completely destroyed. Only a jagged hole marked where it had stood. Then she saw the bodies of Whiskey and Jack lying in the rubble. Were they dead? Where were the others? Horror squeezed her chest. Were they all dead? A sob escaped her. "No," she whispered.

She turned back to Jovan, determined to heal him. She couldn't live if he died, too.

He caught her hand. "No. You can't... not until we know... Ravnaul is dead. King's sword... where...?" His hand slid from her fingers.

The black sword. Where was it? Tara suddenly realized she must have dropped it during the explosion. "I don't care about the sword," she said fiercely. "I won't let you die!"

A freezing chill shot through her. Instinctively, she reached for the normal sword at her right hip, her movements hampered by pain.

"He *will* die!" said a deep voice behind her. "I will make sure of it."

The sound of the familiar southern accent shocked her. How...? Before she could fully unsheathe her blade, Gus strode past and stood looking down at Jovan with eyes full of hate.

"My family died because of you. For that, I send you to the Abyss!" Gripping the hilt with both hands, Gus raised his sword high and stabbed downward, burying the blade in Jovan's chest.

"No!" Tara screamed.

Jovan groaned, his breath dwindling to shallow gurgles.

Gus wrenched out his sword and backed quickly away, his eyes on something behind her. Then he stumbled with a cry and fell, his hand clutching at his side, a knife lodged deep between his ribs.

From the periphery of her vision, Tara became aware of Whittler crawling toward her and pointing behind her, looking terrified. But the image flitted out of her mind. All she could see was Jovan dying. She sliced her palm on her sword blade and pressed her hand over the wound in Jovan's chest. Blood flowed freely between her fingers, his life draining away. *No! Jovan! No!* She tried to marshal the battling powers within long enough to heal him, but the pain... gods... the pain — so excruciating, stealing her will and her ability to focus.

"Lady, leave him. Come with me!" The gravelly voice filtered into her consciousness, breaking what little concentration she had.

Her eyes fixed on the hulking giant who had come up beside her, on the ragged scar livid on his ashen face. In his hand, wrapped in his cloak, he held King Lazarial's black sword. All thoughts of the black sword vanished as another realization sank in. "You! You brought Gus here! I hate you!" She gripped her sword, tears falling freely. "If you try to stop me from saving Jovan, I swear I will kill you this time."

Natiere said nothing, his expression a mix of conflicting emotions.

Tara turned back to Jovan. The faint rise and fall of his chest beneath her hand stopped. "Oh, no." She closed her eyes and fought to heal his death wound. *Please...*

A gnarled hand settled on her shoulder. She tensed, ready to lash out as the touch of Natiere's mind edged around her. Wordlessly and without threat, he offered his strength. Surprise and relief overwhelmed her. She dropped her sword and placed her hand over his, squeezing his fingers in fervent gratitude. Power, solid as the ground beneath her, flooded her mind, strengthening the Light within and filling her soul with the essence of earth and trees and wildlife. She gasped as she realized his magic was as real as hers, inborn, descended from the Ancients. He was earth *Aiykshaav'n*. With a surge of hope, she drank in his power and sent it straight into Jovan. His body jerked once, and his chest rose and fell. *Yes... keep breathing...*

A stab of shocking cold snapped her around.

"Traitorous child! I will destroy you!"

Her mind, still in healing mode, barely had time to register the blue-black flames streaking toward her before Natiere shoved her aside.

The flames struck Natiere full on. With a guttural scream, he fell backward, landing beside Jovan.

Tara scrambled to Natiere's side. "Natiere! Rylan..." She stumbled over the unfamiliar name he'd told her, what seemed like ages ago. A sob escaped her when she saw the charred flesh of his ruined chest and belly.

"I'm sorry," he whispered. He closed his eyes and went still.

Tara's tears flowed again, dripping on his lifeless body. *No!* She'd been right about him after all. The goodness of his boyhood self had broken through the monstrous shell of what he'd become. But now he was dead. He'd never be able to nurture that goodness and live out the rest of the life that should have been his, had his family not been butchered by the bandits. He'd won the battle for his soul, then lost everything. Because of her. She leaned close and kissed his scarred cheek, wishing he could still hear her. "You saved my life. Thank you."

"Such a touching scene." Ravnaul-Gorgrast approached, his evil aura swirling around him like a red shroud. He appeared uninjured.

"That's why it doesn't pay to have friends." He swept his arm outward, indicating her fallen comrades — the corpse of Natiere; Jovan, lying so still beside him; Whittler, who had collapsed before he'd reached her; Whiskey and Jack, still motionless amid the rubble. "They gave their lives. For what? Nothing! You have failed! And now, instead of killing you outright, I will take pleasure in ripping your mind to pieces. You will wish you were dead long before you are. Then I will destroy those insufferable gods" — his voice deepened to an echoing roar as Gorgrast overpowered Ravnaul — "who dared to judge and imprison me on this infernal world!" Growing taller with every step, he strode toward her, the black sword, now more blue than black, held at his side.

Fury welled up inside Tara at the loss of her companions, an anger so deep it raged through her blood like the black sword's fire, giving her the strength to meld the vying powers within until they burned as one. Gorgrast's mental claws slashed at her mind, but he could not pierce the wall of her wrath. She reached beneath Natiere's cloak, lying on the ground beside her. Her fingers curled around the hilt of King Lazarial's sword. Slowly, she rose and faced Gorgrast, who was now more than twenty feet tall. "You will not do any of those things."

Gorgrast snarled and aimed Ravnaul's black sword at her. "You have defied me for the last time."

Tara raised her sword. "And you have destroyed your last soul."

Blue flames streaked with black shot from the end of Ravnaul's sword. Fire burst from Tara's blade, a writhing blend of silver-white, black, blue, and the brownish-green of Natiere's earth magic. She channeled every ounce of power she had into the blast, all her rage and grief. The blast smashed through the blue flames, straight into Gorgrast's chest. Gorgrast roared as the fire burned clean through his body. Ravnaul's sword shattered. A blaze of fire consumed Gorgrast, until all that remained were a pile of ashes and a dead-black lifestone riddled with cracks.

Tara stumbled across to the pile. She savagely kicked the ashes, then pulverized Ravnaul's lifestone with her heel. Never again would Ravnaul or Gorgrast torment her. No more dream dungeon. She was free, and so was Jovan.

She dropped King Lazarial's sword and sank to her knees. *Jovan...* With a sob, she crawled back to where he lay. He was barely breathing. She had to heal him, but she had no strength left. Her trembling limbs gave out and her eyes dimmed. "No... Jovan..."

A cool hand touched her forehead, and she caught a glimpse of a silver-haired man with pale skin bending over her.

Rest easy, child. We will tend to your friends. You have saved us all.

The voice faded from her mind as her world went black.

*****

Flying... Tara felt again like she was flying, though this time she did not fall. She felt safe and cozy, as if wrapped in warm blankets. The pain that had ravaged her mind and body was gone. A silver haze surrounded her as she drifted down and settled on something soft and comfortable.

Sleep, whispered a male Kamarian voice, the same voice she'd heard earlier. *You are safe.*

Her drowsy mind embraced the promise of deep repose, free of the nightmares that had plagued her for so long. Yet an icy prickling kept her on the edge of slumber and wouldn't let her descend into its depths. She felt oddly weak, as if her energy was slowly being siphoned out of her. A touch of coldness crept into her soul, and she had the unnerving feeling that Death was withering part of it away, pursuing not just her, but —

"Jovan!" Tara rolled out of the bed in which she'd been placed, startling the silver-haired man standing beside her. She staggered to the next bed, where Jovan lay silent, still crusted with dried blood. She touched his face. His skin felt unnaturally cool.

Jovan! Fear gripped her when she got no response. She climbed onto the bed, straddling him with her knees, and put her ear to his chest. She heard only the faintest of struggling heartbeats.

"We healed the wounds in his body," the Kamarian said, "but the wounds of his mind and spirit are beyond us."

She rifled her clothing, but found nothing sharp. She whirled on the Kamarian. "Knife, sword — I need a blade. Quickly!"

Blackie de Runo appeared beside her, dirty and blood-stained but apparently whole. He held out his belt knife, hilt first. "Will this do?"

"Blackie! You're alive!" She hugged him so hard he almost fell onto the bed.

"Hey, easy there. I've got a knife in my hand." He held her tight for a moment, then let go.

Tara took the knife and tore aside Jovan's ripped shirt. She made a small cut over his heart and sliced a matching cut on her left palm. Then she pressed her bleeding hand over the wound.

Jovan! You can't leave me. I need you. I love you. Come back!

She delved deeper, infusing her warmth and power into the iciness of his fading soul. Still, he slipped further and further away. She hesitated, confused, sensing a difference within him. She drew in a sharp breath. The wellspring of magic he'd gotten from Gorgrast at Rinpool had vanished, leaving only the Kamarian magic he'd absorbed from her and a touch of Natiere's earth magic. With dawning horror, she realized why her healing power wasn't working. Gorgrast's power had healed the poisoned knife wound he'd received as a boy. If not for that magic power, Jovan would have died. It was that power that had kept him alive ever since. But she'd destroyed Gorgrast, and now that life-giving power was gone. She'd won the war, but lost what mattered most.

"No," she sobbed. "I can't lose you." She bowed her head. *Great Azakai, ruler of the Heavens, please hear me. I've done what you wanted. I defeated the evil within the Kamarian race, and I destroyed your enemy. Please grant me this request — please don't let him die. I can't live without him. I never would have succeeded without his help. Please...* She thought of the smugglers, and Sarita and Gralfar, and Valina, and all that they'd given, and said a desperate prayer for them as well. Then the ashen face of Natiere slipped into her mind, and more tears fell. There was no way to save him. His spirit had already passed. *Please be merciful to his tortured soul...*

Exhaustion overwhelmed her. Dizzy and faint, she sank down onto the bed beside Jovan, her head on his shoulder, her hand still over his heart. Another realization froze her to her very soul, and she suddenly knew why she was so weak. Gorgrast's power had saved her from the spider's poison. Death would soon claim her, too.

Whether in life or in death, please let us be together...

CHAPTER 37

A lone howl, eerie and sorrowful, rose into the starlit night. The black wolf, Kelya, stood on a ridge of solid black rock, the mountain no longer glassy and brittle, but whole again. The transformation had been instantaneous. Ravnaul-Gorgrast's destruction had reversed the damage done by the Cataclysm three centuries before, and life in the Black Mountains was beginning anew.

Kelya howled her grief into the night. Her master had made her promise that she and the other wolves would stay well away while he confronted the human woman. Anxiously, she'd waited for his return, sensing the tension in the air, the threat of impending disaster. She had wanted so much to go to him, to stand with him and protect him, but she had never broken a promise to him before. Her indecision had cost her everything. She'd heard his scream, a horrifying sound that still echoed in her delicate ears. They'd found his body surrounded by silver-haired men and women. With savage growls and a show of teeth, they'd driven them away. Then she'd lain beside Natiere and licked his cold face in despair.

The Gypsy woman had come, and they'd allowed her to say a Gypsy prayer for their master's soul. Afterward, the Gypsy had stroked Kelya's head, murmured a few words, and then disappeared into a mountain tunnel with the other men and women, leaving the wolves alone.

When night fell and the ruins lay silent, the wolves had howled their anguish to the stars. Then the strangest thing had happened. The Wolfmaster's body had sunk into the stone floor of the mountain and vanished. Bereft, she and the other wolves had spent hours searching the area, but had found no trace of him.

Now she knew it was time to leave. There was nothing left to keep them here. She missed the forests of the Western Kingdoms, the sounds and smells of home. With her head lowered and her tail drooping, she padded back to where the six gray wolves waited. They greeted her with soft whines of sympathy.

Another lone howl pierced the night. Kelya's ears pricked sharply at the unknown voice. What wolf was this? She hadn't scented any other canines in the mountains. She listened as the wolf howled again, the sound unfamiliar — and yet there was something... With the six gray wolves following, she bounded down off the ridge toward the sound.

*****

When Tara woke, she felt strong and refreshed, as if she'd slept for a month. She sat up, amazed and thankful to be alive. Jovan lay on his back beside her in the bed, asleep, his breathing deep and steady. All the blood stains had been washed away. They were alone in a small room full of empty beds — an infirmary, she guessed. She felt a pang of worry, and hoped the beds were empty because her friends had been healed, not because they were dead.

Grassy fields thick with flowers and butterflies surrounded them — or at least, that's how it seemed. The richly painted walls were interspersed with tall windows, bright with afternoon sun. She realized with a shock that they had to be in the black castle. Castle Kamar had returned to the living world.

She put her ear to Jovan's chest, reveling in the strength of his heartbeat, and sent up a joyful prayer of gratitude. He stirred, his eyes blinking open. She smiled down at him and caressed his face.

Smiling back, he pushed himself up and brushed back her tousled hair. "Are you all right?"

"I'm fine, but what about you?" She ran her hand over his chest, miraculously free of scars. "How do you feel?"

He caught her hand and brought her fingers to his lips. "I don't think I've ever felt this good."

Then his lips sought hers, and they shared a long and tender kiss, held close in each other's arms.

After a while, they eased back, content to just look at each other, their eyes speaking through the silence.

"I can't believe it's over," Tara said finally.

"Is it truly over? What happened after the explosion? And where are we?" Jovan looked quizzically at the painted walls. "Are we inside or out?"

"We are inside Castle Kamar, I think. The gods must have allowed its return. Ravnaul and Gorgrast have been destroyed."

"You did it!" He embraced her again. "I knew you'd find a way."

She held him tight as the memory of Rylan Natiere's death and the final battle rose in her mind. She closed her eyes and choked back a sob.

Jovan drew back and cupped her face with his hand. "What's wrong?"

"Natiere is dead, too."

"For certain this time?"

Tara nodded and looked away, blinking back tears.

Jovan frowned. "Why does his death distress you? You know what he was."

"No," Tara said vehemently. "No one knew what he was. He was earth *Aiykshaav'n*."

"Natiere — an Ancient?" Jovan looked stunned.

"Descended from them, like me. He helped me heal you. That's how I discovered it. Then he took a blast from Ravnaul's sword that was meant for me. He saved my life. I will never be able to repay him."

Jovan frowned again. "You don't owe him anything. How many times did he try to kill you —"

"He didn't. Not really. If he'd wanted me dead, I would have been dead long ago. He had plenty of opportunities, but he always stayed his hand. And you're wrong. We do owe him. He gave his life for me. If not for him, Ravnaul would have killed me — would have killed all of us. We owe Natiere everything."

A door to their right opened, and the familiar silver-haired man entered.

"Ah, you're awake." He hurried toward them, relief etching his face. "I'm so glad. Our return would mean nothing if it cost your life."

Tara watched him as he moved to their bedside. He was tall and lean, with long, straight hair that fell to the middle of his back. Over a floor-length gray robe, he wore a sleeveless tunic of twilight indigo dotted with star-like silver accents. A luminous gray lifestone hung from a silver chain around his neck.

The Kamarian bowed before them, his silver eyes mirroring his smile. "My name is Dancalan. I am chief advisor to the throne. Please tell me you are well?"

"Yes, we are. Thank you for healing our wounds." Tara swung her legs over the side of the bed and stood, apprehension twisting inside her. "My friends — are they alive? Where are they?"

"Your friends are —"

A commotion just outside the closed door interrupted him. Tara heard Blackie's voice and another unfamiliar voice arguing, but she couldn't discern their words.

Then Brains' voice rose above them. "We're not trying to cause trouble. We just want to see her for ourselves."

Dancalan smiled again. "I'd say they're here."

Tara dashed to the door and whipped it open. A young Kamarian man dressed in gray robes swung around in surprise. Whittler was closest to the door, as if he'd been trying to sneak around behind the distracted Kamarian. Tara let out a joyous whoop and threw her arms around him. Blackie, Brains, Whiskey, Jack, and Gralfar crowded around her, all talking at once. Tara hugged them all repeatedly, wiping away happy tears and thanking the gods for the gift of her friends' lives. Sarita hung back at first, aloof, but then gave in and returned the embrace when Tara hugged her anyway.

"Hey," Brains said, as Jovan stepped through the door. He shook Jovan's hand and clapped him on the back. "Glad to see you made it."

The smugglers welcomed him into the group with more hand shaking and back slapping. Even Blackie shook his hand, a truce called for the moment.

"I knew we did the right thing when we rescued you and your thieving brother all those years ago," Gralfar said with a gruff clearing of his throat. He gave Jovan a firm handclasp and a quick hug. "But I never dreamed I'd be dragged into anything like this. I'm amazed we all survived."

"You can thank the gods for that," Tara said, coming to stand beside Jovan, "as well as our Kamarian friends." She swept her arm toward Dancalan, who'd emerged from the infirmary, and the young Kamarian, who was hurrying away down a side corridor after a word from Dancalan. "They all lent their power to help me fight Ravnaul and Gorgrast, and then healed us in the aftermath."

"Our contribution was nothing, compared to yours," said a whispering voice. The tall, ghostly shape of King Lazarial floated down the hallway toward them, flanked by a young man and a slightly younger woman, both with shoulder-length, wavy silver hair and friendly eyes. They were dressed in white robes — his with a bright yellow sun embroidered on his left shoulder, sun rays blazing down his front, back, and left sleeve, and hers with a silver moon and glittering moonbeams in a similar pattern. Gold crowns with yellow gems and moonstones adorned their heads. The young woman wore a silver chain with a gray lifestone around her neck. The young man had no lifestone, and Tara knew who he must be.

Valina! Valina, can you hear me? she sent urgently, hoping the sorceress had recovered from whatever injury she'd suffered in her attempt to bring her brother to Estiarii Faelle. Valina didn't respond. Worry shadowed Tara's thoughts. What if —? No. She refused to believe that the gods would allow the sorceress to die when Zaniel had just resumed his life. That would be too cruel.

King Lazarial and his two companions halted before Tara and Jovan. "You defeated not only Ravnaul, but Gorgrast as well," the king said. "You restored our people and brought our home back from oblivion." The three bowed deeply. "We are eternally in your debt." They straightened, and the king's arms swung wide, encompassing everyone in the group. "We thank all of you. We owe you all our deepest gratitude."

Gralfar gave a deferential nod. "You are welcome."

The smugglers and Sarita looked at Blackie, as if expecting him to be their spokesperson.

Blackie shifted uncomfortably and cleared his throat.

Brains stepped up beside him and bowed. "We are honored to have been a part of it, Your Highness."

Blackie pointed at Brains. "What he said."

The others nodded.

Brains grinned. "I wouldn't have missed it for anything."

Tara laughed and swept a fond gaze over the group. Then she clasped Jovan's hand and squeezed it. He smiled at her.

Tara...

Tara's heart leaped with hope. *Valina, are you all right?*

Yes, I appear to be. I feel like I've been asleep for ages.

Are you near your mirror? If you are, take a look.

Concern colored the sorceress' voice. *Is something wrong —* Valina's voice caught, and Tara heard a whispered name and soft weeping as she shifted her focus back to the king.

King Lazarial turned to his left, then his right. "This is my son, Zaniel, and my daughter, Zaria. I am ecstatic and humbled to find that two of my children have survived." The king looked at Tara. "You were right about Zaniel."

Tara smiled and nodded. She turned to Zaniel. "I have something that belongs to you."

"To me?" He looked puzzled.

Obviously, the king hadn't told him she had the stone. She wondered why as she lifted the silver chain from around her neck and held out his lifestone, now glowing a soft gray.

His hands trembled as he took it from her. "Where did you get this?"

"Valina gave it to me, to give to you."

"She gave it to you? But how... my father said it's been three hundred years. How could she still be alive?"

"Magic. But she can't leave her home, or she'll revert to her true age."

He studied the lifestone. "If she gave it to you to give me, perhaps... after all this time... she no longer wants it." His voice had grown soft, the pain in his heart bleeding through even though he tried to hide it.

Tara smiled again. "Nothing could be further from the truth."

Zaniel's eyes closed suddenly, and Tara knew the sorceress was telling him exactly how she felt about him.

King Lazarial watched him, a reddish tint of agitation suffusing his ghostly form. Zaria looked uncomfortable.

Zaniel opened his eyes and turned on his father. "Why didn't you tell me she was alive? I told you everything, and yet you kept this from me."

The king sighed, his color shifting to a smoky blue-gray. "I'm sorry. I didn't tell you because I was afraid you would leave again. I'd hoped, my son, that after we'd talked last night, you'd want to stay and, with Zaria, lead our people back to prosperity."

"Father, you know how I feel about that. I never wanted to be king. I have not the head, nor the personality, for such a position. Zaria does. She is more than capable of leading on her own. She'll have Dancalan to advise her, and if she does need my help for any reason, she need only ask, and I will return. Please, Father. I want nothing more than to spend this new life that's been granted to me studying the stars with Valina."

The king regarded him silently for a moment, then spoke. "As king, I am sworn to do whatever is best for my people, though it may not always be what I might wish. However, as a father, I want my children to be happy."

He looked at Zaria.

"Let him go, Father," she said softly. "Life is too precious to spend it away from the one you love."

The king's gaze swung back to Zaniel. "Attend this evening's celebration, then you may go. But you must come back frequently, for the good of the kingdom. You are still Kamarian royalty and cannot completely forsake your birthright."

Zaniel's face lit with happiness. "Thank you, Father. I will do as you ask. Would you please excuse me? I have much to prepare before the celebration."

"Yes, my son, do what you must."

Zaniel bowed once more to Tara and the others. "Thank you again for all you've done." He took Tara's hand and squeezed it. "And thank you for this." He put his other hand over the lifestone around his neck. "For bringing us back together. I am doubly in your debt." His eyes radiant with anticipation, he nodded quickly to his father and sister and hurried back down the hall.

The king sighed again, watching him go.

"He only speaks the truth," Zaria said quietly.

"I know. It is as he says. He is a dreamer and a scholar, like your mother. He does not have the skills of a great leader, nor does he want them." The king smiled at his daughter. "He is lucky that you do. We are all fortunate. You were always the strongest, the most fair-minded, and the most beloved by the people. You will make a great queen."

Zaria bowed her head. "Thank you, Father. I will do my best to serve our people and make you proud."

"I know you will. And I am already proud." The king turned to Tara and Jovan. "Dancalan will show you to your rooms, where you can rest and prepare for tonight's celebration." He raised his arms to include everyone. "We wish for you all to attend as our guests of honor. Please say you'll join us."

Tara smiled. "I think I can speak for us all and say it will be our pleasure."

The king and Zaria bowed again. "We look forward to tonight," the king said, then they turned to go.

Tara's hand brushed her right side and felt something missing. "Oh — wait!"

"Yes?" the king asked.

"Your black sword — I don't know what happened to it. Do you have it?"

King Lazarial smiled sadly. "Yes, we have it. Zaria used its power of *Liuminerii* to purge the dark magic from you while you slept."

"Thank you," Tara said to Zaria.

Zaria nodded gravely. "You are welcome."

"Afterward," the king continued, "we locked the sword in its box and hid it in one of the castle's secret vaults to keep it safe."

"Then you'll want the key." Tara reached for the inner pocket where she'd stashed the jeweled key.

"No, you must keep it."

Tara looked at him in surprise. "But how will you —"

"We won't, and that is as it should be. We are living proof of how much destruction the black sword can cause. The House of Lazarial will never use it again. We entrust the key to you." With a nod, he and Zaria left.

"If you will follow me," Dancalan said.

He led the group through long halls painted like mountain valleys.

"Can you believe these walls?" Brains said to Tara and Jovan as they turned down another hallway. "I've walked through here several times now, and they still take my breath away."

Before Tara could say a word, Brains stopped in the middle of the hall. "You have to see this." He hurried to one of the doors along the passageway and threw it open.

The others halted as Tara went and looked through the doorway. Jovan followed. Tara drew in a breath. It was like stepping into a deep, primordial forest. Massive hardwoods and evergreens painted in rich shades of green and brown and sun gold rose into a cathedral ceiling sky. Forest animals peeked out from around the trunks, and colorful birds nested in the branches.

Whiskey caught Tara's arm and pulled her across the hall. "This one's even better." He opened the door to a sandy beach with azure waves flowing in from a distant horizon. She could almost smell the salt water and hear the cries of the painted gulls.

"They're incredible," Tara said.

"I like my room the best," said Sarita.

"The rainforest." Brains nodded. "I like that one, too. It's so detailed that every time I look at it I see something new."

"It sounds beautiful." Tara moved back to Jovan's side.

Dancalan started to speak, but Brains interrupted him. "Oh, and wait till you see this one." He rushed to another door farther down. "It looks like a giant eagle aerie." He opened the door wide, and Tara heard surprised voices coming from inside the room. "Oops, sorry." Brains swung the door shut and walked back to the group. "I guess you'll have to see that one later."

Tara laughed.

Diamond Jack cuffed Brains on the shoulder. "No one can get any rest when you're around."

"What do you mean?" Brains asked.

"Well, you're either snoring like an axe grinder or barging in on people. You still owe me ten gold pieces, you know."

"I do not!"

"Whittler, I told you not to do that!"

Tara heard Blackie's heated whisper behind her, turned quickly, and saw Whittler carving on one of the door frames. Whittler hastily pocketed his knife and hid behind his hair.

Dancalan sighed. "May we continue?"

Tara tried to keep the smile off her face. "Sorry. Please, lead on."

They made their way to the northern end of the castle. Dancalan stopped before a series of doors resembling caves in a wall of stone.

"This is my kind of painting," Gralfar said.

Dancalan indicated two of the doors. "These adjoining rooms are yours," he said to Tara and Jovan. "I hope they are to your liking. Your friends have the rooms next to you. The celebration begins in an hour. Until then." He swept them a bow and strode away down the hall.

The group dispersed to their rooms.

"I can't believe he left the key with me," Tara said as she and Jovan entered their chambers.

"He trusts you with it, as he should."

They walked into a twilight landscape painted in varying shades of moon silver and indigo.

Jovan looked around. "The rooms in this castle are amazing."

Tara nodded. "I want to go through the entire castle and see them all."

They found fresh clothes laid out for them and hot water drawn for baths.

"That looks inviting." She slipped her fingers under the hem of Jovan's torn shirt and pulled it upward. "Need help undressing?"

He let her pull the shirt off over his head. "That depends."

She tossed the garment onto the floor and raised her arms as he removed her shirt the same way. "On what?" She shook out her hair.

He added her shirt to the pile and slipped his arms around her. "On whether or not you want to be late."

She twined her arms around his neck and reached for his kiss. "I'll let you know," she murmured as the world fell away into bliss.

CHAPTER 38

Lively music, conversation, and laughter spilled from the throne room as Tara and Jovan hurried to join the celebration. Through the open door ahead, they saw rows of occupied tables draped with silver and gold linen and laden with food. Light from the chandeliers reflected brilliantly off the mirrored walls, brightening the festive atmosphere. The vast room radiated warmth and joy.

"I didn't think we were that late," Tara said.

Jovan smiled. "I warned you."

She smiled back. "Yes, you did." She stopped him long enough to give him a quick kiss. "And I don't regret it." She turned back toward the throne room. "Maybe they won't notice."

The moment they stepped through the door, a hush descended, and the Kamarians rose as one, facing them. Tara halted, her cheeks reddening.

Jovan stopped beside her, his hand on her back. He whispered in her ear, "You were saying?"

A graceful Kamarian woman, dressed all in silver, approached them and bowed. The rest of the Kamarians — Tara estimated between three and four hundred — bowed as well.

"Welcome. I am Miressa, Dancalan's consort." The woman smiled warmly. "If you would please come this way?"

She led them to the head of one of the tables near the dais, where four chairs stood empty. She placed them across from each other, next to their friends, who were already devouring the delicious fare of roasted fish and wild fowl, still-steaming potatoes and vegetables, and fresh bread. Apparently, Castle Kamar had returned with a fully stocked larder. Tara's stomach growled appreciatively as she and Jovan took their seats. Gralfar, his mouth full, grunted a greeting as Jovan sat down to his left. On the other side of Gralfar, Sarita, Blackie, and Brains raised their forks or glasses in acknowledgment, as did Whiskey, Whittler, and Jack on Tara's left, too busy enjoying the feast to speak. Miressa sat on Tara's right, on the end, leaving one empty seat across from her, presumably for Dancalan. King Lazarial, Zaniel, and Zaria were absent, and Tara wondered where they were. The rest of the Kamarians had resumed their places, and the blithe music — an enchanting combination of flutes, pipes, and stringed instruments — was rising to the rafters once again.

Tara turned to Miressa. "I apologize for our lateness. We lost track of the time."

"No apologies needed," Miressa said graciously. "You deserve some time to yourselves after all you've been through."

Before Tara could say more, Whiskey nudged her and handed her a stemmed glass full of purplish liquid. "You gotta try this. It's even better than the sorceress' brew."

Tara laughed. "And there's still some left?" Grinning at Whittler, who was fiercely guarding his drink, she tried a sip, then took another, deeper swallow. "You're right. Gods, this is good. What is it?"

"Sweet berry ambrosia, made from the nectar of the flowers of the sweet berry briar and the juice of its berries," said Miressa.

"They grow wild here in the mountains, and we transplanted some to our gardens. The plants are thorny and hard to cultivate, but the taste makes it worth the effort."

"Thorns," Tara murmured, remembering the thorny, flowering briars that had surrounded the ruins of her mother's cottage in Wyndover. The essence of the ambrosia reminded her of them. "Do the plants have small white flowers?"

"Why, yes, they do. And purple berries. How did you know?"

"My mother grew them." Tara smiled wistfully and took another sip to soothe her pang of sadness.

The evening passed quickly with the delicious food and warm company.

As they were finishing their desserts, the music crescendoed into a grand, sweeping finale. The musicians stilled their instruments and acknowledged the applause.

Then everyone rose and bowed as the ghost of King Lazarial entered the room with Zaniel and Zaria, resplendent in their white sun and moon robes. The royal family climbed to the dais and stood before the thrones, smiling at everyone.

Dancalan appeared beside the empty seat across from Miressa, having made his way through the crowd. He gave her a quick wink, at which she blushed, then they both faced the king.

"My friends, you honor me." The king's whispering voice carried remarkably well in the spacious room. "Please, sit." When everyone was again sitting, he spoke, his expression sober. "I do not deserve such deference. I neglected my duty to you — my people. I failed to protect you. I did not take seriously the evil in our midst — an evil I, in my arrogance, helped to create. By the time I realized the extent of it and the paths it had taken, it was too late. The evil was too strong. The resulting Cataclysm..." His voice broke, and he paused. "I will never forgive myself for all the souls lost that day." He bowed his head and was silent a moment, then continued. "The gods' retribution was swift. My brother and I were made to suffer, and deservedly so. It pains me terribly that the remnants of my people suffered along with us."

His voice strengthened. "But after three hundred years, the gods allowed us a glimmer of hope — a chance for redemption in the form of this young woman." He swept his arm toward Tara and beckoned for her to approach.

Tara shifted uncomfortably when everyone turned toward her. Jovan squeezed her hand in encouragement. She took a deep breath, rose, and made her way to the dais.

Zaniel and Zaria smiled at her, their warmth easing her self-consciousness as she ascended the stairs to stand beside the king.

"Tara Triannon risked her life and her very soul to save us. We owe everything to her and to those who helped her on the way." He gestured for Jovan and the others to join them.

The smugglers glanced at each other, most of them looking like they wanted to hide under the table. At Dancalan and Miressa's urging, they stood and followed Jovan, Gralfar, and Sarita onto the dais.

"Behold, our heroes!" The royal family dipped their heads humbly, and the crowd erupted in thunderous applause.

Brains smiled and shook the hand Zaniel offered. Following Brains' lead, the others shed some of their uneasiness and traded handshakes and hugs with Zaniel and Zaria.

Then the king raised his hands for silence. When the crowd had quieted, he faced Tara and her friends. "There is no way we will ever be able to repay you for the horrors you endured and the sacrifices you made. However —" He held up his hands again to stem the objection Tara was about to make. "I know you will say you want no recompense, but please allow us these gestures of our gratitude and trusts for the future."

He turned to Jovan. "To you, I entrust the life of our newly found daughter of Kamar. Protect her and keep her safe."

Standing beside Tara, Jovan slipped his arm around her. He held the king's gaze. "I will." Then he turned his head and winked at Tara. "If she'll let me."

Tara smiled mischievously at him.

Blackie snickered. "Good luck," he said to Jovan.

The ghost king chuckled. He turned to Tara. "We are in need of a liaison between us and the peoples of this world, to help us become an integral part of it again. The liaison we seek would live in a rebuilt Ravnaul's Keep, learn our ways, and help in the restoration of the Kamarian histories that were lost in the destruction of the Keep. As the only living descendant of the House of Ravnaul, you are now Mistress of Ravnaul's Keep. The post is yours, if you wish it."

Tara was speechless. That her royal Kamarian blood might involve some kind of inheritance had never occurred to her. She hadn't thought beyond the return of the Kamarians to what her role might be now that they were back. Although they were her people, she really didn't see herself as one of them. Maybe in time, she might, but right now... No, she couldn't stay. Besides, she just wasn't ready to settle anywhere permanently, she told herself, though she knew in her soul that wasn't the real issue. To stay would make her vulnerable to rejection. She would have to open her scarred heart to these people, and she wasn't sure she could do that. Her childhood in Wyndover had bled her too much.

"I don't know what to say." She searched for words. "Such a position would be a great honor, but I honestly don't think I'm the best person to fit that role. I'm not a historian or a diplomat. I've always settled disputes with a sword, rather than words. However, I do know of someone who I believe would be a perfect liaison, someone who loves learning above all else." She looked at Brains.

Brains' eyes widened, and he appeared as flabbergasted as she'd felt a moment ago.

She turned back to the king. "As Mistress of Ravnaul's Keep, am I allowed to appoint someone to fill the role in my stead — with your approval, of course?"

King Lazarial's gaze followed hers back to Brains. He quirked a smile at Brains' expression. "Yes, that would most certainly be allowed, if the chosen person is interested?"

Brains could hardly contain his excitement. "I — yes! A most emphatic yes! I would be honored, delighted, excited, thrilled —"

Blackie elbowed him. "I think they get the idea."

A chuckle rippled through the crowd.

The king smiled. "Then it is done. A keystone will be made for you."

Zaniel picked up a heavy velvet sack from behind his throne and set it on the seat. He pulled from it a large, leather-bound book.

"I also wished to give you this," said the king. "I sensed you were a scholar and thought you might have a use for it."

Zaniel handed the heavy book to Brains, who accepted it with reverent thanks. Brains opened it, carefully turning the parchment pages. "It's a book of runes, ancient languages, and translations. This is wonderful!" He sat down on the throne seat behind him, then realized what he was doing and hopped up again with a hasty, "Sorry!"

King Lazarial laughed. "Be my guest." He waved Brains back into the chair. Then he turned to Gralfar. "To you, master dwarf, I offer a proposition. Centuries ago, dwarves and Gaians — earth *Aiykshaav'n* — shared the mountains of this world. They worked side by side, learning from each other, united in their love of the mysteries of earth and stone. But wars and the changing of the world brought separation, and the Gaians withdrew to places known only to other Ancients. What I propose is a healing of that separation, a reunion of the master craft of Ancients and dwarves in the rebuilding of Ravnaul's Keep. Do you think your king would be willing to take on such an endeavor?"

Gralfar's eyes were as round as Brains' had been a moment ago. "For a chance to relearn all the Ancient craft that was lost over the centuries? He'd be a fool not to."

"Will you then take this proposal to him, along with this book of Gaian lore, as a token of our good faith?"

Zaniel lifted another heavy tome from the sack and gave it to Gralfar.

"I most certainly will. Thank you." He lovingly traced his finger over the runes on the cover.

The king faced Diamond Jack. "You, sir, have been eyeing every gem in the room."

Jack's face flamed deep red. "I wouldn't take anything, I promise you!"

The king laughed. "Rest assured, I'm not accusing you of anything. I was simply making an observation. Since you obviously appreciate the beauty of gemstones, we would like to give you these, along with this heirloom from the House of Lazarial, as a well-deserved reward for your bravery."

Zaria had drawn from the sack a small velvet bag nearly overflowing with red, green, and blue gems, and a glittering silver ring set with faceted sunstones and polished moonstones.

Jack stared, and Tara could almost see the gemstones reflecting in his eyes. "For me?" he asked in a hushed voice.

"With our profound thanks." Zaria placed the bag of gems and the ring into his cupped hands.

"Thank you," he breathed, never taking his eyes from the bright stones.

The king eyed Sarita's gold chains and bangles. "And since you obviously also appreciate fine jewelry, we've chosen some for you, as well."

Zaria gave Sarita another small velvet bag of gems and a silver necklace with a pendant of sun- and moonstones set in a swirl of silver metal. Sarita thanked them, and Blackie fastened the chain about her neck.

Tara noted the way Blackie's fingers brushed Sarita's throat and how his hands lingered on her shoulders as she smiled at him. Tara grinned to herself. He was definitely hooked.

"For you," the King said to Whittler, "a new whittling knife and some blocks of wood, so you will have something besides our furniture on which to carve."

Whittler ducked his head in embarrassment.

The king laughed again.

"Truly, he is only teasing you," Zaria said to Whittler as she handed him a sheathed knife with smooth moonstones set into the handle and a leather bag of wood pieces.

"Yes," the king said. "Feel free to carve wherever you like. The patterns you create are exquisite."

Whittler smiled and nodded his thanks as he accepted his gifts. He pulled a piece of ebony-colored wood out of the bag and eagerly examined it, then looked up with a question in his eyes.

"It's from the kaladharra trees that grow here in the mountains," said Zaria. "They have silver leaves and bark, and they thrive in moonlight, rather than sunlight."

With a big smile and another thank you nod, he sat down cross-legged on the dais and began carving with his new knife.

"Now then, that leaves the two of you." King Lazarial eyed Blackie and Whiskey. "We were at a loss as to what we could give you to show our appreciation for your heroic actions. Do you have any suggestions?"

Blackie looked uncomfortable, but Tara could tell by his expression that an idea was forming in the devious side of his mind. "Hmm... well... as a matter of fact, I do. What would you say to giving us exclusive rights to sell the ambrosia we were just drinking to the rest of the world? One bottle of that is worth more than ten kegs of Cierran brandy."

"Ah, a businessman," the king said. "Yes, I believe that would be possible. And you?" The king turned to Whiskey. "Might I guess that your suggestion would have something to do with the ambrosia, as well?"

Whiskey glanced down at the glass in his hand that he'd brought from the banquet table and grinned. "Ha. That'd be a good guess, but there's actually somethin' else I'd rather have."

The other smugglers stared at him in shock.

"Really?" Blackie asked.

"Name it," said the king.

A look of longing crossed Whiskey's face. "That magic boat."

"Ah, yes. The boat was crafted by the Bahaariku — the sea *Ai-ykshaav'n*." The king smiled. "I think we can do even better. We can take you to them and let you choose your own craft."

Whiskey nearly dropped his glass. Eyes shining, he stammered a thank you.

"You are most welcome." The king turned, his gaze sweeping Tara and her friends. "All of you are most welcome."

The Kamarians rose to their feet, the walls ringing with their applause.

Tara felt a tingling joy sift through her. She'd done it. She'd defeated the evil, broken the three-hundred-year-old curse, and brought the Kamarians back to the world. Jovan squeezed her shoulders and smiled at her, love and pride in his eyes.

King Lazarial raised his hands again for quiet. "And now it is time for the ceremony."

The royal family escorted Tara and her friends off the dais. Zaniel now carried a silver metal box, a foot square in size. Tara sensed a shifting of the mood, as if a shroud of sadness had suddenly draped the room.

"What ceremony is he talking about?" she asked Miressa and Dancalan.

"The coronation," Dancalan said. "Zaria will become our new queen."

The royal family led the way through a door at the back of the throne room. Everyone followed. They walked down a hallway lined with sculptured trees so lifelike that the leaves rustled with the wind of their passage, then climbed a tall, spiraling waterfall of stairs out onto a flat tiled roof.

Stars filled the indigo sky. A thick crescent moon rode high, shedding silver light over the black castle's tall spires and sweeping the valley with a glow like moondust. The air was cool, but not uncomfortably so, and smelled of evergreens, late summer flowers, and salt water.

The Kamarians continued to file onto the roof. Tara walked with Jovan to the parapet. She studied the statues that rimmed the wall. Carved from black stone, their arms reached upward toward the sky, eyes focused on the stars. They looked so real, as if the touch of a moonbeam would bring them to life.

Tara brushed her fingers along the cool stone arm of the last statue in the row — a woman with long, wind-tossed hair encircled by a crown of moonstones. She looked young. "Who is she?" Tara asked Miressa, who had come up beside her. "Who are they all?"

"Her name was Zaralyn," Miressa said. "She was a kind and benevolent queen, and the mother of Lazarial and Ravnaul. She died giving birth to Ravnaul. The statue of the man on her left was her consort, King Ravnazil. He died in an accident six months before Ravnaul was born. It was a very sad period in Kamarian history. If they had lived, their children might have turned out so differently." Miressa sighed heavily. "Ah, well. We must look to the future now." She smiled. "And a very bright one I believe it will be, thanks to you." She squeezed Tara's arm. "To answer your other question, the statues are all past kings and queens of Kamar. When they pass from this world and become one with the cosmos, their spirits are released and their bodies captured in stone."

Tara sensed a deepening sadness in Miressa. "King Lazarial?"

Miressa bowed her head. "Yes, child. Now, if you will excuse me, I must go to Dancalan." She slipped into the crowd.

"Kamar is quite a city," Jovan said, looking out between the statues toward the valley.

"It is?" Tara had been so taken with the statues, she hadn't looked beyond them. "Oh."

A maze of stone pathways through gardens flush with blooms surrounded the castle and led down to the lake. Spreading outward beyond the gardens lay an intricate panorama of black stone buildings. Closest to the castle rose a series of beautiful, turreted structures arranged in circular patterns around a half-dozen observatory towers so tall that the massive spyglasses protruding from their domed tops could barely be seen against the night sky. Farther down the valley, both to the east and west, were dwellings and shops, smaller in size, but no less eye-catching, with ornate fenestrations and minarets. Beyond those stood workshops, smithies, granaries, and the like, and Tara saw many barns next to pastures of grazing livestock. Farther still lay cultivated fields — acres of silvery green and gold spreading all the way to the feet of the surrounding mountains.

It's all so lovely and peaceful, Tara thought, drinking in the sweet smells and the welcoming warmth radiating from the Kamarians. Maybe she wouldn't mind spending a bit of time here after all, once she'd taken care of a few things, like returning the red griffin ring to the dwarves and making sure Laraina was all right. Had her sister married Kaden and become queen of Dhanarra, or had she left and set out on her own somewhere? Tara itched to use Valina's mirror.

Speaking of Valina, Tara also wanted to find out what had happened to Valina's brother, Validar. No one had mentioned finding his body among the rubble of Ravnaul's Keep, and she hadn't thought to ask. Had Ravnaul killed the wizard when he took back his bloodstone? The last time she'd seen Validar, when Ravnaul had escaped his dungeon prison, she couldn't tell if the wizard was alive or dead. Her thoughts darkened. She hoped he was dead, after all the trouble he'd caused, though his death wouldn't begin to make up for the deaths of those she'd lost...

A breeze riffled the liquid silver of the moon-painted lake, and a twist of sorrow brought tears to Tara's eyes as she thought of the dragon who would guard Echoing Falls no more. It had given its life for her, just as Natiere had, and she mourned its loss.

The royal family climbed the few stairs to a raised platform in the center of the roof. The rest of the Kamarians spread out around them in a great circle. Tara stood with Jovan near the roof's edge as their friends gathered close. Her gaze drifted over the Kamarians, their auras vibrant but pensive, their minds brushing hers in silent, unobtrusive invitation to join their emotional collective. She hesitated, still wary. She found it difficult to grasp that these people — her people, she reminded herself — really wanted her to be a part of their community. Then she remembered Jovan's words: *Choose with your heart and not your head.* Dare she trust this new family? Tentatively, she opened her mind and shared their mingling of sadness and joy. They received her like a long-lost friend.

King Lazarial raised his arms, and the crowd grew quiet. "It is time. Zaniel, the crown, please."

Zaniel set the box on a waist-high pedestal of black marble. Then he opened the lid and carefully lifted free a silver crown encrusted with moonstones. Zaria removed her smaller crown and placed it in the box. She stepped forward and stood before her father.

The ghost king smiled sadly. "My daughter, I wish I could place the crown on your head with my own hands, but alas, I cannot. Zaniel must be my hands." He turned to his son.

Smiling, Zaniel set the silver crown on his sister's head and stepped back. A small smile graced her lips in return.

"We must ask for the blessing of the moon and the gods," King Lazarial said.

He and all the other Kamarians lifted their hands to the sky, mirroring the pose of the statues. Tara and her friends did the same.

A stream of light poured down from the moon and enveloped Zaria in silver radiance. The moonstones embedded in her new crown shone as brightly as the stars for a few heartbeats, before dimming with the fading moonglow to a soft glimmer.

The Kamarians bowed their heads in gratitude for the blessing bestowed.

"Behold — Zaria, your new queen." The king's voice was gruff with pride.

Zaria smiled as everyone bowed low, then cheered and applauded. "Thank you all for having faith in me," she said, when quiet had been restored. "I will do my best to be worthy of your trust." Eyes bright with sudden tears, she faced her father. She took a deep breath. "And now, it is my sad duty to preside over the release of your spirit." A tear trickled down her cheek.

Beside her, Zaniel wiped his eyes with the back of his hand.

"If I could have one wish granted to me, it would be for one last touch — a hug before you leave us." Zaria's voice cracked, and she cleared her throat. "But since that's not possible, I will do what I must and release you from this world." Her voice dropped to a whisper. "Goodbye, Father."

"Goodbye," Zaniel echoed. He put his arm around his sister, their tears falling freely.

Tears slid down Tara's face as the outpouring of grief surging through the Kamarians' mental connection overwhelmed her. Jovan drew her back against him and held her close.

"My children," King Lazarial said brokenly. He reached toward them with nebulous arms, his shadowy fingers unable to touch them.

Moonglow engulfed him, and his body solidified. He stood as he once had, centuries ago, alive.

Zaniel cried out in surprise.

"Father!" Zaria squealed.

They rushed forward, and the three hugged each other as if they would never let go. Then the king's body began to shimmer, losing substance again. Zaniel and Zaria stepped back. King Lazarial's ghostly form dissolved into sparkling lights that drifted upward to join the stars.

"Goodbye, Father," brother and sister both whispered, eyes lost in the night sky. Then they turned toward the parapet.

Tara heard stifled curses from Blackie as a stone figure materialized next to them, beside the statue of Zaralyn. A perfect likeness of King Lazarial reached toward the stars.

A huge splash and an echoing roar filled the night, and Tara whipped around in time to see the massive head and long body of a dragon, its silver-green scales reflecting the moonlight, before it dove beneath the surface of the lake.

Joy sang through her. She gripped the parapet. *Dragon, you survived!*

Yes, Daughter of Kamar. The sea dragon burst from the water again and let out another ear-shattering roar.

Blackie elbowed Whiskey. "I bet you never thought you'd be glad to see that."

Whiskey grinned and saluted the dragon with his ambrosia glass.

Zaniel and Zaria stepped down from the platform. The Kamarians swept back to form a path to the parapet. The new queen and her brother crossed the roof and stopped before the statue of their father. Laying their hands on the stone figure, they closed their eyes and stood with bowed heads in a moment of silence.

Then Zaria turned to Tara. "We all go to our rest now, and in the morning, begin anew." She spread her arms wide, encompassing Tara's friends. "We welcome you all to stay with us for as long as you like."

With weary smiles, she and Zaniel made their way back across the roof and descended the waterfall staircase. The Kamarians ushered Tara and the others in front of them as they followed the royal family down the stairs.

CHAPTER 39

The next morning, Tara paced the grand entry hall, waiting for Zaria to finish meeting with Dancalan so she could take her leave. Jovan and Gralfar stood nearby, discussing in low tones what they would say to the dwarven king when they returned the red griffin ring. Tara knew Jovan dreaded going back to Aldontris. He hadn't slept well, and he'd been tense since rising. She couldn't blame him, after what the dwarves had done to him. Gralfar seemed nervous, too. Tara, however, couldn't wait to get there. She wanted to see the look on King Drordin's face when they proved him wrong: there was honor in humans — some of them, anyway. And returning the ring should square any debt the dwarves felt Jovan still owed them. If they could just get on with it.

The plan was for Valina to bring Tara, Jovan, and Gralfar to Estiarii Faelle, where they would join Zaniel, who would accompany them to the dwarven kingdom to deliver King Lazarial's proposal for the rebuilding of Ravnaul's Keep. The sorceress would transport the four of them to Aldontris, or wherever the dwarven king was at that time.

Not before I look in Valina's mirror, though, Tara thought. She needed to see her sister's face and know that Laraina was all right.

If all went well with the dwarves, Gralfar would begin coordinating the rebuilding project, Zaniel would go back to Estiarii Faelle, and Tara and Jovan would be transported to Laraina's location. Depending on the situation there, she and Jovan would stay for however long they were needed and then return to Kamar. Tara, with Jovan's encouragement, had chosen to give her new family a chance and stay with them for a while.

The smugglers had promised to remain in Kamar until she and Jovan returned. She didn't want them leaving without having time for a proper goodbye. She also wanted to see Brains established as the liaison, and she was looking forward to a ride in Whiskey's new boat.

The smugglers had offered to accompany her to Aldontris as bodyguards, but she didn't think it would be necessary. Valina could whisk them away if there was trouble.

Footsteps interrupted Tara's thoughts as Zaria entered the hall, two attendants following at a distance.

"I'm sorry you had to wait for me," Zaria said. "There's so much to do."

Tara swallowed her impatience and smiled. "You have no need to apologize to us. Is everything ready?"

"Yes. Please tell King Drordin that we have contacted the Gaians. They have agreed to find Gralfar," she nodded to the dwarf, "and reestablish their friendship with the dwarven kingdom. From there, plans can be made for the rebuilding of Ravnaul's Keep."

"We'll tell them," Tara said.

Zaria hesitated. "You will come back, won't you, after visiting your sister?"

Tara was surprised by the touch of anxiety in Zaria's voice. "Yes. For a little while, anyway."

Zaria seemed relieved. "I know you said you would, but I wanted to be sure. Sir Alstyn said you had many stories. I'd really like to hear them. I know I could learn much from you."

"Sir Alstyn?" Gralfar mouthed to Jovan.

"Brains," Jovan whispered back.

Tara laughed. "I'm not sure that what I could teach you would be appropriate for a proper lady queen."

Zaria smiled, a mischievous glint in her eye. "Good. I look forward to it." She hugged Tara and nodded to the others. "Safe journey, my friends." She backed away.

"Thank you." Tara moved close to Jovan and Gralfar and closed her eyes. *Valina?*

Yes, Tara. Are you ready?

We are. Tara found herself holding her breath, even though she knew this transport should go smoothly.

Jovan caught her hand and squeezed it. She heard Gralfar muttering as the white clouds rose up around them and whisked them away from Castle Kamar.

Moments later, they arrived in the observatory at Estiarii Faelle. Valina embraced Tara, who smiled as she noted that the sorceress was wearing Zaniel's glowing lifestone around her neck once more. Zaniel shook hands with Jovan and Gralfar.

Valina laughed and hugged Tara again. "Thank you," she whispered in Tara's ear. "Thank you so much."

"You're welcome," Tara said softly. "I'm so glad for you."

The sorceress stepped back. "Come. The mirror awaits."

She led them to the tall, strangely shaped mirror and pulled off its velvet covering, draping the folds over the end of a nearby spyglass. The morning sky, as reflected in Mirror Lake, filled the mirror's image. "Now, show me who you wish to see."

Tara concentrated on her sister, picturing Laraina as she'd last seen her on the day Tara and Jovan had left Castle Carilon.

Valina closed her eyes for a moment, then looked at the mirror and whispered words of magic. The mirrored sky shifted. The image blurred, resolving into a familiar hall of white stone. Two people were walking down the hall — a tall man with brown hair and a king's cloak, and a red-haired woman in a regal green dress. Both wore crowns. Behind them trailed several guards, attendants, and ladies-in-waiting.

Tara recognized the hall leading to the royal breakfast chamber in Castle Carilon. She realized she was holding her breath again and let it out slowly. Her sister was safe, thank the gods. Laraina was still with Prince — or rather, King — Kaden. Tara wasn't sure how she felt about that. Though she'd known her sister loved Kaden, she'd half hoped Laraina would leave him behind. But she had married him after all. Disappointment threaded through Tara at the thought. She'd missed the wedding. She wished she could have been there to give support to her sister. She knew Laraina had wanted her there. Apparently, her sister had chosen not to wait until Tara's return.

Tara frowned. She felt happy for Laraina, but unhappy at the same time. She didn't relish the idea of dealing with Kaden whenever she visited her sister.

Laraina, Kaden, and their entourage entered the breakfast room.

Tara gasped and took an involuntary step backward as she caught a clear view of her sister's profile. Laraina was carefully leaving room for her slightly bulging belly as she sat down at the table. Now Tara knew why her sister hadn't waited. Laraina was with child. The image of Laraina with a baby at her hip, rather than a sword, was as alien to Tara as seeing antlers on a cat. Her mind just wouldn't accept it.

Valina touched Tara's arm. "Your sister is beautiful. I'm sure her child will be, as well."

"Yes... thank you..." Tara stumbled over her words, overwhelmed by a sense of loss. The life she and her sister had shared as swords-for-hire was now irrevocably in the past. She'd known when she left Carilon that their joint adventures were over, but she realized now she'd still been keeping a tiny candle of hope lit — that Laraina's relationship with Kaden would go sour, or that her sister would decide she'd rather go back to the way things were. That hope had been snuffed out, and Tara felt as though she'd been cast adrift.

Jovan's hands closed over her shoulders. She pressed her back against his chest and realized how accustomed she'd become to leaning on his strength. She may have lost Laraina as a companion, but she'd found so much more. Jovan would always be there for her, his love bearing her up when she teetered on the edge. And she had others who cared about her, a new family who wanted her. Memories of the Kamarians' friendly, welcoming smiles warmed her, like a cozy fire on a cold night, and a revelation startled her. Did *she* really want to go back to her old life?

"Is there more you wish to see?" Valina asked gently.

Tara shook her head. She needed time to think, to sort out her emotions, but there were other things that needed to be finished. "No. Let's find the dwarven king."

The sorceress looked back at the mirror, whispering the spell again. The image of the king and queen of Dhanarra at breakfast faded, and the morning sky returned. The mirrored sky shifted again, then blurred to reveal a vast underground chamber that Tara didn't recognize. Statues of armored dwarves, weapons raised in the heat of battle, lined a wide walkway of polished green and white stone, which led to a dais with a solid gold throne that looked like a giant fist. Thousands of amber earth stones lit the room.

King Drordin, scepter in hand, sat on the fisted throne with a bored expression. He was listening to three dwarves who were talking and gesturing toward the back of the chamber, where another group of dwarves impatiently waited to have their say. Two dozen dwarven guards monitored the proceedings — two at the dais, five with the speaking dwarves, and five more with the group at the back, their bare weapons deterring the group from pressing forward. The other twelve stood at attention along the walkway.

"Where is this?" Tara asked.

"The throne room in Ilgresta, the dwarven capital," Gralfar said, his longing for home spilling into his voice.

"It's beautiful." Tara's gaze traveled over the walls and vaulted ceiling, alive with jeweled carvings and sculpted scenes depicting centuries of dwarven history. The artistry was reminiscent of the interior of Castle Kamar.

"Yes, it is," Gralfar acknowledged with pride. "According to dwarven legend, the halls of Ilgresta were created a millennium ago in the glorious days of the Dwarven-Gaian Alliance, when dwarves and Ancients worked together and shared the mountains in peace. The Gaians lived in the hidden city of Ganaeyal, somewhere in the Cyranel Mountains. The Gaians always found the dwarves when communication was necessary. The dwarves never found them. Only Ancients seem to be able to find other Ancients."

Tara dragged her gaze back to the dwarven king. "Well, since we hope to enlist the aid of your fellow dwarves in rebuilding Ravnaul's Keep, where in Ilgresta should we appear, so as to cause the least offense?"

"Let's try the back of the throne room, between that group of dwarves waiting to be heard and the door," Gralfar said. "Now is a good time, since the room is fairly empty, and I don't see Sauldron. I think he would be the biggest obstacle to our success." He pulled out his book of Ancient lore, his hands caressing the cover.

Tara turned to Jovan, taut as a bowstring beside her. She curled her fingers around his and squeezed them. "Agreed?"

Jovan touched the pocket where he kept the ring, as if to reassure himself it was there, and nodded.

"Whatever Gralfar thinks best," Zaniel said.

"I guess we're ready," Tara said to Valina.

"I will be watching," Valina said.

Tara forced herself to breathe normally as the fog swallowed them once again. She pictured the throne room — twenty-four armed guards, with likely more close by. She almost wished she'd had the smugglers come with them. She no longer had the power of the black sword to fall back on, and greater numbers would be safer if things got ugly. But she hadn't wanted to appear threatening, and she knew Valina would be able to pull them out if need be.

After a slight lurch of displacement, they landed on solid stone. She heard gruff cries and running feet as the white fog melted away. She resisted the urge to draw her sword.

The dozen guards that had been edging the walkway now surrounded them in a loose circle, out of sword range, axes battle ready.

Tara and Jovan held their hands up in front of them, signaling peaceful intent. Zaniel stood silently between them and Gralfar, who was clutching the book of Ancient lore.

Tara faced King Drordin. He sat forward on his throne and scowled at the intruders. The two guards by the dais now blocked the stairs leading up to it. Every dwarf in the chamber regarded Tara's group with surprise and anger.

"We've come to return the ring, as we promised," Tara called out, her voice echoing in the cavernous room.

Jovan produced the ring and held it up for all to see.

"But we will wait our turn for an audience." She gestured toward the group of dwarves ahead of them.

"Your turn is now," King Drordin said sharply. He addressed the guards. "Bring them forward."

The dwarves who had been arguing before the king were herded to the side, much to their displeasure. The contingent of guards escorted Tara and the others to the front of the room.

The king's eyes widened as they approached. He stared at the silver-haired man in their midst. "Who is this you bring with you?" he demanded as they halted before the dais.

"This is Zaniel, Prince of Kamar," Tara said. "The sky *Aiykshaav'n* have returned to the Black Mountains. We broke the curse and set them free."

"Lord King." Zaniel bowed. "It is my honor to meet you."

Never taking his eyes from Zaniel, King Drordin rose slowly and stepped down from the dais. Flanked by his two guards, he stopped before the Kamarian and looked into Zaniel's silver eyes. "By the gods of the earth," the king said softly, his tone of heated anger gone. He took a step back and inclined his head. "You must forgive my skepticism. I never thought I would see, in my lifetime, a true Ancient."

"No offense taken," Zaniel said. "I wish to thank the dwarves for their help in Tara's quest. She said Gralfar was instrumental in leading her and her friends through the tunnels of the Black Mountains. Without his help, they would not have succeeded, and I would not be standing here before you. As a gift to the dwarven kingdom, I would like to present this book of earth *Aiykshaav'n* lore to you and all who dwell here." He glanced about the room, including all he saw — guards, complainants, and those who were now crowding into the archways leading into the throne room, some curious, some indignant, some angry.

Tara watched the growing crowd apprehensively. Niggling chills iced down her spine. *Jovan...*

Yes, Love?

Danger approaches, but I don't know from where. Too many unfriendly auras.

Jovan moved closer to her and scanned the crowd.

Gralfar reverently handed the tome to his king, who accepted it with undisguised eagerness. He seemed to have completely forgotten about the red griffin ring Jovan still held in his hand.

King Drordin opened the book and carefully looked through the first few pages, his attention snatched by the ancient text. After a few moments, he came to himself and remembered his visitors. "You must forgive me once again, Lord Prince. Thank you for your generous and wondrous gift. I have long dreamed of a day when dwarves and Gaians would work side by side as they did long ago. Over the centuries, so much knowledge has been lost. Our artisans are skilled, but they cannot match the exquisite artistry of the Ancients." He swept his arm toward the walls and ceiling.

"I agree that Gaian artistry is unmatched," Zaniel said, "but the dwarves create their own unique style of beauty."

King Drordin nodded his thanks at the compliment.

"This brings me to my other reason for seeking an audience with you," Zaniel continued. "Ravnaul's Keep, the fortress at the entrance to our realm in the Black Mountains, was destroyed, partly in the Cataclysm, and partly in the battle that just took place, in which Tara defeated our enemies. I present you with this proposal: in return for our help in restoring the alliance between the dwarves and earth *Aiykshaav'n*, would you be willing to help rebuild Ravnaul's Keep to its former state?"

"You could do this? You could find the earth Ancients who've been gone from these mountains for hundreds of years?" King Drordin was struggling to keep the disbelief off his face.

Zaniel smiled. "The Gaians never left the Cyranel Mountains. They've only hidden their realm with their earth magic. We have already communicated with them to reestablish our friendship and to offer our proposal to them. They've agreed to come here and seek out Gralfar as a liaison, and renew their old alliance with the dwarves by restoring the Keep. Gralfar would coordinate and oversee the project. Does this seem reasonable to you?" His eyes swept the room again. "You may, of course, take as much time as you need to discuss the proposal with your people."

Fingering the hilt of her sword, Tara kept her eyes roving, watching the swiftly growing mob of dwarves as they spilled into the room. Word of the arrival of one of the dwarves' most hated enemies had swept over the city like an avalanche, rushing all its denizens to the throne room and filling the chamber with cold fury.

Zaniel's proposal, however, had temporarily distracted them from Jovan's presence and cooled their initial rage. Tara noted that the dwarven guards surrounding her group and the other dwarves closest to them, who had heard the proposal firsthand, no longer bristled with hostility.

Anger and hatred still flowed toward her, though, pushing through the crowd from somewhere behind them. Tara was fairly certain she knew who was causing it. Would the guards protect them, or would they be loath to interfere with a vendetta from one of their own?

It's Sauldron, isn't it, she sent to Jovan, more a statement than a question.

Most likely. Jovan shifted, so he could see behind him. *Stay clear of me when he appears. I don't want him attacking you —*

Don't even bother to say it.

King Drordin closed the book of earth Ancient lore and tipped his head toward Zaniel. "I can give you an answer now." He turned and strode up the stairs onto the dais and stood before his throne. The whisperings and mutterings of the crowd ceased. "How many dwarves here would like to reforge our alliance with the Gaians?" he shouted, his gruff voice carrying to the far corners of the room.

An instant of surprised silence hung like a held breath in the air, then thunderous approval roared through the chamber.

The king lifted his scepter. After a few moments, the noise died down. "Are there any who would oppose?"

Not a sound touched the room.

The dwarven king looked at Zaniel. "There, Lord Prince, is your answer."

"Fire and earth stones, will you get out of my way!" The furious voice stabbed the air from the back of the chamber.

All heads turned, searching for the source of the disruption.

Icy shivers of warning raised goose bumps on Tara's skin. She gripped the hilt of her sword, fighting the urge to draw it. Jovan stood tensely beside her. Gralfar cursed under his breath.

Zaniel turned questioningly to Tara. *What is happening?*

An old enemy of Jovan's approaches. Sauldron hates him and wants him dead.

Sauldron burst through the crowd into the small open space between the crush of dwarven citizens and the guards surrounding Tara and the others. Sweat dripped down over the scar above his eye, and he was breathing as if he'd run a great distance.

"You!" Sauldron jabbed his finger at Jovan. "I knew you were here. I could feel it. How dare you defile our mountain again —"

"Sauldron!" King Drordin barked, halting the other's tirade.

"My king," Sauldron growled. He pointed at Jovan again. "Why is he still alive?"

"It is not for you to say whether he lives or dies," the king snapped. "He has brought back the stolen ring." The king set the tome of the earth Ancients on the throne seat, then held out his hand, addressing one of the guards. "Mynan, bring it here."

The guard nearest Jovan extended his hand, and Jovan wordlessly dropped the ring onto his palm. Mynan carried the ring to the dais and gave it to his king.

King Drordin examined the gold setting with its red jewel in the shape of a griffin. Then he looked at Tara and Jovan. "I have misjudged you both." His voice carried clearly throughout the room. "You have proved that you are not like your brother, and that a sellsword can act with honor. Not only have you brought back our heirloom, but you've provided the means to restore so much of what was lost to us when the Gaians withdrew to their hidden realm. We thank you and will welcome your presence from this moment forward."

A freezing chill speared down Tara's spine. She saw the flash of a dagger as Sauldron whipped it from his belt.

"No! I will see him dead first!" Sauldron leaped forward, knocked aside the intervening guard, and lunged at Jovan.

Sword drawn, Tara moved at the same time. Shoving Jovan out of the way, she slid between him and Sauldron, her blade angled to deflect Sauldron's knife thrust.

A step before he reached her, thick fog swallowed him and then vanished, taking him with it.

Tara blinked in surprise, then relaxed and sheathed her sword. She'd forgotten Valina was watching.

Tara, are you all right? the sorceress asked anxiously.

Yes, thank you. What did you do with him?

I deposited him in a distant tunnel, north of the city. It should take him a couple of hours to find his way back.

Jovan, Zaniel, and Gralfar surrounded Tara protectively. She knew that Jovan was angry with her, but she'd had to step in. He couldn't have reacted as quickly as she had.

"What happened? Is anyone hurt? Where is Sauldron?" King Drordin demanded.

"No one is hurt," Tara answered. "The sorceress, Valina Mellarian, feared for our safety and transported him to a tunnel somewhere north of the city. He has not been harmed in any way."

"She also apologizes for removing one of your dwarves without your permission," Zaniel added, "but, as Tara said, she feared for the safety of our group."

"Apology accepted," the king said slowly, and Tara could see he was still thinking over what had just happened. "How did she know? Does she have some magical eye that allows her to see things beyond where she is?"

"She has not an eye, but a mirror, with which she can see if she chooses," Tara said. "She uses it for good. There is not an evil bone in her body."

"I see," the king said. He obviously didn't like the idea, but was apparently reserving judgment for the moment. "I must apologize, as well, for Sauldron's behavior. Dwarves have long memories and do not easily forgive. Mynan, take some of the northern guards and go find him. Let him cool his anger in a holding cell for now."

Mynan bowed his head and left through the parting crowd.

Gasps arose, and a hush descended on the opposite side of the room.

"What new intrusion is this?" the king asked with a scowl.

The dwarven crowd split again as three tall figures approached the dais.

Broad-shouldered and muscular, the newcomers, two male and one female, had long, greenish-brown hair, pale brown skin, and brown leather clothing trimmed with gold and fur. But it was their eyes, black as coal, that held Tara's attention — so much like Natiere's.

Zaniel smiled and welcomed them with outstretched hands and words spoken in a rough-edged language Tara had never heard. They responded in kind, their voices deep and gravelly.

"By the gods of the earth," the dwarven king said in an awed voice. "The Gaians have returned."

CHAPTER 40

"Well, I'm glad that's settled," Tara said, as she, Jovan, and Zaniel stepped free of the dissipating fog into Valina's observatory. "I thought it went well, mostly."

"Yes," Zaniel agreed. He embraced Valina and kissed her, held her close for a lingering moment.

"The Gaians and the dwarves are renewing their friendship, and they've both agreed to help us rebuild Ravnaul's Keep," Zaniel told Valina. "Gralfar said they would collect the necessary tools and equipment and be ready to start their journey to the Black Mountains in a few days."

"That's wonderful." Valina glanced out the window to the west, where the orange sun hung low over the horizon, setting fire to the thin clouds that draped the mountaintops. "It's so late in the day." She turned to Tara. "Do you wish to go to your sister now, or wait until morning?"

"I'd like to wait, if you don't mind our staying here for the night," Tara said. She needed time to work through the tumult of emotions surrounding her sister, and she wanted Jovan to have time to relax. She brushed her arm against his as he stood grimly beside her, felt his answering pressure. He'd been tense and silent all day. She'd sensed his uneasiness like prickles on her skin. It was as if he'd thought the dwarves might change their minds at any moment and try to throw him back into the Pit. There'd been no problems, though. After the incident with Sauldron, all had gone smoothly.

"Of course you may stay," Valina said. "The rooms you had the last time you were here are ready, if you'd like to refresh yourselves. I'll go prepare us a grand supper to celebrate the day's success."

"Before you go," Tara said, "and while we're near your mirror, there's one other thing I need to ask about."

Sadness crept across Valina's face. "You want to know about my brother."

"I'm sorry. I don't mean to cause you pain, but... yes. Do you know where he is? Is he alive? The last time I saw him, I couldn't tell."

Valina took a deep breath, and Zaniel squeezed her hand.

"I believe he's still alive," Valina said. "I don't feel the emptiness in my heart I know I would feel if he were dead. But as to where he is..." She lifted her hand helplessly. "I don't know." She walked back to the mirror, the others following. "I've looked for him. Zaniel said he was not found among the rubble. I thought when Ravnaul's bloodstone was destroyed, Validar would die, too, since he had somehow tapped into its power." She spoke the words to activate the mirror. "But this is what happens when I search for him."

The sunset sky in the mirror shifted, the reflected clouds circling far around in the mirrored sky. The image blurred, then went completely black.

"You see? There's just... nothing." Valina shrugged in perplexity. "I don't know what it means."

Tara frowned. "It's almost like when Gorgrast interfered when we were looking for Jovan."

"But the image was clouded then, not just blank," Valina said. "And in the past, when his strength was at its peak, my brother would prevent me from seeing where he was by cloaking himself and his surroundings with a swirling red mist."

"Could he be underground or in a cave?" Jovan asked.

"Or maybe he was buried by rocks during the explosion of Ravnaul's Keep," Tara said.

Valina shook her head. "He's not anywhere near Ravnaul's Keep. The sun's position in the mirror is wrong for that." She stepped to the window and looked down at the sunset sky reflected on the surface of Mirror Lake, far below. The others joined her. "The setting sun you see on the lake is in the same position as what you saw in the mirror. It indicates a location far to the northeast. Underground might be a possibility, or a deep cave, as you said." She nodded to Jovan. "I know he had the ability to work the transport magic, though he used a different method. All I can think is that he must have found the strength to transport himself somewhere and then collapsed."

Tara went back to the mirror and studied the empty black glass. A faint tinge of orange like the flicker of firelight caught her eye, and she suddenly sensed heat, as though a roaring flame burned nearby. Then the mirror went black and cold again. She glanced about. No fires warmed the observatory.

"What is it?" Valina asked. "Did you see something?"

Tara nodded. "For a moment, I saw an orange cast to the black, and I felt a burst of intense heat. But it's gone now."

"If Validar is underground, as Jovan suggested, perhaps he is deep enough to have found molten rock — a lava flow — somewhere," Zaniel said. "I can ask the Gaians if they know of such a place."

"Eastern legends say he had a stronghold in Gor Mountain in the Barren Mountain range in the Northlands," Jovan said, "but I don't recall ever hearing of a volcano there — only near the southern seas."

"I will ask about Gor Mountain as well," Zaniel said.

"What will happen to him if he's found?" Valina asked hesitantly.

For what he did to Laraina and Jovan and what he tried to do to me, I'd kill him, Tara thought to herself. Out loud, she said, "I'm not exactly sure. He should be tried for his crimes, by either men or Kamarians, or both, but I doubt there's a lockup anywhere that could hold him. I'm sorry to say it," she added gently, "but I fear he will be a danger to everyone as long as he's alive."

Valina turned away, eyes glistening with tears. "Yes. I fear the same." She sighed, her shoulders sagging with the weight of her grief. Zaniel slipped his arm around her. "We will do our best to find him in the coming days." She summoned a smile. "But enough of such thoughts for now. I refuse to let them dampen today's success." She took Zaniel's hand. "We have a meal to prepare. Come down to the dining hall when you're ready."

"Thank you. We'll be down shortly," Tara said.

As Valina and Zaniel headed for the kitchen, Tara and Jovan hurried to their rooms to freshen up.

*****

The meal of roast pheasant had been delicious, and as Tara filled her stomach, she'd felt a pleasant tiredness settle into her bones as some of the tension from the past two days dissipated. But now, as she sat in her room in her night shirt, brushing out her damp hair before a plain oval mirror, her jitters were crawling over her again like ants swarming an oat cake. Tomorrow, she would go back to Castle Carilon to visit her sister and Kaden. She couldn't get the image of her sister's bulging belly out of her mind. Her sister — a mother. Why was that so hard for her to imagine? Because she'd always lived for the moment, Tara realized, and never for the future. She and Laraina were swords-for-hire — that was who and what they were, what she thought they'd always be — and sell-swords generally didn't live long enough to have a future. That had never bothered Tara before. She'd just accepted it and moved on to the next job. As long as each day brought a new adventure, she didn't care.

But now... Her hand on the hairbrush slowed in its downward motion as she stared at herself in the mirror — really looked at herself, for the first time in a long time. She was surprised at how much she'd aged over the past few months. Care lines wrinkled the corners of her eyes and mouth, even though she was barely past twenty-five summers, and her silver-blue eyes had a haunted look in their depths that hadn't been there before. Gone was the arrogance and carelessness of youth. Caution framed her thoughts now, whereas before, she would have barged in heedlessly. She'd never thought that adventurous life would end.

Just because Laraina no longer wants to be a soldier of fortune, it doesn't mean I have to change, Tara thought to herself. She and Jovan could go to the Twin Cities, find some jobs, live by the sword again... but after all she'd been through, that life wasn't nearly as tempting. So what then — babies and motherhood for her too? What a frightening thought. She ran from that idea like a person fleeing a burning house. It wasn't that she didn't like children, though her experiences with them as a child growing up were all bad. She just couldn't imagine being tied down that way, being responsible for such a tiny, helpless bundle of life.

But what if Jovan wanted children? She'd never thought about it before. What did he want? She realized with chagrin that she had no idea. Gods, how selfish she was. He'd saved her life more times than she could count. He'd stayed with her through it all, even through his own horror and pain. He'd loved her through everything. And she'd been so focused on herself and her quest that she'd never considered his or anyone else's needs.

Jovan stepped into the chamber, shirtless, a towel wrapped around the lower half of his body. She set the brush down and rose to meet him.

"What troubles you so?" he asked softly, eyes dark with concern.

She slipped her arms around his neck and pressed against him. "Everything."

He held her close, one hand caressing her hair. He kissed her forehead. "Your sister?"

"Yes, but it's more than that," she murmured against his chest.

"What else?"

She eased back. "You. Me. The way I've been treating you."

A trace of confusion flickered through his expression. "What do you mean?"

"I mean I've never asked you what *you* wanted."

"What I wanted? For what?"

"For the future. Laraina wanted a family, a stable life. She'll have that now. I always thought I'd be what I was, but now I don't know anymore. And I realized I don't know what you want. I never thought to ask. What if you want a settled life, too? A home with children, or I don't know — a farm or a business or something. Or what if we don't want the same things or what if I can't give you what you want? Will you feel you need to move on —"

He kissed her, pulling her close again, stroking her back, arousing the flames inside her until they consumed her frantic thoughts.

"Mmmmmmmmm," she murmured. "How do you do that?"

"Do what?" His lips drifted down to her neck.

"You kiss me like that, and nothing matters anymore."

"I love you, and all that matters is that we're together."

She nuzzled his ear. "Truly?"

He raised his head, his eyes catching hers. "What did I say you should never do?"

"Doubt you."

"Do you?"

"No. I love you. And I want you. Right now."

He smiled. "I'm all yours."

His lips closed over hers.

*****

The next morning found them standing again before the scrimoire with Valina and Zaniel. In the mirror, Laraina and Kaden and their entourage had just entered the breakfast chamber of Castle Carilon. Two straight-backed guards stood by the door.

"Do you want me to transport you to that room?" Valina asked.

"No, I think I'd rather enter the city the normal way," Tara said. "If you could land us here, we'll walk in through the gates." She thought of a field, sheltered by low hills, about two miles north of the city.

"As you wish." Valina embraced Tara. "Just let me know when you're ready to come back."

"Thank you. I will." Tara clasped Jovan's hand. "Ready?"

He nodded. "Whenever you are."

The four said their goodbyes, and a few moments later, Tara and Jovan found themselves in a recently mown hayfield, the stubble stiff beneath their boots. The smell of cut grass lingered in the fresh morning air.

Tara looked around and saw no one. They'd arrived unobserved, as she had hoped. The last thing she wanted was to revive talk of witches and strange magic, and have the people turn against Laraina because they feared Tara. When Tara had been in Carilon, after the retaking of the castle from the Sulledorns, the people had treated her with cautious respect. They honored her part in the war with General Caldren — she'd saved their king's life more than once — but they still weren't entirely comfortable in her presence.

Jovan squeezed her hand. "Shall we go?"

Tara nodded, and they strode across the field. As much as she wanted to see her sister, she couldn't escape the tiny slivers of dread pricking her heart. How much would Laraina's crown and impending motherhood have changed her? Would there be anything left of the sister who'd been Tara's constant companion through the years, or would Laraina be a total stranger?

Jovan raised Tara's hand to his lips. "Stop worrying. It'll be fine."

Tara sighed. She'd rather face a gang of cutthroats than have to figure out relationships.

They crossed another meadow, then paralleled a dusty road wide enough for three wagons abreast, keeping a comfortable distance between themselves and the increasing number of horse-drawn carts and foot traffic heading for Carilon. Before long, they reached the city gates. No one spoke to them as they entered the white stone city, but Tara saw startled recognition on the faces of the gate guards and wondered how quickly word of their arrival would travel.

Quite quickly, it appeared. Tara had to smile when, before they were a third of the way through the city, two mounted soldiers in royal livery found them, saluted respectfully, and gave them rides to the castle. They were shown to a small but elegantly furnished parlor just inside the castle proper.

"Tara!" Laraina cried as they stepped through the parlor door. She swept her sister into a bear hug and wouldn't let go. "I've been so worried about you."

Tara hugged her awkwardly, all too aware of Laraina's altered figure.

Laraina stepped back for a moment and caught Tara's glance at her belly. Laraina put her hands on her hips. "Sister, it's me. Just because I'm with child, doesn't mean I'll break. I want a proper hug."

Tara laughed and embraced her again. "Sorry. It's just hard to get used to. I missed you, sister."

They held each other for a long moment, then stepped back, smiling.

Laraina hugged Jovan. "It's so good to see you both again. It feels like it's been an age."

Tara glanced around, noticing that other than a young, dark-haired handmaiden, the room was empty. She wondered where Kaden was, though she felt glad for his absence.

"You are well?" Laraina asked. "You look well." She studied their faces and sobered a bit. "Though I can see your paths have not been easy." She embraced Tara once more. "But at least you're alive. I prayed to the gods every day for your safe return."

"Thank you, sister. We needed all the help we could get."

Laraina led them to a comfortable sofa. "You must tell me everything." She sat on a matching sofa across from them. "Ramilla, fetch us some cider and some cheese and oat bread, will you please? And maybe some oat cakes and honey and some of those pickled cucumbers."

"Yes, Milady." The girl curtsied and left the room.

"I can't believe I'm hungry again," Laraina said. "I eat all the time, now. The only time I'm not eating is when I'm throwing up."

Tara grimaced. "That... sounds... very unpleasant."

Laraina laughed. "Yes, I suppose it does. It's really not that bad. My stomach is still queasy in the mornings, but it's getting better. I'm sorry Kaden couldn't be here to see you, but he's meeting with some ambassadors from Barony. They just brought in this beautiful herd of three dozen horses. Kaden is looking for some more breeding stock and hopes to broker a deal —" Laraina stopped. "Listen to me chattering away, when it's your story I want to hear."

There was a soft knock at the door, and Ramilla entered. When the girl had spread the food and drink out on a low table between the sofas, Laraina thanked her and sent her away.

"Now," Laraina said, as she forked honey-drenched oat cakes and pickled cucumbers onto a plate, then sat back with the plate in her lap, "I want you to begin from the moment you left Carilon, and don't stop until the moment you reached the city gates just now."

Tara and Jovan glanced at each other with raised eyebrows.

"Be my guest," Jovan said to Tara.

Tara poured two glasses of cider and handed one to Jovan. She took a deep swallow. "This is going to take a while."

*****

The royal garden lay green and quiet as Tara and Laraina walked along the mossy stone pathway, winding their way to the arbor bench where, so many weeks before, Laraina had shared the startling revelation of their parentage that had sent Tara on her quest. Jovan had gone to see the new horses and give the sisters time alone.

The late afternoon sun filtered down through the vine-laced arbor, tracing patterns of light and shadow on the stone bench. Tara sat and raised her face to the sun, enjoying its warmth after the coolness of the castle. Laraina sat beside her. Tara tried to think of some way to dispel the awkwardness between them, but she didn't know how. Laraina was still her sister, familiar in many ways, but in others... It was going to take some time for Tara to get used to the new facets of Laraina's personality.

"I'm glad you're still with Jovan," Laraina said. "He seemed so right for you."

"He is." Tara smiled, as she always did when she thought of Jovan. "And I'm glad you're still here in Carilon, if that's what makes you happy."

Laraina smiled, too. "I am happy here. I love this new life. It's fascinating and ever-changing, yet stable and safe. Sometimes the constant give and take of diplomacy and politics feels like a huge game that can never be won, but I've discovered that, as queen, I have tremendous influence, and I can help people. It's so rewarding. And Kaden and I love each other and work well together. He respects my opinions and ideas, and the people of Dhanarra have accepted me."

"That's wonderful. I'm really glad for you."

Laraina sighed and looked down at the bench, tracing shadows with her finger. "I know he worries about the baby — what it will be like — but I keep telling him that whatever the outcome, the child is ours and will be what we make of it."

Tara looked away and clamped her jaw. She knew if she said anything about Kaden now, she'd regret it.

"So," Laraina said after a moment. "How is Blackie, that old pirate?"

"Same as ever," Tara said. "He'd hardly been with the Kamarians for more than a few days, and he'd already come up with a money-making scheme."

Laraina laughed. "Sounds like he hasn't lost his touch. You should have brought him with you. We could have talked old times."

"I asked him, but he refused and wouldn't tell me why."

It was Laraina's turn to look away, her smile disappearing. "I guess he hasn't forgiven me yet."

"Forgiven you for what?"

"Do you remember when we were hired to rescue that kidnapped noble from Dunregor's castle, just outside the Twin Cities?"

"How could I forget? That was our last job before we left Blackie's band. Something went wrong, and we were lucky to escape with our lives."

"Yes, well, that was partly my fault."

"It was?"

"Juggler and I were lookouts. You remember Juggler, don't you?"

Tara nodded.

"We'd been flirting for a while, and since all was quiet and everything was going as planned, we got a bit... distracted." She looked down at the bench again. "Blackie and Bow and the rest of the band had taken out the guards, and you and Speed had gotten the noble out of his cell and were headed for a side gate, where Blackie and the others were waiting." She took a deep breath, then continued.

"I'm not sure what happened next, but from what Blackie said later, two guards appeared up on the wall where we didn't expect them, and because of our 'distraction,' we missed seeing them and failed to give warning. They were archers — good ones. They wounded Speed. You took an arrow in your shoulder. They had you in their sights, and you would have been dead, but Blackie got to you first. Bow took out the archers — thank the gods he was an even better shot than they were — but the alarm had already been sounded, so we grabbed the noble and scattered.

"We met up later at the Cave. You and Blackie didn't show up until the next day. Apparently, he'd had to take you into the mountains to escape pursuit."

"Is that what happened? No one would ever tell me all the details." Tara recalled the memory that had come back to her on the boat during her amnesia — she and Blackie, alone in the mountains, holding hands while he slept, so she could warn him of danger.

"After that, Blackie kicked Juggler out of the band and said I wasn't welcome anymore, either. You could stay, but he no longer trusted me. And since you refused to stay without me, we left."

"I hated leaving his band," Tara said softly. "They'd become the family I'd never had. Why didn't you tell me?"

Laraina met her eyes. "I'm sorry. I was so ashamed, and scared. You could have been killed, and I... I've done some stupid things in my lifetime. That was one of the worst."

They fell silent, both staring out across the sunlit garden. Tara hardly noticed the sweet smell of the late-blooming flowers or the rustle of foliage in the breeze, her mind lost in memories.

"Blackie loved you, you know," Laraina said finally.

Tara's gaze dropped to her hands, her fingers fidgeting with the pommel of her dagger. "I didn't know. I never realized." She let out a long breath. "He's a good man, and I did love him, just not in that way."

"He was good most of the time." Laraina quirked a hesitant smile. "But even on his bad days, he would have been a lot better than that snake, Myles."

Tara smiled grimly. "Yes, I won't argue that."

"I have to say, though, that Jovan beats the two of them by a long shot. I think you've found something special with him."

"He is very special. Sometimes, when I think about all we've been through, I can't believe he's still here, that he didn't run for the hills long ago."

"What will the two of you do when you get back to Kamar? Are you going to stay there for a while, make that your home?"

"I don't know. I haven't decided. We'll be there for a little while, anyway."

"I wish it wasn't so far away." Laraina turned and clasped Tara's hands in hers. "Sister, I don't want us to lose our bond. I know I've changed, and so have you, but I want our bond to stay strong. I want it to grow and change with us. I will always be there for you if you need me."

"And I'll be there for you." Tara held her sister's eyes. "We're sisters, aren't we? That will never change."

CHAPTER 41

Tara rode briskly across the dewy meadow, reveling in the open space around her and the wind whipping her hair back from her face. The cool evening air was refreshing. After three weeks in Castle Carilon, it felt good to be free, even if only for a short time. The crowded confines of the castle and the city had tied her nerves into knots. For the life of her, she couldn't see what there was about court life that intrigued her sister so much. Tara found the politics annoying, and the repetitive domesticity was about as interesting as watching a slug crawl across the floor.

When she reached the end of the meadow, she slowed her mount and reluctantly turned back toward the city. Normally she wouldn't have gone riding so late, but she'd had to get out of the castle, out of the city — just *out*. She'd needed to breathe. Laraina had been smothering her lately. Every time Tara approached her sister to tell her it was time for her and Jovan to head back to Kamar, Laraina would find another reason for them to stay — some event that was about to happen or some ceremony they couldn't miss. Each time, Tara had humored her and let her sister talk her into staying a bit longer. Jovan had kept busy helping train the new horses. He was finishing up the day's work with the horse masters now. He'd said the decision to leave or stay was hers and hadn't tried to sway her either way.

Kaden had been coolly polite, but he could never quite get the "why did you have to come back" look off his face. She knew her presence disrupted his court. Some of his courtiers couldn't get past her strange hair and eye color and the rumors of her magical abilities. Laraina hadn't told anyone else about Tara's powers or her connection to the Ancients, but rumors had run rampant, and old prejudices refused to die.

But even beyond that, Tara's presence was a constant reminder to Kaden that his and Laraina's baby could be a "witch child." Tara knew he would like nothing better than to see her and Jovan disappear over the horizon.

Well, she would be happy to oblige him, though at the moment, she wasn't certain that going back to Castle Kamar would be much of an improvement. Wouldn't she be trading one confining castle for another? She shook her head, trying to shrug off her moodiness. Being in Kamar would have to be better, simply because the people there loved and accepted her for what she was. There were no sideways glances, no whispering behind her back, no hurrying away whenever she came near. And she would have more interesting things to do — learning about her own people and her heritage. Besides, she didn't have to stay there any longer than she wanted to.

She would talk to Laraina first thing in the morning, and this time, they would leave. She knew she'd have to promise to return when the baby was born, but that would be months from now. By then, she knew she'd feel better, too. These last few days she just hadn't been herself. She felt different in ways she couldn't explain, not really sick, but just... off. She'd likely picked up a touch of some illness. There were always various sicknesses floating through cities, though she hadn't heard of any in the castle currently. Whatever the case, the queasiness in her stomach this morning hadn't lasted long and... *Oh, gods!*

She pulled her horse up short as the obvious reason for her discomfiture stared her in the face. No, she couldn't be — well, of course, she could be, but... Panic seized her, and for a moment she couldn't breathe. Her horse danced sideways, upset by her sudden tension.

Love, what's wrong? Where are you? Jovan's urgent thought pressed into her mind.

She reined in her mount and took a few deep breaths to steady herself.

Nothing's wrong. I'm fine. I'm out riding, and I was startled by something. I'm on my way back now. I need to talk to you.

I'll meet you at the gate.

She sent her acknowledgment and urged her horse into a canter, her thoughts swirling around her like storm clouds. What if she was with child? It certainly wasn't impossible. She always carried dried millewort with her, but with everything that had happened, she hadn't always been able to take the herb regularly. She took another deep breath. Maybe it was just an illness, and she was worrying for nothing.

A memory flashed into her mind. One of Jovan's visions from Rinpool had been of a young man leading an army into battle — a young man who had looked much like Jovan, but wasn't him. Her breath caught. A son...

A sudden movement near a low hill up ahead snapped her out of her distracted thoughts. Several gray shadows detached from the twilight darkness at the base of the hill. Her horse's nostrils flared, catching their scent. Wolves. The horse shied violently and reared, nearly pitching her from the saddle. She fought to control her mount and keep it from bolting. She knew she should let it run and escape the predators, but something stopped her, kept her fighting her frightened horse until she'd calmed it to a quivering standstill.

The wolves had gathered a dozen yards away, six pairs of yellow eyes watching her intently. She sensed no danger. Could it be? Tears filled her eyes as the memory of Natiere's sacrifice swelled in her again.

Two more shadows, black as the coming night, slipped from behind the hill and joined the gray pack. She drew in a sharp breath, her chest tightening painfully. They turned as one toward her, silent, waiting.

"Kelya?" she whispered over the lump in her throat.

One of the black wolves ambled forward a few steps and whined softly.

Tara's horse rolled its eyes and backed away. She reined the beast in sharply, then dismounted and knotted the reins tightly around the trunk of a nearby juniper tree.

Trembling with grief, she walked slowly to Kelya's side and dropped to her knees. "I'm so sorry." Tears flowed down her face as she stroked the soft black fur. "He gave his life for me, and I'll never be able to repay him, or even thank him."

Kelya whined and licked Tara's face, then turned and looked back at the other black wolf.

Tara wiped her eyes on her sleeve. "Who is your friend?"

The other wolf took a step forward and stopped.

"Please, don't be shy." Tara held out her hand to the wolf. He — Tara sensed it was a male — was a little bigger than Kelya and had a thin white ruff on his chest.

The wolf's ears flicked sideways and forward, then he came to Tara and nosed her palm. She smoothed back the fur on his face, felt a rough line beneath her fingers — a ragged scar that ran from forehead to muzzle. She gasped, shocked by a sudden realization.

The wolf jerked away, poised to run.

"No, no, please! Don't run away!"

The wolf hesitated.

Kelya barked softly. Tara's horse snorted and yanked at the reins, but they held firm.

Tara held out her hand again to the black male wolf and opened her mind. She sensed the familiar spirit within the wolf, and a wild gladness rose within her. "You're him, aren't you?" She laughed, spreading her joy on the night air and thanking every god in the heavens. "If you know me and understand what I'm saying, please come back."

Kelya nudged her wolfen companion, and he padded slowly back to Tara and rubbed his head against her hand.

Tentatively, she slid her arms around the wolf's neck and hugged him. He didn't pull away. "Thank you for saving my life — for saving us all."

She let go and sat back on her heels. The wolf licked a tear from her face.

She smiled. "You gave your life for me. Now I'd like to do something for you." She took her knife from her belt, sliced her palm, and placed her bleeding hand over the scar on the black wolf's face. The wolf stood quietly while she let her power flow, healing the scar. It was so good to be able to use her power without fear of a mental attack.

When she was done, she ran her fingers through the soft fur over the new, unbroken skin. "There, you're whole now."

The wolf made a guttural noise and licked her hand.

She leaned forward and kissed the wolf's face where the scar had been, then rose to her feet. "Live well, my friends. *Urani metrista elan.*" *Until we meet again.*

Tara's horse neighed, and she heard rapidly approaching hoofbeats coming from the direction of the city. Jovan. He'd come looking for her. She sensed his closeness, though she couldn't yet see him in the deepening twilight.

The wolves faded silently into the shadows.

With her soul still singing a joyful air, she moved back to her mount's side and spoke soothingly to the nervous beast.

Jovan galloped around the base of the hill, pulled up beside her, and swung down from the saddle. "What happened? Are you all right?"

She stepped into his embrace. "I'm fine. And you won't believe what just happened."

"Tell me."

"When we get back to the castle."

She untied her horse, and they swung aboard their mounts and cantered back to the city.

*****

"So he's still with us."

From her seat on the bed, Tara heard Jovan curse under his breath as he paced their bedchamber.

He stopped by the window and glared out into the darkness. "Apparently, there's no killing him."

She sighed inwardly. She'd known he wouldn't be as happy as she was to find out about Natiere's transformation. "But he redeemed his soul when he sacrificed his life. The gods have forgiven him."

"Maybe they have, but the fires of the Abyss will burn cold before I'll forgive him for what he put us through."

She curled her leg underneath her, nervousness beginning to gnaw at her again. "There's something else I need to talk to you about."

Jovan crossed the room and sat beside her on the bed. "Something's troubling you again. I can feel it. What is it?"

"Do you remember my asking you what you wanted for the future?"

"Yes."

"You said it was enough that we were together, but what do you want beyond that? I need to know."

"Why?"

"You first, then I'll explain."

He held her gaze for a moment, then looked out across the room. "Well, honestly, I've never thought about it. I've spent half my life in thrall to Gorgrast, never knowing from one day to the next if I'd be alive. I had no future, so there was no point in wishing for things that would never be."

Tara covered his hand with hers at the bitterness in his voice. "But that's over now. You're free, and so am I. No more nightmares for either of us."

He looked down at their hands, their fingers interlacing. "Yes, I know, but sometimes I still wake up in a cold sweat, fearing I'll hear that voice again in my head, ordering me to do some horrific thing."

She put her arms around him and drew him to her. "I'm sorry you had to go through such torment."

He leaned his head against hers. "All I know for certain is that I want to be with you. So to answer your question — for right now, I'm content to just live each day as it comes and try to find some sense of peace. I don't care where we are as long as we're together. Perhaps in a few weeks, or months, if nothing crops up to throw our lives in disarray again, I might be able to consider what a real future might be."

Tara sat back and chewed her lip. "That sounds reasonable." She hesitated, still not sure how he would take her second piece of news. As much as she'd tried to convince herself that her queasiness wasn't what it seemed, her instincts told her otherwise, and she knew, to her dismay, that her instincts were never wrong. She plunged ahead. "I'm afraid, though, that our lives are about to be thrown in disarray again, but I don't know whether it will be for good or bad."

His head jerked up. "Why? What happened? Has Laraina or Kaden —?"

"No, no, it has nothing to do with them. Or Natiere," she added. She could feel the mixture of tension and dread slinging through him. "Do you remember your visions from Rinpool? You said one involved a young man leading an army into battle, and that he looked something like you. Do you think he could be... your son?"

Thoughtful surprise crossed Jovan's face. "I don't know. That never occurred to me. I —" He stopped short and looked in her eyes.

Neither spoke for a few heartbeats, then he asked in a tone of wonder, "Are you...?"

"I think so," she said softly.

He cupped her face, brushed his thumb over her cheek. "That kind of disarray will be a blessing."

"You're sure?" The idea still scared her.

Jovan smiled. "I've never been more sure of anything in my life — other than you."

She took a deep breath and gave him a half smile. "Well, then." She took his hand and laid it gently on her belly. "Meet your son."

"*Our* son," he said, and kissed her tenderly.

END BOOK 2

ABOUT THE AUTHOR

Lori L. MacLaughlin traces her love of fantasy adventure to Tolkien and Terry Brooks, finding *The Lord of the Rings* and *The Sword of Shannara* particularly inspirational. She's been writing stories in her head since she was old enough to run wild through the forests on the farm on which she grew up.

She has been many things over the years – tree climber, dairy farmer, clothing salesperson, kids' shoe fitter, retail manager, medical transcriptionist, journalist, private pilot, traveler, wife and mother, Red Sox and New York Giants fan, muscle car enthusiast and NASCAR fan, and a lover of all things Scottish and Irish.

When she's not writing (or working), she can be found curled up somewhere dreaming up more story ideas, taking long walks in the countryside, or spending time with her kids. She lives with her family in northern Vermont.